Only One Love
Or, Who Was The Heir

by

Charles Garvice

Double 9
BOOKS

Only one love
Or, who was the heir
by Charles Garvice

ISBN: 978-93-64280-21-1

Published by
DOUBLE 9 BOOKS
2/13-B, Ansari Road
Daryaganj, New Delhi – 110002
info@double9books.com
www.double9books.com
Tel. 011-40042856

ABOUT THE AUTHOR

Charles Garvice (1850-1920) was a prolific British novelist who wrote predominantly in the late 19th and early 20th centuries. He was known for his romantic fiction, which was immensely popular during his time. Garvice published over 150 novels throughout his career, making him one of the most widely read authors of his era. His novels typically featured themes of romance, adventure, and melodrama, catering to the tastes of a predominantly female audience. Garvice's works often portrayed strong heroines and dashing heroes in exotic or dramatic settings, appealing to readers seeking escapism and emotional engagement. His novels were serialized in magazines and were also published as standalone books, contributing significantly to popular fiction in the late Victorian and Edwardian periods.

CONTENTS

CHAPTER I

One summer's evening a young man was tramping through the Forest of Warden. "Forest of Warden" sounds strange, old-fashioned, almost improbable; but, thank Heaven, there yet remain, in over-crowded England, some spots, few and far between though they may be, still untouched by the greedy fingers of the destroyers, whom men call Progress and Civilization.

To this grand old forest, for instance, whose dim shades echo the soft pit-pat of the deer and the coo of the wood-pigeon, comes not the tourist, with hideous knapsack and suit of startling check; no panting locomotive belches out its cloud of coal smoke to dim the brightness of the sky and choke the elms and oaks which reared their stately heads before their fell enemy, the steam engine, was dreamt of.

So remote and unfrequented is the forest that there is scarcely a road from end to end of its umbrageous length, for the trail made by the rough carts of the woodmen and charcoal burners could scarcely be dignified by the title of thoroughfare, and a few footpaths that wind about the glades are so faint and seldom used as to be scarcely distinguished from the undergrowth of ferny moss around.

Along one of the footpaths the young man tramped, occasionally stopping for a moment to look up at the sky which shone redly through the openings of the trees or to watch some frightened hare scamper across the glade.

Every now and then a herd of deer would flit through the undergrowth, turning toward him distended eyes of alarm and curiosity, for of the two kinds of men with whom they were acquainted—charcoal burners and woodmen—he was neither; nor did he belong to the tribe of tourists, for he carried no knapsack, and instead of the inevitable check and knickerbockers, was clad in a loose Cheviot suit, which, though well worn, bore about it the unmistakable stamp of Saville Row.

That he was young and light-hearted was evident from the fact that he broke out into an occasional snatch of an air from the last new popular *opera bouffe*, notwithstanding that the evening was closing in and he had most completely and emphatically lost his way.

Now, to lose your way in a forest reads rather romantic and entertaining than otherwise, but like shipwreck, or falling into the hands of Greek banditti, it is a much pleasanter thing on paper than in reality.

A bed of moss, though very charming in the daytime, is not nearly so comfortable as a spring mattress, and is sure to be damp, and primeval oaks, majestic and beautiful as they are, do not keep out the draught. The worst room in the worst inn is preferable to a night's lodging in the grandest of forests.

But, though he had never been in the Warden Forest before, the young man knew it would be midsummer madness to hope for an inn and was wandering along on the chance of coming across some woodman's hut, or by meeting a stray human being of whom he could inquire his way.

He was tired—he had been walking since morning, and he was hungry and athirst, but he tramped on, and smoked and sang as carelessly as if he were strolling down the shady side of Pall Mall.

Slowly the sun set, and the glades, which had been dusky an hour ago, grew dark. The faint footpath grew still more indistinct, the undergrowth denser and more difficult for persons walking.

The pedestrian fought on for some time, but at last, as he stumbled over one of the gnarled roots which a grand chestnut had thrust up through the ground, he stopped and, looking round, shook his head.

"A regular babe in the wood, by Jove!" he exclaimed. "I shall have to make a night of it, I expect. Wonder whether the robins will be good enough to cover me over in the proper nursery-book style? Is it any good halloing, I wonder? I tried that an hour ago, much to the disgust of the live animals; and I don't think I can kick up a row at this time of night. Let's see how the 'bacca goes. Hem! about three—perhaps four pipes. I wish I had something to eat and drink; what a fool I was to leave that piece of steak at breakfast. Steak! I mustn't think of it—that way madness lies. Well, this looks about as sheltered a spot as I could find—I'll turn in. I wonder if anybody has, ever since the world began, hit upon a short cut? I never have, and hang me if I'll try it again. By George! the grass is wet already. Such a likely place for snakes—find my pocket full when I wake, no doubt."

Then, with a laugh, he dropped down amongst the long brake; but the idea of going to bed in a forest, at the early hour of nine, was too much for him, and instead of composing himself to rheumatic slumber, he began to sing:

"Oh, wake and call me early, mother,
Call me early, mother, dear."

Scarcely had he finished the line when there came through the darkness, as if in response, a short, sharp bark of a dog.

The wanderer leapt to his feet as if something had bitten him, and after listening intently for a moment, exclaimed:

"Another chance, by Jove!" and sent up a shout that, ringing through the stillness, echoed from tree to tree, and at last called forth the answering bark from the distant dog.

Knocking out his pipe as he ran, he made his way as best he could toward the sound, shouting occasionally and listening warily to the dog's response.

At last, after many a stumble, he found himself in a narrow glade, at the end of which, faintly defined against the patch of sky, stood the figure of a man.

"Saved, by George!" exclaimed the youth, with mock melodramatic emphasis.

"Halloa! Hi! Wait a moment there, will you?" he shouted.

The figure stopped and turned its head, then, after what seemed a moment's hesitation, brought back the dog, which was running toward the belated youth, and suddenly disappeared.

The wanderer pulled up and stared about the glade with an astonishment which immediately gave place to wrath.

"Confound his impudence!" he exclaimed, fiercely. "I'll swear he saw me! What on earth did he mean by going off like that? Did the fool think I was a ghost? I'll show him I'm a ghost that carries a big stick if I come up with him. Confound him, where——" Then, as a sudden thought struck him, he set off running down the glade, barking like a dog.

No live, real dog could withstand such an invitation. The dog ahead set up an angry echo, through which the youth could hear the man's angry attempt to silence the animal, and guided by the two voices, the wanderer struck into a footpath, and running at a good pace, came suddenly into a small clearing, in which stood a small wooden hut, before the door of which man and dog were standing as if on guard.

For a moment the two men stood and regarded each other in silence, the youth hot and angry, the man calm and grim.

Each, in his way, was a fine specimen of his class; the man, with his weather-beaten face and his thick-set limbs, clad in woodman's garb; the youth, with his frankly handsome countenance and patrician air.

"What the deuce do you mean by leaving a man in the lurch like this?" demanded the young man, angrily. "Did you take me for a ghost?"

The woodman, half leaning on his long-handled axe, regarded him grimly.

"No. I don't come at every man's beck and call, young sir. What's your will with me?"

"Why didn't you stop when I called to you just now?" retorted the youth, ignoring the question.

"Because it didn't suit me," said the man, not insolently, but with simple, straightforward candor. "You are answered, young sir; now, what do you want?"

The young man looked at him curiously, conquering his anger.

"Well, I've lost my way," he said, after a moment's pause.

"Where are you going?" was the quiet response.

"To Arkdale."

The woodman raised his eyes, and looked at him for a moment.

"Arkdale? Yes, you are out of the way. Arkdale lies to the west. Follow me, young sir, and I'll show you the road."

"Stop a moment," said the other; "though you declined to wait for me just now, you would not refuse to give me a glass of water, I suppose."

The man turned, he had already strode forward, and laid his hand on the latch of the cottage door.

The young man was following as a matter of course; but the woodman, with his hand still on the latch, pointed to a wooden seat under the window.

"Take your seat there, sir," he said, with grim determination.

The other stared, and the hot blood rose to his face; but he threw himself on the bench.

"Very well," he said; "I see you still think me a ghost; you'll be more easy when you see me drink. Look sharp, my good fellow."

The woodman, not a whit moved by this taunt, entered the cottage, and the young man heard a bolt shot into its place.

A few moments passed, and then the man came out with a plate and a glass.

"Thanks," said the young man. "What's this?"

"Cider—cake," was the curt answer.

"Oh, thanks," repeated the other; "jolly good cider, too. Come, you're not half a bad fellow. Do you know I meant to give you a hiding when I came up to you?"

"Very like," said the man, calmly. "Will you have any more?"

"Another glass, thanks."

With his former precaution in the way of bolting and barring, the man entered the cottage and reappeared with a refilled glass.

This the young man drank more leisurely, staring with unconcealed curiosity at his entertainer.

It was a kind of stare that would embarrass six men out of ten, and madden the remaining four; but the woodman bore it with the calm impassiveness of a wooden block, and stood motionless as a statue till the youth set down the glass, then he raised his hand and pointed to the west.

"Yonder lies Arkdale."

"Oh! How far?"

"Four miles and a half by the near road. Follow me, and I will put you into it."

"All right, lead on," said the other; but as he rose he turned, and while refilling his pipe stared at the closely locked cottage.

"Comfortable kind of crib that, my man."

The woodman nodded curtly.

"You are a woodman?"

Another nod.

"And poacher too, eh? No offense," he added, coolly. "I only supposed so from the close way in which you keep your place locked up."

"Suppose what you please," retorted the woodman, if words so calmly spoken could be called a retort. "Yonder lies your road, you'd best be taking to it."

"No hurry," retorted the young man, thrusting his hands in his pockets and smiling at the ill-concealed impatience which struggled through the grave calm on the weather-beaten face. "Well, I'm coming. You're not half such a bad sort, after all. What have you got inside there that you keep so close, eh? Some of the crown jewels or some of the Queen's venison? Take my advice, old fellow—if you don't want people to be curious, don't show such anxiety to keep 'em out of your crib."

The man, pacing on ahead, knit his brows as if struck by the idea.

"Curious folk don't come this way, young sir," he said, reluctantly.

"So I should think," retorted the other. "Well, I'm not one of the curious, though you think I am. I don't care a button what you've got there. Will you have a pipe? I've got some 'bacca."

The man shook his head, and they walked on in silence for some minutes, the footpath winding in and out like a dimly-defined serpent. Presently it widened, and the woodman stopped short and pointed down the leafy lane.

"Follow this path," he said, "until you come to a wood pile; take the path to the left of it, and it will bring you to Arkdale. Good-night, young sir."

"Here, stop!" said the young man, and he held out his hand with a dollar in it. "Here's a trifle to drink my health with."

The woodman looked at the coin, then shook his head slowly; and with another "good-night" turned and tramped off.

Not at all abashed the young man restored the coin to his pocket, laughed, and strode on.

The woodman walked back a few yards, then stopped, and looked after the stalwart figure until it deepened in the gloom, a thoughtful, puzzled expression upon his face, as if he were trying to call up some recollection.

With a shake of his head, denoting failure, he made his way to the cottage, unlocked it and entered.

The door opened into what appeared to be the living room. It was small and plainly furnished, after the manner of a woodman's hut, and yet, after a moment's glance, a stranger would have noticed a subtle air of refinement in common with better habitations.

The table and chairs were of plain deal, the walls were of pine, stained and varnished, but there was a good thick carpet on the floor, and on one side of the room hung a bookcase filled with well-bound volumes.

Beside the table, on which was spread the supper, stood a chair, more luxurious than its fellows, and covered with a pretty chintz. The knife and fork laid opposite this chair was of a better quality than the others on the table; and beside the knife and fork lay a white napkin and a daintily engraved glass; the other drinking vessels on the table were of common delf. As the woodman entered, a woman, who was kneeling at a fire in an adjoining room, looked round through the doorway.

"Is't you, Gideon?"

"Yes," he answered. "Where is Una?"

"Una? Isn't she with you? I heard voices. Who was it?"

"Where is Una?" he said, ignoring her question.

"In the clearing, I suppose," said the woman. "She went out a few minutes ago. I thought she went to meet you?"

The man opened the door and called the dog, who had been wandering round the room in an uneasy fashion.

"Go, Dick," he said. "Go fetch her!"

Then he came and stood by the fire thoughtfully.

"No," he said, "it was not Una. I wish she wouldn't leave the cot after dusk."

"Why not? What's the fear? What has happened? Who was that I heard with you?"

"A stranger," he said, "a young gentleman lost his way. How long has she been gone?"

"Not ten minutes. A young gentleman. Think of that! How came he here?"

"Lost his way. He followed me through the Chase. He has gone on to Arkdale."

"Lost his way," repeated the woman. "Poor fellow! Five miles it is to Arkdale! A gentleman! A gentleman, did thee say?"

"Ay," responded the man, frowning. "An outspoken one, too; I heard him at the bottom of the Chase and thought to give him the slip, but he was cunning, he teased the dog and ran us down. I had hard work to get rid of him; he looked sore tired. No matter, he's gone," and he gave a sigh of relief. "'Tis the first stranger that has come upon us since she came."

"Lost his way," murmured the woman, as she lifted a saucepan from the fire, "and a gentleman. It is a rare sight in Warden Forest. Why, Gideon, what has happened to thee?" and saucepan in hand, she stared at her husband's cloudy brow.

"Tut—nothing!" he answered, thrusting a projecting log into the fire with his foot. "The young man's face seemed—as I thought—'twas but a passing fancy—but I thought it was familiar. It was the voice more than the face. And a bold face it was. I wish," he broke off, "that the lass would come in. From to-night I will have no more wanderings after sunset! One stranger follows another, and it is not safe for her to be out so late— —"

"Hush!" interrupted the woman, holding up a forefinger. "Here she comes."

"Not a word!" said Gideon, warningly.

As he spoke the door opened, the dog bounded in with a short yelp of satisfaction, and close behind him, framed like a picture in the dark doorway, stood a young girl.

CHAPTER II

She had evidently run some distance, for she stood panting and breathless, the color coming and going on her face, which shone out of the hood which half covered her head.

She was dressed in a plain cotton dress which a woodman's daughter might wear, and which was short enough in the skirt to reveal a shapely foot, and scant enough in the sleeves to show a white, shapely arm.

But no one would have wasted time upon either arm or foot after a glance at her face.

To write it down simply and curtly, it was a beautiful face; but such a description is far too meager and insufficient. It requires an artist, a Rembrandt or a Gainsborough, to describe it, no pen-and-ink work can do it. Beautiful faces can be seen by the score by anyone who chooses to walk through Hyde Park in the middle of the season, but such a face as this which was enframed by the doorway of the woodman's hut is not seen in twenty seasons.

It was a face which baffles the powers of description, just as a sunset sky laughs to scorn the brush of the ablest painter. It was neither dark nor fair, neither grave nor sad, though at the moment of its entrance a smile played over it as the moonbeams play over a placid lake.

To catalogue in dry matter-of-fact fashion, the face possessed dark brown eyes, bright brown hair, and red, ripe lips; but no catalogue can give the spirit of the face, no description convey an idea of the swift and eloquent play of expression which, like a flash of sunlight, lit up eyes and lips.

Beautiful! The word is hackneyed and worn out. Here was a face more than beautiful, it was soulful. Like the still pool in the heart of a wood, it mirrored the emotion of the heart as faithfully as a glass would reflect the face. Like a glass—joy, sorrow, pleasure, mirth, were reflected in the eloquent eyes and mobile lips.

Of concealment the face was entirely ignorant; no bird of the forest in which she lived could be more frank, innocent of guile, and ignorant of evil.

With her light summer cloak held round her graceful figure, she stood in the doorway, a picture of grace and youthful beauty.

For a moment she stood silent, looking from the woodman to his wife questioningly, then she came into the room and threw the hood back, revealing a shapely head, shining, bronze-like, in the light of the lamp.

"Did you send Dick for me, father?" she said, and her voice, like her face, betokened a refinement uncommon in a woodman's daughter. "I was not far off, only at the pool to hear the frogs' concert. Dick knows where to find me now, he comes straight to the pond, though he hates frogs' music; don't you, Dick?"

The dog rubbed his nose against her hand and wagged his tail, and the girl took her seat at the table.

To match face and voice, her mien and movements were graceful, and she handled the dinner-napkin like—a lady. It was just that, expressed in a word. The girl was not only beautiful—but a lady, in appearance, in tone, in bearing—and that, notwithstanding she wore a plain cotton gown in a woodman's hut, and called the woodman "father."

"You did not come by your usual path, father," she said, turning from the deerhound, who sat on his haunches and rested his nose in her lap, quite content if her hand touched his head, say once during the meal.

"No, Una," he replied, and though he called her by her Christian name, and without any prefix there was a subtle undertone in his voice and in his manner of addressing her, which seemed to infer something like respect. "No, I went astray."

"And you were late," she said. "Was anything the matter?" she added, turning her eyes upon him, with, for the first time, an air of interrogation.

"Matter? No," he said, raising himself and coming to the table. "What should be? Yes, I came home by another path, and I don't think you must come to meet me after dark, Una," he added, with affected carelessness.

"No?" she asked, looking from one to the other with a smile of surprise. "Why not? Do you think I should get lost, or have you seen any wolves in Warden Forest, father? I know every path from end to end, and wolves have left merry England forever."

"Not quite," said Gideon, absently.

"Yes, quite," and she laughed. "What Saxon king was it who offered fivepence for every wolf's head? We were reading about it the other night, don't you remember?"

"Reading! you are always reading," said the woman, as she put a smoking dish on the table, and speaking for the first time. "It's books, books, from morn to night, and your father encourages you. The books will make thee old before thy time, child, and put no pence in thy father's pocket."

"Poor father!" she murmured, and leaning forward, put her arms round his neck. "I wish I could find in the poor, abused books the way to make him rich."

Gideon had put up his rough hand to caress the white one nestling against his face, but he let his hand drop again and looked at her with a slight cloud on his brow.

"Rich! who wants to be rich? The word is on your lips full oft of late, Una. Do *you* want to be rich?"

"Sometimes," she answered. "As much for your sake as mine. I should like to be rich enough for you to rest, and"—looking round the plainly furnished but comfortable room—"and a better house and clothes."

"I am not weary," he said, his eyes fixed on her with a thoughtful air of concealed scrutiny. "The cot is good enough for me, and the purple and fine linen I want none of. So much for me; now for yourself, Una?"

"For myself?" she said. "Well, sometimes I think, when I have been reading some of the books, that I should like to be rich and see the world."

"It must be such a wonderful place! Not so wonderful as I think it, perhaps, and that's just because I have never seen anything of it. Is it not strange that for all these years I have never been outside Warden?"

"Strange?" he echoed, reluctantly.

"Yes; are other girls so shut in and kept from seeing the world that one reads so pleasantly of?"

"Not all. It would be well for most of them if they were. It has been well for you. You have not been unhappy, Una?"

"Unhappy! No! How could one be unhappy in Warden? Why, it's a world in itself, and full of friends. Every living thing in it seems a friend, and an old friend, too. How long have we lived in Warden, father?"

"Eighteen years."

"And I am twenty-one. Mother told me yesterday. Where did we live before we came to Warden?"

"Don't worry your father, Una," said Mrs. Rolfe, who had been listening and looking from one to the other with ill-concealed anxiety; "he is too weary to talk."

"Forgive me, father. It was thoughtless of me. I should have remembered that you have had a hard day, while I have been idling in the wood, and over my books; it was stupid of me to trouble you. Won't you sit down again and—and I will promise not to talk."

"Say no more, Una. It grieves me to think that you might not be content, that you were not happy; if you knew as much of the world that raves and writhes outside as I do, you would be all too thankful that you are out of the monster's reach, and that all you know of it is from your books, which— Heaven forgive them—lie all too often! See now, here is something I found in Arkdale;" and as he spoke he drew from the capacious pocket of his velveteen jacket a small volume.

The girl sprang to her feet—not clumsily, but with infinite grace—and leaned over his shoulder eagerly.

"Why, father, it is the poems you promised me, and it was in your pocket all the while I was wearying you with my foolish questions."

"Tut, tut! Take your book, child, and devour it, as usual."

Once or twice Gideon looked up, roused from his reverie by the rustling of the trees as the gusts shook them, and suddenly the sky was rent by a flash of lightning and a peal of thunder, followed by the heavy rattle of the rainstorm.

"Hark at the night, father!" she said, raising her eyes from the book, but only for a moment.

"Ay, Una," he said, "some of the old elms will fall to-night. Woodman Lightning strikes with a keen ax."

Suddenly there came another sound which, coming in an interval of comparative quiet, caused Una to look up with surprise.

"Halloa there! open the door."

Gideon sprang to his feet, his face pale with anger.

"Go to your room, Una," he said.

She rose and moved across the room to obey, but before she had passed up the stairs the woodman had opened the door, and the voice came in from the outside, and she paused almost unconsciously.

"At last! What a time you have been! I've knocked loud enough to wake the dead. For Heaven's sake, open the door and let me in. I'm drenched to the skin."

"This is not an inn, young sir."

"No, or it would soon come to ruin with such a landlord. It's something with four walls and a roof, and I must be content with that. You don't mean to say that you won't let me come in?"

"I do not keep open house for travelers."

"Oh, come," exclaimed the young man, with a short laugh. "It's your own fault that I am back here; you told me the wrong turning. I'll swear I followed your directions. I must have been walking in a circle; anyhow I lost my way, and here I am, and, with all your churlishness, you can't refuse me shelter on such a night as this."

"The storm has cleared. It is but an hour's walk to Arkdale; I will go with you."

"That you certainly will not, to-night, nor any other man," was the good-humored retort. "I've had enough of your confounded forest for to-night. Why, man, are you afraid to let me in? It's a nasty thing to have to do, but— —" and with a sudden thrust of his strong shoulder he forced the door open and passed the threshold.

But the woodman recovered from the surprise in a moment and, seizing him by the throat, was forcing him out again, when, with a low cry, Una sprang forward and laid her hand on his arm.

At her touch Gideon's hands dropped to his side. The stranger sprang upright, but almost staggered out with discomfited astonishment.

For the first time in her life she stood face to face with a man other than a woodman or a charcoal-burner. And as she looked her heart almost stopped beating, the color died slowly from her face. Was it real, or was it one of the visionary heroes of her books created into life from her own dreaming brain?

With parted lips she waited, half longing, half dreading, to hear him speak.

It seemed ages before he found his voice, but at last, with a sudden little shake of the head, as if he were, as he would have expressed it, "pulling himself together," he took off his wide hat and slowly turned his eyes from the beautiful face of the girl to the stern and now set face of the woodman.

"Why didn't you tell me that you had a lady—ladies with you?" half angrily, half apologetically. Then he turned quickly, impulsively, to Una. "I hope you will forgive me. I had no idea that there was anyone here excepting himself. Of course I would rather have got into the first ditch than have disturbed you. I hope, I do hope you believe that, though I can't hope you'll forgive me. Good-night," and inclining his head he turned to the door.

Una, who had listened with an intent, rapt look on her face, as one sees a blind man listen to music, drew a little breath of regret as he ceased speaking, and then, with a little, quick gesture, laid her hand on her father's arm.

It was an imploring touch. It said as plainly as if she had spoken:

"Do not let him go."

"Having forced your way into my house you—may remain."

"Thanks. I should not think of doing so. Good-night."

"No; you must not go. He does not mean it. You have made him angry. Please do not go!"

The young man hesitated, and the woodman, with a gesture that was one of resigned despair, shut the door.

Then he turned and pointed to the next room.

"There's a fire there," he said.

"I'd rather be out in the wood by far," he said, "than be here feeling that I have made a nuisance of myself. I'd better go."

But Gideon Rolfe led the way into the next room, and after another look from Mrs. Rolfe to Una, the young man followed.

Una stood in the center of the room looking at the door behind which he had disappeared, like one in a dream. Then she turned to Mrs. Rolfe.

"Shall I go, mother?"

"Yes. No. Wait till your father comes in."

After the lapse of ten minutes the woodman and the woodman's guest re-entered. The latter had exchanged his wet clothes for a suit of Gideon's, which, though it was well-worn velveteen, failed to conceal the high-bred air of its present wearer.

Meanwhile Mrs. Rolfe had been busily spreading the remains of the supper.

"'Tis but plain fare, sir," she said; "but you are heartily welcome."

"Thanks. It looks like a banquet to me," he added, with the short laugh which seemed peculiar to him. "I haven't tasted food, as tramps say, since morning."

"Dear! dear!" exclaimed the wife.

Una, calling up a long line of heroes, thought first of Ivanhoe, then—and with a feeling of satisfaction—of Hotspur.

Figure matched face. Though but twenty-two, the frame was that of a trained athlete—stalwart, straight-limbed, muscular; and with all combined a grace which comes only with birth and breeding.

Wet and draggled, he looked every inch a gentleman—in Gideon's suit of worn velveteen he looked one still.

Silent and motionless, Una watched him.

"Yes," he said, "I got some lunch at the inn—'Spotted Boar' at Wermesley—about one o'clock, I suppose. I have never felt so hungry in my life."

"Wermesley?" said the wife. "Then you came from——"

"London, originally. I got out at Wermesley, meaning to walk to Arkdale; but that appears to be easier said than done, eh?"

Gideon did not answer; he seemed scarcely to hear.

"I can't think how I missed the way," he went on. "I found the charcoal burner's hut, and hurried off to the left——"

"To the right, I said," muttered Gideon.

"Right, did you? Then I misunderstood you. Anyhow, I lost the right path, and wandered about until I came back to this cottage."

"And you were going to stay at Arkdale? 'Tis but a dull place," said Mrs. Rolfe.

"No; I meant taking the train from there to Hurst Leigh—— Hurst Leigh," repeated the young man. "Do you know it? Ah," he went on, "don't suppose you would; it's some distance from here. Pretty place. I am going to see a relative. My name is Newcombe—Jack Newcombe I am generally called—and I am going on a visit to Squire Davenant."

Gideon Rolfe sprang to his feet, suddenly, knocking his chair over, and strode into the lamplight.

The young man looked up in surprise.

"What's the matter?" he asked.

With an effort Gideon Rolfe recovered himself.

"I—I want a light," he said; and leaning over the lamp, he lit his pipe. Then turning toward the window, he said: "Una, it is late; go to bed now."

She rose at once and kissed the old couple, then pausing a moment, held out her hand to the young man, who had risen, and stood regarding her with an intent, but wholly respectful look.

But before their hands could join, the woodman stepped in between them, and waving her to the stairs with one hand, forced the youth into his seat with the other.

CHAPTER III

A hearty meal after a long fast invariably produces intense sleepiness.

No sooner had the young gentleman who was called, according to his own account, Jack Newcombe, finished his supper than he began to show palpable signs of exhaustion.

He felt, indeed, remarkably tired, or be sure he would have demanded the reason of the woodman's refusal to allow his daughter to shake hands.

For once in a way, Jack—who was also called "The Savage" by his intimate friends—allowed the opportunity for a quarrel to slide by, and very soon also allowed the pipe to slide from his mouth, and his body from the chair.

Rousing himself with a muttered apology, he found that the woodman alone remained, and that he was sitting apparently forgetful of his guest's presence.

"Did you speak?" said Jack, rubbing his eyes, and struggling with a very giant of a yawn. Gideon looked round.

"You are tired," he said, slowly.

"Rather," assented the Savage, with half-closed eyes; "it must have been the wind. I can't keep my head up."

The woodman rose, and taking down from a cupboard a bundle of fox-skins, arranged them on the floor, put a couple of chair-cushions at the head to serve as pillows, and threw a riding-cloak—which, by the way, did not correspond with a woodman's usual attire, and pointed to the impromptu bed.

"Thanks," said Jack, getting up and taking off his coat and boots.

"It is a poor bed," remarked the woodman, but the Savage interrupted him with a cheerful though sleepy assurance that it needed no apologies.

"I could sleep on a rail to-night," he said, "and that looks comfortable enough for a king! Fine skins! Good-night!" and he held out his hand.

Gideon looked at it, but refusing it, nodded gravely.

"You won't shake hands!" exclaimed the Savage, with a little flush and an aggrieved tone. "Come, isn't that carrying the high and imposing rather too far, old fellow? Makes one feel more ashamed than ever, you know. Perhaps I'd better march, after all."

"No," said Gideon, slowly. "It is not that I owe you any ill-will for your presence here. You are welcome, but I cannot take your hand. Good-night," and he went to the stairs.

At the door, however, he paused, and looked over his shoulder.

"Did you say that—Squire Davenant was your uncle, Mr. Newcombe?"

"Eh—uncle? Well, scarcely. It's rather difficult to tell what relationship there is between us. He's a sort of cousin, I believe," answered Jack, carelessly, but yet with a touch of gravity that had something comical about it. "Rum old boy, isn't he? You know him, don't you?"

Gideon shook his head.

"Oh, I thought you did by the way you looked when I mentioned his name just now. Good thing you don't, for you might have something to say about him that is not pleasant, and though the old man and I are not turtle doves just now, I'm bound to stand up for him for the sake of old times."

"You have quarreled?" the old man said; but the Savage had already curled himself up in the fox-skins, and was incapable of further conversation.

Gideon Rolfe crossed the room, and holding the candle above his head, looked down at the sleeper.

"Yes," he muttered, "it's the same face—they are alike! Faces of angels and the hearts of devils. What fate has sent him here to-night?"

Though Jack Newcombe was by no means one of those impossible, perfect heroes whom we have sometimes met in history, and was, alas! as full of imperfections as a sieve is of holes, he was a gentleman, and for a savage, was possessed of a considerable amount of delicacy.

"Seems to me," he mused, "that the best thing I can do is to take my objectionable self out of the way before any of the good folks put in an appearance. The old fellow will be sure to order me off the premises directly after the breakfast; and I, in common gratitude, ought to save him the trouble."

To resolve and to act were one and the same thing with Jack Newcombe. Going into the adjoining room, he got out of the woodman's and into his own clothes, and carefully restored the skins and the cloak to the cupboard. Then he put the remainder of the loaf into his pocket, to serve as breakfast later on, then paused.

"Can't go without saying good-by, and much obliged," he muttered.

A bright idea struck him; he tore the blank leaf from an old letter which he happened to have with him, and after a few minutes' consideration—for epistolary composition was one of the Savage's weakest points—scribbled the following brief thanks, apology, and farewell:

"Very much obliged for your kindness, and sorry to have been such a bore; shouldn't have intruded if I'd known ladies were present. Will you oblige me by accepting the inclosed"—he hesitated a moment, put back the sovereign which he had taken from his pocket, and filled up the line—"for your wife."

Instead of the coin, he wrapped up a ring, which he took from his little finger.

He smiled, as he wrapped it up, for he remembered that the wife had particularly large hands; and he thought, cunningly, "*she* will get it."

Having placed this packet on the top of the cheese, he took a last look round the room, glanced toward the stairs rather wistfully—it was neither the woodman nor his wife that he longed to see—gently unbarred the door, and started on his road.

Choosing a sheltered spot, the Savage pulled out his crust, ate it uncomplainingly, and then lay down at full length, with his soft hat over his eyes, and while revolving the strange events of the preceding night, and striving to recall the face of the young girl, fell asleep.

CHAPTER IV

A more beautiful spot for a siesta he could not have chosen. At his feet stretched the lake, gleaming like silver in the sun, and set in a frame of green leaves and forest flowers; above his head, in his very ears, the thrushes and linnets sang in concert, all the air was full of the perfumes of a summer morning, rendered sweeter by the storm of the preceding night, which had called forth the scent of the ferns and the honeysuckle.

As he lay, and dreamt with that happy-go-lucky carelessness of time and the daily round of duties which is one of the privileges of youth, there rose upon the air a song other than that of the birds.

It was a girl's voice, chanting softly, and evidently with perfect unconsciousness; faintly at first, it broke upon the air, then more distinctly, and presently, from amongst the bushes that stood breast high round the sleeping Savage, issued Una.

The night had had dreams for her, dreams in which the handsome face, with its bold, daring eyes, and quick, sensitive mouth, had hovered before her closed eyes and haunted her, and now here he lay at her feet.

How tired he must be to sleep there, and how hungry! for, though she had not seen the note—nor the ring—she knew that he had gone without breakfast.

"Poor fellow!" she murmured—"his face is quite pale—and—ah——!" she broke off with a sudden gasp, and bent forward; a wasp, which had been buzzing around his head for some time, swept his cheek.

Too fearful of waking him to sweep the insect aside, she knelt and watched with clasped hands and shrinking heart; so intent in her dread that the wasp should alight on his cheek and sting him as almost to have forgotten her fear that he should awake.

At last the dreaded climax occurred; the wasp settled on his lips; with a low, smothered cry, she stretched out her hand, and, with a quick movement, swept the wasp off. But, lightly as her finger had touched his lips, it had been sufficient to wake him, and, with a little start, he opened his eyes, and received into them, and through them to his heart the girl's rapt gaze.

For a minute neither moved; he lest he should break the dream; she, because, bird-like, she was fascinated; then, the minute passed, she rose, and drew back, and glided into the brake.

The Savage with a wild throb of the heart, saw that his dream had grown into life, raised himself on his elbow and looked after her, and, as he did so, his eye caught a small basket which she had set down beside him.

"Stay," he called, and in so gentle a voice that his friends who had christened him the Savage would have instantly changed it to the Dove.

"Stay! Please stay. Your basket."

"Why did you run from me?" asked the Savage, in a low voice. "Did you think that I should hurt you?"

"Hurt me? No, why should you?" and her eyes met his with innocent surprise.

"Why should I, indeed! I should have been very sorry if you had gone, because I wanted to thank you for your kindness last night."

"You have not to thank me," she said, slowly.

"Yes," he assented, quietly. "But for you——" then he stopped, remembering that it was scarcely correct to complain of her father's inhospitality; "I behaved very badly. I always do," he added—for the first time in his life with regret.

"Do you?" she said, doubtfully. "You were wet and tired last night, and—and you must not think ill of my father; he——"

"Don't say another word. I was treated better than I deserved."

"Why did you go without breakfast this morning?" she said, suddenly.

"I brought it with me," he replied. "You forgot the loaf!" and he smiled.

"Dry bread!" she said, pityingly. "I am so sorry. If I had but known, I would have brought you some milk."

"Oh, I have done very well," he said, his curt way softened and toned down.

"And now you are going to Arkdale?" she said, gently.

"That is, after I have gone to rest for a little while longer; I am in no hurry; won't you sit down, Una? Keep me company."

To her there seemed nothing strange in the speech; gravely and naturally she sat down at the foot of an oak.

"You think the forest is lonely?" she said.

"I do, most decidedly. Don't you?"

"No; but that is because I am used to it and have known no other place."

"Always lived here?" he said, with interest.

"Ever since I was three years old."

"Eighteen years! Then you are twenty-one?" murmured Jack.

"Yes; how old are you?" she asked, calmly.

"Twenty-two."

"Twenty-two. And you have lived in the world all the time?"

"Yes—very much so," he replied.

"And you are going back to it. You will never come into the forest again, while I shall go on living here till I die, and never see the world in which you have lived. Does that sound strange to you?"

"Do you mean to say that you have never been outside this forest?" he said, raising himself on his elbow to stare at her.

"Yes. I have never been out of Warden since we came into it."

"But—why not?" he demanded.

"I do not know," she replied, simply.

"But there must be some reason for it? Haven't you been to Arkdale or Wermesley?"

"No," she said, smiling. "Tell me what they are like. Are they gay and full of people, with theaters and parks, and ladies riding and driving, and crowds in the streets?"

"Oh, this is too much!" under his breath. "No, no—a thousand times no!" he exclaimed; "they are the two most miserable holes in creation! There are no parks, no theaters in Arkdale or Wermesley. You might see a lady on horseback—one lady in a week! They are two county towns, and nothing of that kind ever goes on in them. You mean London, and—and places like that when you speak of theaters and that sort of thing!"

"Yes, London," she says, quietly. "Tell me all about that—I have read about it in books."

"Books!" said the Savage, in undisguised contempt; "what's the use of *them!* You must see life for yourself—books are no use. They give it to you all wrong; at least, I expect so; don't know much about them myself."

"Tell me," she repeated, "tell me of the world outside the forest; tell me about yourself."

"About myself? Oh, that wouldn't interest you."

"Yes," she said, simply, "I would rather hear about yourself than about anything else."

"Look here, I don't know what to tell you."

"Tell me all you can think of," she said, calmly; "about your father and mother."

"Haven't got any," he said; "they're both dead."

"I am sorry," she said.

"Yes, they're dead," he said; "they died long ago."

"And have you any brothers and sisters?"

"No; I have a cousin, though," and he groaned.

"I am so glad," she said, in a low voice.

"Don't be. I'm not. He's a—I don't like him; we don't get on together, you know."

"You quarrel, do you mean?"

"Like Kilkenny cats," assented the Savage.

"Then he must be a bad man," she said, simply.

"No," he said, quietly; "everybody says that I am the bad one. I'm a regular bad lot, you know."

"I don't think that you are bad," she said.

"You don't; really not! By George! I like to hear you say that; but," with a slow shake of the head, "I'm afraid it's true. Yes, I am a regular bad lot."

"Tell me what you have done that is so wrong," she said.

"Oh—I've—I've spent all my money."

"That's not so very wrong; you have hurt only yourself."

"Jove, that's a new way of looking at it," he muttered. "And"—aloud—"and I've run into debt, and I've—oh, I can't tell you any more; I don't want you to hate me!"

"Hate you? I could not do that."

He sprang to his feet, paced up and down, and then dropped at her side again.

"Well, that's all about myself," he said; "now tell me about yourself."

"No," she said; "not yet. Tell me why you are going to Arkdale?"

"I'm going to Arkdale to take a train to Hurst Leigh to see my uncle, cousin, or whatever he is—Squire Davenant."

"Is he an old man?"

"Yes, a very old man, and a bad one, too. All our family are a bad lot, excepting my cousin, Stephen Davenant."

"The one you do not like?"

"The same. He is quite an angel."

"An angel?"

"One of those men too good to live. He's the only steady one we've got, and we make the most of him. He is Squire Davenant's heir—at least he will come into his money. The old man is very rich, you know."

"I see," she said, musingly; then she looked down at him and added, suddenly: "You were to have been the heir?"

"Yes, that's right! How did you guess that? Yes, I was the old man's favorite, but we quarreled. He wanted it all his own way, and, oh—we couldn't get on. Then Cousin Stephen stepped in, and I am out in the cold now."

"Then why are you going there now?" she asked.

"Because the squire sent for me," he replied.

"And you have been all this time going?"

"You see, I thought I'd walk through the forest," he said, apologetically.

"You should be there now—you should not have waited on the road! Is your Cousin Stephen—is that his name?—there?"

"I don't know," he said, carelessly.

"Ah, you should be there," she said. "Squire Davenant would be friendly with you again."

"I'm afraid you haven't hit the right nail on the head there," he said. "I rather think he wants to give me a good rowing about a scrape I've got into."

"Tell me about that."

"Oh, it's about money—the usual thing. I got into a mess, and had to borrow some money of a Jew, and he got me to sign a paper, promising to pay after Squire Davenant's death; he called it a *post obit*—I didn't know what it was then, but I do now; for the squire got to hear of it, but how, hanged if I can make out; and he wrote to me and to the Jew, saying that he shouldn't leave me a brass farthing. Of course the Jew was wild; but I gave him another sort of bill, and it's all right."

"Excepting that you will lose your fortune," said Una, with a little sigh. "What will you do?"

"That's a conundrum which I've long ago given up. By Jove! I'll come and be a woodman in the forest!"

"Will you?" she said. "Do you really mean it?—no, you were not in earnest!"

"I—why shouldn't I be in earnest?" he says, almost to himself. "Would you like me to? I mean shall I come here to—what do you call it—Warden?" and he threw himself down again.

"Yes," she said; "I should like you to. Yes, that would be very nice. We could sit and talk when your work was done, and I could show you all the prettiest spots, and the places where the starlings make their nests, and the fairy rings in the glades, and you could tell me all that you have seen and done. Yes," wistfully, "that would be very nice. It is so lonely sometimes!"

"Lonely, is it?" he said. "Lonely! By George, I should think it must be! I can't realize it! Books, it reads like a book. If I were to tell some of my friends that there was a young lady shut up in a forest, outside of which she had never been, they wouldn't believe me. By the way—where did you go to school?"

"School? I never went to school."

"Then how—how did you learn to read? and—it's awfully rude of me, you know, but you speak so nicely; such grammar, and all that."

"Do I?" she said, thoughtfully. "I didn't know that I did. My father taught me."

"It's hard to believe," he said, as if he were giving up a conundrum. "I beg your pardon. I mean that your father would have made a jolly good schoolmaster, and I must be an awful dunce, for I've been to Oxford, and I'll wager I don't know half what you do, and as to talking—I am not in it."

"Yes, my father is very clever," she said; "he is not like the other woodmen and burners."

"No, if he is, they must be a learned lot," assented Jack; "yes, I think I had better come and live here, and get him to teach me. I'm afraid he wouldn't undertake the job."

"Father does not like strangers," she said, blushing as she thought of the inhospitable scene of the preceding night. "He says that the world is a cruel, wicked place, and that everybody is unhappy there. But I think he must be wrong. You don't look unhappy."

"I am not unhappy now," said Jack.

"I am so glad," she said; "why are you not?"

"Because I am with you."

"Are you?" she said, gently. "Then it must be because I am with you that I feel so happy."

The Savage flushed and he looked down, striving to still the sudden throb of pleasure with which his heart beat.

"Confound it," he muttered, "I must go! I can't be such a cad as to stop any longer; she oughtn't to say this sort of thing, and yet I—I can't tell her so! No! I must go!" and he rose and took out his watch.

"I am afraid I must be on the tramp."

"Yes," she assented; "you have stayed too long. I hope you will find that the Squire Davenant has forgiven you. I think he cannot help it. And you will have your fortune and will go back into the world, and will quite forget that you lost your way in Warden Forest. But I shall not forget it; I shall often think of it."

"No," he said, "I shan't forget it. But in case I should, will you give me something—no, I won't ask it."

"Why not?" she said, wonderingly. "Were you going to say, will I give you something to help you to remember?"

"Yes, I will. What shall I give you?" and she looked around.

Jack looked at her. His bad angel whispered in his ear, "Ask her to give you a kiss," but Jack metaphorically kicked him out of hearing.

"Give me a flower," he said, and his voice was as gentle as its deep ringing bass could be.

Una nodded, and plucking a dog rose held it out to him.

"There," she said; "at least you will remember it as long as the rose lasts. But it soon dies," and she sighed.

Jack took it and looked at it hard. Then he put it to his lips.

"There is no smell to a dog rose," said Una.

"Ah no! I forgot. Just so. Well, good-by. We may shake hands, Una. That is your name, isn't it? How do you spell it?"

"U—n—a," she said, giving him her hand.

"It's a pretty name," he said, looking at her.

"Is it?" she said, dreamily. "Yes, I think it is, now. Say it again."

"Una, good-by. We shall meet again."

"Do you think so? Then you will have to come to Warden again."

"And I will. I will come soon. Oh, yes, we shall meet again. Good-by," and, yielding to the temptation, he bent and touched her hand—Heaven knows, reverently enough—with his lips.

A warm flush spread over the girl's face and neck, and she quivered from head to foot. It was the first kiss—except those of her father and mother—that she had ever received.

"Good-by," he repeated, and was slowly relinquishing her hand, the hand that clung to his, when a hand of firmer texture was laid on his arm and swung him round.

It was Gideon Rolfe, his face white with passion, his eyes ablaze, and a heavy stick upraised.

The Savage had just time to step back to avoid the blow and plant his feet firmly to receive a renewed attack; but with an effort the old man restrained himself, and struggling for speech, motioned the girl away with one hand and pointed with the other to Jack.

"You scoundrel!" he gasped, hoarsely. "Go, Una, go. You scoundrel! I warmed you at my hearth, you viper! and you turn to sting me. Go, Una—go at once. Do you disobey me?"

White and trembling, the girl shrank into the shade.

"You villain!" went on the old man, struggling with his passion.

"Stop!" exclaimed Jack, the veins in his forehead swelling ominously. "You must be mad! Don't strike me!—you are an old man!"

"Strike you! No, no; blows are of no avail with such as you! Curs take no heed of blows! What other way can one punish the scoundrel who repays hospitality by treachery? Was it not enough that you forced your way into my house, broke my bread, but you must waylay a credulous girl and lead her in the first step to ruin. Oh, spare your breath, viper! I know you and your race too well. Ruin and desolation walk hand in hand with you; but you have reckoned without your host here. My knowledge of you arms me with power to protect a weak, innocent girl from your wiles. Scoundrel!"

"You use strong words," he said, and his voice was low and hoarse. "You are an old man and—you are her father. You call me a scoundrel; I call you a fool, for if I were half the scoundrel you think me, you'd be to blame for any harm I might have done. I've done none. But that's no thanks to you, who keep such a girl as she is shut up as you do, and leave her to wander about unprotected. You know me, you say, and you know no good of me; that's as it may be, but I say when you call me a scoundrel, you lie!"

"Yes, I know you. I know the stock from whence you sprung, villains all! I thought that here, at least, I was safe from your kind; but Fate led you here—thank Fate that I let you go unhurt. Take an old man's advice, and, unlike your race, for once leave the prey which you thought so easy to destroy. Go!"

"I am going," he said, grimly. "I shall go, because if I stayed all night I should not convince you that I am not the scoundrel you suppose me. But, if you think that I am to be frightened by these sort of threats, you are mistaken. I have said that I will come back, and I *will!*" and with a curt nod he strode off.

CHAPTER V

It was the evening of the day on which Jack Newcombe had parted from Gideon and Una, and the young moon fell peacefully on the irregular pile of the ancient mansion known familiarly for twenty miles of its neighborhood as The Hurst.

The present owner was one Ralph Davenant, or Squire Davenant, as Jack Newcombe had called him, and as he was called by the county generally.

He was an old man of eighty, who had lived one-half his life in the wildest and most dissipated fashion, and the other half in that most unprofitable occupation known as repenting thereof.

I say "known as," for if old Squire Davenant had really repented, this story would never have been written.

If half the stories which were told of him were true, Ralph Davenant, the present owner of Hurst, deserves a niche in the temple of fame—or infamy—which holds the figures of the worst men of his day. He had been a gambler, a spendthrift, a rogue of the worst kind for one half his life; a miser, a cynic, a misanthrope for the other.

And he now lay dying in his huge, draughty bed-chamber, hung with the portraits of his ancestors—all bad and filled with the ghosts of his youth and wasted old age.

As it was, he lay quite still—so still that the physician, brought down from London at a cost of—say, ten guineas an hour, was often uncertain whether he was alive or dead.

There was a third person in the room—a tall, thin young man, who stood motionless beside the bed, watching the old man, with half-closed eyes and tightly compressed lips. This was Stephen Davenant, the old man's nephew, and, as it was generally understood, his heir. Stephen Davenant was called a handsome man, and at first sight he seemed to merit that description. It was not until you had looked at him closely that you began to grow critical and to find fault. He was dark; his hair, which was quite black, was smooth, and clung to his head with a sleek, slimy closeness that only served to intensify the paleness, not to say pallor, of the face. Pallor was, indeed, the prevailing characteristic, his lips even being of a subdued and half-tinted red; they were not pleasant lips, although for every forty minutes out of the sixty they wore a smile which just showed a set of large and even teeth, which were, if anything, too faultless and too white. Jack said that when Stephen smiled it was like a private view of a cemetery.

In short, to quote the Savage again, Stephen Davenant was an admirable example, as artists would say, of "a study in black and white."

As he stood by the bed, motionless, silent, with the fixed regard of his light gray eyes on the sick man, he looked not unlike one of those sleek and emaciated birds which one sees standing on the bank of the Ganges, waiting for the floating by of stray dead bodies.

And yet he was not unhandsome. At times he looked remarkably well; when, for instance, he was delivering a lecture or an address at some institute or May meeting. His voice was low and soft, and not seldom insinuating, and some of his friends had called him, half in jest, half in earnest, "Fascination Davenant."

It will be gathered from this description that to call all the race of Davenants bad was unfair; every rule has its exception, and Stephen Davenant was the exception to this. He was "a good young man."

Fathers held him up as a pattern to their wayward sons, mothers patronized and lauded him, and their daughters regarded him as almost too good to live.

The minutes, so slow for the watchers, so rapid to the man for whom they were numbered, passed, and the old cracked clock in the half-ruined stables wheezed out the hour, when, as if the sound had roused him, old Ralph moved slightly, and opening his eyes, looked slowly from one upright figure to the other.

Dark eyes that had not even yet lost all their fire, and still shone out like a bird's from their wrinkled, cavernous hollows.

Stephen unlocked his wrist, bent down, and murmured, in his soft, silky voice:

"Uncle, do you know me?"

A smile, an unpleasant smile to see on such a face, glimmered on the old man's lips.

"Here still, Stephen?" he said, slowly and hollowly. "You'd make a good—mute."

A faint, pink tinge crept over Stephen's pale face, but he smiled and shook his head meekly.

"Who's that?" asked Ralph, half turning his eyes to the physician.

"Sir Humphrey, uncle—the doctor," replied Stephen, and the great doctor came a little nearer and felt the faint pulse.

"What's he stopping for?" gasped the old man. "What can he do, and—why don't he go?"

"We must not leave you, uncle, till you are better."

A faint flame shot up in the old man's eyes.

"Better, that's a lie, you know. You always were— —" Then a paroxysm of faintness took him, but he struggled with and overcame it.

"Is—is—Jack here?" he asked.

"I regret to say," he replied, "that he is not. I cannot understand the delay. I hope, I fervently hope, that he has not willfully— —"

"Did you tell him I was dying?" asked Ralph, watching him keenly.

"Can you doubt it?" murmured Stephen, meekly. "I particularly charged the messenger to say that my cousin was not to delay."

The old man looked up with a sardonic smile.

"I'll wait," he muttered, and he closed his eyes resolutely. The minutes passed, and presently there was a low knock at the door, and a servant crept up to Stephen.

"Mr. Newcombe is below, sir."

Stephen looked warningly at the bed, and stole on tiptoe from the room—not that there was any occasion to go on tiptoe, for his ordinary walk was as noiseless as a cat's—down the old treadworn stairs, into the neglected hall, and entered the library.

Bolt upright, and looking very like a Savage indeed, stood Jack Newcombe.

With noiseless step and mournful smile, Stephen entered, closed the door, and held out his hand.

"My dear Jack, how late you are!"

With an angry gesture Jack thrust his hands in his pockets, and glared wrathfully at the white, placid face.

"Late!" he echoed, passionately. "Why didn't you tell me that he was dying?"

"Hush!" murmured Stephen, with a shocked look—though if Jack had bellowed in his savagest tone, his voice would not have reached the room upstairs. "Pray, be quiet, my dear Jack. Tell you! Didn't my man give you my message? I particularly told him to describe the state of my uncle's health. Slummers is not apt to forget or neglect messages!"

"Messages!" said Jack, with wrathful incredulity; "he gave me none— left none, rather, for I was out. He simply said that the squire wanted to see me."

"Dear, dear me," murmured Stephen, regretfully. "I cannot understand it. Do you think the person who took the message delivered it properly? Slummers is so very careful and trustworthy."

"Oh," said Jack, contemptuously. "Do you suppose anyone would have forgotten to tell me if your man had told them that the squire was dying? I don't if you do, and I don't believe you do. You're no fool, Stephen, though you have made one of me," and he moved toward the door.

"Stay," said Stephen, laying his white hand gently on Jack's arm. "Will you wait a few minutes? Though by some unfortunate accident you were not told how ill my uncle is, I assure you that he is too ill now to be harassed——"

"Oh, I know what you mean without so many words," interrupted Jack, scornfully. "Make your mind easy, I am not going to split upon you. Bah!" he added, as Stephen shook his head with sorrowful repudiation. "Do you suppose that I don't know that your man was instructed to keep it from me? What were you afraid of—that I should cut you out at the last moment? You judge me by your own standard, and you make a vast mistake. It isn't on account of the money—you are welcome to that—and you deserve it, for you've worked hard enough for it; no, it's not on that account, it's—but you wouldn't understand if I told you. I am going up now," and he sprang up the stairs quickly.

Stephen followed him, and entered the room close behind him. The old man looked up, motioned with his hand to Jack, looked at the other two and quietly pointed to the door.

Stephen's eyes closed and his lips shut as he hesitated for a moment, then he turned and left with the physician.

"I think," said Sir Humphrey, blandly, and looking at his watch—one of a score left him by departed patients, "I think that I will go now, Mr. Davenant; I can do no good and my presence appears only to irritate your uncle."

The great doctor departed, just thirty guineas richer than when he came, and Stephen went into the library and closed the door, and as he did so it almost seemed as if he had taken off a mask and left it on the mat outside.

The set, calm expression of the face changed to one of fierce, uncontrollable anxiety and malice. With sullen step he paced up and down the room, gnawing—but daintily—at his nails, and grinding the white tombstones.

"Another half hour," he muttered, "and the fool would have been too late? Will he tell the old man? Curse him; how I hate him! I was a fool to send for him—an idiot! What is he saying to him? What are they doing? Thank Heaven, that old knave Hudsley isn't there! They can't do anything—can't, can't! No, I am safe."

Stephen Davenant need not have been so uneasy; Jack was not plotting against him, nor was the old man making a will in the Savage's favor.

Jack stood beside the bed, waiting for one of the attacks of faintness to pass, looking down regretfully at the haggard, death-marked face, recalling the past kindnesses he had received from the old man, and remorsefully remembering their many quarrels and eventful separation.

"Bad lot" as he was, no thought of lucre crossed the Savage's mind; he forgot even Stephen and the cowardly trick he had played him, and remembered only that he was looking his last on the old man, who, after his kind, had been good, and so far as his nature would allow it, generous to him.

At last old Ralph opened his eyes.

"Here at last," he said; and by an effort of the resolute will, he made himself heard distinctly, though every word cost him a breath.

"I'm sorry I'm so late," he said; and his voice was husky. "I didn't know——"

The old man looked at him shrewdly.

"So Stephen didn't send? It was just like him. A good stroke."

"Yes, he sent," said Jack; "but— —"

The old man waved his hand to show that he understood.

"A sharp stroke. A clever fellow, Stephen. You always were a fool."

"I'm afraid so, sir," he said quietly.

"But Stephen is a knave, and a fool, too," murmured the old man. "Jack, I wish—I wish I could come back to the funeral."

"To see his face when the will's read," explained old Ralph, with a grim smile.

Jack colored, and, I am ashamed to say, grinned.

A sardonic smile flitted over the old man's face.

"Be sure you are there, Jack; don't let him keep you away."

"Not that you will be disappointed—much," said the old man.

"Don't think of me, sir," said Jack, with a dim sense of the discordance in such talk from such lips.

"I have thought of you as far—as—as I dared. Jack, you are an honest fool. Why—why did you give that *post obit?*"

"I don't know," said Jack, quietly. "Don't worry about that now."

"Stephen told me," said the old man, grimly. "He has told me every piece of wickedness you have done. He is a kind-hearted man, is—Ste— phen."

"We never were friends, sir," he said. "But don't talk now."

"I must," murmured the old man. "Now or never, and—give me your hand, Jack."

"I've had yours ever since I came in," said Jack, simply.

"Oh, I didn't know it. Good-by, boy—don't—don't end up like this. It—and—for Heaven's sake don't cry!" for Jack emitted a suspicious little choking sound, and his eyes were dim. "Good-by; don't be too disappointed. Justice, Jack, justice. Where is Stephen?—send him to me. I"—and the old sardonic smile came back—"I like to see him—he amuses me!"

The eyes closed; Jack waited a moment, then pressed the cold hand, and crept from the room.

Half way down the stairs he leaned his arm on the balustrade and dropped his face on it for a minute or two, then choking back his tears, went into the library—where Stephen was sitting reading a volume of sermons—and pointed up-stairs.

"My uncle wants me?" murmured Stephen. "I will go. Might I recommend this book to you, my dear Jack; it contains——"

Jack, I regret to say, chucked the volume into a corner of the room, and Stephen, with a mournfully reproachful sigh, shook his head and left the room.

CHAPTER VI

"Villains," says an old adage, "are made by accident." Now mark how accident helped to make a villain of the good Stephen Davenant.

He passed up the stairs and entered the bedroom. As he did so his foot struck against a chair and caused a little noise. The dying man heard it, however, and opening his eyes, said, almost inaudibly:

"Is that you, Hudsley?"

Stephen was about to reply, "No, it is I—Stephen," but stopped, hesitated, and as if struck by a sudden idea, drew back behind the bed-curtains.

Whatever that idea was, he was considerably moved by it; his hands shook, and his lips trembled during the interval of silence before the old man repeated the question:

"Is that you, Hudsley?"

Then Stephen, wiping his lips, answered in a dry voice utterly unlike his own, but very remarkably resembling that of the old solicitor, Hudsley:

"Yes, squire, it's Hudsley."

The dying man's hearing was faint, his senses wandering and dimmed; he caught the sense of the words, however, for with an effort he turned his head toward the curtains.

"Where are you?" he asked, almost inaudibly; "I can't see you; my sight has gone. You have been a long while coming. Hudsley, you thought you—knew—everything about the man who lies here; you were wrong. There's a surprise for you as well as the rest. Did you see Jack?"

Stephen had no need to reply: the old man rambled on without waiting, excepting to struggle for breath.

"He is down-stairs. Poor boy! it's a pity he is such a fool. There was always one like him in the Newcombe family. But the other—Stephen—the man who has been hanging about me all this time, eager to lick my boots so that he might step into them when I was gone; he is a fool and a knave."

Stephen's face went white and his lips twitched. It is probable that he remembered the adage: "Listeners hear no good of themselves."

"He is the first of his kind we have had in the family. Plenty of fools and scamps, Hudsley, but no hypocrites till this one. Well, he'll get his deserts. I'd give a thousand pounds to come back and hear the will read, and see his face. He makes so sure of it, too, the oily eel!"

Stephen writhed like an eel, indeed, and his lips blanched. Was the old man delirious, or had he, Stephen, really played the part of sycophant, toady and boot-licker all these years for nothing?

Great drops of sweat rolled down his face, his tongue clove to the roof of his mouth, and his knees shook so that he had to steady himself by holding the curtain.

"Yes, disappointed all. You don't understand. You think that you know everything. But no; I trusted you with a great deal, but not with all. How dark it is! Hudsley, you are an old man; don't finish up like—like this. Only one soul in the wide world is sorry that I'm going; and he's a fool. Poor Jack! I remember——"

Then followed, half inaudibly, a string of names belonging to the companions of his youth. Most of them were dead and forgotten by him until this hour, when he was about to join their shades.

"Ah, the old time! the old time. But—but—what was it I was saying? I—I—Hudsley—quick! for Heaven's sake! I—the key—the key——"

Stephen came round, in his eagerness risking recognition.

"The key?" he asked, so hoarsely that his voice might well be taken for an old man's. "What key?"

"Feel—under my pillow!" gasped Ralph Davenant.

Stephen thrust his trembling hand under the pillow, and, with a leap of the heart, felt a key.

"The safe!" murmured a faltering voice. "The bottom drawer. Bring them to me! Quick!"

Stephen glided snake-like across the room to a small safe that stood in a recess, opened the door, and with trembling hands drew out the drawer. His hands shook so, his heart beat to such an extent, that as a movement in the next room struck upon his ears, he could scarcely refrain from shrieking aloud; but it was only the nurse, whom the old man would only allow to enter the room at intervals; and setting his teeth hard, and fighting for calm, Stephen took out two documents.

One was a parchment of goodly proportions.

Both were folded and endorsed on the back—the parchment with the inscription, "Last will and testament of Ralph Davenant, Gent., Jan. 18—."

With eyes that almost refused to do their task, Stephen turned the other paper to the light, and read, "Will, July 18—." This inscription was written in an old man's hand—the parchment was engrossed as usual.

Two wills! The one—the parchment, however, was useless; the other— the sheet of foolscap—was the last.

"Well," rose the voice from the bed, hollow and broken, "have you got them?"

Stephen came up and stood behind the curtain, and held the wills up.

"Yes, yes," he said. "The first is—is in whose favor?"

The old man struggled for breath. White, breathless himself with the agony of anxiety and fear—for any moment someone might enter the room—Stephen stood staring beside him. He dared not undo the tapes and glance at the wills, in case of interruption—dared not conceal them, for Hudsley might appear on the scene. With the wills clasped in his hand, he stood and waited.

The faintness passed—old Ralph regained his voice.

"One is parchment—the other is paper. The parchment one you drew up; you know its contents—I want it destroyed, or, stay, keep it. It will add to the deceitful hound's disappointment. The other—ah, my God—it is too late—Hudsley, there is a cruel history in that paper. No hand but mine could pen it. But—but—I have done justice. Too late!—why do you say—too late? Why do you mock a dying man? Mind, Hudsley, I trust to you. It is a sound will, made in sound body—and—mind. Don't leave that hypocritical hound a chance of setting it aside. I trust to you. Stop, better burn the first will; burn it here now—now," and in his excitement he actually raised his head. Raised it to let it drop upon the pillow again with exhaustion.

Stephen stood and glared, torn this way and that by doubt and uncertainty.

"Justice," he whispered hoarsely. "The first will, my will leaves all to— —"

"To that hound Stephen!" gasped the old man. "I did it in a weak moment and repented of it. Leaves all to him; but not now."

Stephen hesitated no longer. With the quick, gliding movement of a cat he reached the iron safe, replaced the parchment in the drawer and locked the outer door, and thrust the paper will into his pocket.

Scarcely had he done so, before he had time to get to his place, the door opened and Hudsley, the lawyer, entered.

He was an old man, as thin and bent as a withy branch, with a face seamed and wrinkled, like his familiar parchment, with the like spots; his dark, keen gray eyes, which looked out from under his shaggy eyebrows, like stars in a cloudy sky.

As he entered, Stephen came forward, his back to the light, his face in the shadow, and held out his hand.

Hudsley took it, held it for a moment, and dropped it with a little, irritable shudder—the slim, white hand was as cold as ice—and, turning to the bed, looked anxiously at the dying man.

"Great heaven!" he said, "is he dead?"

A savage hope shot up in Stephen's heart, but he looked and shook his head.

"No. You have been a long time coming, Mr. Hudsley."

"I have, sir, thanks to your man's stupidity," said the lawyer, in an angry whisper. "He came for me in a confounded dogcart!"

"The quickest vehicle to get ready," murmured Stephen. "I told him, to take the first that came to hand."

"And the result," said the lawyer impatiently. "The result is that we lost half an hour on the road! Does your man drink, Mr. Stephen?"

"Drink! Slummers drink!" murmured Stephen. "A most steady, respectable—I may say conscientious—man."

"He may be conscientious, but he's a very bad driver. I never saw such a clumsy fellow. He drove into a ditch half a mile after we had started."

"Dear, dear," murmured Stephen regretfully. "Poor Slummers. It is not his fault. He is a worthy fellow, but too sympathetic, and my uncle's illness quite upset him——"

"Hush!" interrupted Mr. Hudsley, holding up his finger and bending down.

"Squire, do you know me? I am Hudsley."

The dying man moved his hand faintly in assent.

"Yes. Have you done as I told you?"

"You have told me nothing yet."

"The safe!—the key!—the pillow!" said the Squire.

Hudsley caught his meaning and felt under the pillow, and Stephen, as if to assist, thrust his hand under, and withdrew it with the key in his fingers.

"Why—again?" came the voice, broken and impatient. "You have done it! you have burnt the first."

"What is he saying?" he asked.

"You have burned it; show me the other—the last; let me—touch it."

Hudsley opened the safe and took the first will from the drawer.

"Two, did he say?" he muttered: "there is only one here—the will;" and he came to the bed with it.

"There is only one will here, of course, squire," he said, bending down and speaking slowly and distinctly.

"Yes—you, you have—burned the other. Speak. I cannot see, but I can hear you."

"I have burned none," said Hudsley. "Have only just come—there is only one will here."

"Which?" gasped the dying man.

"The will of January—Mr. Stephen——"

Before they could finish, they saw, with horror, the dying man half raise himself, his face livid, his hands wildly clutching the air, his eyes, by accident, turned toward Stephen.

"You—you thief!" he gasped. "Give it to me!—give—give—oh, God! Too late?—too la——"

It was too late. Before the nurse and Jack could rush into the room, horrified by the shriek which rang from Stephen's white lips, old Ralph Davenant had fallen back dead!

CHAPTER VII

Half an hour afterward Stephen Davenant passed down the stairs on tiptoe, though the tramp of an armed host could not disturb old Ralph Davenant now—passed down with his hand pressed against his breast pocket, in which lay the stolen will. Had the sheet of blue foolscap been composed of red-hot iron instead of paper, Stephen could not have felt its presence more distinctly and uncomfortably; it seemed to burn right through his clothes and scorch his heart; he could almost fancy, in his overstrained state, that it could be seen through his coat.

He paused a moment outside the library door, one white hand fingering his pale lips, the other vainly striving to keep away from his breast pocket, and listened to the tramp, tramp of Jack as he walked up and down the room. Any other face would have been more endurable than Jack's, with its fiercely frank gaze and outspoken contempt.

At last he opened the door and entered, his handkerchief in his hand. Jack stopped and looked at him.

"I have been waiting for you," he said.

"My poor uncle!"

Jack looked at him with keen scrutiny, mingled with unconcealed scorn.

"I have been waiting for you, in case you wished to say anything before I went."

"What?" murmured Stephen, with admirably feigned surprise and regret. "You will not go, my dear Jack! not to-night."

"Yes, to-night," said Jack quietly. "I couldn't stop in the house—I shall go to the inn."

"But——"

"No, thanks!" said Jack, cutting him short.

"Oh, do not thank me," murmured Stephen, meekly. "I may have no right to offer you hospitality, the house may be yours."

"Well, I think you could give a pretty good guess on that point," said Jack, bluntly; "but let that pass. I am going to the 'Bush.' If you or Mr. Hudsley want me—where is Hudsley?" he broke off to inquire.

"Mr. Hudsley is up-stairs sealing up the safe and things," said Stephen humbly. "He wished me to assist him, but I had rather that he should do it alone—perhaps you would go through the house with him?"

Jack shook his head.

"As you please," murmured Stephen, with a resigned sigh. "Mr. Hudsley is quite sufficient; he knows where everything of importance is kept. You will have some refreshments after your journey, my dear Jack?"

"No, thanks," said Jack; "I want nothing—I couldn't eat anything. I'll go now."

"Are you going, Mr. Newcombe?" said Mr. Hudsley, entering and looking from one to the other keenly.

"I am going to the 'Bush;' I shall stay there in case I am wanted."

"The funeral had better be fixed for Saturday. You and Mr. Stephen will be the chief mourners." Then he turned to Stephen. "I have sealed up most of the things. Is there anything you can suggest?"

"You know all that is required; we leave everything to you, Mr Hudsley. I think I may speak for my cousin—may I not, Jack?"

Jack did not reply, but put on his gloves.

"I will go now," he said. "Good-night, Mr. Hudsley."

The old lawyer looked at him keenly as he took his hand.

"I shall find you at the 'Bush?'" he said.

"Yes," replied Jack, and was leaving the room when Stephen rose and followed him.

"Good-night, my dear Jack," he said. "Will you not shake hands on—on such an occasion?"

Jack strode to the door and opened it without reply, then turned and, as if with an effort, took the hand which Stephen had kept extended.

"Good-night," he said, dropping the cold fingers, and strode out.

Stephen looked after him a moment with his meek, long-suffering expression of face changed into a malignant smile of triumph, and his hand went up to his breast pocket.

"Good-night, beggar!" he murmured, and closed the door.

Mr. Hudsley was still standing by the library-table, toying absently with the keys, a thoughtful frown on his brow, which did not grow any lighter as Stephen entered, making great play with the pocket-handkerchief.

"I think I also may go now, Mr. Stephen," he said. "Nothing more can be done to-night. I will be here in the morning with my clerk."

"I suppose nothing more can be done. You have sealed up all papers and jewels? I am particularly anxious that nothing shall be left informal."

"I don't think there is anything unsealed that should have been."

"A very strange scene, the final one, Mr. Stephen."

"Awful, awful, Mr. Hudsley. My poor uncle seemed quite delirious at the last."

"Hem!" grunted the old lawyer, putting his hat to his lips and looking over it at the white, smooth face. "You think he was delirious— —"

"Don't you, Mr. Hudsley? Do you think that he was conscious of what he was saying? You have been his legal adviser and confidant for years; you would know whether there was any meaning in his wild and incoherent statement about the will. As you are no doubt aware, my poor uncle never broached the subject of his intentions to me."

"I know of only one will—that of last year. That will I executed for him; it is the will locked up in the safe up-stairs. I have a copy at the office," he added, dryly

"You—you don't think there is any other—any other later will?" he asked, softly.

"I didn't think so until an hour ago. I am not sure that I think so now. Do you?"

"No," he said, shaking his head. "My uncle was not the man to draw up a will with his own hand, and his confidence, and I may say affection for you, were so great that he would not have gone to any other legal adviser to do it for him. No, I do not think there is any other will; of course, I do not know the contents of the will in the safe."

"Of course not," said Mr. Hudsley, in a tone so dry that it seemed to rasp his throat.

"And yet I cannot understand, my poor uncle's outbreak, except by attributing it to delirium."

"Hem!" said Mr. Hudsley. "Well, in case there should have been any meaning and significance in it, my clerk and I will make a careful search to-morrow."

"Yes," murmured Stephen, "and I devoutly trust that should a later will be in existence, you may find it."

"I hope we may," said Mr. Hudsley. "Good-night!"

Stephen accompanied him to the door as he had accompanied the doctor and Jack, and saw him into the brougham, and then turned back into the house with a look of release, which, however, gradually changed to one of lurking fear and indefinite dread.

"Conscience makes cowards of us all."

It makes a worse coward of Stephen Davenant than he was naturally.

As he stood in the deserted hall, and looked round, at its vast dimness, at the carved gallery and staircase, somber and dull for want of varnish, and listened to the faint, ghostly noises made by the awe-stricken servants moving to and fro overhead, a chill crept over him, and he wished that he had kept one of them, even Jack, to bear him company.

With fearful gaze he peered into the darkness, scarcely daring to cross the hall and enter the library. For all the stillness, he fancied he could hear that last shriek of the dying man ringing through the house; for all the darkness, the slim, bent figure seemed to be moving to and fro, the dark piercing eyes turned upon him with furious accusation. Even when he had summoned up courage to enter the library, locking the door after him, the eyes seemed to follow him, and with a shudder that shook him from head to foot he poured out a glass of brandy and drank it down.

The Spirit of Evil certainly invented brandy for cowards.

Stephen set down the empty glass and looked round the room—another man.

He even smiled in a ghostly kind of fashion as he took the will from his pocket and opened it.

"Poor Jack!" he murmured, with a sardonic display of the white teeth. "This no doubt makes you master of Hurst Leigh; but Providence has decreed that the spendthrift shall be disappointed. Yes, I am the humble instrument chosen. I am——"

He stopped suddenly with a start, for he had been reading as he soliloquized, and he had come upon words that struck him to the very heart's core.

Was he dreaming, or had his senses taken leave of him?

With beating heart and white, parched lips he stared at the paper until the lines of crabbed handwriting danced before his astounded eyes.

If brevity is the soul of wit, old Ralph Davenant's will was wit itself. It consisted of five paragraphs.

The first was merely the usual preamble declaring the testator to be of sound mind.

The second ran thus:

"To John Newcombe I will and bequeath the sum of fifty thousand pounds, the said sum to be realized by the sale or transfer of bonds and stocks, at the discretion of James Hudsley."

Enough in this to move Stephen, but it paled into insignificance before what followed:

"To my nephew, Stephen Davenant, I will and bequeath the set of Black's sermons in twenty-nine volumes, standing on the second shelf in the library, having remarked the affection which the said Stephen Davenant bore the said volumes, and accepting his repeated assertions that his attendance upon me was wholly disinterested."

An ugly flash and an evil glitter swept over Stephen's white face and eyes, and his teeth ground together maliciously.

"To each and every one of my servants I bequeath the sum of one hundred pounds, such sum to be forfeited by each and every one who assumes mourning for my death, which each and every one has anxiously looked forward to.

"And lastly, I will and bequeath the remainder of my property of whatsoever kind, be it money, houses, lands, or property of any description, to my only daughter and child, Eunice Davenant, the same to be held in trust for her sole use and benefit by James Hudsley.

"And I hereby inform him, and the world at large, that the said Eunice Davenant is the only issue of my marriage with Caroline Hatfield; that the said marriage was celebrated in secret at the Church of Armfield, in Sussex, in June, 18—. And that the said Eunice Davenant, my daughter, is in the keeping of one Gideon Rolfe, woodman, of Warden Forest, who has reared her as his own child, and who is unacquainted with the facts of my secret marriage, and I decree and appoint James Hudsley sole guardian, trustee, and ward of the aforesaid Eunice Davenant, and at her hands I crave forgiveness for my neglect of her mother and herself.

"(Signed)Ralph Davenant,
"Hurst Leigh.
"Witness—George Goodman,
"Coachman, Hurst Leigh.
"Martha Goodman,
"Cook, Hurst Leigh."

White, breathless, Stephen held the paper in his clinched hands and stared at the astounding contents.

Eunice Davenant the squire's daughter.

His overstrained brain refused to realize it.

Old Ralph Davenant married! Married! It was impossible.

Oh, yes, that was it. A smile, a ghastly smile shone on his face. *It was a joke*—a vile, malicious joke, worthy of the crabbed, misanthropical old man! A villainous joke, set down just to bring about litigation, and create trouble and confusion between the two young men, himself and Jack Newcombe. And yet—and the smile died away and left his face fearful and haggard— and yet that awful fury of the dying man when he knew that the will had been stolen.

No, it was no jest. The marriage had taken place; there *was* a daughter, and she was the heiress of all that immense, untold wealth, except the fifty thousand pounds left to Jack Newcombe, while he—he, Stephen Davenant, the next of kin, the man who had been working, lying, toadying for the money, was left with a set of musty sermons.

Rage filled his heart; stifling, choking with fury, the disappointed schemer struck the senseless paper with his clinched fist, and ground his teeth at it; then, suddenly, as if by a swift inspiration, he remembered that this accursed will, which would reduce him to beggary, and leave an unknown girl and his hated cousin wealthy, was in his hands; that he and he only knew of its existence. With a sudden revulsion of feeling he sprang to his feet, and held the paper at arm's length and laughed softly at it, as if it were endued with sense, and could appreciate its helplessness.

Then he drew the candle near, folded the paper into a third of its size, held it to the candle—and drew it back again, overcome by that fascination which almost invariably exercises itself on such occasions—that peculiar reluctance to destroy the thing whose existence can destroy the possessor.

The flame flickered and licked the frail paper; the smoke curled round its edge; and yet—and yet he could not destroy it.

Instead, he sat down, and with clinched teeth unfolded the will and read it—read it again and again, until every word was burned and seared into his brain.

"Eunice Davenant! Eunice Davenant! Curse her!" he groaned out.

But even as the words left his lips a sound rose, the unmistakable tap—tap of something—some finger striking the window-pane.

Biting his bloodless lips to prevent himself calling out in his ecstasy of fear, he thrust the will into his pocket, caught up the candle, swept the curtains aside, and started back.

The light fell full upon the face of a young girl.

CHAPTER VIII

The face at the window was that of a young girl of about two-and-twenty.

It would be hard to say whether Stephen Davenant was pleased or annoyed by this apparition. That he was surprised there could be no doubt, for he almost dropped the candle in his astonishment, and fumbled at the lock of the window for some moments before he could open it.

"Laura!" he exclaimed, "can it be you? Great Heavens! Impossible!"

With a little gasp of relief and suppressed excitement, the girl stepped into the room, and leaned upon his arm, panting with a commingling of weariness and fear.

"My dear Laura," he said, still holding the candle, "how did you come here? Why——"

"Oh, Stephen, is it really you? I was afraid that I had made some mistake—that I had come all this way——"

"You do not mean to say you have come all the way from London alone—alone!"

"Yes, I have come all the way from London. Do not be angry with me, Stephen. I—I could not wait any longer. It seemed so long! Why did you leave me without a word? I did not know whether you were alive or dead. Three weeks—think, three weeks! How could you do it?"

"Hush! hush! Do not speak so loud," he whispered. "Did anyone see you come in?"

"No one. I have been waiting in the shrubs for—oh, hours! I saw the visitors go away—an old gentleman and a young one—and I saw your shadow behind the blind," and she pointed to the window. "I have been outside waiting, and dreading to knock in case you should not be alone."

"You—you saw my shadow?" he said, with an uneasy smile. "Did you see—I mean, what was I doing?"

"I did not see distinctly; I was listening for voices. Oh, Stephen, I am so weary!"

He drew a chair for her, and, motioning her to sit, mixed a glass of brandy-and-water, and stood over her holding her wrist and looking down at her with an uneasy smile.

"Now," he said, taking the glass from her, "tell me all about it—how you came, and why? Speak in a whisper."

"You don't need to ask me why, Stephen," she said, leaning forward and laying her hand upon his arm, her dark eyes fixed on his half-hidden ones. "Why did you leave me so long without a word?"

"I will tell you directly," he answered. "Tell me how you came—alone! Great Heaven!"

"Alone, yes; why not? I was not afraid. I came by the train."

"But—but— —" he said, with a little flush and a shifting glance, "how did you know where I was?"

"You would never guess! You do not deserve that I should tell you. Well, I followed Slummers!"

"Followed Slummers!" he echoed, with a forced smile.

"Yes, I met him in the street; you are going to ask me why I did not ask him where you were," she broke off with a smile and a shake of her head.

"Because I knew he would not tell me. Stephen, I do not like that man, and he does not like me. Why do you trust him so?"

"You followed Slummers—well?"

"To the station. I was behind him when he took his ticket, and I took one for the same place. I was quite close behind him, but he did not see me. I got into the train at the last moment, and I followed him from the station here."

"My dear Laura," he murmured, soothingly; "how rash, how thoughtless!"

"Was it?" she said. "Perhaps it was. I did not stop to think."

"But now—now what are you to do?"

"Don't be angry with me, Stephen, now I *am* here. You must tell me what I am to do." Then her eyes wandered round the house. "What a large house! Is it yours, Stephen?"

"Eh?" he said, starting slightly. "I—I—don't know—I mean it was my uncle's. I was going to write to-night and tell you where I was, and why I did not write before."

"Why didn't you?" she said, with gentle reproach.

"Because," he replied, "I could not—it was impossible. I could not leave the house, and could not trust the letter to a servant. My uncle has been very ill: he—he—lies dead up-stairs."

"Up-stairs! Oh, Stephen!"

"You see," he exclaimed reproachfully, "that I have a good excuse, that I have not desert—left you without a word for no cause."

"Forgive me, Stephen, dear!" she murmured, penitently. "Do not be angry with me. Say you are glad to see me now I have come."

"Of course I am glad to see you, but I am not glad you have come, my dear Laura. What am I to do with you? I am not alone here, you know. The house is full of servants; any moment someone may come in. Think of the awkward position in which your precipitancy has placed me—has placed both of us!"

"I never thought of that—I did not know. Why did you not tell me you were with your uncle? Oh, Stephen, why have you hidden things from me?"

"Hidden things?" he echoed, with ill-concealed impatience. "I did not think that it was worth telling. I did not know that I was coming—I was fetched suddenly. Now that I come to think of it, I told Slummers to call and tell you."

"And he forgot it—on purpose. I hate Slummers!"

"Poor Slummers!" murmured Stephen. "Never mind him, however. We must think now of what is to be done with you. You—you cannot stay here."

"Can I not? No, I suppose not. I can go back," she added, with a touch of bitterness.

"My darling," he said, coaxingly, "I am afraid you must go back. There is an up-train—the last—in half an hour."

The girl leaned back and clasped her hands in her lap.

"I am very sorry," he said, grasping her arm; "but what can I do? You cannot stay here. That's impossible. There is only one inn in the place, and your appearance there would arouse curiosity, and—oh, *that*, too, is quite impossible! My poor Laura, why did you come?"

"Yes," she said, slowly, "it was foolish to come. You are not glad to see me, Stephen."

He bent over her and kissed her, but she put him from her with a touch of her hand, and rose wearily.

"I will go," she said. "Yes, I was wrong to come. Tell me the way," and she drew her jacket close.

"Don't look so grieved, dear," he murmured. "What am I to do? If there was any place—but there is not. See, I will come with you to the station. We shall have to walk, I am afraid; I dare not order a carriage. My poor child, if you had only foreseen these difficulties."

"Do not say any more," she interrupted coldly. "I am quite convinced of my folly and am ready to go."

"Sit down and wait while I get my hat. We must get away unobserved. Suspicious eyes are watching my every movement to-night. I can't tell you all, but I will soon. Sit down, my darling; I will not be gone a moment. If anyone comes to the door, step through the window and conceal yourself."

Unlocking the door noiselessly he went out, turning the key after him.

Barely a minute elapsed before he was in the room again.

Warm though the night was he put on an overcoat and turned up the collar so that it hid the lower part of his face.

Locking the door after him, he came up to the table, poured out another glass of brandy-and-water, and got some biscuits.

"Come," he said, "you must eat some of these. Put some in your pocket. And you must drink this, my poor darling, or you will be exhausted."

She put back the glass and plate from her with a gesture of denial.

"I could not eat," she said. "I do not want anything, and I shall not be exhausted. Let us go; this house makes me shudder," and she moved to the window and passed out.

"Laura, my dear Laura," murmured Stephen, in his most dulcet tones, "why are you angry with me?"

"I am not angry with you," she said, and the voice, cold and constrained, did not seem the same as that in which she had greeted him a quarter of an hour ago. "I am angry with myself; I am filled with self-scorn."

"My dear Laura," he began, soothingly, but she interrupted him with a gesture.

"You are quite right; I was wrong to come. You have not said so in so many words, but your face, your eyes, your very smile have told me so plainly."

"What have I said?"

"Nothing," she answered, without hesitation, and with the same air of cold conviction. "If you had said angry words, had been harsh and annoyed openly, and yet been glad to see me, I could have forgiven myself, but you were not glad to see me. If I had been in your place—but I am a woman. Don't say any more. Is the station near?"

"My dear Laura," murmured Stephen for the third time, and now more softly than ever, "more must be said. I am anxious, naturally anxious, to learn whether this—this sudden journey can be concealed."

It was quite true, he was anxious, very anxious—on his own account.

CHAPTER IX

"Come," he said; "it is all right, then. Do not take the matter so seriously, my darling Laura. The worst part of it is that you should have made such a journey alone, and have to go back alone, and at night! That is what grieves me. If I could but go with you—and yet that would scarcely be wise—but it is impossible under the circumstances. Come, give me your arm, my dear Laura."

A little shiver ran through her frame, and she caught her breath with a stifled sob.

"Come, come, my darling," he murmured; "don't look back, look forward. In an hour or two you will be home."

"Do you think I am afraid?" she asked, and her voice trembled, but not with fear. "No, I am looking back. Oh, Stephen, do you remember when we met first?"

"Yes, yes," said Stephen, soothingly, and with an anxious, sidelong look about—to be seen promenading the high road with a young woman on his arm on the night of his uncle's death would be the ruin of his carefully built-up reputation. "Yes, yes," he murmured. "Shall I ever forget? How fortunate you lost your way, Laura, and that you should have come up to me to ask it, and that I should have been going in that direction. And yet the thoughtless speak of chance!"

And he cast up his eyes with unctuous solemnity, though there was no one in the dark road to be impressed by it.

"Chance," said the girl, sadly—"an evil or a good chance for me—which? Stephen, I sometimes wish that we had never met—that I had not crossed your path, and so have left the old life, with its dull, quiet and sober grayness; but the die was cast that afternoon. I went back to the quiet home, to the old man who had been my father, mother and all to me, and life was changed."

"Your grandfather has no suspicion?"

"No, he trusts me entirely. If he asks a question when I go to meet you, he is satisfied when I tell him that I am going to a neighbor. Stephen, if I had had a mother, do you think I should have deceived her also?"

"Deceived? Deceived is too harsh a word, my dear Laura. We have been obliged, for various reasons, to use some reserve—let us say candidly, to conceal our engagement. You have not mentioned my name to anyone?" he broke off.

"To no one," she answered.

"Such concealment was necessary. My uncle was a man of rough and hasty temper, ill-judging and merciless."

"But," she said, with a sudden eagerness, and a slight shudder, "he—he is dead now, Stephen. There is no need for further concealment."

"Softly, softly, dear Laura. We must be patient—must keep our little secret a little while longer. I can trust my darling to confide in me—yes, yes, I know that——"

"Stephen, to-night for the first time—why, I know not—I have doubted—no, not doubted, for I have fought hard against the suspicion that I was wrong to trust you."

"My dearest!" he murmured reproachfully.

"You were wrong to leave me for so long without a word—you put my love to too severe a test. I—I cannot say whether it has stood it or not. To-night I am full of doubt. Stephen—look at me!"

He turned his face and looked down. He had not far to look, for she was tall, and in the moment of excitement had drawn herself to her full height. The moon, sailing from amongst the clouds, shone on her upturned face; her lips were set, and the dark eyes gleamed from the white face.

"Look at me, Stephen. If—I say if—there is the faintest idea of treachery lurking in your mind——"

"My dearest——"

"Cast it out! Here, to-night, I warn you to cast it out! Such love as mine is like a two-edged sword, it cuts both ways, for love—or hate! Stephen, I have loved, I have trusted you—for mine, for your own sake, be true to me!"

He was more impressed than alarmed. This side of her character had been presented to him to-night for the first time. Hitherto the beautiful girl had been all smiles and humble devotion. Was she bewitched, or had he been mistaken in her. Perhaps it was the moon, but suddenly his face looked paler than ever, and the white eyelids drooped until they hid the shifting eyes, as he put his arm around her.

"My dearest! What can you mean? Deceive you! Treachery! Can you deem me—*me*—capable of such things. My dearest, you are overtired! And your jacket has become unbuttoned. Listen, that is the railway bell. Laura, you will not leave me with such words on your lips?"

"Forgive me, Stephen."

"I have done so already, dearest, and now we must part! It is very hard—but—I cannot even go with you to the platform. Someone might see us. It is for your sake, darling."

"Yes, yes, I know," she said, with a sigh. "Good-bye—you will write or come to me—when?"

"Soon, in a day or two," he said. "Do not be impatient. There is much to be done; my poor uncle's funeral, you know. Good-bye. See! I will stay here and watch the train off. Good-bye, dear, dear Laura!"

She put her arm round him and returned his kiss, and glided away, but at the turn of the road leading to the station she turned and, holding up her hand, sent a word back to him.

It was:

"Remember!"

Stephen waited until the train puffed out of the station, and not until it had flashed some distance did the set smile leave his face.

Then, with a rather puzzled and uneasy expression, he turned and walked swiftly back to the house.

His brain was in a whirl, the sudden appearance of the young girl coming on the top of the other causes of excitement bewildered him, and he felt that he had need of all his accustomed coolness. The sudden peril and danger of this accursed will demanded all his attention, and yet the thought of the girl would force itself upon him. He had met her, as she had said, in the streets, and had commenced an acquaintance which had resulted in an engagement. Alone and unprotected, save for an old grandfather, and innocent of the world, Laura Treherne had been, as it were, fascinated by the smooth, soft-spoken Stephen, from whose ready tongue vows of love and devotion rolled as easily as the scales from a serpent in spring-time. And he, for his part, was smitten by the dark eyes and quick, impulsive way of the warm-hearted girl.

But there had come upon him of late a suspicion that in binding himself to marry her he had committed a false step; to-night the suspicion grew into something like certainty.

To tell the truth, she had almost frightened him. Hitherto the dark eyes had ever turned on his with softened gaze of love and admiration; to-night, for the first time, the hot, passionate nature had revealed itself.

The deep-toned "Remember!" which came floating down the lane as she disappeared rang unpleasantly in his ears. Had he been a true-hearted man the girl's spirit would have made her more precious in his eyes; but, coward-like, he felt that hers was a stronger nature than his, and he began to fear.

"Yes," he muttered, as he unlocked the library window, and sank into a chair. "It was a weak stroke, a weak stroke! But I can't think of what is to be done now, not now!"

No, for to-night all his attention must be concentrated on the will.

Wiping the perspiration from his brow, he lit another candle. This time nothing should prevent him from destroying the accursed thing which stood between him and wealth; he would burn it at once—at once. With feverish eagerness he thrust his hand in his coat, then staggered and fell back white as death.

The pocket was empty. The will was not there.

"I—I am a fool!" he muttered, with a smile. "I put it in the other coat," and he snatched up the overcoat, but a glance, a touch showed him that it was not there either.

Wildly, madly he searched each pocket in vain, went on his knees and felt, as if he could not trust his sight alone, every inch of the carpet; turned up the hearth-rug, almost tore up the carpet itself, shook the curtains, and still hunted and searched long after the conviction had forced itself upon his mind that in no part of the room could the thing be hidden.

Then he paused, pressing his hand to his brow and biting his livid lips. Let him think—think—think! Where could it be? He had not dropped it on the stairs or in any other part of the house, for he remembered, he could swear, that he had felt the thing as he stood in the study buttoning up his overcoat. If not in the house, where then?

Throwing aside all caution in his excitement, he unfastened the window, and, candle in hand, examined the grand terrace, traced every step which he had taken across the lawn—and all to no purpose.

"It is lying in the road," he muttered, the sweat dropping from his face. "Heaven! lying glaring there, for any country clown to pick up and ruin me. I must—I will find it! Brandy—I must have some brandy—this—this is maddening me!"

And indeed he seemed mad, for though he knew he had not passed it, he went back, still peering on the ground, the candle held above his head. Suddenly he stumbled up against some object, and, looking up, saw the tall figure of a man standing right in his path. With a wolfish cry of mingled fear and rage, he dropped the candle and sprang on to him.

"You—you thief!" he cried, hoarsely; "give it to me—give it me!"

The man made an effort to unlock the mad grasp of the hands round his throat, then scientifically and coolly knocked his assailant down, and, holding him down writhing, struck a match.

Gasping and foaming, Stephen looked up and saw that it was Jack Newcombe—Jack Newcombe regarding him with cool, contemptuous surprise and suspicion.

"Well," he said contemptuously, "so it's you! Are you out of your mind?" and he flung the match away and allowed Stephen to rise.

Trembling and struggling for composure, Stephen brushed the dust from his black coat and stood rubbing his chest, for Jack's blow had been straight from the shoulder.

"What have you got to say for yourself?" said Jack, sternly. "I asked you if you had gone mad. What are you doing here with a candle, and behaving like a lunatic?"

Stephen made a mighty effort for composure, and a ghastly smile struggled to his face.

"My dear Jack, how you startled me!" he gasped. "I was never so frightened in my—my life!"

"So it appeared," said Jack, with strong disgust in his voice. "Pick up the candle—there it is."

And he pointed with his foot. But Stephen was by no means anxious for a light.

"Never mind the candle," he said. "You are quite right—I must have seemed out of my mind. I—I am very much upset, my dear Jack."

"Are you hurt?" inquired Jack, but with no great show of concern.

"No, no!" gasped Stephen; "don't distress yourself, my dear Jack—don't, I beg of you. It was my fault, entirely. The—the fact is that I——"

He paused, for Jack had got the candle, lit it, and held it up so that the light fell upon Stephen's face.

"Now," he said, his tone plainly intimating that he would prefer to see Stephen's face while he made his explanation.

"The fact is," Stephen began again, "I have had the misfortune to lose a pocketbook—no, not a pocketbook, that is scarcely correct, but a paper which I fancied I had put in my pocketbook, and which must have dropped out. It—it was a draft of a little legal document which my lawyer had sent me—of no value, utterly valueless—oh, quite——"

"So I should judge from the calm way in which you accused the first man you met of stealing it," said Jack, with quiet scorn.

Stephen bit his lip, and a glance of hate and suspicion shot from under his eyelids.

"Pray forgive me, my dear Jack," he said, pressing his hand to his brow, and sighing. "If you had sat up for so many nights, and were so worn and overwrought, you would have some sympathy with my overstrained nerves. I am much shaken to-night, my dear Jack—very much shaken."

And indeed he was, for the Savage's fist was by no means a soft one.

Jack looked at him in silence for a moment, then held the candle toward him.

"You had better go to the house and get some of the servants to help you look for the paper," he said. "Good-night."

"Oh, it is of no consequence," said Stephen, eagerly. "Don't go—stop a moment, my dear Jack. I—I will walk with you as far as the inn."

"No, thanks," said Jack, curtly; then, as a suspicious look gleamed in Stephen's eyes, he added: "Oh, I see! you are afraid I should pick it up in the road. You had better come."

Stephen smiled, and laid his hand on Jack's arm.

"You—you are not playing a joke with me, my dear Jack? You haven't got the—document in your pocket all the time?"

"If I said that I hadn't you wouldn't believe me, you know," he replied. "There, take your hand off my coat!"

"Stop! stop!" exclaimed Stephen, with a ghostly attempt at a laugh. "Don't go, my dear Jack; stop at the house to-night. I should feel very much obliged, indeed, if you would. I am so upset to-night that I—I want company. Let me beg of you to stop."

And in his dread lest Jack should escape out of sight, he held on to his arm.

Jack shook him with so emphatic a movement of disgust that Stephen was in imminent danger of making a further acquaintance with the lawn.

"Go indoors," he said sternly, "and leave me alone. I'd rather not sleep under the same roof with you. As for your lost paper, whatever it may be, you had better look for it in the morning, unless you want to get into further trouble," and he turned on his heel and disappeared.

Stephen waited until he had got at a safe distance, and, blowing out the candle, followed down the road with stealthy footsteps, keeping a close watch on the rapidly-striding figure, and examining the road at the same time. But all to no purpose; Jack reached and entered the inn without stopping, and neither going nor returning could Stephen see anything of the missing will.

Two hours afterward he crept back and staggered into the library more dead than alive, one question rankling in his disordered brain.

Had Jack Newcombe found the will, and, if not, where was it?

After a time the paroxysm of fear and despair passed, and left him calmer. His acute brain, overwhelmed but not crushed out, began to recover itself, and he turned the situation round and round until he had come to a plan of action.

It was not a very definite one, it was rather vague, but it was the most reasonable one he could think of.

There in Warden Forest, living as the daughter of a woodman, who was himself ignorant of her legitimacy, was the girl. I am sorry to say that he cursed her as he thought of her. Where was the will? Whoever had got it would no doubt come to him first to make terms, and, failing to make them, would go to the real heiress.

Stephen, quick as lightning, resolved to take her away.

But where?

He did not much care for the present, so that it was somewhere under his eyes, or in the charge—the custody, really—of a trustworthy friend.

The only really trustworthy friend whom Stephen knew was his mother.

"Yes, that is it," he muttered. "Mother shall take this girl as—as—a companion. Poor mother, some great ignorant, clodhopping wench who will frighten her into a nervous fit. Poor mother!" And he smiled with a feeble, malicious pleasure.

There are some men who take a delight in causing pain even to those who are devoted to them.

"Dear mother," he wrote, "I have to send you the sad news of my uncle's death. Need I say that I am utterly overwhelmed in grief. I have indeed lost a friend!" ("The malicious, mean old wolf," he muttered, in parenthesis.) "How good he was to me! But, mother, even in the midst of our deepest sorrows, we must not forget the calls of charity. I have a little duty to perform, in which I require your aid. I fear it will necessitate your making a journey to Wermesley station on this line. If you will come down by the 10:20 on Wednesday, I will meet you at Wermesley station. Do not mention your journey, my dear mother; we must not be forgetful that we are enjoined to do good by stealth.

"In great affliction,
"Your loving son,
"Stephen Davenant."

It was a beautiful letter, and clearly proved that Stephen was not only a bad man, but an extremely clever and dangerous one—for he could retain command over himself even in such moments as these.

CHAPTER X

Let us hasten from the gloomy atmosphere of Hurst Leigh, and, leaving the presence of the thwarted old man lying upstairs, and the no less thwarted young man writhing in torturing dread in the darkened library, return to Warden Forest.

With fleet feet Una fled from the lake, the voices of the woodman and Jack Newcombe ringing in her ears, a thousand tumultuous emotions surging wildly in her heart.

Until the preceding night Gideon Rolfe had seemed the calmest and most placable of fathers; nothing had occurred to ruffle his almost studied impassability. New and strange experiences seemed to crowd upon her so suddenly that she scarcely accepted them as real. Had she been dreaming, and would she wake presently to find the handsome young stranger, with his deep musical voice, and his dark, eloquent eyes, the phantom of a vision?

As she came in sight of the cottage she turned aside and, plunging into the depths of the wood, sank down upon a bank of moss and strove to recall every word, every look, every slight incident, which had passed since the arrival of the stranger; and, as she did so, she seemed vaguely conscious that a change, indefinite yet undeniable, had fallen upon her life. The very trees, the atmosphere itself, seemed changed, and in place of that perfect, unbroken calm which had hitherto enwrapped her life, a spirit of unrest, of vague longing, took possession of her.

A meteor had crossed the calm, serene sky of her existence, vanishing as quickly as it had come, and creating a strange, aching void.

Still it was not at all painful, this novel feeling of wistfulness and unrest; a faint echo of some mysterious delight rang in the inner chambers of her young soul, the newly awakened heart stirred within her like an imprisoned bird, and turned to the new light which had dawned upon her. That it was the celestial light of love she was completely ignorant. She only knew and felt, with all the power of mind and soul, that a spirit had fallen upon her life, that she had, half-blinded, left the road of gray, unbroken calm, never to return—never to return.

Step by step she recalled all that had passed, and sat revolving the strange scene with ever-increasing wonder.

What did it mean? Why should her father be angry with the youth? Why should he accuse and insult him, and drive her away as if from the presence of some wild animal who was seeking to devour her?

Wild animal! A smile, sad and wistful, flitted over her beautiful face as she called up the handsome face and graceful form of the youth. Was it possible that one so base as her father declared him to be could look as this youth had looked, speak as he had spoken? With a faint, tremulous, yet unconscious blush, she remembered how graceful he looked lying at her feet, his lips half parted in a smile, his brow frank and open as a child's.

And yet he himself had said, half sadly, that he was wild and wicked. What could it mean?

Innocent as a nun, ignorant of all that belonged to the real living world, she sat vainly striving to solve this, the first enigma of her inner life.

Once, as she sat thinking and pondering, her eyes cast down, her brows knit, her fingers strayed to her right arm with a gentle, almost caressing touch. It was the arm upon which Jack's hand had rested: even now she seemed to feel the pressure of the strong fingers just as she heard the ring of his deep, musical voice, and could feel the gaze of his dark, flashing eyes; they had looked fierce and savage when she had first seen them at the open door of the cottage last night, but this morning they had worn a different expression—a tender, half-pitying, and wholly gentle expression, which softened them. It was thus she liked to remember them—thus she would remember them if she never saw them again.

And as this thought flashed across her mind a wistful sadness fell upon her, and a vague pain came into her heart. Should she never see him again? Never! She looked round mournfully, and lo! the whole world seemed changed; the sun was still shining, the trees were still crowned in all their glory of summer leafage, but it all looked gray and dark to her; all the beauty and glory which she had learned to love had gone—vanished at the mere thought that she should never see him again.

Slowly she rose, and with downcast eyes moved toward the cottage. She passed in at the open door and looked round the room—that, too, seemed altered, something was missing; half-consciously she wandered round, touching with the same half-caressing gesture the chair on which Jack Newcombe had sat, opened the book at the page which she was reading while he was eating his supper; a spell seemed to have fallen upon her, and it was with a start like one awakening from a dream that she turned as a shadow fell across the room and Gideon Rolfe entered.

She turned and looked at him questioningly, curiously, but without fear. The cry of alarm when he had broken in upon them by the lake had been on Jack's account, not her own; never since she could remember had Gideon Rolfe spoken harshly to her, looked angrily; without a particle of fear, rather with a vague wonder, she looked and waited for him to speak.

The old man's face wore a strange expression; all traces of the fierce passion which had convulsed it a short time ago had passed away, and in its place was a stern gravity which was almost sad in its grim intensity.

Setting his ax aside, he paced the room for a minute in silence, his brows knit, his hands clasped behind his back.

Una glided to the window and looked out into the wood, her head leaning on her arm.

"Una," he said, suddenly, his voice troubled and grave, but not unkind.

She started, and looked around at him; her spirit had fled back to the lake again, and she had almost forgotten that he was in the room.

"Una, you must not wander in the forest alone again."

"No! Why not?"

He hesitated a moment, as if he did not know how to answer her; then he said, with a frown:

"Because I do not wish it—because the man you saw here last night, the man you were with by the lake, may come again"—a faint light of gladness shone in her eyes, and he saw it, and frowned sternly as he went on—"and I do not wish you to meet him."

She was silent for a moment, her eyes downcast, her hands tightly clasped in front of her; then she looked up.

"Father, tell me why you spoke so angrily to him—why do you not want him to come to Warden again?"

"I spoke as he deserved," he answered; "and I would rather that Warden should be filled with wild beasts than that he should cross your path again."

Her face paled slightly, and her eyes opened with wonder and pain.

"Is he so very bad and wicked?" she asked, almost inaudibly.

Gideon Rolfe strode to and fro for a moment before he answered. How should he answer her?—how warn and caution her without destroying the innocence which, like the sensitive plant, withers at a touch?

"Is it not sufficient that I wish it, Una?" he said. "Why are you not satisfied? Wicked! Yes, he's wicked; all men are wicked, and he's the most wicked and base!"

"You know him, father?" she asked. "You would not say so if you did not. I am sorry he is so bad."

"Look at me, Una," he said.

She turned, her eyes downcast and hidden, her lips trembling for a moment.

"Yes, father."

"Una," he said, "what is the meaning of this? Why are you changed—why do you shrink from me?"

She looked up with a curious mixture of innocent pride and dignity.

"I don't shrink from you, father," she said in a low voice.

Gideon's hand dropped from her shoulder, and the frown gave place to a sad expression. "Has the time I looked forward to with fear and dread come at last?" he murmured, inaudibly, and he paced to and fro again, as if endeavoring to arrive at some decision.

Una watched him with dreamy, questioning eyes, in which shone a tender mournfulness. Why were all men wicked? Why was this one man, with the handsome face and the musical voice, more wicked than the rest? What was it that her father knew that should make him hate the youth so? These were the questions that haunted her as she waited silent and motionless.

At last, with a wave of the hand, as if he were putting some decision on one side, Gideon Rolfe turned to her and motioned her to the window-seat. "Una," he said, "last night you were wondering why your lot should be different from that of other girls; you were wondering why I have kept you here in Warden, and out of the world. It is so, is it not?"

She did not answer in words, but her eyes said "yes," plainly.

Gideon Rolfe sighed, and passed his hand over his brow; it was a hand hardened by toil, but it was not the hand of a peasant, any more than was his tone or his words those of one.

"Una, I have foreseen this question; I have been expecting it, and I had resolved that when it came I would answer it. But," and his lips twitched, "I cannot do it—I cannot," and his brow contracted as if he were suffering some great, mental anguish. "For my sake, do not press me. In time to come, sooner or later, you must know the secret of your life, you must learn why and wherefore your whole life has been spent in seclusion; you have guessed that there is some mystery, some story—there is. It must remain a mystery still. For your own sake I dare not draw aside the veil which conceals; for your own sake my lips are for the present sealed. Child, can you tell me that, secluded and lonely as your life has been, it has been an unhappy one?"

"Father!" she murmured, and her eyes filled slowly.

"God forgive me if it has been!" he said, sadly. "I have striven to make it a happy one."

Silently she rose and laid her hand upon his arm and put up her lips to kiss him, but with a gentle gesture he put her away from him.

"Una, listen to me. All my life I have had but one aim, one purpose, your happiness and welfare. For your sake I left the world and an honored name——" he stopped suddenly, warned by the gentle wonder of her gaze, and with a faint color in his face hurried on—"for your sake, and yours only. Do you think that it is by choice that I have kept you hidden from the world? No, but of necessity. Una, between the world and you yawns a wide gulf. On this side are peace, and innocence, and happiness; on the other," and his voice grew grave and solemn, "lie misery and shame." White and wondering, she gazed at him, and the innocent wonder in the beautiful face recalled him to himself. "Enough! You can trust me, Una; it is no idle, meaningless warning. Remember what I have said, when your thoughts turn to the world beyond the forest, when you grow weary and impatient with the quiet life which, though it may seem sad and weary, is the only one you can ever know without passing that gulf of which I have spoken."

"And now I want you to give me a promise, Una."

"A promise, father?" she echoed, in a low voice.

"Yes; I want you to promise me that if this—this young man should come, as he has threatened to do—that if he should come to you, and speak to you, you will not listen, will not speak to him."

An impatient frown knitted Gideon Rolfe's brow.

"Is this so much to ask you?" he said, in a low voice. "Is it so grave a thing to demand of you that you should avoid a man whom you have seen but twice in your life, one whom you know to be wicked and worthless?"

"Girl," he exclaimed, in low, harsh accents, "has the curse fallen upon you—already? Has he bewitched you? Speak? Why do you not speak? Has all the careful guarding of years been set at naught and rendered of no avail by the mere sight of one of his race, by a few idle words spoken by one of his hateful kin?"

He grasped her shoulder; instantly, with a revulsion of feeling, he withdrew his hand, and bent his head with a gesture almost of humility.

"Una, forgive me. You see how this unmans me—can you not understand how great must be the danger from which I wish to save you? Promise me what I ask you, for your own sake—ay, and for his."

"For his?" she murmured.

"Yes, for his. Let him but attempt to cross your path again, and I will not hold my hand. I held it once—would to Heaven I had not! I say, for his sake, promise that you will hold no speech with him!"

"Father, what has he done to make you hate him so?" she asked.

"I cannot, I will not tell you more than this: His race has ruined my life and yours—ruined it beyond all reparation here and hereafter. No more. I wait for your promise."

"I promise," she said.

"Good," he said. "I can trust you, child."

"Yes, you can trust me," she said, in a low voice; then with slow, listless steps she crossed the room and stole up-stairs.

CHAPTER XI

The Savage, wholly unconscious of, and totally indifferent to, the fact that his every footstep was watched by Stephen, entered the "Bush" Inn and went straight to his room, the little knot of regular customers, who were drinking and smoking in the parlor, either rising respectfully as he entered or maintaining an equally respectful silence until he was out of hearing.

"Mr. Jack's a fine fellow," said the landlord, looking at the fire solemnly. "Did you notice his face as he went through? I'm afraid it's all over with the old squire. Well, well, rest his soul, I say. I'm not one to bear grudges against the dead."

There was, if not a hearty, a unanimous assent to this dutiful sentiment, and the landlord, encouraged, ventured a little further, looking first over his shoulder to see if the door was shut, and then glancing at a little wrinkled faced man who sat in the corner by the fireplace, and looked, in his rusty black suit, like a lawyer's clerk, as indeed he was.

"All over now, Mr. Skettle," said the landlord, with a little cough. "I wonder—ahem—who'll be the next squire?"

The old clerk peered out from under his hairless brows, and shook his head with a dry smile; it was a very fair imitation of his master's, Mr. Hudsley's, manner, and never failed to impress the company at the "Bush."

"Aha!" he breathed. "Hem—yes. Time will prove—time will prove, Jobson."

Jobson, the landlord, looked round and winked with impressive admiration, as much as to say, "Deep fellow, Skettle; knows all about it, mind you, but not a word!"

"Well," said the parish clerk, with a shake of the head, "if wishing would make the mare to go, I know who'd be the Squire o' Hurst," and he pointed with his pipe to the ceiling, above which the Savage was thoughtfully pacing to and fro.

"We've had enough o' Davenants," began the miller; but Jobson stopped him with a warning gesture.

"No names, South—no names; this air a public house, and I'm a man as minds my own business."

"So was the last squire," retorted the miller, who was not to be put down—"leastways, he didn't meddle or help his neighbors. Not one shilling have I took from the Hurst since I was that high. Is there a man in this room as can say he'll be a penny the worse for Squire Ralph's death?

"And from what I see it seems to me that if things go on as they appear to be going, we shan't be much better for the new squire, if the name's to be the same."

"A nice spoken gentleman, Mr. Stephen," muttered the tailor, from behind the table.

The miller smiled and shook his head.

"There's some grain as grinds so soft that you can't keep it on the ground from the wind; but it don't make good bread, neighbor. No! Now the youngster up above," and he jerked his head toward the ceiling, "he comes of a different branch—same tree, mind yer, but a healthier branch. It will be good news for Hurst Leigh if it's found that Master Jack is to be our head."

"Nothing soft about Mr. Jack. If all we hear be true, it's a pretty wild branch of the tree he comes from."

"They say he's wild. No doubt; he always was. I can remember him a boy home for the holidays. He used to come down to the mill and poach my trout—a bit of a boy no higher than that"—and he put his hand against the table—"as fine a boy as ever I see. One day I caught him, and told him I'd either give him a thrashing or tell his uncle; for, do yer see, we allus called the old squire his uncle.

"'All right,' said he, 'wait till I've landed this fish and we'll settle it between us like gentlemen.' Another time I found him in the orchard. 'Well, Master Jack,' says I, 'bean't you got enough apples at the Hurst, but you must come and plague me?' He thought a moment, then he looks up with that audacious flash in his eyes, and says, quiet enough: 'Stolen fruit is the sweetest, South. If you feel put upon, take it out of the Hurst Orchard. I give you leave.' What was to be done with a boy like that? Fear! He didn't know what fear was. Do any o' you remember that roan mare as the old parson had? Well, Master Jack hears us talking o' the spiteful beast one day, and nothing 'ud do but he must go off and ask the parson to let him ride 'un. Of course the old fellow said no. Two nights after that the young varmint breaks open the stables, takes out the mare, saddles her, and rides her out to the common. I was late at the mill that night, and I hears her come clattering down the yard like a fire-engine, with Master Jack on her back, his eyes flashing and his hair a-flying, and him a-laughing as if it was the rarest bit o' fun in the world. I'd just time to cut across the meadow to the five-barred fence, and here he come past me, making straight for the fence, waving his hand and shouting someut about Dick Turpin. Ah, and he took the fence, too, and when that vicious beast threw him, and we came up to him, lying all o' a heap, with his arm broke, and the blood streaming from his face—what's he do but laugh at us, and swear as we'd startled her! And as for fighting! There warn't a week but what he'd come to the mill, all cut and mauled, for the missis to wash him and put him to rights. He'd never go home to the Hurst those times. Even then the old squire and him didn't agree. The old man called him a Savage, and I hear as that's what they call him up in London, and yet there warn't a house in Leigh as he warn't welcome in. Many and many a time he's slept up in the mill loft after one of his harum-scarum tricks, and many's the time I've faced the old squire when he's come after him with a horsewhip."

"They say that he run through all the money, as was his by rights, up in London in fast living," said the parish clerk, gravely.

"May be," said the miller, curtly. "If fast living means open-handed living, it's like enough; he never could keep a shilling when he was a boy, the first tramp as passed had it, safe as a gun. What's bred in the bone must come out in the flesh. Here's to the new squire—if it be Master Jack," and the sturdy old man raised his glass and emptied its contents at one vigorous but steady pull.

Meanwhile the subject of the discussion paced to and fro, pulling at his brier, and indulging in a study of the brownest description.

Never perhaps in his life had Jack been so upset, so serious and so sobered.

In the first place the sudden—or rather sudden to Jack—death of the old man with whom he had lived and quarreled as a boy, affected him more deeply than even he was aware. There in the silent room in the inn, he recalled all the old man's good qualities, all the little kindnesses he had done him, Jack, and more than all, the few last solemn and quite unexpectedly affectionate words which had dropped from his dying lips.

Jack, puffing at his pipe and rubbing his short hair with a puzzled frown, went over the scene again and again, and with no mercenary thoughts of the old man's declaration that he had remembered Jack in his will, but with reference to the mysterious allusions in the disposal of the large part of the property; then Jack's mind would fly off to the fearful scene at the actual death.

The wild cry, the white and horrified face of Stephen, the puzzled and sternly questioning one of the old lawyer. What did it mean?

And still more mysterious, what was the meaning of Stephen's conduct on the lawn? What was he hunting for with such intense eagerness as to make him fly at Jack like a madman?

Jack—as no doubt the reader will have surmised—was not clever.

He could not piece this and that together, and from disjointed incidents form an intelligent whole, as a child does with a box of puzzles.

The whole thing was a mystery to him, and grew more confusing and bewildering the more he thought of it.

It takes a villain thoroughly to appreciate a villain, a thief to understand and catch a thief; and Jack, being neither one nor the other, utterly failed to understand Stephen.

That he disliked him, with a feeling more like contempt than hatred, was a matter of course, but if any one had told Jack straight out that Stephen had abstracted the will, Jack would in all probability have refused to credit it. Will stealing and all such meanness was so thoroughly out of his line that he would not have understood how Stephen, led on step by step, could have possibly been guilty of it.

Then again, something else came forcing itself on these thoughts concerning the strange events at the Hurst. For the life of him he could not forget the Forest of Warden and all that had happened to him within its leafy shades.

At one moment it seemed as if years must have elapsed since he lost his way and forced an entrance at the woodman's hut, at another he was half inclined to believe that he had dined rather heavily at the club and dreamed it all. Like Una, he could not realize that they had met, touched hands and exchanged speech.

Jack could not get the beautiful face out of his mental vision; it mingled with the wan face of the dying man, with Stephen's pale, distorted countenance; it seemed to beam and shine upon him from the dark corners of the room with the same frank, pure, innocent smile with which it had shone down upon him as he lay at her feet in the woods.

And then the girl's surroundings! The extraordinary father, with his laborer's dress and his refined speech and bearing. What mystery enveloped the little group of persons buried in the depths of a wood, living apart from the world?

Jack rumpled his hair and drew a long breath eloquent of confusion and bewilderment.

It was certainly extraordinary! Three days ago he had left London, prosaic London, and was now plunged to the neck in a sea of romance and secrecy.

On one thing he was, however, resolved. He would keep his threat or promise. He would go to Warden Forest and see that beautiful face again, though he had to brave the anger of twenty mysterious woodmen. He thought at first that he would start on the morrow, but some feeling— perhaps some reverence and respect for the dead man—made him change his mind.

"No," he said to himself, as he knocked the ashes out of his pipe and prepared for bed; "I'll stay here over the funeral, and then— —"

But, though he felt tired and worn out, it was hours before he could sleep, and when he did, his spirit fled back to Warden Forest, and the face that had haunted him waking hovered about him in dreams.

Was it love; love at first sight? Jack would have been first to laugh at the idea; but it is worthy of note that all the loves which had occurred in his wild, reckless life had never, in their warmest epochs, moved him as the remembrance of Una had done; not one had had the power to disturb his sleep or to bring him dreams.

Jack kept to his resolution. Five days passed, and he stuck to the "Bush" manfully. They were, perhaps, the dreariest days he ever spent in his life, and he never thought of them afterward without a shudder.

Every day he was tempted to take flight and go to London until the day of the funeral; but his promise to Hudsley kept him at his post. He would not even leave the "Bush."

On the first day, a note, written on the deepest of mourning paper, had come from Stephen, begging him to come to the Hurst; but he had written a firm and what was for him a polite refusal. Of Stephen himself he saw nothing. Mr. Hudsley had also sent, and asked him to stay at his house; and this, too, Jack had declined.

The fact was he wanted to be left alone, to think over the strange adventures in the forest, to dwell with unceasing wistfulness on the beautiful face and sweet, musical voice.

So he clung to the inn; taking a morning dip in the river; strolling about, with his brier pipe in his mouth and his hands in his pockets, exchanging a word with this man and the other, and bestowing his odd change on any children he happened to meet. Sometimes he would drop in at one of the cottages, where he was so welcome when a boy, and smoke and chat; but usually he kept to his room.

But wherever he went he was the observed of all observers. Every night the little club that met in the "Bush" parlor talked about him, and wondered why he didn't go to the Hurst, and whether he would be the new squire.

The day of the funeral arrived at last—a cold, wet day, that foreshadowed the approaching autumn; and Jack put on his black suit—made by the village tailor who had described Stephen as a nice-spoken gentleman—and went up to the Hurst.

It was the first time he had been near it since the night he had the scuffle with Stephen on the lawn; and, to Jack's eyes, it looked gloomier than ever.

As he entered the hall, a shrunken figure in shabby black came to meet him; it was old Skettle, Hudsley's clerk.

The old man peered at him curiously, and made him a respectful bow in response to Jack's blunt greeting, and opened the library door.

Mr. Hudsley was standing at the table, and looked up with his wrinkled face and keen eyes—not a trace of expression beyond keenness in them. Jack shook hands with him and looked around.

"Where is Stephen?" he said.

As he spoke the door opened and Stephen entered. Jack, frank and candid, stared at him with astonishment.

"Are we ready?"

And they passed out.

In silence they stood beside the grave while all that was mortal of Ralph Davenant was consigned to the earth, and in silence they returned to the library.

With the same stony, impassive countenance, Mr. Hudsley seated himself at the head of the table; Stephen sank into a chair beside him, and sat with his eyes hidden under the white lids; Jack stood with folded arms beside the window, glancing at the far-stretching lawns and watching the servants as they filed in, a long line of black.

When they had all entered Mr. Hudsley drew from his pocket a folded parchment, slowly put on his spectacles, and without looking round, said:

"I am now about to read the last will and testament of Ralph Davenant."

There was a pause, a solemn pause, then he looked up and said:

"This will was drawn up by me on January—last year. It is the last will of which I have any cognizance. A careful search has been made, but no other document of the kind has been found. That is so, Mr. Stephen, is it not?" and he turned to Stephen so suddenly that all eyes followed his.

Stephen paused a moment, then raised his lids, and with a shake of his head and a sigh murmured an assent.

Mr. Hudsley allowed his keen eyes to rest on him for an instant, then slowly looked in the direction of Jack.

"A most careful search," he repeated.

Jack, feeling that the remark was addressed to him, nodded and looked at the lawn again.

Mr. Hudsley cleared his throat, and opened the crackling parchment.

There was an intense silence, so intense that Stephen's labored breathing could be heard as plainly as the rain on the windows.

In the same dry, hard voice Mr. Hudsley began to read. Clause by clause, wrapped in the beautiful legal jargon in which such documents are, for some inscrutable reasons, worded, no one understanding the import, but suddenly familiar words struck upon the ear. They were the servants' legacies, and a mourning ring to Mr. Hudsley; then, in a stillness that was oppressive, there fell the words:

"To my nephew, Stephen Davenant, I will the whole and sole remainder of all I possess, be it in lands or money, houses or securities, all and of every kind of property, deducting only the afore-mentioned legacies."

A thrill ran through the assemblage, every eye turned, as if magnetized, to the white, death-like face of the heir.

There he sat, the new squire, the owner of Hurst Leigh and the uncounted thousands of old Ralph Davenant, motionless, white, too benumbed to tremble.

Slowly Mr. Hudsley read over the signatures, and then slowly commenced to fold the parchment.

Then, from the shadow of the curtains, Jack emerged, pale, too, but with cool, calm dignity.

Quite quietly, and with perfect self-possession, he came to the table and looked at the dry, wrinkled face.

"So I understand, Mr. Hudsley, that the squire has left me—nothing."

Mr. Hudsley looked up, no trace of expression on his face.

"Quite right, Mr. Newcombe," he replied.

"He has not named me," said Jack.

"He has not named you in this will."

Jack bowed, and was turning from the table when Stephen started to his feet.

For one moment his eyes rested on Jack's face with an awful, piercing look of scrutiny, then his eyes lit up with a malicious gleam of triumph, but it disappeared instantly, and with a gesture of honest generosity and regret, he exclaimed:

"Not named! My dear Jack! But stay! I see how it is. My uncle felt that he could trust to my feeling in the matter. He knew that you would not have to look to me in vain."

Jack turned and looked at him with infinite contempt and unbelief, and then slowly passed out.

CHAPTER XII

Two days passed since Una had given her promise that should Jack Newcombe come to seek her she would hold no converse with him. How much that promise had cost her no one could say; she herself did not know. She only knew that whereas her life had always seemed dull and purposeless, it had, since Jack Newcombe's visit, grown utterly dreary and joyless.

Was it love? She did not ask herself the question. Had she done so, she could not have answered it.

Any school-girl of fifteen feeling as Una felt would have known that she was in love, but Una's only schooling had consisted of the few stern lessons of Gideon Rolfe.

"I can never see him, hear him, speak to him again," was her one sad reflection; "but if I could be somewhere near him, unseen!"

Then, through her brain, her father's words rang with melancholy persistence. This youth, whose eyes had seemed so frank and brave, whose voice rang with music so new and sweet, was, so her father said, unutterably wicked. One to be avoided as a dangerous animal! It could not but be true; she thought her father was truth itself.

But if it were so, then how false the world must be, for one to look and speak so gently, and yet be so wicked!

All day she wandered in the woods, returning to the cottage pale and listless, to leave her plate untouched or at best trifled with. Gideon Rolfe saw the change which had befallen her, but held his peace, though a bitter rage filled his heart; Martha Rolfe chided her for her listlessness, and tried to tempt her to eat; but Una put chiding and coaxing aside with a gentle smile, and escaped to the lake where she could dream alone and undisturbed.

The two days passed—on the third, as she was sitting beside the spot which had grown sacred in her eyes, with its crushed and broken ferns, she heard steps behind. Thinking that they were those of her father or one of the charcoal burners, she did not turn her head. The footsteps drew nearer, and a man came out from the thick wood and stood on the margin of the lake, and remained for a moment looking about him.

Una was so hidden by the tall brake that she remained unseen, and sat holding her breath watching him.

He was tall, thin, and dressed in black, and when he turned his face toward her, Una saw that he was not ill-looking. She might have thought him handsome but for that other face which was always in her mental vision. He was very pale, and looked anxious and ill at ease; and as he stood looking before him his right hand took his left into custody. It was Stephen Davenant.

For a few moments he stood with a half-searching, half-absent expression on his pale face, then turned and entered the wood again.

Pale with wonder and curiosity, Una rose and looked after him, and to her infinite surprise saw a carriage slowly approaching.

A lady was seated in it, a lady with a face as pale as the man's but with a still more anxious and deprecating expression.

Una, with the quickness of sight acquired by a life spent in communion with nature, could see, even at that distance, that the lady's eyes were like those of the man's, and, furthermore, that she was awaiting his approach with a nervous timidity that almost amounted to fear.

With fast beating heart Una watched them wondering what could have brought them to Warden, wondering who and what they were, when suddenly her heart gave a great bound, for the gentleman, turning to the driver, said, in a soft, low voice:

"We are looking for the cottage of a woodman, named Gideon Rolfe."

"Never heard of it, sir. Do you know what part of the forest it is in?"

"No," said Stephen.

"Then it's like looking for a needle in a bundle of hay," retorted the man.

"However difficult, it must be found," said Stephen. "Drive on till you come to some road and follow that. It may lead us to some place where we can ascertain the direction of this man's cottage."

The man touched his horse with the whip, and still Una stood as if spell-bound, but, suddenly remembering that they were going in the opposite direction to the cottage, she was about to step forward, when she heard the bark of the dog, and almost as if he had sprung from the ground, Gideon Rolfe stood beside the carriage.

"Ah, here is someone," said Stephen. "Can you tell us the road to the cottage of Gideon Rolfe, the woodman, my man?" he asked.

"And what may be your business with him?"

"Why do you ask, my good man?" he replied.

"Because I am he you seek," said Gideon.

"You are Gideon Rolfe? How fortunate."

"That's as it may prove," said Gideon, coldly. "What is your business?"

"It is of a nature which, I think, had better be stated in a more convenient spot. Will you kindly permit me to enter your cottage and rest?"

Gideon looked searchingly into Stephen's face for a moment that seemed an age to Una, then nodded curtly, and said: "Follow me."

"Will you not ride?" asked Stephen, suavely.

But Gideon shook his head, and shouldering his ax, strode in front of the horse, and Stephen motioning to the driver, the carriage followed.

"A charming spot, Mr. Rolfe—charming! Rather shall I say, retired, if not solitary, however."

"Say what you please, sir," retorted Gideon, grimly and calmly. "I am waiting to learn the business you have with me."

"Mother," he said—"this lady is my mother, Mr. Rolfe—I think, I really think you would find it pleasant and refreshing on the bench which I observed outside the door."

With a little deprecatory air the lady got up and instantly left the cottage.

Then Stephen's manner changed. Leaning forward he fixed his gray eyes on Gideon Rolfe's stern face and said:

"Mr. Rolfe—my name is Davenant——"

Gideon started, and, with a muttered oath, raised the ax.

Stephen's face turned as white as his spotless collar, but he did not shrink.

"My name is Davenant," he repeated—"Stephen Davenant. I am afraid the name has some unpleasant associations attached to it. I beg to remind you, if that should be the case, that those associations are not connected with any fault of mine."

"Go on. Your name is Stephen Davenant?"

"Stephen Davenant. I am the nephew of Squire Davenant—Ralph Davenant. The nephew of Ralph Davenant. I think you can guess my business with you."

"Do you come from—him?" he asked, hoarsely.

"In a certain sense, yes," he said. "No doubt you have heard the sad news. My uncle is dead."

"Dead!" he repeated fiercely.

"Dead. My uncle died three days ago."

"Dead!" repeated Gideon, not in the tone of a man who had lost a friend, but in that of one who had lost an enemy.

"Yes," said Stephen, wiping his dry eyes with his spotless handkerchief; "my poor uncle died three days ago. I am afraid I have not broken it as softly as I should have done. You knew him well?"

"Yes, I knew him well."

"Then you know how great a loss the county has suffered in——"

"Spare your fine phrases. Come to your business with me. What brings you here?"

"I am here in consequence of a communication made to me by my uncle on his death-bed. Are you alone?"

Gideon waved his hand with passionate impatience.

"That communication," Stephen continued, "concerns a certain young lady——"

"He told you?" he exclaimed.

"My uncle told me that I should find a young lady, in whose future he was greatly interested, in the charge of a certain person named Gideon Rolfe."

"Well, did he tell you any more than that?"

Stephen made a gesture in the negative.

"So," said Gideon Rolfe, "he left it to me to tell the story of his crime. You are Ralph Davenant's nephew. You are the nephew of a villain and a scoundrel!"

It was true, then, that the man knew nothing of the secret marriage of Ralph Davenant and Caroline Hatfield.

"A scoundrel and a villain!" repeated Gideon, leaning forward and clutching the table. "You say that he told you the story of his crime, glossed over and falsified. Hear it from me. Your uncle and I were schoolfellows and friends. I was the son of the schoolmaster at Hurst. Your uncle left school to go to college. I remained at Hurst in my father's house. I could have gone to college also, but I would not leave Hurst, for I was in love. I loved Caroline Hatfield. She was the daughter of the gamekeeper on the Hurst estate, and we were to be married. Two months before the day fixed for our marriage your uncle, my friend—my friend!—came home to spend the vacation. We were friends still, and I—cursed fool that I was—took him to the gamekeeper's lodge to introduce him to my sweetheart. Six weeks afterward he and she had fled."

Stephen watched him closely, his heart beating wildly.

"They had fled," continued Gideon, in a broken voice. "My life was ended on the day they brought me the news. I left Hurst Leigh and came here. A year later she came back to me—came back to me to die. She died and left me——. She left me her child. I—I loved her still and swore to protect that child, and I have done so. There is my story. What have you to say?"

"It is terrible, terrible!" he exclaimed.

"I have kept my vow. Her child has grown up ignorant of the shame which is her heritage. Here, buried in the heart of the forest, away from the world, I have kept and guarded her for her mother's sake. There is the story, told without gloss or falsehood. What have you to say?"

"You have discharged your self-appointed trust most nobly! But—but that trust has come to an end."

"Who says so?"

"I say so. You have done your duty—more than your duty—I must do mine. My uncle, on his deathbed, bequeathed his daughter to my charge."

"To yours?"

"To mine," said Stephen, gravely.

"Where is your authority?"

"That I do not come without authority is proven by the mere fact of my presence here and by my knowledge of my uncle's secret. No one but yourself, your wife and I know of the real identity of this girl. It was my uncle's wish that the story of her birth should still remain a secret—that it should be buried, as it were, in his grave. Why should the poor girl ever learn the truth, when such knowledge can only bring her shame and mortification?"

"Grant that," said Gideon, "where could she better be hidden than here? Her secret, her very existence, have been concealed from the world."

"True, but—but the future, my dear sir—the future! You are not a young man——"

"I am still young enough to protect her."

"My dear Mr. Rolfe, you may live—you look as if you would—to be a hundred; you have discharged your self-imposed task most nobly, but you must not forget that it has now devolved upon one who is bound by ties of blood to fulfill it, if not so well, certainly with the best intentions. Mr. Rolfe, I am the young girl's cousin."

"You speak of ties of blood; say rather, the ties of shame! Suppose—I say suppose—that I refuse to deliver her up to your care?"

"I do not think you will do that. You forget that, after all, we have little choice in the matter."

Gideon Rolfe eyed him questioningly.

"The young girl is now of age, and——"

"Go on."

"And supposing that you were to refuse to hand her over to my charge, I should feel compelled to tell the story of her life, and——. Pray—pray be calm. I beg you to remember that I am not here of my own desire; that I am merely fulfilling my duty to my uncle, and endeavoring to obey his last wishes. I do not blame you for your reluctance to part with her. It does you credit, my dear Mr. Rolfe—infinite credit. But duty—duty; we must all do our duty."

"Has anyone of your name ever yet done his duty?" repeated Gideon, sternly.

"For my part, Mr. Rolfe, I have always striven to do mine; yea, even in the face of great temptation and difficulties. I must do it now. After all, why should you resist my uncle's wish? Consider, she, who was once a child, is now a woman. Do you think it possible to keep her imprisoned in this wood for the whole of her days?"

Gideon Rolfe turned toward the window. For the first time Stephen had found a weak spot in his armor. It was true! Already she was beginning to pine and hunger for the world. Could he keep her much longer?

"Come," said Stephen, quick to see the impression he had made. "Do not let us be selfish; let us think of her welfare, as well as our own wishes. Candidly, I must confess that I should be perfectly willing to leave her in her present obscurity."

Gideon Rolfe broke in abruptly.

"Where will you take her?" he asked, hoarsely.

"It is my intention," he said, "to place her in my mother's charge. She lives in London, alone. There my cousin will find a loving home and a second mother. Believing that you would naturally have some reluctance at parting with her, not knowing with whom and where she was going, I have brought my mother with me."

Gideon glanced at the quiet, motionless figure seated on the bench outside, and then paced the room again.

"Does she know?" he asked hoarsely.

"She knows nothing," said Stephen. "My mother can trust me implicitly. She has long wanted a companion, and I have told her that I know of a young girl in whom I am interested."

"You intend to keep her secret?" said Gideon.

"Most sacredly," responded Stephen, with solemn earnestness.

Gideon went to the door and opened it.

"Wait," he said, and disappeared.

CHAPTER XIII

Stephen rose softly and watched him from behind the window curtains until Gideon had vanished amongst the trees; then Stephen went out and smiled down upon his mother with the air of a man who had just succeeded in accomplishing some great work for the good of mankind at large.

"Sorry to keep you waiting, mother," he said. "I have been making some arrangements with the worthy man, her father."

Mrs. Davenant looked up with the nervous, deprecatory expression which always came upon her face when she was in the presence of her son.

"It does not matter, Stephen; I am glad to rest. Where has the man gone? He—he—doesn't he look rather superior for his station, and why does he look so stern and forbidding?"

"A life spent in solitude, away from the world, has made him reserved and cold," replied Stephen, glibly, "and, of course, he feels the parting from his daughter."

"Poor man—poor girl!" murmured Mrs. Davenant.

Stephen looked down at her with a contemplative smile, while his ears were strained for the returning footsteps of Gideon Rolfe.

"Yours is a sweetly sympathetic nature, my dear. I can already foresee that the 'poor girl' will not long need anyone's sympathy. You are already prepared to open your arms and take her to your heart. Is it not so?"

Mrs. Davenant looked up—just as if she wanted to see what he expected of her to say, and seeing that he meant her to say "yes," said it.

"Yes, I shall be very glad to have a young girl—a good young girl—as a companion, Stephen. My life has been very lonely since you have been away."

"And I may be away so much. But, mother, you will not forget what I said during our drive? There are special reasons why the girl's antecedents should not be spoken of. The friend who interested me in her wishes her to forget, if possible, everything concerning her early life."

"I understand, Stephen."

"And, by the way, do not allow any expression of astonishment to escape you if, when you see her, you feel astonished at her appearance or manner. Remember that she has spent all her life here, buried in the forest, her sole companions a woodsman and his wife."

"Her mother and father?" said Mrs. Davenant.

"I said her mother and father, did I not? Just so—her mother and father. Well, we must not expect too much. And after all, it will be far more interesting for you to have a fresh and unsophisticated nature about you, although she may be rather rough and rustic——"

"I shall be quite content if she is a good girl."

"Just so. Virtue is a precious gem though incased in a rough casket."

Gideon Rolfe had returned, but not alone. Emerging from the deep shadow of the trees was what looked to their astonished and unprepared eyes a vision of some wood nymph.

Gideon Rolfe strode forward, his face set hard and sternly cold, and as he reached the cottage he took Una's hand in his, and looking steadily into Stephen's eyes, said:

"Mr. Davenant, I have informed my daughter of your mother's offer to take her under her charge, but I have asked her to postpone her answer until she saw you."

Stephen bowed, and laid his white hand on his mother's arm.

"Miss Rolfe," he said, in a low voice in which paternal kindness and social respect were delicately blended, "this lady is my mother. Like most mothers whose children have flown from the nest, she lives alone and feels her solitude. She is desirous of finding some young lady who will consent to share it with her. It is not only a home she offers you, but—I think I may add, mother—a heart."

"Yes, indeed," said Mrs. Davenant, and as she held out her hand her voice trembled and a tear shone in her eye.

Una, who had been looking from one to the other, with the breath coming in little pants through her half parted lips, drew near and put her hand in the outstretched one, but the next moment turned and clung to Gideon's arm with a sudden sob.

"Oh, father, I cannot leave you!" she murmured.

Gideon bent his head, perhaps to hide his face, which was working with emotion.

"Hush! it is for the best. Remember what I have said. You wanted to see the world— —"

"Yes—with you," said Una, audibly.

"The world and I have parted forever, Una."

"But shall I never see you again?"

"Yes, yes, we shall meet now and again."

"I trust, Miss Rolfe, that we shall wean your father from his long seclusion. You must be the magnet to draw him from his retreat into the busy haunts of men."

"You will come and see me?" she murmured.

"Yes, Una. Go where you will," and he glanced over her head at Stephen, "you may feel that I am watching over you, as I have always watched and guarded you. If any harm comes to you— —"

"Harm?" she breathed, and looked up into his face with questioning gaze.

"Come, Mr. Rolfe, you mustn't alarm your daughter," said Stephen, softly. "She will think that the world is filled with lions and wolves seeking whom they may devour. I think you may feel safe from any harm under my mother's protection, Miss Rolfe."

"Yes. I have never had a daughter. If you come you shall be one to me."

"You think me ungrateful?" said Una to her, in her simple, frank way.

"No, my dear," replied Mrs. Davenant. "I think you only show a naturally affectionate heart. You have never been from home before."

"Never," said Una. "Never out of the woods."

"My poor child. No, I do not think you ungrateful. I like to see that you feel leaving home so much. For you will come, will you not? I shall be disappointed and grieved if you do not, now that I have seen you."

"Now that you have seen me," said Una.

"Yes, my dear. For I am sure that I shall love you, and I hope that you will grow fond of me."

"Do you?" said Una, musingly. "Yes," she said, after a pause, "I shall love you."

"Will you kiss me, my dear," she said; and Una bent and kissed her.

"And now that you think—that you are sure you will like me—you will come," said Mrs. Davenant.

Una looked before her thoughtfully, almost dreamily, for a moment, then replied:

"Yes, my father wishes me to go. Why does he wish me to go into the world he hates and fears so much? It was only the other day that he warned me against wishing for it, and told me that I should never be happy if I left Warden. Why has he changed so suddenly?"

"I—I think it must have been Stephen who persuaded him. I heard them talking together."

"Stephen—that is your son," said Una.

"Yes, he is my son; he is very good and clever—so very clever! He has been a most affectionate son to me, and has never caused me a day's uneasiness."

"All sons are not so?" she asked.

"No, indeed," responded Mrs. Davenant.

"Is he ill?" asked Una, after a pause.

"Ill!"

"Because he is so pale," she said.

"Yes, Stephen is pale. It is because he thinks and reads so much, and then he is in great trouble now; his uncle died three days ago."

"Is that why he is dressed in black—and you, too? I am very sorry."

"Thank you, my dear," said Mrs. Davenant, "that was very nice of you to say that. I can see you have a kind heart. Yes, his uncle is just dead, Mr. Ralph Davenant—Squire Davenant. Why did you start?"—for Una had started and turned to her with a sudden flash of intense interest in her eyes—"did you know him? Ah, no, you could not, if you have not been out of the forest—how strange it seems!—- but you have heard of him, perhaps?"

"Yes, I have heard of him."

At that moment the door opened, and Stephen and Gideon Rolfe came out.

The usual smile sat upon Stephen's face, in strange contrast to the stern, set look on his companion's.

Raising his hat to Mrs. Davenant as he approached, Gideon put his hand on Una's shoulder.

"Go indoors, Una, to your mother," he said quietly.

Una rose, and after a momentary glance at each of their faces, went inside. Stephen opened and held the door for her, then closed it and came back to the others.

"Mother," he said, "Mr. Rolfe and I have made our arrangements, and he agrees with me that it would be wiser, now that the news is broken to Miss Rolfe, for her to accompany you back to town this afternoon."

Mrs. Davenant nodded, and glanced timidly at Gideon's stern face.

"We have won Mrs. Rolfe over to our side, and she is already making the few preparations necessary for Miss Rolfe's journey."

Gideon Rolfe inclined his head as if to corroborate this, then he said:

"Will you come inside, madam, and partake of some refreshment?"

"I would rather wait here. Mr. Rolfe, I hope you feel that, in trusting your daughter to my charge, that she will at least have a happy home, if I can make one for her?"

"That I believe, madam."

"Yes, I have quite convinced Mr. Rolfe that the change will be beneficial to Miss Rolfe, and that she will be taken every care of. I suppose you are quite old friends already, eh, mother?"

"I think she is a beautiful girl whom one could not help loving," murmured Mrs. Davenant.

Half an hour passed, and then Una and Martha came out. Una was pale to the lips, the other was red-eyed with weeping, and her tears broke out afresh when Mrs. Davenant shook hands with her and assured her that her daughter should be happy.

"Thank you, ma'am," said Martha. "It's what I said would come to pass. Gideon couldn't expect to keep her shut up here, like a bird in a cage, forever and a day. It was against reason, but it is so sudden," and her sobs broke into her speech and stopped her.

Mrs. Davenant's eyes were wet, and she glanced at Stephen, half inclined to postpone the journey; but Gideon Rolfe had called the carriage to the door, and the box was already on the seat.

With the same set calm which he had maintained throughout, Gideon took Una in his arms, held her for a moment and whispering, "Remember, wherever you are I am watching over you!" put her in the carriage in which Stephen had already placed his mother.

He, too, had a word to whisper. It was also a reminder.

"Remember, mother, not another word of the past. Her life begins from today."

Then he looked at his watch, and said aloud:

"You will just have time to catch the train. Good-bye."

With the most dutiful affection, he kissed his mother, then went round, and, bare-headed, offered his hand to Una.

"Good-bye, Miss Rolfe," he said. "You are now starting on a new life. No one, not even your father, can more devoutly wish you the truest and fullest happiness than I do."

Una, half-blinded with her tears, put her hand in his; but almost instantly drew it away, with something like a shudder. It was cold as ice.

The next moment the carriage started, and the two men were left alone.

For fully a minute they stood looking at it, till it had been swallowed up by the shadows of the trees; then Gideon turned, his face white and working.

"Stephen Davenant," he said, in slow, measured tones, "one word with you before we part. You have gained your end—be what it may; I say for your sake, let it be for good; for if it be for evil, you have one to deal with who will not hold his hand to punish and avenge. Rather than let her know the heritage of shame which hangs over her, I have let her go. If you value your safety, guard her, for at your hands I require her happiness and well being."

Stephen's face paled, but the smile struggled to its accustomed place.

"My dear Mr. Rolfe," he began, but Gideon stopped him with a gesture.

"Enough. I set no value on your word. There is no need for further speech between us. From this hour our roads lie apart. Take yours, and leave me mine."

"This is very sad. Well, well; as you say, I have gained my end, but, as I would rather put it, I have done my duty, and I must bear your ungrounded suspicions patiently. Good-bye, my dear sir—good-bye."

"I have sworn never to touch the hand of a Davenant in friendship," he said, grimly. "There lies your path"—and he pointed to the Wermesley road—"mine is here, for the present."

And with a curt nod, he turned toward the cottage.

With a gentle sigh and shake of the head, Stephen, after lingering for a moment, as if he hoped that Gideon's heart might be softened, turned and entered the wood.

Once in the shadow and out of sight, the smile disappeared, and left his face careworn, restless and anxious.

"Fate favors me," he muttered. "That boor knows—guesses—nothing of the truth. I never thought to get the girl out of his clutches so easily! Now she is under my watch and ken—I hold her in my hand. But—but"—he mused, his lips twitching, his eyes moving restlessly to and fro—"what shall I do with her? Beautiful—she is lovely! How long will she escape notice in London? Someone will see her—some hot-headed fool—and fall in love. She might marry. Ah!"

And he stooped amongst the brakes and ferns, and looked up, with a sudden, dull-red flush on his pale cheek, a bright glitter in his light eyes, while a thought ran like lightning through his cunning brain.

"Marry her! Why—why should not I?"

An answer came quickly enough in the remembrance of the pale dark face of Laura Treherne, the girl to whom he was pledged.

But with a gesture of impatience he swept the obtrusive remembrance aside.

"Why not?" he muttered. "Then, at one stroke, I should secure myself. By Heaven—I will! I will!"

So elated was he by the thought that he stopped and leaned against a tree and took off his hat, allowing the cool breezes to play upon his white forehead.

"Beautiful, and the real heiress of Hurst Leigh," he muttered. "Why should I not? By one stroke I should make myself secure, and set that cursed will at defiance, let it be where it may! I will! I will!" he repeated, setting his teeth; then, as he put on his hat, he smiled pitifully and murmured:

"Poor Laura, poor Laura!"

CHAPTER XIV

Una saw her last of Warden Forest through a mist of tears; while a tree remained in sight her face was turned toward it, and in silence she bade farewell to the leafy world in which her life had passed with so much uneventfulness—in silence listened to the soughing of the breeze that seemed to voice her a sad good-bye.

Her companion sat in silence, too, holding the soft, warm hand which clung to hers with an eloquent supplication for protection and sympathy.

But youth and tears are foes who cannot abide long together, and by the time the little railway village of Wermesley was reached, Una's eyes were full of interest and curiosity.

As the fly rumbled over the unkept streets toward the station, past the few tame shops and the dead-and-alive hotel, her color came and went in rapid fluctuations.

"Is—is this the world?" she asked, in a low voice.

Mrs. Davenant looked at her with a smile, the first which Una had seen on the thin, pale face. She had yet to learn that Mrs. Davenant never smiled in her son's presence.

"The world, my dear?" she replied. "Well, yes; but a very quiet part of it."

"And yet there are so many people in the streets, and—ah!" she drew back with an exclamation as the train shrieked into the station.

Mrs. Davenant started—she was nervous herself, and had not yet realized that she had for companion one who was as ignorant of our modern high-pressure civilization as a North American Indian.

"That is the train; don't be frightened, my dear," she said.

"Forgive me. I know it is the train—I have read about it. I am not frightened," she added, quietly, and with a touch of gentle dignity that puzzled Mrs. Davenant.

"My dear," she said, "I am not finding fault, or chiding you, it is only natural that you should be surprised, but you will find a great deal more to be surprised at when we get to London."

Una inclined her head as she mentally registered a resolution to conceal, at any cost, any surprise or alarm she might feel on the rest of the journey.

Nevertheless, she kept very close to Mrs. Davenant as they passed to the train, and shrank back into the corner of the carriage driven there by the stupid stare of one or two of the passengers.

"Now we are all right," said Mrs. Davenant, gently. "We shall not sleep now till we get to town."

"To London—we are going to London?" asked Una in a low voice.

"Yes," said Mrs. Davenant. "That is where I live; I live in a great square at the West-end."

"I know the points of the compass," said Una, with a smile; "my father taught me," and she sighed—"poor father!"

"I think your father must be a very clever man, my dear. He appears to have taught you a great deal—I mean"—she hesitated—"you speak so correctly."

"Do I?" said Una. "Yes, my father is very clever. He knows everything."

"It is very curious," she said. "I mean—I hope you won't be offended—but men in his position are not generally so well informed."

"Are they not?" said Una, quietly. "I don't know. Perhaps my father learned all he knows from books."

"And taught you in the same way. Tell me what books you have read."

Una smiled softly, and as she did so, Mrs. Davenant started, and looked around at her with something like fright in her grave, still eyes.

"What is the matter?" asked Una.

"No—nothing," replied the other. "I—you reminded me of somebody when you laughed, I can't tell whom. But the books, you were going to tell me about the books."

"I can't remember all," said Una, and then she mentioned the titles of some of the well-bound volumes which stood on the little bookshelf in the hut.

Mrs. Davenant regarded her curiously.

"Those are all books of a world that existed long ago," she said. "You have never read any novels—any novels of present day life?"

"No, I think not."

"Then you are absolutely ignorant of life as it is," said Mrs. Davenant.

"Yes, I suppose so," assented Una.

"I can understand now how useful fiction really is," murmured Mrs. Davenant. "It is by it alone that a future age will understand what ours is. You are entering upon some strange experiences, Miss Rolfe."

Una started; the name was so unfamiliar to her that she hardly recognized it.

"Please don't call me that," she said, laying her hand on Mrs. Davenant's arm. "My name is Eunice—Una. Call me Una."

"I will," said Mrs. Davenant.

"You have promised to love me, you know."

"A promise easy to keep, my dear," she said, and her eyes grew moist. "I little thought when my son Stephen telegraphed to meet him that he was taking me to a daughter."

"Your son Stephen—he sent for you!" said Una, with frank curiosity. "How did he know of my existence?"

"Through some friend," said Mrs. Davenant, with much hesitation and nervous embarrassment. "My son is a very good man, and always interesting himself in some good cause or other—something that will benefit his fellow creatures. You—you will like my son when you know more of him," she added, and though she spoke with pride there was a touch of something like fear in her voice, which always came when she mentioned his name or spoke of his goodness.

"Yes," said Una, simply, "I will for your sake."

"Thank you, my dear," murmured Mrs. Davenant.

"But how," went on Una, after thinking a moment, "how did his friend know anything about me? Did my father——"

"I don't know, Una," said Mrs. Davenant, nervously. "Stephen doesn't always tell me everything; you see he has so much to think of, and just now he is in great trouble, you know."

"Ah! yes," said Una, gently; "and he had not time to tell you. But he will. I am sorry he is in such trouble." Then, after a pause, she said: "Are you rich?"

Mrs. Davenant started. The question, so unusual and so strange, bewildered her by its suddenness and its frankness.

"Rich, my dear?" she said. "Yes—I suppose I am rich."

"And he is rich?"

"He will be, perhaps; we do not know until his uncle's will is read."

"I know what a will is," said Una, with a smile. "It is the paper which a man leaves when he dies, saying to whom he wishes his money to go. And Stephen——"

"You should say Mr. Stephen, or Mr. Davenant, my dear," she said. "I don't mind your calling him Stephen, but—but——" She looked round in despair. How was she to explain to this frank, beautiful girl the laws of etiquette? "But everyone who speaks of those to whom they are not related say Mr., or Mrs., or Miss."

"I see," said Una. "Then Mr. Davenant expects to get his uncle's money, and then he will be rich. I am very glad. And he does not live in the same house with you?"

"No," replied Mrs. Davenant—and surely there was something like a tone of relief in her voice—"no; when he is in London he lives in chambers in rooms by himself; but he has been staying at Hurst Leigh."

"At Hurst Leigh!" echoed Una, softly, and a faint color stole over her face. How wonderful it was! That other—he whose face was always with her, was going there!

"At Hurst Leigh," repeated Mrs. Davenant. "Do you know it?"

Una shook her head silently. She longed to ask more, to ask if Mrs. Davenant knew the youth who had taken shelter in the cottage, but she simply could not. Love is a wondrous schoolmaster—he had already taught her frank, out-spoken nature the art of concealment.

"It is a grand place," continued Mrs. Davenant. "A great, huge place," and she shivered faintly, "and—and if Squire Davenant has left it to Stephen, he will live there."

"You don't like it?" said Una, with acute intuition.

"No," replied Mrs. Davenant, with unusual earnestness. "No, oh no! it frightens me. I was never there but once, and then I was glad—very, very glad to get away, grand and beautiful as it was!"

"But why?" asked Una, eagerly.

"Because—have you never heard of Ralph Davenant?"

Una hesitated a moment. She had heard of him.

"He was a wonderful man, but terrible to me. His eyes looked through one, and then he had been so wicked."

She stopped short, and Una sighed. So there was another person who was wicked.

"Why are men so wicked?" she asked, in a low voice.

"I—I—don't know. What a singular question," said Mrs. Davenant. "No one knows. Perhaps it is because they have different natures to ours. But you need not look so grieved, my dear," she added, with a little smile, "you need not know any wicked men."

"Who can tell? One does not know; wicked men are just like the others, only we like them better."

Mrs. Davenant stared at her, and utterly overwhelmed by the strange reply, sank into her corner and into silence.

The panting engine tore along the line, and presently the clear atmosphere was left behind, and the cloud of smoke which hangs over the Great City came down upon them and took them in, and infolded them

To Una's amazement the train seemed to glide over the tops of houses, houses so thick that there seemed but two, or three inches between them. With suppressed excitement—she had resolved to express no surprise or fear—she watched through the window. Sometimes she caught sight of streets thronged with people, and with commingled alarm and curiosity, wondered what had happened to draw them all together so.

She would not ask Mrs. Davenant, for wearied by her double journey, she was leaning back with closed eyes.

Suddenly the train stopped—stopped amidst the noise and confusion of a large terminus—Mrs. Davenant woke, a porter came to the door, received instructions as to the luggage and handed them out.

Notwithstanding her resolution, Una felt herself turning pale.

From Warden Forest to a London railway station.

"Keep close to me, dear," said Mrs. Davenant, who seemed only nervous and helpless in her son's presence. "Come, there is a cab."

In silence Una followed. Men—and women, too,—turned to look at the tall, graceful figure in its plain white dress, and stared at the lovely face, with its half-frightened, half-curious, downcast eyes, and Una felt the eyes fixed on her.

"Why—why do they look at me so?" she asked, when they had entered the cab.

Mrs. Davenant regarded her with a smile, and evaded the frank, open eyes. Was it possible that the girl was ignorant of her marvelous beauty?

"People in London always stare, my dear Una," she replied, "and they see that you are strange."

"It is my dress," said Una, who had been looking out of the window at some of the fashionably-attired ladies. "It is different to theirs. See—look at that lady! Why does she wear so long a dress? she has to hold it up with one hand."

"It is your dress, no doubt, my dear," she said. "We must alter it when we get home."

The cab rolled into the street, and Una was rendered speechless.

But for her resolve she would have shrunk back into the farthest corner of the cab. The number of people, the noise, alarmed her, and yet she felt fascinated.

Were all the people mad that they hurried on so with such grave and pre-occupied faces. She had never seen her father hurry unless he had cut down a tree that had been struck by lightning, and which might injure others in its fall unless cut down with greatest care.

Presently they passed into one of the leading thoroughfares, already lit up, its shops gleaming brightly with the gas-light, its ceaseless line of cabs, and omnibuses, and carriages.

At last, when her eyes were weary with looking, she murmured: "This—this—is the world then at last."

"Yes," said Mrs. Davenant, with a sigh. "This is the world, Una!"

"And are those palaces!" asked Una, as they passed through the West End streets and squares.

"No," said Mrs. Davenant; "they are only houses, in which rich people dwell, as you would call it."

"And the trees! Are there no trees?" asked Una, with, for the first time, a sigh.

"Not here, dear. There are some in the parks; some even in the middle of the city itself. You will miss your trees, Una."

"Yes, I shall miss my trees. But this—this world seems so large; I thought that——"

"Well," said Mrs. Davenant, amused with her bewilderment.

"I thought that people in the world knew each other; but that is impossible."

And she sighed, as she thought that, after all, now that she was in the world, she was no nearer that one being who, for her, was the principal person in it.

"Very few people know each other, Una. It's a big world, this London. I wonder whether you will be happy?"

Una turned to her with a look upon her face that would have melted a sterner heart than Mrs. Davenant's.

"I shall be happy, if you will love me," she said.

Something in the frank, simple reply made Mrs. Davenant tremble. What had she undertaken in the charge of this simple, pure-natured girl, whose beauty caused people to turn and stare at her, and whose innocence was that of a child?

Through miles and miles of streets, as it seemed to Una, the cab made its slow, rumbling way; houses, that were palaces in her eyes, flitted past; and at last they stopped before a palace, as it seemed to Una, in a quiet square.

The door of the house opened, and a servant came out and opened the cab door.

In silent wonderment Una entered the hall, lit with its gas-lamps and lined with flowers, and followed Mrs. Davenant into what was really the drawing-room of a house in Walmington Square; but which seemed to Una to be the principal apartment in some enchanted castle.

But true to her resolve, she stood calm and silent, feeling, rather than seeing, that the eyes of the servant were fixed upon her with curious interest.

"Come upstairs, Una, dear," said Mrs. Davenant, and Una followed her into another fairy chamber. Flowers, of which Mrs. Davenant, like most nervous persons, was inordinately fond, seemed everywhere: they lined the staircase and the landing, and bloomed in every available corner.

Mrs. Davenant entered her own room, then opened a door into an adjoining one.

"This is your room, my dear," she said. "If—if—you like it——"

"Like it!" said Una, with open eyes and beating heart. "Is—is this really mine?" and she looked round the dainty room with incredulous admiration.

"If—if you like it, my dear," said Mrs. Davenant.

"How could I do otherwise? It is too beautiful for me——"

"I don't think anything could be too beautiful for you, Una," said Mrs. Davenant, with a significance that was entirely lost on Una. "If there is anything you want—I can't give you any trees, you know."

"I shan't want trees while the flowers are here. It is nothing but flowers."

"I am very fond of them," said Mrs. Davenant, meekly. "You will hear a bell ring in half an hour; come to me then, I shall wait in the next room for you. I will not lock the door," and she left her.

Una felt dazed and stunned for a few minutes, then she made what preparations were possible. She chose from her box, which had been conveyed to her room by some invisible agency apparently, a plain muslin dress, and, more by instinct than any prompting of vanity, fastened a rose in her hair.

She had scarcely completed her simple toilet when the bell rang, and she went into the next room.

A maid servant—Una noticed that it was not the one who had opened the door—was in attendance upon Mrs. Davenant, and dropped a courtesy as Mrs. Davenant said, in her nervous, hesitating fashion:

"This is Miss Rolfe, Jane."

Una smiled, and was about to hold out her hand, but stopped, seeing no movement of a similar kind on the part of the neatly-dressed girl.

"Jane is my own maid, Una," said Mrs. Davenant. "She will attend to you when you want her."

Jane dropped another courtesy, but Una detected a glance of curiosity and scrutiny at the plain white muslin.

"Come," said Mrs. Davenant, "let us go down. Dinner is ready," and she led the way down-stairs.

Another fairy apartment broke upon Una's astonished vision as they entered the dining-room.

Small as the houses are in Walmington Square, Una, accustomed only to the small room in the hut, thought that this dining-room was large enough to be the banquet hall of princes.

But, whatever surprise Una felt, she, mindful of her resolve, concealed.

Not even the maid in waiting could find anything to condemn. When she went down-stairs her verdict was favorable.

"Whoever she is," she said, "she's a lady. But where on earth she comes from, goodness only knows. A plain muslin dress that might have come out of the ark."

Dinner was over at last. A "last" that seemed to Una an eternity. Mrs. Davenant rose and beckoned her to follow, and they went into the drawing-room.

"Are you very tired, Una?"

"No," said Una, thinking of her long wanderings in Warden Forest, "not tired at all, but very surprised."

"Surprised?" said Mrs. Davenant, questioningly.

"Yes. Do all the people in London live like this—in such beautiful houses, with people to wait upon them, and with so many things to eat, and with such pretty things in the houses?"

"Not all," said Mrs. Davenant, watching the tall, graceful figure as it moved to and fro—"not all. But it would take too long to explain. You think these are pretty things; what will you say when you see the great sights—sights which we Londoners think nothing of?"

Una did not answer; she had been looking round the room at the pictures, mostly portraits, on the walls.

"Are these pictures of friends of yours?" she said. "Who is that?"

"That? That is the portrait of a man I was speaking of in the train. That is Ralph—Squire Davenant—when he was a young man."

It was a portrait of Ralph Davenant in his best—and worst—days. It had been painted when men wore their hair long, and brushed from their foreheads. One hand, white as the driven snow, was thrust in his breast, the other held a riding-whip.

Una looked at it long and earnestly, and Mrs. Davenant, impressed by her long silence, rose and stood beside her.

"Yes," she said, "that is Ralph Davenant. It was painted when he was about your age, my dear. Ah— —"

"What is the matter?"

Mrs. Davenant, pale and excited, took up a hand-mirror from one of the tables and held it in front of Una.

"Look!" she exclaimed.

"Well?" she said.

"Well?" echoed Mrs. Davenant. "Don't you see? Look again. The very image! It is himself come to life again; it is Ralph Davenant turned woman!" she exclaimed.

And before Una could glance at the glass a second time Mrs. Davenant threw it aside.

"Am I so like?" said Una, with a smile. "How mysterious! And that is so beautiful a face."

"Beautiful eyes, and you are— —" said Mrs. Davenant, but stopped in time, warned by Una's frank, questioning gaze. "If you like to look at portraits," she said, "there is an album there; look over that."

Una took up the album and turned over its pages; suddenly she stopped, and the color flew to her face.

With unconcealed eagerness she came toward Mrs. Davenant with the open album in her hand.

"Look!" she said; "who is that?"

"That," said Mrs. Davenant, peering at it, "that is—Jack Newcombe."

"Jack Newcombe," said Una, breathlessly. "You know him?"

"Yes," said Mrs. Davenant, with a sigh. "Poor Jack! Shut the book, my dear."

"Why do you say 'Poor Jack?'" said Una, with a hollow look in her beautiful eyes.

"Because—because he is a wicked young man, my dear," said Mrs. Davenant. "Poor Jack!"

CHAPTER XV

Amidst a profound silence Jack walked slowly and quietly out of the house. There was no anger in his heart against the old man whose favorite he had once been—for the moment there was scarcely any anger against Stephen; surprise and bewilderment overwhelmed every other feeling.

He had not expected a large sum of money—had certainly not expected the Hurst; and but for the words spoken by the dying man, he would not have expected anything at all, after having offended him in the matter of the money-lenders and the post-obit. But most assuredly the squire had intimated that there would be something—something, however small.

And now he was told that there was nothing, that his name was not even mentioned.

Apart from any mercenary consideration, Jack was cut up and disappointed; if there had been a simple mourning ring, a few of the old guns out of the armory—anything as a token of the old man's forgiveness, he would have been satisfied; but nothing, not one word.

Then, again, he could not understand it, near his end as he was when he spoke to him. The squire was as sane and clear-headed as he had been at any time of his life, or at least so it seemed to Jack; and he certainly had given him to understand that he had left him some portion of his immense wealth.

It was another link in the chain of mysteries which had seemed to coil around Jack since he started from London.

Slowly and thoughtfully he made his way back to the "Bush," and began to pack up the small portmanteau which had been sent from town.

Hurst Leigh was no place for him; every minute he remained in it seemed intolerable to him. He would go straight back to town by the next train.

Suddenly a thought struck him, and he paused in his task of packing the portmanteau, an operation which he reduced to its simplest by thrusting in anything that came first and jamming it down tight with his fist; he stopped and looked up with a red flush on his handsome face. Why shouldn't he go to Warden Forest on his way back?

In a moment, the idea thrilled him with the delight of anticipation, the next, a shade came over his brow. Why shouldn't he? Rather, why *should* he? What was the use of his going? If he had no business there before, he had less excuse now. He was next door to a beggar—and— —

Realizing for the first time the blow that had been dealt him by the squire's neglect, he continued at the jamming process, jumped and kicked at the portmanteau till it consented to be locked, and then went down to the bar and called for his bill.

There were several people hanging about—a funeral is a good excuse for a holiday in a country village—but Jack, in his abstraction, scarcely noticed the little group of men who sat and stood about, and merely nodded in response to the respectful and kindly greetings.

"But, Mr. Jack," said Jobson, with a deeply respectful air of surprise, "you don't think of going right away at once, sir?"

"Yes, I'm off, Jobson," said Jack. "What's the next train?"

"To London?" said a dry, thin voice behind him; and Jack turned and saw Mr. Hudsley's clerk—old Skettle. "There's no train to London till seven o'clock; there's a train to Arkdale in an hour, but it stops there."

"All right," he said, "I'll go to Arkdale; and, by the way, Jobson, I don't want to be bothered with the portmanteau; send it on by rail to my address—Spider Court, the Temple, you know."

Jobson touched his cap, and while he was making out the bill Jack lit his pipe and paced up and down, his hands in his pockets, the knot of men watching him out of the corners of their eyes with sympathetic curiosity.

Jack paid the bill—so moderate a one that he capped it with half a sovereign over; and with a "good-day" all round, started off. He had not got further than the signpost, when he felt a touch on his arm, and, turning, saw that old Skettle had followed him.

"Halloa," said Jack, in his blunt way, "what's the matter?"

The old man looked up at him from under his wrinkled lids, and fumbled at his mouth in a cautious sort of a way.

"I'm very sorry things have gone on so crooked up at the Hurst, Master Jack," he said, respectfully.

"But not more sorry than I am, Skettle, thank you."

"I'm afraid it's rather unexpected, Master Jack," he continued, his small, keen eyes fixed, not on Jack, but on his second waistcoat-button, counting from the top.

"Well, yes, it is," said Jack, tugging at his mustache. "Very much so. I've got a hit in the bread-basket this time, Skettle, and I'm on my back again."

Old Skettle looked a keen glance at the handsome face and frank eyes that were looking rather ruefully at the ground.

"Hitting below the belt is not considered fair, is it, Master Jack?" he asked.

"Eh, what?" said Jack, who had not been paying much attention. "No, according to the rules; but what do you mean by the question? You are always such a mysterious old idiot, you know. You can't help it, I suppose."

Old Skettle smiled, if the extraordinary contortion of the wrinkled face could be called by so flattering a designation.

"I've seen such mysterious things since I first went into Mr. Hudsley's office to sweep the floor— —"

"Now, then," said Jack, "none of that game; going into the old story, which I have heard a hundred times, of how you went as an office boy, and have risen to the proud position of confidential clerk. You're like one of the old fellows in the play, who draws a chair up to the footlights, and says, 'It's seven long years ago— —' and the people begin to clear out into the refreshment bar, and wait there till he's done. Where were you? Oh, 'mysterious experiences.' Well, go on."

But old Skettle had, apparently, nothing to say; he had, while Jack had been speaking, changed his mind.

"I beg pardon for stopping you, Master Jack," he said. "I felt I couldn't let you go out of the old place without expressing my sympathy."

"Thanks, thanks," said Jack, holding out his hand. "You're one of the right sort, Skettle, and so's Hudsley. I believe he's sorry, too. Looks a little puzzled, too. Puzzled isn't the word for what I feel. I've got the sensation one experiences when he's been sitting through one of the old-fashioned melo-dramas. Not even a mourning-ring, or a walking-stick. Poor Squire— well, I forgive him. He had a right to do what he liked with his own."

"Just so, Master Jack, but it's hard for you," said Skettle. "Not a mourning-ring. By the way, sir," and something like a blush crept over his wrinkled face. "If—if you should be in want of a little money——"

Jack stared, then laughed grimly.

"Well, you certainly must be mad, Skettle," he interrupted. "Want money! When didn't I want it? But don't you be idiot enough to lend me any. It would be a jolly bad speculation, old fellow. There is not a Jew in London would take my paper. No, Skettle, it would be downright robbery, and I don't think I could rob you, you know."

"Do you remember the day you swam across the mill-pond, and fished my little boy out, Master Jack?"

"You take care I shan't forget it, Skettle," said Jack, with a smile. "It was a noble deed, wasn't it? Every time you mention it, I try to feel like a hero, but it won't come. How is little Ned?"

"He's well, sir; he's in London now, working his way up. He'd have been in the church-yard if it hadn't been for you."

"Why, Skettle, this is worse than ''Twas seven long years ago!'" exclaimed Jack.

"On that day, Master Jack, I swore that if ever a time came when I'd a chance of serving you, I'd do it. It did not seem very likely then, for we all thought you'd be the next squire; but now, Master Jack, I should be grateful if you'd borrow ten pounds of me."

"Nonsense," cried Jack. "Don't be an idiot, Skettle. You a lawyer! why, you're too soft for anything but a washerwoman. There, good-bye; remember me to little Ned when you write, and tell him I hope he'll grow up a little harder than his father. Good-bye," and he shook the thin, skinny claw heartily.

Old Skettle stood and looked after him, his right hand fumbling in his waistcoat pocket; and when Jack had got quite out of sight he pulled the hand out, and with it a small scrap of paper with a few words written on it, and a seal. It was just such a scrap of paper which might have been torn from a letter, and the seal was the Davenant seal, with its griffin and spear plainly stamped.

Old Skettle looked at it a moment curiously, then shook his head.

"No, I was right after all in not giving it to him; it may be nothing— nothing at all. And yet—it's the squire's handwriting, for it's his seal, and what was it lying outside the terrace for? Where's the other part of it, and what was the other part like? I'll keep it. I don't say that there's any good in it, but I'll keep it. Not a mourning-ring or a walking-stick! All—house, lands, money—to Mr. Stephen, with the sneaking face and the silky tongue. Poor Master Jack! I—I wish he'd taken that ten-pound note; it burns a hole in my pocket. Not—a—mourning-ring," he muttered. "It's not like the squire, for he was fond of Master Jack, and if I'm not half the idiot he called me, the old man hated Mr. Stephen. I seem to feel that there's something wrong. I'll keep this bit of paper;" and he restored the scrap to its place and returned to the "Bush" with as much expression on his face as one might expect to see on a blank skin of parchment.

Jack was more moved than he would have liked to admit by old Skettle's sympathy and offer of assistance, and in a softened mood, produced by the little incident, sat and smoked his pipe with a lighter spirit.

After all he was young, and—and—well, things might turn up; at any rate, if the worst came to the worst, he could earn his living at driving a coach-and-four, or, say, as a navvy.

"I shouldn't make a bad light porter," he mused, "only there are no light porters now. I wonder what will become of me. Anyhow, I'd rather live on an Abernethy biscuit a day than take a penny from Stephen or borrow ten pounds from Skettle. Stephen. Squire of Hurst Leigh! He'll make a funny squire. I don't believe he knows a pheasant from a barn-door fowl, or a Berkshire pig from a pump-handle. I should have made a better squire than he. Never mind; it's no use crying over spilt milk!"

Jack was certainly not the man to cry over milk spilt or strewn, and long before the train had reached Arkdale he had forgotten his ill-luck and the mystery attending the will, and all his thoughts were fixed on the beautiful girl who dwelt in a woodman's hut in the midst of Warden Forest.

Forbidden fruit is always the sweetest, and Jack felt that the fruit was forbidden here. What on earth business had he, a ruined man, to be lounging about Warden, or any other forest, in the hope of getting a sight of, or a few words with, a girl, whom, be she as lovely as a peri, could be nothing to him? What good could he do? On the contrary, perhaps, a great deal of harm; for ten to one the woodman would cut up rough, and there would be a row.

But he felt, somehow, that he had made a promise, and promises were sacred things to Jack—excepting always promises to pay—and a row had rather a charm for him.

Nevertheless, when the train drew up at Arkdale Station, he had quite resolved to wait until the London train came up, and as such resolutions generally end, it ended in giving up the idea and starting for Warden.

Jack was not sentimental. Men with good appetites and digestions seldom are; but his heart beat as he entered the charmed center of the great elms and oaks which fringed the forest, and the whole atmosphere seemed full of a strange fascination.

"I wonder what she will say, how she will look?" he kept asking himself. "I'd walk a thousand miles to hear her voice, to look into her eyes. Oh, I'm a worse idiot than old Skettle! What can her eyes and her voice be to me? By Jove, though, I might turn woodman and—and——" marry her, he was going to say, but the thought seemed so bold, so—well, so coarse in connection with such a beautiful person, that Jack actually blushed and frowned at his effrontery.

He found no difficulty in recognizing the way, and strode along at a good pace, which, however, grew slower as he neared the clearing in which stood Gideon Rolfe's cottage, and just before he emerged from the wood into it he stopped, and felt with a faint wonder that his heart was beating fast.

It was a new sensation for Master Jack, and it upset him.

"This won't do," he said; "I must keep cool. A child would get the better of me while I am like this; and I mustn't forget I've got to face that wooden-faced woodman. Courage, my boy, courage!"

And with a resolute front he stepped into the clearing.

Yes, there was the cottage, but why on earth were the shutters up.

With a strange misgiving he walked up to the door and knocked.

There was no answer. He knocked again and again—still no answer.

Then he stepped back and looked up at the chimney. There was no smoky trail rising through the trees. He listened—there was no sound. His heart sank and sank till he felt as if it had entered his boots.

With a kind of desperate hope he knelt on the window-sill and looked through a hole in the shutter into the room.

It was bare of furniture—empty, desolate.

He got down again and looked about him like one who, having buried a treasure, goes to the spot and finds that it has gone.

Gone—that was the word—and no sign!

It was incredible. Three days—only three days. What had happened? Was—was anyone dead? And at this thought his face grew as pale as the tan would allow it.

No; that was absurd. People—she—could not have died and been buried in three days! Then, where was she? Was it possible that the old man had actually left the wood—thrown up his livelihood—because of his (Jack's) visit to the cottage?

A great deal more disturbed and upset than he had been over the squire's will, he paced up and down. He sat down on the seat outside the window—the seat where he had drunk his cider and eaten his cake—the seat where Mrs. Davenant sat so patiently—and he lit his pipe and smoked in utter bewilderment.

Disappointment is but a lukewarm word by which to describe his feelings.

He felt that he had looked forward to seeing Una as a sort of set-off against the terrible blow which the squire's will had dealt him, and now she was gone!

I am afraid to say how many hours he sat smoking and musing, in the vain hope that she, or Gideon Rolfe, or someone would come to tell him something about it; but at last he realized that she had indeed flown; that the nest which had contained the beautiful bird was empty and void; and with a heart that felt like lead, he set out for Wermesley.

By chance, more than calculation, he caught the up-train, and was whirled into London.

Weary, exhausted rather, he signaled a hansom, and was driven to Spider Court.

Spider Court is not an easy place to find. It is in the heart of the Temple, and consists of about ten houses, every one of which, like a Chinese puzzle, contains a number of houses within itself.

Barristers—generally briefless—inhabit Spider Court; but it is the refuge of the hard-working literary man, and of the members of that strange class which is always waiting for "something to turn up."

Jack ascended the stairs of No. 5, passed various doors bearing the names of the occupants on the other side of them, and opened a door which bore the legend:

"Leonard Dagle.

"John Newcombe."

painted in small black letters on its cross-panel.

It was not a large room, and it was plainly furnished; but it looked comfortable. Its contents looked rather incongruous.

At the end of the room, close by the window, which only allowed about four hours of daylight to enter it, stood a table crowded with papers, presenting that appearance which ladies generally call "a litter." The table and book-shelf, filled with heavy-looking volumes, would give one the impression that the room belonged to a barrister or a literary man, if it were not for a set of boxing-gloves and a pair of fencing foils, which hung over the fireplace, and the prints of ballet-girls and famous actresses which adorned the walls.

As Jack entered the room, a man, who was sitting at the table, turned his head, and peering through the gloom which a single candle only served to emphasize, exclaimed:

"Jack, is that you?"

The speaker was the Leonard Dagle whose name appeared conjointly with Jack's on the door of the chambers.

Seen by the light of the single candle, Leonard Dagle looked handsome; it was left for the daylight to reveal the traces which life's battle had cut in his regular features. One had only to glance at the face to be reminded of the old saying of the sword wearing the scabbard. It was the face of a man who had fought the hard fight of one hand against the world, and had not yet won the victory.

Leonard Dagle was Jack's old chum; friends he had in plenty—dangerous friends many of them—but Leonard was his brother and companion in arms. They had shared the same rooms, the same tankard of bitter, sometimes the same crust, for years.

There was not a secret between them. Either would have given the other his last penny and felt grateful for the acceptance of it. It was a singular friendship, for no two men could be more unlike than Leonard Dagle, the hard-working barrister, and Jack Newcombe, the spendthrift, the ne'er-do-well, and—the Savage.

"Is that you, Jack?" exclaimed Leonard, straightening his back. "Home already?"

"Yes, I'm back."

"What's the matter—tired?"

"Tired—bored—humbled—thoroughly used up! I've got news for you, Len."

"Bad or good?"

"Bad as they can be. First the squire's dead!"

"Dead?"

"Yes, dead and buried. Poor old fellow!"

"I am very sorry. Then you—then you—am I addressing the Squire of Hurst Leigh?"

"You are addressing the pauper of Spider Court."

"Jack, what do you mean?"

"I mean that the poor old fellow has died and left me nothing—not even a mourning-ring."

"I'm very sorry. Left you nothing, my dear old man!"

"Don't pity me. I can't stand that. Say serves you right, say anything. After all, what did I deserve?"

"But you expected something," said Leonard.

"Yes, and no. I expected nothing till I got there, and then did. I saw him for a few minutes before he died, and he said—certainly said—that I—well, that there would be something for me."

"And there is nothing."

"Not a stiver. Mind I don't complain, Len. I didn't deserve it."

"Where has it all gone? He was a rich man, was he not?" asked Leonard.

"Rich as a Crœsus," replied Jack, "and it has all gone to Stephen Davenant."

"That is the man that goes in for philanthropy and all that sort of thing."

"That's the man," replied Jack.

"Tell me all about it," said Leonard, after a long pause.

And, with many pauses, Jack told his story.

Leonard Dagle listened intently.

"It's a strange story, Jack," he said. "I—I—it rather puzzles me. There could be—of course, there could be nothing wrong."

"Wrong, how do you mean?" exclaimed Jack.

"Well, Stephen Davenant's conduct is rather peculiar—isn't it?"

"Oh, he's half out of his mind," said Jack, carelessly. "He has been playing a close game for the money, and hanging about the old man till he has got as hysterical as a girl. What do you think could be wrong? Everything was as correct as it could be—family lawyer, who made out the will, and all the rest of it."

"Then you think the squire was wandering in his mind at last?"

"That's it," said Jack. "He wanted to provide for me—to leave me something, and he fancied he'd done it. It's often the case, isn't it?"

"I've met with such cases," said Leonard.

"Just so," said Jack. "Is there anything to drink?" he asked, abruptly, as if he wanted to change the subject.

"There's some whiskey——"

Jack mixed himself a tumbler and sat on the edge of the table, and Leonard Dagle leaned back and watched him.

"There's something else, Jack," he said. "Out with it; what is it?"

"What a fellow you are, Len. You are like one of those mesmeric men; there's no keeping anything from you. Well, I've had an adventure."

"An adventure?"

"Yes, I'm half under the impression that it's nothing but a dream. Len, I've seen the most beautiful—the most—Len, do you believe in witches? Not the old sort, but the young ones—sirens, didn't they call them; who used to haunt the woods and forests and tempt travelers into quagmires and ditches. The innocent-looking kind of sirens, you know. Well, I've seen one!"

"Jack, you've been drinking; put that glass down."

"Have I? Then I haven't. Look here," and he told the story of his wanderings in Warden, and all it had led up to.

"How's that for an adventure?" he said, when he had finished.

"It would do for a mediæval romance. And she has gone, you say?"

"Clean gone," said Jack, with a sigh and a long pull at the tumbler. "Gone like a—a dream, you know. How is that for an adventure? You don't believe in them, though."

Leonard Dagle looked up, and there was a strange, half-shy expression in his face.

"You are right, Jack. I didn't till the day before yesterday."

"The day before yesterday? What do you mean?"

"Simply that I, too, have had an adventure."

"Seems to me that we're like those confounded nuisances who used to meet on a coach and tell stories to amuse themselves. Go on; it's your turn now."

"Mine's soon told. After you started for Hurst Leigh I got a letter from a man at Wermesley——"

"Wermesley!" exclaimed Jack. "Why——"

"Yes, it is on the same line. He wanted me to go down to look over some deeds, and I went. I took a return ticket and got into the last train. When I got into the carriage—I went 'first' on the strength of the business—I saw a young lady—mind, a young lady—seated in a corner. It struck me as rather odd that a young girl should be traveling alone at this time of night, and I shifted about until I could get a good look at her. Jack, you're not the only man that has seen a beautiful girl within the last week."

"Beautiful, eh?" cried Jack, interested.

"Beautiful in my eyes. The sort of face that Cleopatra might have had when she was that girl's age. I never saw such eyes, and I had plenty of opportunity of seeing them, for she seemed quite unconscious of my presence. Jack, I'm a shy man, and I'm often sorry for it, but I was never sorrier than I was then, for I'd have given anything to have been able to speak to her and hear her speak. There she sat, looking like a picture, quite motionless, with her eyes fixed on the flare of the lamp; and there I sat and couldn't pluck up courage to say a word. At last we got to London; they came for the tickets, and she couldn't find hers. I went down on my hands and knees, and at last I found the ticket under the seat. I looked at it as I gave it to the porter; and where do you think it was from?"

Jack shook his head. He didn't think it much of an adventure after Una and Warden Forest.

"You'll never guess. What do you say to Hurst Leigh?"

"Hurst Leigh! Why, who was she? Somebody I know, perhaps."

"I found my tongue at last, and said, 'You have had a long journey. Hurst Leigh is a beautiful place.' And what do you think she said?"

Jack shook his head.

"She said, 'I don't know. I have never been there before today.' That's all until we got to the terminus, then I asked her if I could get her luggage. 'I haven't any,' she said. 'Could I get her a cab?' I asked. Yes, I might get her a cab. I went and found a cab and put her in it; and, if I had a shadow of a doubt as to her being a lady, the way in which she thanked me would have dispelled it. I asked her where I should direct the cabman to drive, and she said 24 Cheltenham Terrace. And—and then she went."

"Well?"

"Well, I—of course you'll call me a fool, Jack, I am quite aware of that—I followed in another cab."

"Good heavens! You've been drinking!"

"No. I followed, and when she had gone I knocked at the door of the next house and asked the name of the people who lived next door. They—for a wonder—were civil, and told me. She lives with her grandfather, and her name is Laura Treherne."

CHAPTER XVI

"Her name is Laura Treherne," said Leonard.

"Laura Treherne. Never heard the name before."

"Nor I, but it belongs to the most beautiful creature I have ever seen."

"That's because you haven't seen Una Rolfe," put in Jack, coolly. "But I say, Len, what has come to us? We've both caught the universal epidemic at the same time. It's nothing wonderful in me, you know—but you—*you*, who wouldn't look at a woman! Have you got it bad, Len?"

"Very bad, Jack. Yes, the time which Rosseau calls the supremest in one's life, has come to me. As a novice in the art of love-making, I come to you for advice."

"Why, it's easy enough in your case. You know where to put your hand upon the lady. What are you to do? Why, disguise yourself as a sweep, and go and sweep the chimneys at 24 Cheltenham Square, or pretend you're the tax collector, or 'come to look at the gas meter.' You've got half a dozen plans, but I—what am I to do? I've seen the most beautiful creature in existence, and if I'm not in love with her— —"

"I should say you were," said Leonard, gently.

"Yes, I am. I knew it when I found that confounded cottage empty. But what am I to do? I haven't the faintest clew to her whereabouts. The old gentleman with the hatchet may have murdered his whole family—her included—or emigrated to Australia."

"It is very strange. Didn't you notice any sign of a move about the place the first night you were there?"

"No, none. Everything looked as if it had been going on for a hundred years—excepting Una—and meant to go on for another hundred. Len, I'm afraid we've been bewitched. Perhaps it's all a dream; I haven't been down to Hurst and you haven't been down to Wermesley. We shall wake up directly—oh, no! The poor squire! Len, it's all true, and we're a couple of young fools!"

"Speak for yourself, old fellow. I have been a fool until three days ago, now I am as wise as Solomon, for I have learned what love is."

"So have I—I have also learned the vanity of human wishes, and the next thing I shall have to learn will be some way of earning a livelihood. I should prefer an honest one, but—poor men can't afford to be particular, and honesty doesn't seem to pay now-a-days. I feel so hard up and reckless that I could become a bank director or a member of Parliament without feeling a pang of conscience."

Leonard looked up at him, for the vein of bitterness was plainly to be detected running through Jack's banter; and Leonard knew that when Jack was bitter—which was but once a year, say—he was reckless.

"We must talk it over. Sit down—get off that table; you're making a perfect hash of my papers—and let's talk it over. You won't go out tonight."

"Yes, I shall. I shall go down to the club."

"No, no, keep away from the club tonight, Jack."

"What are you afraid of? Do you think I shall want to gamble? I've no money to lose."

"That's the very reason you'll want to play. Do keep at home tonight."

"I couldn't do it, old man," he said. "I'm on wires—I'm all on fire. If I sat here much longer, I should get up suddenly, murder you, and sack the place. The Savage has got his paint on, and is on the trail."

"Don't be a fool, Jack. You are hot and upset. Keep away from the club tonight. Well, well—let the *ecarte* alone, at any rate."

"All right, I'll promise you that. I won't touch a card tonight. *Ecarte!* I couldn't play beggar-my-neighbor tonight! Len, I wish you were a bigger man; I'd get up a row, and have a turn-to with you. Sit down here! I couldn't do it. I want to be doing something—something desperate. You can sit here and dream over your complaint; I can't—I should go mad! Don't sit up for me."

Leonard looked after him as he disappeared into one of the two bedrooms which adjoined the common sitting-room, and, with a shake of his head, muttered, "Poor Jack!" and returned to his work.

Jack took a cold bath, dressed himself, and merely pausing to shout a good-night, as he passed down the stairs, went into the street, and jumped into a hansom, telling the man to drive to the Hawks' Club.

It was rather early for the "Hawks," and only a few of them had fluttered in. It was about the last club that such a man as Jack should have been a member of. It was fast, it was expensive, it was fashionable, and the chief reason for its existence lay in the fact that play at any time, and to any extent, could be obtained there.

When Jack entered the cardroom, that apartment was almost empty, but the suspicious-looking tables were surrounded by chairs stuck up on two legs, denoting that they were engaged, and those men who were present were all playing.

Every head was turned as he entered, and a buzz of greeting rose to welcome him.

"Halloa; you back, Jack!" said a tall, military-looking man, who was known as the "Indian Nut," because he was one of the most famous of our Indian colonels. "You're just in time to take a hand at loo."

"No; come and join us," said young Lord Pierrepoint, from another table, at which nap was being played.

But if you could only wring a promise out of Jack, you could rest perfectly certain that he would keep it; and he shook his head firmly.

"Nary a card."

"What! Don't you feel well, Jack?"

"No, I'm hungry. I'm going to get something to eat."

"Dear me, I didn't know you did eat, Jack. However, man, come and sit down, and don't fidget about the room like that."

"Len's right, the club won't do neither. I couldn't hold a card straight tonight. I'll get some dinner, and go back, and we'll have it all over again."

It was a wise and virtuous resolution; and, unlike most resolves, Jack meant to keep it. But alas! before he had got through with his soup, the door opened and two men strolled in.

They were both young and well-known. The one was Sir Arkroyd Hetley; the other, the young Lord Dalrymple, whose coronet had scarcely yet warmed his forehead, as the French say.

Both of them uttered an exclamation at seeing Jack, and made straight for his table.

"Why, here's the Savage!" exclaimed Dalrymple. "Back to his native forest primeval."

"Been on the war trail, Jack?" asked Sir Arkroyd. "How are the squaws and wigwams? Seriously, where have you been, old man?"

"Yes, I have been on the war trail," he said.

"And got some scalps, I hope," said Dalrymple. "What are you doing—dining? What do you say, Ark, shall we join him? It's so long since I've eaten anything that I should like to watch a man do it before I make an attempt."

The footman put chairs and rearranged the table, and the two men chatted and conned over the *carte*.

"You don't look quite the thing, Jack. Been going it in the forest, or what?"

"Yes, I've been going it in the forest, Dally."

"Been hunting the buffalo and chumming up with his old friend, Spotted Bull," said Arkroyd. "Bet you anything he hasn't been out of London, Dally."

"Take him," said Jack. "I've been out of London on a little matter of business."

"He's been robbing a bank," said Arkroyd, "or breaking one."

"Neither. Stop chaffing, you two, and tell a fellow what's going on."

"Shall we tell him, Dally? Perhaps he'll try to cut us out. It wouldn't be a bad idea to start a joint stock company, all club together, you know, and work it in that way, the one who wins to share with the other fellows."

"Wins what? What on earth are you talking about? Is it a sweepstake, a handicap, or what——"

"No, my noble Savage. It's the heiress."

"Oh," said Jack, indifferently, and he sipped his claret critically.

"What has come to you, Jack? Have you decided to cut the world or have heiresses become unnecessary? Perhaps someone has left you a fortune, old man; if so, nobody will be more delighted than I shall be—to help you spend it."

A flush rose to Jack's face, and his eyes flashed. He had been drinking great bumpers of the Hawks' favorite claret—a heady wine which Jack should never have touched at any time, especially not tonight.

"No, no one has left me a fortune; quite the reverse. But you'd better tell me about this heiress, I see, or you'll die of disappointment. Who is she—where is she?—what is she? Here's her good health, whoever she is," and down went another bumper of the Lafitte; and as it went down, it was to Una he drank, not to the unknown one.

"Do you remember Earlsley?" said Arkroyd. "Oh, no, of course not, you must have been in your cradle in the wigwam in that time. Well; old Wigsley died and left his money to a fifty-second cousin, who turned out to be a girl. No one knew anything about her; no one knew where to find her; but at last there comes a claimant in the shape of a girl from one of the Colonies—Canada. That isn't a colony, is it, though? Australia—anywhere—nobody knows, you know. She came over with her belongings—a rum-looking old fellow, with a white head of long hair, like, a—a—what's got a long head of white hair, Dally?"

"Try patriarch," murmured the marquis.

"Well, in addition to the money, and there's about a million, more or less—she's got the most beautiful, that isn't the word, most charming, fascinating little face you ever saw. If she looks at you, you feel as if you never could feel an ache or pain again as long as you lived."

"Ark, you've had too much champagne."

"No; 'pon my honor. Isn't it right, Dally?"

"Yes, and if she smiles," said Dalrymple, "you never could feel another moment's unhappiness. The prettiest mouth—and when it opens, her teeth——"

"Oh, confound it!" exclaimed Jack, brusquely. "You needn't run over her points as if she were a horse; I don't want to buy her."

As a matter of fact, he had only caught the last word or two, for while Arkroyd had been talking he had been thinking of that other beautiful girl—not a doll, with teeth and a smile, but an angel, pure and ethereal—a dream—not a fascinating heiress.

"Buy her!" exclaimed Arkroyd. "Listen to him! Don't I tell you she's worth a million?"

"And I'd make her Countess of Dalrymple tomorrow if she hadn't a penny, and would have me," said Dalrymple.

"Try her," said Jack, curtly.

"No use, my dear Savage," he said, tugging at his incipient fringe of down ruefully. "She won't have anything to say to yours truly, or to any one of us for that matter. She only smiles when we say pretty things, and shows her teeth at us. Besides, the title wouldn't tempt her. She's got one already. Don't I tell you she's one of the Earlsley lot? No; we've all had a try, even Arkroyd. He even went so far as to get a fellow to write a poem about her in one of the society journals, and signed it 'A. H.;' but she told him to his face that she didn't care for poetry. It was a pretty piece, too, wasn't it, Ark?"

"First-rate," said Arkroyd, with as much modesty as if he had written it. "But it was all thrown away on Lady Bell."

"On whom?" said Jack, waking up again.

"On Lady Bell—Isabel Earlsley is her name. You're wool-gathering tonight, Jack."

"Oh, Lady Bell, is it?" said Jack, carelessly. "Go ahead. Anything else?"

"No, that's all, excepting that I'll wager a cool thousand to a china orange that you'll change your tone when you see her, Savage."

"Perhaps," said Jack, "but your description doesn't move me; not much, Ark. You're not good at that sort of thing. It isn't in your line. The only things you seem to have remarked are her smile and her teeth."

"Savage, you are, as usual, blunt, not to say rude. Let us have another bottle of Cliquot."

Jack shook his head, but another bottle came up, and he sat and took his share in silence, and, indeed, almost unconsciously. For all the attention he paid to the chatter of his two friends they might not have been present.

His thoughts flew backward to the shady grove of Warden Forest, to the girl who, like a vision of purity and innocence and loveliness, had floated like a dream across his life.

He gave one passing thought to Len, too, and his story.

It was a strange coincidence that they should both have met their fates at one and the same time, or nearly so.

He would have thought it stranger still if he could have lifted the veil of the future and seen how closely the web of his life was woven with the woof, not only of Una's, but of Laura Treherne, and also of Lady Bell Earlsley.

All unconscious he had turned a leaf of his life's book, and had begun a new chapter in which these three women were to take a part.

But he sat and drank the champagne, knowing nothing of this, and—I am sorry to have to say it—he was rapidly arriving at that condition in which it is dangerous to be within a mile of that fascinating fluid. When a man passes from a state of half-feverish restlessness and dissatisfaction to one of comparative comfort, and that by the aid of the cheering glass, it is time to put the cheering glass aside and go home.

Jack did not go home; on the contrary, he went into the billiard-room, and Cliquot followed, as a matter of course.

For a time Jack had managed to forget everything excepting his promise to Len; he would not enter the card-room, but he stuck to pool and champagne.

CHAPTER XVII

I am not going to apologize for our hero, nor am I going to gloss over his faults with any specious special pleading. No man is either wholly good or wholly bad; certainly Jack was not wholly good; he was human, very human, and blessed, or cursed, with a hot, passionate blood, which made him more liable to trip than most men. But, at the same time, this in justice must be said of him, that he very rarely sinned in this way.

Tonight his blood was at full heat; the love which had sprung up like a tongue of flame in his heart burned and maddened him, and to this newly-born love was added the disappointment and bewilderment of Una's sudden disappearance. Add, too, that he had been overstrained and upset, and—well, there are the excuses and apologies, after all.

Somewhere about two o'clock, when the club was full with men who had dropped in from theater and ball-room, and amidst the popping of corks and click of pool balls, a certain feeling came over poor Jack that he had taken quite as much, and more, of the sparkling juice than was good for him; and with that consciousness came the resolution to go home.

The game was just over, and without a word he put up his cue, motioned to a footman to bring him his hat, and, scarcely noticed in the crowd and bustle, slowly descended the broad and indeed magnificent staircase for which and its palatial hall the club was famous.

He descended very slowly, with his hand on the balustrade, and having reached the bottom, he filled a glass with water from the crystal filter that stood on a side table in the porter's box, and sallied out.

The night air struck upon his hot brow in a cool and welcome fashion, and Jack stood for a moment or two, fighting with the hazy and stupefying effects of the night's work.

"I won't go home yet," he muttered. "Len will be cut up; he always is. He's as bad as a father—almost as bad as a mother-in-law. Well, I didn't touch the cards, anyhow. And if it had not been for those two idiots, Ark and Dally, I shouldn't have got so far into the champagne. How bright the stars shine—an unaccountable number of them tonight." Poor Jack! "Never saw such a quantity! No, I won't go home yet. I'll walk it off if I have to walk till tomorrow morning. Where am I? Ah! where is *she*? Thank Heaven, she isn't near me now! I'm glad she's gone; I'm glad I shall never see her any more. I'm not fit to see her; not worthy to touch her hand. But I did touch it," and, with a kind of wonder at his audacity, he stretched out his hand and stared at it under the gas-lamp.

Then he walked on perfectly indifferent to the direction, perfectly indifferent to the weariness which was gradually—no, rapidly—coming on him.

Just at this time, while he was walking off the drowsy dream that had got possession of him, a stream of carriages was slowly moving down Park Lane, taking up from one of the best known houses in town—Lady Merivale's.

Lady Merivale was one of the leaders of *ton* and had been one as long as most middle-aged people could remember. To be seen at Lady Merivale's was to be acknowledged as one of that small but powerful portion of humanity known as "the upper ten."

It was one of her ladyship's grand balls, and not only were the ball and drawing-rooms full, but the staircase also, and any one wishing to enter or exit had to make his way down a narrow line flanked on either side by the youth and nobility of the best kind of society.

That it had been a great success no one who knows the world—and Lady Merivale—needs to be told. It had, perhaps, been one of her greatest, for in addition to two princes of the blood royal, she had secured the great sensation of the day, the young millionairess, Lady Isabel Earlsley.

And this was no slight achievement, for Lady Bell, as she was generally called, was a wilful, uncertain young personage, from whom it was very hard to procure a promise, and who, not seldom, was given to breaking it when made, at least, so far as acceptation of invitations went.

But she was there tonight; as the next issue of the *Morning Post* would testify.

Jack had been really too careless and scornful in his indifference. Lady Bell was not only beautiful, she was—what was more rare than beauty—charming. She was rather short than tall; but not too short. She had a beautiful figure; not a wasp waist by any means, but a natural figure, full of power and grace. Her skin was, well, colonial; delicately tinted and creamy; and her eyes—it is difficult to catalogue her eyes, because their lights were always changing—but the expression which generally predominated was one of half-amused, half-mocking light.

With both expressions she met the open admiration of the gilded youths who thronged round her, amused at their foppery, mocking at their protestations of devotion.

Tonight she was dressed neither magnificently nor superbly, but with, what seemed to the women who gazed at her with barely concealed envy, artful simplicity.

Her dress was of Indian muslin, priceless for all its simplicity; and she wore glittering in her hair, on her arms, and on her cream-white bosom, pearls, that, in quantity and quality would have made the fortune of any enterprising burglar.

By her side stood—for they were moving toward the door, on their way to an exit—an elderly woman, with an expressionless face, simply and plainly dressed. She was generally spoken of as the watch dog; but she scarcely deserved that name, for Lady Bell was quite capable of watching over herself; and Mrs. Fellowes, the widow of the Indian colonel, was too mild to represent any sort of dog whatever.

Surrounded by a crowd of devoted courtiers, the great heiress and her companion moved toward the door where the hostess stood receiving the farewells and thanks of her guests; and when one thinks of the many hundred times Lady Merivale had stood by that door, and undergone that terrible ordeal, one is filled with amazement and awe at her courage and physical strength.

For forty years she had been standing at doors, receiving and meeting guests; yet she stood tonight as smiling and courageous as ever.

At last Lady Bell reached her hostess, and Lady Merivale, tired and done up as she was, gave her special recognition.

"Must you go, Lady Bell? Well, good-night. And thank you for making my poor little dance a success. Thank you very much."

Lady Bell said nothing, but she smiled "in her old colonial" way, as they called it, and threaded through the lane of human beings on the stairs.

"Lady Earlsley's carriage!" shouted the footman in the gorgeous Merivale livery, and a little brougham drove up.

Lady Bell hated show and magnificence.

Her stables and coach-houses were crowded with horses and carriages, her wardrobes filled to repletion with Worth's costumes and Elise's "confections," as bonnets are called now-a-days, but a plain little brougham was her favorite vehicle, and the simplest of costumes pleased her best.

All the way down the stairs she had to nod and smile and exchange farewells, and at the bottom, in the hall, on the stone steps themselves, she was surrounded by men eager to secure the privilege of putting her into her little brougham.

But she avoided them all, and sprang in as if she had not been dancing for four hours, and throwing herself back into the corner, exclaimed:

"Thank goodness, that is over. Poor old Fellowes! you are worn out. Confess it."

"I am rather tired, my dear," said Mrs. Fellowes, who had been sitting against a wall all the evening.

"Tired! of course you are; it's ever so much more tiring looking on than dancing, and joining in the giddy round. I don't feel a bit tired; I'm a little bored."

"Bored! what a word, my dear Bell," murmured Mrs. Fellowes, sleepily.

"It's a good word—it's an expressive word—and it just means really what I feel."

"And yet you received more attention than any woman—any girl—in the room, my dear," murmured Mrs. Fellowes.

"My money-bags may have done so," said Lady Bell, scornfully; "not I. Do you think that if I were as penniless as one of Lady Southerly's daughters, I should receive as much attention? Fellowes, don't you take to flattering me. I couldn't stand that."

"I don't want to flatter you, my dear Bell; but when the prince himself dances twice with you——"

"Of course he did. I am a celebrity. I am the richest young woman in the kingdom, and he would have done it if I had been as ugly as sin—which isn't ugly, by the way."

"What strange things you say," murmured Mrs. Fellowes, with mild rebuke. "I'm sure no girl received more attention than you have tonight. I sat and watched you, my dear, and a spectator sees more of the game than a player."

"You are right, it is all a game, a gamble," retorted Lady Bell. "All those nice young men were playing pitch and toss who should make the hardest running with the great heiress. Do you think I am blind? I can see through them all, and I despise them. There isn't a man among them but would pay me the same court if I were as plain as Lucifer— —"

"My dear Bell— —"

"But it is true," said Lady Bell. "I can read them all. And if they knew how I despised them, even while I smile upon them, they would keep at arm's length for very shame. I wish I hadn't a penny in the world."

"My dear Bell!" ejaculated Mrs. Fellowes, really and truly shocked at such a fearfully profane wish.

"I do! I do! I should then find out if any one of them cared for me—for myself. You say I am beautiful, but you are so partial; do you think I am beautiful enough to cause any man to risk his all in life for my sake?"

"I don't know. I don't just follow you," said poor Mrs. Fellowes.

"No, you are half asleep," retorted Lady Bell. "There, curl yourself up and snooze. I shan't talk any more."

Lady Bell leaned forward, and looked up at the stars—the same stars that seemed so numerous to poor Jack—and pondered over the events of the evening.

It was true that a prince of the blood had danced there with her; it was true that, all through the evening, she had been surrounded by a court of the best men in London; it was true that she had sent one half the women home burning with envy and malice and all uncharitableness; but still she was not happy.

"No," she murmured, unheard by the sleeping companion; "the dream of my life has not yet been fulfilled. I have not yet met the man to whom I could say, 'I am yours, take me!' Perhaps I never shall; and until I do, I will remain Lady Bell, though they buzz round my money-bags till I am deaf with their hum."

The brougham was going at a great pace, simply because the coachman very reasonably desired to get home and to bed; and Lady Bell saw the houses flit past as if they had been part of a panorama got up for her special amusement.

But suddenly the brougham swerved, and, indeed, nearly upset, and the stillness of the night was broken by what seemed remarkably like an oath by the coachman.

Lady Bell felt that something was wrong; but she neither turned color nor lost her presence of mind.

Putting her head, with a thousand pounds of jewels on it, through the window, she said, in clear tones:

"What is the matter, Jackson?"

"I—whoa! I don't quite know, my lady; I think it is a man. Something came right across the road. Yes, it is a man."

Lady Bell opened the brougham door, stepped into the road—the light from the lamp flashing on her pearls—and went toward the horse.

"Keep away from her hind legs, for goodness' sake, my lady," ejaculated Jackson. "Keep still, will you!" this was of course addressed to the horse.

"What is it? what is it?" asked Lady Bell, peering about.

"Here, my lady, on the near side—on the left. It's down in the road, whatever it is."

Lady Bell went behind the brougham to the near side—she was too well acquainted with horses and their moods to cross in front of the horse's eyes—and looked about her. For a moment she could see nothing, but presently, when her eyes had become used to the darkness, she saw a man lying, as it seemed, right under the horse's body.

Her impulse—and she always acted on that impulse—was to pull him out. But to pull a man even an inch is a difficult task even for the strongest girl, and after a moment's tug she was about to tell Jackson to alight while she stood at the horse's head, when suddenly the prostrate man staggered to his feet, and leaned against the brougham as if it had been specially built and brought there for that purpose.

Lady Bell went up to him and laid her hand upon his arm.

"What has happened?" she said, anxiously. "Were you run over—are you hurt?"

Jack—for it was Jack—opened his eyes and stared at her with the gravity of a man suddenly sobered.

"No," he said, "I am not hurt. Don't blame the man, it was my fault. Not hurt at all. Good-night."

And he feels for his hat, which at that moment was lying under the carriage a shapeless mass.

As he spoke Lady Bell saw something drop on to his hand, and looking at it saw that it was a drop of blood.

With a shudder—for she could not bear the sight of blood—she said:

"Not hurt! Why, you are bleeding."

"Am I?" said Jack, gravely and curtly. "It will do me good. Don't you be alarmed, miss. I am used to being upset, and my bones are too hard to break. Good-night."

And he made for the pavement pretty steadily. But a hand, soft and warm, and strong also, stayed him.

"Stop," said Lady Bell; "I am sure you are hurt. How did you come to be run over?"

"Got in the way of the horse, I suppose," said Jack, quietly. "That is the usual way."

"But—but," said Lady Bell; and she looked at the handsome face scrutinizingly.

Then she stopped, for her scrutiny had discovered two facts; first, that the individual who had been run over was a gentleman; secondly, that he had been drinking.

"Wait," she said, still keeping her hand on his arm; "you are not fit to go alone without some assistance, and I am sure you are hurt. Look, you are bleeding."

"A mere nothing," said Jack; "don't trouble. Allow me to put you in—I shall get home all right."

Lady Bell, still keeping her eyes fixed on his face, shook her head.

"I couldn't leave you like this," she said. "Where do you live?"

"Where do I—live?" repeated Jack. "Spider Court, Temple. It's no distance from here."

"The Temple!" exclaimed Lady Bell. "It must be miles away."

"A hansom," smiled Jack.

"But there are no cabs here, not one. I cannot leave you like this—you must get into the brougham."

"Not for worlds! I have given you quite enough trouble," he said. "I shall find my way home somehow."

"No," she said; "I cannot let you go without seeing you safe into a cab. There are none here. You do not know—I do not know—how much you are hurt. You must let me take you to your home."

"I assure you I am all right," he said.

"And I refuse to accept your assurance," said Lady Bell, with a little shudder at the streak of blood which oozed from his forehead. "Come, you will not refuse to obey a lady. I wish you to enter my brougham."

"No, I can't refuse to obey a lady," he said.

"Then come with me," said Lady Bell.

"Where to, my lady?" asked Jackson, who was used to her ladyship's willfulness, and sat, patient as Job, waiting for the issue of this strange adventure.

"To—where did you say?" asked Lady Bell.

"Spider Court," said Jack; "but I wish you'd let me go out and walk. It must be right out of your way."

"Spider Court, Temple," said Lady Bell, and the brougham rolled on.

Through it all Mrs. Fellowes had remained in the deep sleep which the gods vouchsafe to good women of her age, and the two—Lady Bell and Jack—were, to all intents and purposes, alone.

Lady Bell looked at him as he sat in his corner, the thin, red stream trickling down from his forehead, and shuddered; not at him, but at the blood.

"How did you come to be run over?" she asked. "Did you fall?"

"Must have done," he said, coolly; "anyway I'll swear it wasn't the coachman's fault."

"I am not going to blame the coachman," said Lady Bell, with the shadow of a smile.

"That's right," said Jack. "It was all my fault. I'd been—been to see a favorite aunt."

"You had been to your club," said Lady Bell.

"How did you know that?" he said.

Lady Bell smiled again, and Jack, his eyes fixed upon her, thought the smile wonderfully fascinating.

"A little bird told me," she said.

"The little bird was right," said Jack, shaking his head, with penitence and remorse written on every feature. "I have been dining at my club. Perhaps the little bird told you everything else?"

"Yes; the little bird also whispered that you had— —"

"Drank too much champagne? Confound those fellows! Wonderful little bird!" muttered Jack.

"It is very wicked of you," said Lady Bell, gravely, her eyes fixed on his face, that, notwithstanding its streak of red, looked wonderfully handsome.

While she looked, she almost convinced herself that she had never seen such a handsome face, nor such frank eyes.

"It was very wicked of you," she repeated, in a voice pitched in a low key, no doubt out of consideration for the sleeping watch dog.

"Yes," he said, "I am a bad lot; I am not fit to be here with you. I have been dining at my club; but how you knew it, I can't conceive. And—and— —"

"Don't tell me any more," said Lady Bell. "I am sorry that you should have been run over, and I hope you are not hurt. That—that is blood running down your face. Why do you not wipe it off? I can't bear it."

"I beg your pardon," said Jack, and he fumbled for his pocket-handkerchief, which at that moment was lying under the seat in the billiard-room.

"Here, take this," said Lady Bell, and she put her own delicate lace-edged one in his hand.

Jack mopped his forehead diligently.

"Is it all off?" he asked.

"No, it keeps running," replied Lady Bell, with a little thrill of horror. "I believe you are much hurt."

"I'm not; I give you my word," said Jack. "There—no, I'll keep it until it's washed." And he thrust the delicate cobweb into his pocket.

Lady Bell leaned back, but her eyes wandered now and then to the handsome face, pale through all its tan.

Presently, wonderfully soon, as it seemed to her, the brougham came to a stop, and Jackson, bending down to the window, said:

"Spider Court, my lady."

"Spider Court," said Jack. "Then I'm home. I'm very much obliged to you, and I wish I didn't feel so much ashamed of myself. Hark! who's that?" for someone had come to the carriage door.

"It is I—Leonard. Is that you, Jack?"

"Yes," said Jack, and he got out and closed the door. "This lady——"

Lady Bell leaned out and looked at Leonard Dagle's anxious face earnestly.

"Your friend has met with an accident," she said, "and I have brought him home."

"Thank you, thank you," sighed Leonard.

"I hope he is not much hurt," said Lady Bell. "His forehead is cut. Will you—will you be so kind as to let me know if it is anything serious?"

"Anything serious! A mere scratch," ejaculated Jack, carelessly.

But Lady Bell did not look at him.

"Here is my card," she said, taking a card-case from the carriage basket. "Will you please let me know? Good-night."

And she held out her hand.

Leonard did not see it, and merely raised his hat. But Jack, who was nearest, took the hand and held it for a moment.

"Good-night, good-night," he said. "I shall never forgive myself for causing you trouble."

And in his earnestness his hand, quite unconsciously, closed tightly on her white, warm palm.

Lady Bell dropped back into her seat, a warm flush spreading over her face; and Mrs. Fellowes, awakened by the stopping of the brougham, exclaimed, with a yawn:

"Home at last!"

"No, miles away," said Lady Bell. "Go to sleep again, my dear."

Leonard took Jack's arm within his, though there was no occasion for it, for Jack was sober enough now, and led him upstairs.

"My dear Jack," he exclaimed, reproachfully, "what have you been doing?"

"Falling under a cab," said Jack, gravely.

"A cab!" retorted Leonard; "a lady's brougham, you mean!"

And he took the card to the light.

"Why!" he exclaimed, with an expression of amazement. "Lady Isabel Earlsley! Good Heaven! that's the heiress."

"Eh?" said Jack, indifferently. "What's her name? She's a brick, if ever there was one. Oh, Jupiter, I wish I was in bed!"

CHAPTER XVIII

It was Una's first night in London. Weary as she was she could not find sleep; the dull roar of the great city—which those who are used to take no heed of—rang in her ears and kept her awake. Her brain was busy, too; and even as she closed her eyes the endless questions, which the strange events of the day had given birth to, pursued and tormented her. She could scarcely realize that she had left Warden Forest, that she was here in London, the place of her most ardent dreams! And then how singular, how mysterious was that coincidence which had brought it about.

Until Jack Newcombe, the young stranger, had come to Warden, she had never heard the name of Davenant, and now she was actually living under the roof of Stephen Davenant's mother.

With half-closed eyes she recalled all that Jack had said about Stephen Davenant, and it did not require much effort to recall anything Jack had said, for every word was graven on her heart, and it had seemed to her as if he had spoken disparagingly of this Stephen, and had implied that he was not as good as he was supposed to be.

She herself, as she lay, her beautiful head pillowed on her round white arm, was conscious of a strange feeling which had taken possession of her in Stephen's presence—not of dislike, but something of doubt, something also of a vague fear.

And yet he could not but be good and generous, for was it not to him that she owed all that had happened to her? And did not his mother, the timid, gentle woman who had already won Una's heart, speak of him as great and good?

Alas! and a faint flush stole over her cheek, and a long sigh stole from her lips—alas! it was that other—Jack Newcombe—who was bad; it was he whom she was to avoid.

And so, notwithstanding that she was in the very city of her dreams, she fell asleep with a vague sadness in her heart.

Quiet as Walmington Square is, the noise of the market carts passing to Covent Garden awoke her soon after dawn.

She looked round with a stare of amazement as her eyes fell upon the dainty room, with its costly furniture and rich hangings, and listened for a moment, as if expecting to hear the rustle of the great oaks which surrounded the cottage at Warden; then she remembered the change that had befallen her, and springing out of bed, ran to the window.

All the square was asleep; the blinds were closely drawn in all the houses, and only the birds on the trees seemed thoroughly awake.

She could hear the market carts rumbling in the great thoroughfare beyond, and as she had gone asleep with the rattle of wheels in her ears, she asked herself, wonderingly:

"Does London never rest?"

She remembered that Mrs. Davenant had showed her a bathroom communicating by a door from her own room, and then—with her cold water was as necessary as air—went and had her bath; then she dressed herself, and, opening her door, went downstairs.

To her amazement, all the house seemed wrapped in slumber.

At home, at the cottage at Warden, Gideon and all of them were up with the lark, and life began with the morning sun.

She stole into the drawing-room, and, unfastening the shutters with some little difficulty, opened the window and leaned out to breathe the fresh air; but it seemed as if the air was asleep, too, or, in its journey from the country, had lost itself in the maze of houses, and failed to reach Walmington Square.

Una looked out dreamily, wondering who and what sort of people lived in the huge blocks of dwellings that surrounded her, and wondered, faintly, whether she could be looking at the spot where Jack Newcombe dwelt.

She could not guess that Jack had not come back from Hurst Leigh yet, but was waiting for the squire's funeral.

Instinctively she turned to the table and took up the album and went back to the window with the book open at the page which contained Jack's portrait.

How beautiful the face was! And yet, she thought, with a warm glow in her eyes, that she had seen it look still more beautiful, as she had looked down at it the morning he lay sleeping at her feet.

Presently a servant came into the room, and startled at the sight of the white figure by the window, uttered an exclamation.

"Good-morning," said Una.

Closing the book she came forward and held up her face to be kissed, as she had always done to Mrs. Rolfe.

The maid—a pretty young girl, fresh from Devonshire—stared at her and looked half-frightened, while a crimson flush of embarrassment came into her face.

"Good-morning, miss," she said, nervously, and hastily turned and fled.

Una looked after her a moment, and pondered; and she would have made a superb study for a painter at that moment.

How had she frightened the pretty girl, and why had she declined to kiss her?

Una could not understand it. Hitherto she had lived only with equals, and could not be expected to guess that it was a breach of the proprieties to kiss this pretty, daintily-dressed little hand-maiden.

As for Mary, the maid, she flew into the kitchen and sank into a chair, gasped at the cook, speechless for a moment.

"What do you think, cook?" she exclaimed, "that young lady—Una, as the mistress calls her—is up already. I found her in the drawing-room, and—and she said 'Good-morning,' and came up to me as if she—she wanted me to kiss her."

"You must be out of your mind, Mary," said the cook, sternly.

But Mary stuck to her assertion, and at last it was decided that Una was either out of *her* mind, or that she was no lady.

"And that I am sure she is," exclaimed Mary, and the other servants assented heartily. "If there ever was a true lady, this one is, whoever or whatever she may be. Perhaps she's just come from boarding-school."

But the cook scoffed at the idea.

"Boarding-school!" she exclaimed incredulously. "Do you think they don't know the difference between mistress and servants there? It's the first thing that is taught them."

Meanwhile, quite unconscious of the discussion which her ingenuous conduct had caused, Una wandered about the room, examining, with unstinted curiosity, the exquisite china and valuable paintings, the Collard and Collard grand piano, and the handsomely-bound books.

An hour or two passed in this way; then she heard a bell ring and Mary entered, and, eying her shyly, said:

"Mistress says will you be kind enough to step up to her room, miss."

Una went upstairs and knocked at Mrs. Davenant's door, and in answer to the "come in," entered, and found Mrs. Davenant in the hands of her maid Jane.

Una crossed the room with her swift, light step, and kissed the face turned up to her with a timid, questioning smile on it.

"My child," exclaimed Mrs. Davenant, "have you been up all night? I sent Jane to your room to help you dress."

Una started, and a smile broke over her face.

"To help me dress?" she repeated, Jane regarding her with wide open eyes the while. "Why should she do that? I have always dressed myself ever since I can remember."

Mrs. Davenant flushed nervously.

"I—meant to brush your hair and tie your ribbons—as she does mine; but it does not matter if you would rather not have her."

"I should not like to trouble her," said Una.

"And how long have you been up, my dear?"

"Since five," said Una, quietly.

Mrs. Davenant stared aghast, and Jane nearly dropped the hair-brush.

"Since five! My dear child! Ah! I see, you—you have been used to rising early. I am afraid you will soon lose that good habit. We Londoners don't rise with the lark."

"I don't think there are any larks here," remarked Una, gravely; "and at this time of the year the lark begins to sing at four. I have often watched him rise from his nest in the grass."

"My poor child, you will miss the country so much."

"No," said Una; "I am so anxious to see the world, you know."

"Well, we will begin today."

"Una, you know I wish you to be quite—to be very happy with me. And—and I hope if there is anything that you want you will ask for it without hesitation."

"Anything I want?" repeated Una, with a smile. "Is it possible that any one could want anything more than is here? There seems to be everything. I was thinking, as you spoke, of what my father would say if he saw this table, with all the things to eat, and the silver and glass."

"My dear child, this is nothing. I live very simply. If you saw, as you will see, some of the homes of the wealthy, some of the homes of the aristocracy, you would discover that what you deem luxury is merely comfort."

"I was never uncomfortable at the cottage," said Una, gravely.

"That is because you were unused to anything better, and—and—you must not speak of the past life too much, Una. I mean to strangers. Strangers are so curious, and—and my son, Stephen, does not wish everyone to know where you come from and how you lived."

"Does he not? Well, I will not speak of it; but I do not understand— quite——"

"Neither do I. I am afraid I do not always understand Stephen; but—but I always do as he tells me."

And she looked up with the anxious, questioning expression which Una noticed was always present when Stephen Davenant was mentioned. Was Mrs. Davenant afraid of her son?

Una mused for a minute in silence; then she looked up and said:

"I ought to do what Mr. Stephen wishes. Do you know what he wants me to do?"

"You are to be companion to me, my dear."

"I am very fond of fairy tales," she said; "but I have never read one more strange and beautiful than this."

"Let me show you how to put on your gloves, dear," she said. "Yes, you have got a small hand, and a beautifully-shaped one, too. Strange, small hands are a sure sign of high birth."

"Perhaps I am a princess in disguise. No! I am a woodman's daughter in the disguise of a princess, that is it."

Mrs. Davenant looked at her curiously.

"You are not ashamed of being a woodman's daughter, Una," she said; "but yet—perhaps the time will come when you will——"

Una's opened-eyed surprise stopped her.

"Ashamed?" she echoed, with mild astonishment. "Why?"

"I—I don't know. Never mind, my dear," said Mrs. Davenant, as the brougham stopped.

"You are a strange child, and—and you say such strange things so naturally that I am puzzled to know how to speak to you."

CHAPTER XIX

As the days passed on, Mrs. Davenant grew to understand more fully the innocent but frank and brave nature of the beautiful girl whom her son Stephen had so strangely committed to her charge; grew to understand and to love her, and, bit by bit, her nervousness and timidity wore off in Una's presence. Insensibly she grew to lean and rely on the girl, who, with all her innocence and ignorance of the world, was so gently calm and self-possessed, and Una, in return, lavished her love upon the timid, shrinking woman.

Mrs. Davenant had heard no word from Stephen; she was accustomed to such silence, and almost dreaded to hear, lest it should be a message tearing Una from her side. She did not know that Stephen was master of Hurst Leigh and all the immense wealth of Ralph Davenant.

Una did not know that Jack Newcombe was back here in London, almost within half an hour of her. When she thought of her father and mother there in Warden, it was always with the confident trust that they were well, for she felt that if it were otherwise, Gideon would somehow let her know. She was quite ignorant that the cottage was empty and deserted.

Indeed, there was not much time for thought. Day after day brought its succession of wonderful sights and experiences, as the little green brougham bore them about town, and Mrs. Davenant showed her all the marvels of the great city.

Una was dazzled, bewildered sometimes: but her instinctive good taste helped her to keep back all extravagant expressions of surprise on her voyage through Fairyland.

One day, however, an exclamation of delight escaped her, as she came in sight of a jeweler's window, opposite which the brougham had stopped.

To her who had only read of precious stones, and regarded them as objects almost fabulous, the window looked as if it contained the wealth of the Indies and of Aladdin's palace combined.

They entered and Mrs. Davenant asked to see some ladies' watches, selected one and a handsome albert, and, with a smile, arranged them at

Una's waist, in which, to her equal amazement, she found a pocket already provided.

Pale with emotion, she could not utter a word, and to hide the tears that sprang into her eyes, turned aside to look at a case containing a magnificent set of brilliants. The jeweler politely unlocked the case, and placed the bracelet in her hand.

"A really magnificent set. It is sold. They were purchased by Lady Isabel Earlsley."

"Lady Earlsley," said Mrs. Davenant. "Ah, yes; she is fond of diamonds, is she not?"

"Yes, and of other precious stones, too, madam. She has excellent taste and discrimination. Perhaps you have seen her set of sapphires?"

"No," said Mrs. Davenant, in her quiet way, "I have met Lady Earlsley, but I have not seen them."

The jeweler opened an iron safe, and took out a case containing a superb, a unique set of sapphires, and handed them to her.

"This is it—I have it to alter. They are the purest in the world—finer even than her ladyship's rubies, which are considered, but wrongly, matchless."

Una stared open-eyed, and the jeweler, pleased by her enthusiasm and admiration, took the set from its case and laid it in her hands.

As Una was bending over them fascinated, a handsome carriage drew up, and the shop door was opened by a footman in rich livery.

Una looked up, and saw a beautiful girl who, pausing in the doorway, stood regarding her.

The eyes of the two girls met, Una's with an instant frank admiration in her calm depths—a curious, half-amazed, but also admiring stare in the bright, dark eyes of the other.

The jeweler glanced from the new-comer to the gems in Una's lap, and changed color. Mrs. Davenant started nervously, and turned pale.

With a quick, bird-like, but thoroughly graceful movement, the richly-dressed lady turned, and with a smile of recognition, bowed.

"Mrs.——" she said, and hesitated.

"Davenant," said Mrs. Davenant. "How do you do, Lady Earlsley?"

Lady Isabel Earlsley, the great heiress and queen of fashion, held out her hand in her quick, impulsive way, but turned her quick glance on Una, whose eyes had never left the dark, bewitching face.

"Your daughter, Mrs. Davenant?"

Poor Mrs. Davenant trembled with nervous agitation.

"No—no—a young friend, Miss Rolfe," she answered, tremulously.

Lady Bell went straight up to Una and held out her hand, her eyes fixed on the now flushed face.

"How do you do?" she said, in the almost blunt fashion which her admirers declared so charming, and which, though envious tongues declared an affectation, was a perfectly natural consequence of her early life.

Una put her hand in the delicate white gloved one, and the two women looked at each other for a moment in silence.

Was it possible at that moment that some prophetic instinct whispered to the heart of each that the threads of both their lives were doomed to be entangled together?

Then Una suddenly remembered that she had in her hand the jewels belonging to this young lady, and with a grave smile she put them back in their case.

"You are looking at my sapphires, I see," said Lady Bell, in a tone which set the soul of the alarmed jeweler at rest. "Do you admire them? Are they fine, do you think?"

Una smiled.

"I do not know. They are very beautiful. I have never seen anything like them before."

"Really," said Lady Bell, with a nod; "I don't care for them. They don't suit me; there is not enough color in them." Then, turning to the jeweler, she said, in that quiet tone of command which for the first time fell upon Una's ears: "Give me the rubies, please."

The man hastened to hand her a case from the safe, and Lady Bell placed the contents in Una's lap.

"Ah!" she said, with a smile, as Una's eyes opened wide with admiration, at once childish and yet dignified, "you are of my opinion, too. But the sapphires would suit you best. I wish I were your husband."

Una looked up with a smile of grave astonishment; and Lady Bell turned with a light laugh to Mrs. Davenant.

"How puzzled she looks! I mean," she went on to Una, "that if I were your husband I would give you the sapphire set; though a lover would be more suitable, would it not?"

Then seeing Una's grave, open-eyed wonder, Lady Bell turned to Mrs. Davenant, and in a low tone, said:

"Who is she, Mrs. Davenant?—has she just come out of a convent? She is simply lovely; her eyes haunt me—who is she?"

Mrs. Davenant stammered, and fidgeted speechlessly.

"Ah!" said Lady Bell, quickly, in the same low tone. "You think I'm rude and ill-bred. They all do when I ask a simple question, or show the slightest interest in anything." She glanced at Una lingeringly: "I mustn't ask, I suppose?"

"I—I—she is new to London," said Mrs. Davenant. "It is her first day——"

"Her first day!" echoed Lady Bell, her eyes twinkling. "Do you mean that she was never in London before? How I envy her; I who am sick and weary of it! Yes, the glamour is on her; I can see it in her eyes—on her face. She is like some beautiful wild bird who has settled on an inhabited island for the first time, and is marveling at the strange sights and faces—look at her!" and she touched Mrs. Davenant's arm.

Una, quite unconscious of their scrutiny, was sitting looking dreamily into the street with its ceaseless throng of carriages and people. Lady Bell had hit upon a happy simile; she looked like some beautiful bird, half stupefied by the strange life moving around her.

Mrs. Davenant rose; but Lady Bell, with a gentle pressure, forced her back into her seat.

"Not this minute; leave her for a minute. See what a beautiful picture she makes! New to London! Do you know what will happen when London finds that she is in its midst?"

Mrs. Davenant looked up helplessly. She, too, looked like a bird—like some frightened pigeon in the clutch of a glittering hawk.

"You can't guess," went on Lady Bell, with a smile. "Well, it will make a queen of her—all London will be at her feet within a month, and I—I shall be dethroned."

The last few words were spoken—- murmured—almost inaudible, and in a tone that was half sad, half mocking. But suddenly her mood changed; and with a smile that lit up her face, and seemed to dance like a flash of sunlight from eyes to lips and back again, she said:

"At any rate be mine the credit of discovering her. I am the first at the shrine of the new goddess!" and touching Una's hand with the top of her gloved finger, she said: "Miss Rolfe, Mrs. Davenant has been kind enough to promise to come and see me tomorrow night. Are you fond of dancing?"

"I don't know," said Una, with a smile. "I do not know how to dance——"

"Heavens!" murmured Lady Bell.

"You forget, Lady Bell," murmured poor Mrs. Davenant.

"Ah, yes, yes; I remember," said Lady Bell, hastily. "Well, you will come and see how you like it, won't you?"

Una looked at Mrs. Davenant inquiringly, and Lady Bell looked from one to the other impatiently.

"Do not say 'No,' pray, Mrs. Davenant," she said, with her dark, bright eyes. "I have set my heart upon it, and a disappointment is intolerable. Besides, why should you say 'No?' You would like to come?"

"Yes, I should like to come," said Una gravely.

Lady Bell looked at her as if fascinated.

"From a convent, certainly," she murmured.

"Then it's settled. Remember! I shall look for you—shall wait for you with impatience. Mrs. Davenant, I count upon you."

"But—but I cannot go out, Lady Earlsley—I am in mourning."

Lady Bell sighed impatiently.

"I am so sorry! I have never set my heart upon anything so much in my life," she said. "Something tells me that we shall be great friends! Are you fond of jewels, lace, books?—what are you specially fond of?" And she seemed to dazzle Una with her smile. "You shall see them all—everything. Yes, let her come, and I will take such care of her as if she were something too precious to be touched; she shall not leave my side all the evening. Let her come, Mrs. Davenant!"

Mrs. Davenant paled and flushed in turn. What would Stephen say—would he be displeased or gratified? What should she do? She could not resist the half-imploring, half-commanding eyes which Lady Bell flashed upon her, and at last murmured a frightened "Yes."

With a smile that seemed to set the diamonds scintillating, Lady Bell shook hands with Mrs. Davenant, and taking Una's, held it for a moment in silence, then, with a sudden gravity, she said:

"Good-bye. I will take care of you. I will be your *chaperon*. We shall meet again," and was gone.

So interested and absorbed had she been in Una that she had quite forgotten her purpose in entering the shop, and had gone without another word to the jeweler.

He showed no surprise, however, but smiled complacently as he put the jewels back into their cases, being quite used to Lady Bell's vagaries, and he bowed Mrs. Davenant and Una out with increased respect and deference.

Lady Bell, attended by the two footmen, entered her carriage, and Mrs. Fellowes, her friend and companion, who had been sleeping peacefully, awoke with a little start.

"Well, my dear, have you got the rubies?"

"The rubies?" said Lady Bell. "No, I quite forgot them."

"Forgot them!" said Mrs. Fellowes.

"Yes. What are stupid rubies compared with an angel?"

"My dear Lady Bell!" exclaimed Mrs. Fellowes, "what are you talking about?"

Lady Bell leaned back with her hands folded in her lap, and her eyes musingly staring at nothing.

"Yes, an angel," she repeated. "I never believed in them until today, but I have seen one this morning—in a jeweler's shop."

"Lady Bell, how strangely you talk. I am getting alarmed."

"You always are," said Lady Bell, coolly. "I repeat, I have seen an angel. You are always trying to flatter me by talking of my beauty and such nonsense; but I have seen today a real beauty. Not a mere pretty pet mortal like myself, but one of the celestials! With eyes like a wild bird's, and a lady, too, I'll be sworn!"

"My dear Bell, what language!" murmured Mrs. Fellowes.

"A perfect lady; her hands, her voice would vouch for that. Her voice is like a harp. If I had been a man I should have fallen in love with her on the spot."

"Fallen in love," said Mrs. Fellowes. "My dear Bell," with a politely suppressed yawn, "I am half inclined to think you have taken leave of your senses, and you will drive me out of mine. One night it is a young man whom we nearly run over; a—I must say—a tipsy young man."

"No; he had only taken too much wine."

"Well, if that isn't being tipsy——"

"Don't, don't," said Lady Bell, pleadingly; "we might have killed him."

"I don't know that he would have been much loss to the world at large," said Mrs. Fellowes.

"Home!" said Lady Bell to the footman; and she sank back with a brilliant flush on her face.

Mrs. Davenant drove home also, and in considerable perturbation. What had she done? What would Stephen say?

Fortunately for that young man's peace of mind, he was resting at ease at Hurst Leigh, little dreaming that Lady Bell, or any one else, would meet Una, and coax her out of his mother's nerveless hands.

Una, with quick sympathy, saw that her companion was distressed, and with a gentle touch of her hand, said:

"You do not like me to go to this lady's house. I will not go. No; I will not go."

"My dear," she replied, with a sigh, "it isn't in our hands now. You don't know Lady Bell—nor do I very well; but I know enough of her to be convinced that if you do not go tomorrow night, she would come and fetch you, though she left all her guests to do so."

"Is she then so—so accustomed to having her own way?"

"Always; she always has her own way. She is rich—very, very rich—and petted; and she is even more than that; she—she—I don't know how to explain myself. Well, my dear, she is a sort of queen of society, and more powerful than many real queens."

"So that when she commands such as I am I must obey," said Una, with her low, musical laugh.

"Just so," said Mrs. Davenant, with a sigh. "But you will be careful, my dear. I mean, don't—don't let her put you forward, remind her of her promise to keep you at her side."

"I think I would rather not go."

"Don't be frightened, my dear," said Mrs. Davenant, kindly; but Una's calm, steady look of response showed her that there was no fear in the young, innocent heart.

"No, I am not frightened," she said. "I do not know what I am to fear."

Having consented to Una's going, Mrs. Davenant lost no time in making the few necessary preparations. She selected a plain but rich evening dress, set her own maid to make the required alterations, selected from her own store a sort of old Honiton, and gave orders that some white flowers should be bought at Covent Garden the next morning.

"White flowers, my dear," she said, nervously. "Because I—I am not sure that Stephen would not consider that your being in the house with me you are not in mourning. But, then, you are no relation, my dear."

"I wish I were," said Una, kissing her.

CHAPTER XX

At nine o'clock the next evening the quiet-looking green brougham came round to the door, and took them rapidly to Park Lane.

Una had already grown almost weary of staring out of the carriage window, but her wonder and interest revived as she saw in the dusky twilight the green trees and flowers in the most beautiful park in the world, and amazed at the magnificent buildings past which they rolled.

Presently the brougham drew up at a corner house facing the park; an awning was suspended from the gateway to the pavement, and three footmen in splendid liveries, which she recognized as those she had seen worn by the servants attending Lady Bell's carriage, were standing to receive the guests; one of them opened the brougham door and escorted them into the hall, which seemed to Una, with its flowers and mirrors, its rich hangings and statues, a fairy palace, and was about to usher them into the drawing-room, when, upon hearing Mrs. Davenant's name, he bowed, and took them into a small room at the side, which was Lady Bell's boudoir.

"I will tell her ladyship," he said.

Una had scarcely time to take in the exquisite beauty of the room, with its antique furniture and costly knicknacks, when the door opened and Lady Bell entered. She was exquisitely dressed; diamonds—the diamonds Una had seen at the jeweler's—glittering in her hair and on her neck and on her arms, and seemed to Una like some vision which at a breath would vanish and leave the room to its subdued twilight again.

With outstretched hands she came toward them, with her eyes dancing and her cheeks flushed.

"You have kept your word and brought my wild bird! I knew you would come," and she took a hand of each, but suddenly reached up and kissed Una. "Yes, I felt that you would come, but it is good of you all the same, and to show you that I am grateful, I will let you go at once, this minute, dear Mrs. Davenant!"

Mrs. Davenant looked relieved.

"Thank you! thank you, Lady Bell!" she said. "You—you——"

"Will take care of your bird? Yes, that I will. You may trust her to me; not a feather shall be ruffled."

Mrs. Davenant murmured something about the time she would come for her, and then with a timid look from one to the other was gone.

"And now," said Lady Bell, "let me look at you," as if she had not been doing so ever since she entered the room. "My dear, my dear, you are——" she stopped short. "No, I'll not be the first to teach you vanity. But tell me, do you ever look in your glass, Miss Rolfe—Miss Rolfe, I don't like that name, I mean between you and me. My name is Bell, and yours is——"

"Mine is Una."

"Una! That is delightful! And have you your lion? Where is he?"

Una had never read the story of "Una and the Lion," and looked calmly puzzled.

"Well, if you have not one already, you soon will have. You don't understand me. I am glad of that. But will you come now? This is a very, very quiet little party, but you may be amused. And I will keep you by my side all the evening. Come," and she drew Una's arm through her own white one and led her through the corridor into the ball-room.

It was not a large room. Lady Bell detested huge and crowded assemblies too much to permit them at her own house, but it was, as a ball-room, perfect. There was light, and just enough light, to show the tasteful magnificence of the decorations, and nothing of that fearful glare from innumerable lights, and their reflections in huge mirrors, which make most ball-rooms so trying and unbearable. The band had just commenced as they entered, and the whole scene, the beautiful room with its soft draperies of Persian damask, the Venetian mirrors, the rich dresses of the ladies, and the soul-moving strains of the best band in London, for the moment overawed and startled the girl fresh from the primeval forest.

For a moment her eyes dilated almost with fear, and she unconsciously drew back, but Lady Bell, with a gentle pressure of the arm, drew her forward, and skillfully avoiding the dancers, took her to the further end of the room, where, in a recess lined with ferns and tropical plants, were arranged some seats so placed as to be almost hidden from the room, while they allowed the sitter a full view of it.

Lady Bell drew a fauteuil still further into the recess, and playfully forced Una into it.

"There, my wild bird, is your cage. You can see all the world without being seen, and here you and I will take a peep at it. Now, don't you want to know all their names and all about them?"

Una smiled. She was a little pale and was trembling slightly.

"No; I am too surprised and astonished at present. How beautiful it is, and how lovely they are."

"The women?" said Lady Bell, with a laugh, and a glance at the unconscious face beside her, which she knew outshone all others there. "You think so! Well, there are some pretty women here. There is Lady Clarence—the one in light blue and swansdown—and Mrs. Cantrip—she was the beauty last season. You don't understand?"

"Last season!" said Una. "Who is the beauty this?"

Lady Bell laughed and flushed a little.

"Never mind, child," she said. "One who doesn't care a farthing about it, at any rate. But look, do you see that tall lady there, dancing with the short man with whiskers? She is the Countess of Pierrepoint, and he is the Duke of Garnum——"

"A duke?" said Una, surprised.

"You expected to see a man seven feet high in his ducal robes?" she said. "See those two men who have just come in? The dark one is Sir Arkroyd Hetley, the other, the boy—the baby they call him—is a marquis, the Marquis of Dalrymple. They are always together. They are coming to shake hands with me."

Una drew further into the shade as the two men, after hunting about the room, came up to the recess, and listened as they paid their compliments and seemed anxious to remain, but Lady Bell sent them off quite plainly and distinctly, and sat looking toward the door, and presently she ceased talking, and her bright, beautiful face grew quiet and almost sad, certainly wistful, and at last she sighed and murmured:

"No, he will not come."

"Who will not come?" said Una. "Are you expecting any one?"

"Did I speak?" she said. "Yes, I am expecting someone, but he will not come. People one expects and wants never do—never do. You will find that out in time, wild bird; you will find—ah!" and she started and turned pale, and her hand, which had been laid on Una's arm, closed over it with a sudden grip and flutter.

Una looked up, and her face went deadly white.

The room seemed to spin round with her, and the lights to flood her brain and paralyze her, for there, towering above the throng, stood Jack Newcombe.

Jack Newcombe—not in his rough tweed suit, but in evening dress; Jack, not with the frank, tender, pleasant smile which always rested upon his face as it appeared in her dreams, but with a cold, half-irritable, and wholly bored expression.

Slowly she rose and glided into the shadow of the recess and hid herself, her heart beating wildly, her whole form trembling with a strange ecstasy of mingled fear and delight.

At last she saw him again.

CHAPTER XXI

Poor Jack! How came he to be in Lady Bell's ball-room?

The morning after she had nearly driven over him he woke to find Leonard Dagle, his friend and fellow lodger, standing beside his bed and looking down at him with a grave smile on his intellectual face.

"Hallo!" said Jack, "the house on fire?"

"Not at present," said Leonard, "though it would soon be if you lived in it alone. Why don't you blow your candle out, and not chuck your slippers at it? How are you this morning?"

"How am I?" said Jack, staring. "How should I be? Quite well of course," which was quite true, for Jack and the headache had not been introduced to each other.

"That's all right," said Leonard, with a smile. "Perhaps you remember last night's tragic occurrence, then?"

Jack thought for a moment, then shook his head gravely.

"Len, I'm an idiot. I always was. It's a good job idiocy isn't catching or you'd have caught it of me long ago. I made a confounded idiot of myself last night. It was all Dalrymple and Hetley's fault, and I wish they'd knock champagne off the club wine list. Did I take too much, Len?"

"What do you think?" said Leonard, grimly.

"I'm afraid I did. For the first time in my life, or nearly—but I didn't touch a card, Len."

"I knew you wouldn't do that."

"No, a promise is a promise with me," said Jack. "And I didn't drink much, Len, 'pon my honor; but I was upset, and when a man is upset he——"

"He generally tries to get run over," said Leonard, with a smile.

Jack stared, then he laughed.

"By George! yes. I remember!"

"But always does not get the luck to be rescued by a beautiful young lady—who is an heiress—and who, instead of giving him in charge for blocking the queen's highway, brings him home in her brougham."

"It was a kind thing to do, certainly," said Jack, with a yawn.

"Kind is a mild way of putting it," remarked Leonard.

"It was more than I deserved," said Jack; "much more, and she's a brick."

"The man who calls Lady Isabel Earlsley a brick should be a bold man."

At last Jack looked up, and pressing his chair back, said:

"And now, old man, let's hold a council of war. Subject to be considered: the future of a young man who has been cut off with a shilling—by George! the poor old fellow didn't even leave me that—who knows no trade, who cannot dig, and to beg is ashamed, and who is penniless."

"Quite penniless, Jack?" asked Leonard.

Jack rose, and sauntering to a drawer, pulled forth an old tobacco pouch, and pouring the contents on to the table proceeded to count the small—very small—heap of coin.

"Twenty-one pounds six-and-fourpence farthing—no; it's a brass button—and a brass button."

"Can't carry on this way long with that small amount of ammunition, Jack."

"Just so, old Solomon. Well, what's to be done?"

"You might enlist."

"Get shot, and break your heart. No, I'm too fond of you, Len. Go on; anything else?"

"Upon my word, you can't do anything."

"Nary thing," admitted Jack, with frank candor.

"What do men—well-born and high-bred men like you——"

"What will you take to drink?" said Jack, bowing low.

"Who have no money, and no brains——"

Jack bowed again, and pitched the sugar tongs at him.

"What do they do? They generally marry an heiress, Jack."

"I shall never marry."

"I've heard that remark before. The last it was from a man who married a fortnight afterward."

"I'm not going to marry in a fortnight. Go ahead."

"I've done," said Leonard with a shrug.

"Solomon is dried up," said Jack. "You don't keep a large stock of wisdom on hand, old man."

"I've given you the best I've got, and good advice too, with a foundation to go upon. Your heiress is ready to your hand."

"What do you mean?" said Jack.

Leonard was about to reply, when the housekeeper entered and brought him a card. He looked at it; it bore Lady Isabel Earlsley's name, and on the back was written:

"To inquire whether Mr. Newcombe was hurt last night?"

Leonard pitched it across the table, as an answer to Jack's question.

Jack read the card and flushed hotly, then threw it down again.

Leonard took up a piece of paper, and rapidly wrote:

"Mr. Newcombe's compliments, and he was not in any way injured by last night's accident, which he deeply regrets as having caused Lady Earlsley so much trouble," and gave it to the housekeeper.

"What have you written?" asked Jack sulkily.

"What you are too much of a bear to write," said Leonard, with a smile—"an answer and an apology. Jack, you are a favorite of fortune. Half the men in London would give the forefinger of their right hand to get such a message from Lady Bell. I know her——"

"So do I," broke in Jack, roughly; "I heard all about her at the club last night. Hetley and Dalrymple bored me to death about her. She's a great heiress and a beauty, and all the rest of it. I know, and I don't want to hear any more."

Jack went up to Len and laid his hand on his shoulder.

"Forgive me, old fellow; but I—my heart is full. Only one woman in the world has any interest for me, and she has gone—up to the sky again, I suppose. What do I care for Lady Bell, or Lady anyone else? I tell you I laid awake half the night thinking of that beautiful face, and dreamed of her eyes the rest of the night; and I'd give all the world if I had it, to find her. And much good it would do me if I succeeded? I couldn't ask her to share twenty-one pounds six and a brass button!"

"Forgive *me*, Jack," said Leonard, quietly. "I know what you mean. I'm in love myself. But—but at any rate you can't treat Lady Bell rudely. You must call and thank her."

"Confound her!" said Jack, and hurried out of the room.

Leonard looked after him, and then went on with his work. He saw no more of him until late in the evening, when Jack came in and threw himself into a chair, looking weary if not exhausted.

"What have you been doing, Jack?" asked Leonard.

"Looking for a needle in a bundle of hay," replied Jack, grimly.

Leonard nodded.

"I've been walking about ever since I left you, with scarcely a rest. I've walked through every thoroughfare in London. I've looked into windows and into shops. I've been warned off and told to move on by the police, who thought I was a burglar on the search for a job; and here I am and there is she as far off as ever. And yet I feel—Heavens knows why—that she is here in London. Len, if you smile I shall knock you down."

"I was never farther from smiling than I am at this moment," said Leonard quietly.

"Do you know what I would do if—if the squire had left me any money?" went on Jack, fiercely; "I would spend every penny of it in searching for her. I'd have a hundred—a thousand detectives at work. I'd never give them rest night or day till they found her."

"And then?" said Leonard.

Jack groaned and lit his pipe. Leonard looked at him.

"I thought you had gone to call on Lady Earlsley," he said.

Jack looked very much as if he really meant to knock him down, and marched off to bed.

When he came in to breakfast the next morning Leonard noticed that he was dressed in proper walking attire, instead of the loose, free and easy, well-worn suit of cheviot, but he said nothing. Jack looked up.

"You are staring at my get-up, Len. Well, I'll do it; but mind it is only to please you. What should I care what she thinks? though I ought to do it, I know. I'll call and thank her, and then let there be an end of it. I can't bear any chaff of that sort even from you, old fellow."

Leonard nodded without a word, for he saw that the once frank face had lost its careless *sang froid* expression, and looked harassed and even haggard.

Jack smoked a pipe in silence, watching Leonard's rapidly moving pen; then, without a word, went out.

Two hours later he came in, and with an air of relief and even a smile, said:

"Well, I've done it, and it's over."

"Well?" said Leonard, curiously.

"Well, nothing; she wasn't at home," said Jack, triumphantly.

"Not at home. What sort of a place was it?"

"The best place in Park Lane," said Jack. "No end of flunkeys about, and the rest of it. Looks as if she rolled in gold, as she must do to have the place at all."

"And you didn't see her?" asked Leonard.

Jack colored and frowned.

"What a curious beggar you are! Yes, I did see her; her carriage drove up just as I was going away."

"And you spoke to her?"

"No, I just raised my hat and walked away," said Jack, gravely.

Leonard shrugged his shoulders.

"She will think you a boor."

"So I am," said Jack. "What does it matter? Tell me something about yourself. I am sick of myself. What have you been doing?"

Leonard's pale face flushed.

"I've been to Cheltenham Terrace," he said.

"Well, did you see her?"

"No," said Leonard, sadly. "I saw that the blinds in the upper windows were down, and I went to the next door, and asked if anyone was ill."

"Well?"

"Yes, her grandfather, old Mr. Treherne, was ill, they said, and I came away."

"Well," said Jack, "at any rate you know where to find her—while I——"

"I saw her shadow on the blind," said Leonard, simply. "I could swear to it among a hundred. I watched her beautiful profile for an hour in that railway carriage."

"Treherne, Laura Treherne," said Jack. "It is a pretty name. What took her to Hurst Leigh that night, I wonder? The night the squire died. Len, it is a romance, but I envy you. If I knew where Una lived I'd hang about the house night and day until I saw her. Len, do you know what it is to be hungry, to be parched and dried up with thirst so that you would give all you possessed—ten years of your life for a draught of water? That is just how I feel when I think of that beautiful face, with its soft brown eyes and innocent smile! And when do I not think of her?"

"And you didn't speak to Lady Bell?" said Leonard.

Jack made a hasty explanation and made for the door, nearly running against the housekeeper.

"A letter for you, sir," she said.

Jack tore it open, read it and threw it to Leonard.

The envelope was a dainty gray color, and stamped with an elaborate coat of arms, with the initials I. E. in cipher underneath, and inside was a card of invitation to a ball, filled in by a lady's delicate hand, with a line in addition.

"With Lady Earlsley's compliments and regret that she was from home when Mr. Newcombe called."

"Jack, what condescension. You must go!"

Jack stammered, and argued, and protested. He was too honest to plead that he was in mourning; but he simply swore that he would not go.

The day came round and the evening fell, and Jack came into the sitting-room in evening dress, his tall form seeming to fill the room.

Leonard used to say that it was a treat to see Jack in evening dress; that he was one of the few men who looked to advantage in it, and he turned from his eternal pen and ink to look at him with an approving smile.

"Yes," said Jack, fiercely, "I am going; I am a fool, but how can a man stand against such a perpetual old nuisance as you are? But mind, I am just going in and out again, and after this there is an end of it. I shall enlist!" and out he went.

CHAPTER XXII

Jack called a hansom—of course he could have walked, but he had no idea of economy or the value of money—and was driven to Park Lane.

Half a dozen times on the way he felt inclined to stop the cab, jump out and go to the club—anywhere but Lady Bell's; but nevertheless, he found himself in Park Lane, and ascending the staircase. He saw at once, by a few unmistakable signs, that the party was a small and select one, and furthermore, judging by the tasteful magnificence of the appointments, that Lady Bell's wealth had not been very much exaggerated.

He made his way slowly, for a dance was just over, and the stairs were lined, as usual, with people mostly whom he knew, and had to stop to speak to. Amongst them were Sir Arkroyd Hetley, and Dalrymple, of course together.

"Hullo, here's the Savage!" cried Hetley. "How do you do, Jack? You've soon got on the war trail, old fellow," he added in a low voice and with a significant smile.

Jack growled something and made his way into the room.

For a moment he could see nothing of Lady Bell, then as she came out of the fernery and advanced toward him her dark eyes flashing, or rather gleaming softly, with a faint, delicious color mantling on her cheeks, he felt almost the same shock of surprise which had fallen on Una.

He had scarcely noticed her the other night, had scarcely, indeed, seen her, and he now saw, as it were for the first time, her beauty, set off and heightened by the aid of one of Worth's happiest dresses, and Emanuel's diamonds. In spite of himself he was dazzled, and his frank eyes showed that he was.

And Lady Bell? Well, though his face had scarcely left her mind's eye since she had seen it, she was not disappointed.

Notwithstanding the rather bored and surly—not to say ferocious expression which set upon it—she thought him handsomer than even she had remembered him.

"This is very kind of you, Mr. Newcombe," she said speaking first, for Jack had contented himself with bowing over her hand.

"Kind?" said Jack, in his straightforward way.

Lady Bell hesitated, and for the first time, perhaps, in her life, smiled shyly.

"I heard—they tell me—that it is as difficult to get Mr. Newcombe to a dance as a prince of the blood royal."

"It isn't much in my way," said Jack, quietly; "I am not a dancing man—that is, I don't care for it."

"Then it was kind," said Lady Bell, recovering her courage and smiling at him with that wonderful smile which Hetley and all the rest of them talked so much about.

Jack looked at her. Yes, certainly she was very beautiful, and there was a subtle something in that smile.

His ill-temper began to disappear.

"I should say," he said, "that a man ought to feel lucky at the chance of getting here."

"They also told me," said Lady Bell, archly, "that you never paid compliments."

"Someone seems to have been taking a great deal of trouble to make me out a regular boor," said Jack, with his curt laugh. "Did they also tell you that I lived in the woods up a tree, and existed on wild animals?"

"Like a savage?" said Lady Bell, wickedly.

Jack flushed and looked at her; then her smile conquered and he laughed.

"Yes, that is what they call me, confound their impudence! But I'm a very tame kind of a savage, Lady Earlsley; I shan't scalp you."

"It wouldn't matter much, would it?" she retorted. "They make such beautiful false hair now."

Jack looked down on the soft, glossy head, with its thick, light coils, and smiled.

"Are you going to change your mind and scalp me, after all?" she said. "You make me tremble when you look like that."

Jack laughed right out.

"No," he said; "even a savage is incapable of such ingratitude. I have come to-night, Lady Earlsley, to thank you for your kindness the other night, and to tell you how sorry I am that—that you should have had so much trouble!"

And a blush managed to show itself under the tan.

Lady Bell looked down.

"It was no trouble," she said. "I was afraid that you were hurt. It was very clumsy and stupid of my man."

"It was all my fault," said Jack, penitently. "I——"

"Do not say any more," she said, gently, and she put her finger tips on his arm.

Jack looked at her, and met her gaze, full of concealed interest, and his own eyes fell before it.

They had been standing near the fernery, behind which stood Una; she could hear every word, see every look.

Pale and almost breathless she stood, her hands clasped in front of her, her heart beating fast, her eyes fixed on Jack's face. She longed to fly, yet could not move a foot. Something, his very presence, his very voice, held her like a chain.

She felt that if he were to turn and, seeing her, say, "Follow me!" she must follow him, though it were to the end of the earth.

A storm of conflicting emotions battled within her for mastery; a wild delight at his presence, an intense longing that his eyes might turn and rest on her, and at the same time an awful miserable feeling, which she did not know was jealousy.

How beautiful they looked, these two, Lady Bell, the heiress, in her rich dress and splendid jewels, and he, with his tanned face and bold, fierce eyes, his stalwart frame towering above all others, and sinking them into insignificance. How well matched they seemed. Why—why did Lady Bell smile at him like that? No wonder his face had grown brighter. Who could resist that bewitching smile?

The music of a waltz commenced and recalled her to a sense of her position. With a start she drew still further back, so that she was quite out of sight.

"There's a dance," said Jack, in his blunt way. "I would ask if you were free to give it to me, but I cannot dance to-night. I am in mourning. Don't let me keep you, though."

"That is a plain intimation," said Lady Bell; "but I am sorry that you are in trouble. In sober earnest it was kind of you to come. I hope it was no one near to you."

"No," said Jack, and his face clouded at the recollection of Hurst Leigh. "It was a very dear old friend who had been very good to me."

Lady Bell inclined her head, and her voice grew wonderfully soft.

"I see that I must not keep you. I shall not be offended if you leave us at once. If I had known— —"

Now here was Jack's opportunity. Why did he not seize it and go?

"Thanks," he said; "although I won't dance I'll stay a little while if you'll permit me."

Lady Bell bowed.

"Thank you," she said, almost humbly, as if he had granted her a great favor, as it seemed to Una.

At this moment the great—or little—duke came up with a smile.

"Am I fortunate enough to find you free for this, Lady Earlsley?"

Lady Bell looked at her card, carefully keeping it out of his reach, and shook her head.

"I'm so sorry! My partner will be here directly, I expect."

The duke bowed, expressed his regret, and moved off, not without a glance at Jack, who stood calm and possessed; and Una knew, notwithstanding all her ignorance, that Lady Bell was not engaged, but had refused the duke that she might keep Jack by her side; and with this knowledge the demon jealousy sprang into life, and made himself fully known.

With an awful aching of the heart she sank into a seat and hid her face in her hands.

What right had she there—she, the ignorant, untaught forest girl, among these grand people? Even supposing that he saw her he would not remember her, and if he did he would not care to waste a glance or a word on her, while such a beautiful creature as Lady Bell was willing to refuse a duke for his sake.

Suddenly the brilliant scene seemed to grow dark and joyless; the music sounded harsh and out of tune; all the beauty had vanished, and she longed to be sitting in the depths of Warden Forest.

"Your partner doesn't seem to turn up," said Jack. "He's an ungrateful idiot."

Lady Bell laughed and sank down in a fauteuil just in front of the recess.

"I forgive him," she said, and she swept her skirts aside to make room for him.

Jack sat down, not gratefully, but quite courtly.

Lady Bell was silent for a moment, then she said:

"I would have sent a card for your friend, but I could not remember his name."

"Oh, Len," said Jack, shaking his head. "I'm afraid he would not have come. He never goes out—at least not to this sort of thing. He's a book worm, and doesn't care for the gaieties. His name is Leonard Dagle."

"He is a great friend of yours?"

"The best that ever man had," said Jack, quietly; "more than a brother."

"You live with him?" she said, with an interest only too palpable to the listening Una, whom Lady Bell had quite forgotten.

"Yes, we live together—have done so for years—always shall, I hope, till——"

He paused.

"Till death, were you going to say?" said Lady Bell.

"No, I wasn't," said Jack, simply. "I was going to say till I took his advice and—enlisted."

"Enlisted!" she repeated, turning her beautiful face full upon him.

Jack colored and frowned.

"Yes," he said, stoutly; and though he said not a word more, Lady Bell knew that he was poor and in trouble.

It was just the one thing wanted to finish the romance. He was poor and in trouble, while she was rich beyond the dreams of avarice. Why should she not say as she longed to do:

"You want money. See, here am I who have more than I know what to do with; take some of it and make me happy!"

Instead, she thought it only, and remained silent.

"How hot it is," she said presently. "It is more than time to leave London. One longs for the green fields and the sea."

"It is late," said Jack.

"We are staying in town," she said, "because my father is a bookworm and can only live near a library—he only exists elsewhere. I cannot find it in my heart to tear him away from the British Museum; but we make the best of it. We are going to have a water-party to-morrow at Richmond."

"Yes," said Jack.

She waited for him to ask for an invitation; then, pressing her lip with her fan, said:

"Will you join us?"

Jack hesitated a moment.

"I shall be delighted," he said.

"You don't look it," she said. "But I forgot—savages rarely smile. At any rate, we start to-morrow at twelve o'clock. Sir Arkroyd is going to drive us down in Lord Dalrymple's drag."

"Perhaps there isn't room," said Jack.

"Are you trying to find an excuse for not coming?" she said, smiling on him.

Jack frowned, and then laughed.

"I'll come," he said.

Yes, there was a nameless charm about her which had made itself felt already. Was it her beauty or her frankness—the latter so different to the cut-and-dried and measured manner of the ordinary women of society?

"I'll come," he said.

Then he looked around.

"This is a beautiful room. Where did you get all the flowers from? Some of them I never saw before in London."

"Do you like them?" she said. "Many of them we brought over with us from 'across the seas,' the others I ransacked London to get—at least, poor Mrs. Fellowes did."

"Why poor?" he said.

"Because she has the misfortune to be my companion, and I worry her to death."

"A pleasant death," he muttered.

"Thanks," she said. "That is the second compliment you have paid me. And yet they say you are not gallant, as the French have it."

"It's the heat," said Jack, in his grim way.

"You will find some ices in the ante-room there, behind that lace curtain."

"Shall I get you one?" said Jack.

She nodded.

"Thanks! Yes, that is the way," and she rose to point to a winding path made through the rows of ferns and tropical plants.

He had to pass her in going, and in doing so he struck a spray of a palm with his head; it recoiled, and caught some of its soft, spiky leaves in her hair.

She uttered a half-laughing cry, and Jack turned.

"I beg your pardon," he said. "I am awfully clumsy. Allow me."

She bent her head toward him, laughing, and Jack disentangled the silken threads from the great clinging leaf. In doing so he again proved his clumsiness, for the silken threads got round his fingers.

He could feel her soft, peach-like face against his wrist, and being human his blood thrilled.

Lady Bell looked up. Her face was pale, and her eyes drooping and languid.

"Are you going to scalp me after all?" she murmured.

Jack's heart beat strangely.

"I—I am very sorry," he muttered below his breath, and with lowered eyes he went on.

Lady Bell looked after him and drew a long breath. A sigh that almost echoed hers startled her, and turning she saw Una, sitting where she had left her, with her hands clasped in her lap.

"My child," said Lady Bell, "I had almost— —"

"Yes, you had quite forgotten me," said Una, with a strange smile.

Lady Bell flushed and looked at her. Her lovely face was pale and her eyes clouded with a strange look of pain and weariness.

"Forgive me, my child," she said. "You are quite pale—you are tired. It is too hot. Wait! there are some ices coming."

"No, no," said Una, with a sudden shrinking. "Please leave me—do not bring him here—I mean— —" she stammered, "I would rather be alone. Go and dance, Lady Bell."

"What a timid fawn it is," said Lady Bell, caressingly. "There, go and sit in the shade there. Don't be frightened; I promised to take care of you."

"I am not frightened," said Una, quietly, "but I would rather— —"

"I understand," said Lady Bell, quickly; then she said, trying to speak carelessly and toying with her fan: "Did you see the gentleman I was speaking to, dear?"

"Yes," said Una, calmly.

"Don't you think that he is very handsome?"

Una's heart beat so fast that she could scarcely speak.

"Yes," she answered, at last.

"What a cold Diana it is!" said Lady Bell, caressingly. "What an icy 'yes.' My dear, he is the handsomest man in the room."

"Yes," said Una, sadly.

Lady Bell looked at her.

"I see, for all your yesses, that you don't think so," she said, with a laugh. "Do you know they call him the Savage, and that it is quite an achievement on my part to get him here? I made his acquaintance by accident. Mrs. Fellowes is quite shocked over it. But I always do as I like. I've got a fancy, Una—you'd never guess it."

"What is it?" said Una, raising her dark eyes gravely to the beautiful, witching face.

Lady Bell smiled.

"I have a fancy for taming the Savage," she said, more to herself than to Una; "it will be so amusing."

Una turned her head aside.

"For him, do you mean?" she asked, in a low voice.

Lady Bell stared at her, and her color came and went amusedly.

"What a strange child it is! For him? No, for me! And—yes, for him too. What right has he to pretend to be invincible? Do you think I shall succeed?"

Una looked at her with an aching heart.

"Yes," she answered; "I think you will succeed."

"What a flatterer it is!" said Lady Bell, playfully. "Hush! here he comes; half tamed already. Now for the first lesson," and, to Una's surprise she glided from the recess and was instantly lost in the crowd. A moment after Una saw her dancing with the duke.

She drew back into the shadow and watched Jack. He came along slowly, the ice in his hand, and looked around for Lady Bell, with astonishment and something like anger in his face for a moment. Then he saw her dancing with the duke in the center of the room, looked round for some place to put the ice down, and, seeing none convenient, gently pitched it, plate and all, into a fountain, to the considerable astonishment of the gold fish.

Then he sat down and thrusting his hands into his pockets, seemed lost in thought; his head thrown back, almost touched Una's arm, and she wondered whether he would be glad or sorry, or simply indifferent, if she rose and stood before him, or called him by name.

Yes, there he sat, within reach of her hand. She had often dreamed of him as being near her, but it was no dream now.

An infinite longing to touch, to speak to him, possessed her, and if he would but turn and look at her as he had looked that morning by the lake!

She struggled hard against the temptation, and sat motionless, all her heart going out toward him.

If she had known that Jack, even at that moment, was thinking of her, and recalling her every look and word. It was one of Strauss' waltzes they were playing, but he heard it not; in his ears was the rustle of the forest trees and the ripple of the lake; before him was one of the most beautiful ball-rooms in London, before him moved, in a glittering pageant, the pick of London's beauty and rank, but he saw them not; he was looking in fancy into the lovely face of the innocent forest girl.

The dance was over, but still Lady Bell did not come; couples, arm-in-arm, promenaded past him, but still Jack sat, and dreaming of the girl who sat longing, longing for a word or look from him, just behind him. Suddenly Una felt something drop into her lap. It was a blossom from one of the tropical plants.

She took it up and looked at it absently; then, as if by a sudden inspiration, she raised it to her lips and kissed it, and rising, dropped it on his knee and fled.

Jack started, and stooping picked up the flower, looked at it for a moment, and then turned and looked up to see whence it had come.

As he did so he saw reflected dimly in a mirror framed in palm leaves a girl's face.

With a bound he darted to his feet, and naturally enough made for the reflection; but ere he could reach the mirror the face had vanished.

Pale and trembling with eagerness he turned—but Una had glided through the ferns and reached the ante-room—and came face to face with Lady Bell.

She was flushed and laughing, her eyes dancing with the excitement of the dance.

"Well," she said, "where is my ice?"

Jack, startled and bewildered, stared at her.

"I must have been dreaming," he muttered.

"Dreaming," she said. "What do you mean?"

He passed his hand over his brow.

"Your ice!" and he glanced at the fountain. "I—I beg your pardon. What did I do with it? I will get you another."

"Never mind!" said Lady Bell, laughing; "I do not care for it now; I am too hot. Have you been asleep?"

"Asleep!" he said, striving to recover his coolness; "nearly. What could I do when you left me?"

"The third compliment," she said, with a smile. "Where are you going now?" for Jack, with his eyes fixed on the end of the fernery, was moving slowly away.

"I—I'm afraid I must go," he said.

"Good-night!" she said, turning away coldly.

Jack "pulled himself together," as he would have called it, and sat down beside her.

"No," he said, "I will stay if I may."

She turned to him with a gentle smile.

"No; go now, please. I am not ungrateful. It was very kind of you to come. You will not forget tomorrow?"

"No," said Jack, fingering his crush hat. "I will not forget tomorrow—how could I?"

She held out her hand—not a tiny, meaningless one, but a long, shapely eloquent hand—and put it into his broad, strong one.

"Good-night!" she said, and her voice grew wondrously low and gentle in its caressing, clinging tones. "Good-night!"

Jack felt the slender fingers, warm through the thin gloves, cling round his fingers.

"Good-night," she said, hurriedly. "Good-night."

CHAPTER XXIII

Jack walked leisurely enough through the fernery looking this way and that in search of the phantom girl; but once clear of the ball-room, he hurried through the ante-rooms and down the staircase—utterly ignoring the adieus which were sent after him by the crowd on the stairs—and reached the hall.

The carriages were already taking up, and without ceremony he pushed through the footmen into the open air.

"Has a carriage left just now—five minutes ago?" he asked.

"Two or three, sir," said the footmen, and, too busy to answer any further questions, he dashed off.

Jack waited just outside the stream of light for nearly an hour, his coat collar turned up, his hands thrust in his pockets. But though many a beautiful face passed him and was driven away, Una's lovely face was not amongst them.

"I must have fallen asleep and been dreaming," he muttered. "How could she possibly have been there?"

Then he called a hansom, and was driven to the club.

His blood was on fire, his brain was in a whirl; two faces—Una's and Lady Bell's—seemed to dance before his eyes. Do something he must to get rid of them, or they would drive him mad.

There was only one thing to do—play. Before the morning he had lost every penny of his twenty-one pounds six and fourpence, and a couple of hundred besides.

Chance had favored Una in her escape; no sooner had she reached the staircase than she heard Mrs. Davenant's carriage announced. To get her shawl and make her way down the staircase was the work of a few moments, and the brougham was rolling away toward Walmington Square before Jack had got down to the hall.

"Well, my dear," said Mrs. Davenant, "have you enjoyed yourself? You look pale and tired."

Una shrunk into her corner.

"I am rather tired," she said, in a low voice, "it was all so new and strange."

"And was Lady Bell kind?"

"Very kind," answered Una, with a sigh. "How beautiful she is!"

"Yes," said Mrs. Davenant, "she is a very fortunate girl. Youth and beauty and wealth, she has much to make her happy. Tell me whom you saw, my dear."

Una flushed and trembled. She went over the names of some of the great people, but she said nothing of Jack. She could not bring her trembling lips to frame his name.

"All the best people in town," said Mrs. Davenant, with a smile. "You will be a fashionable young lady before long, Una."

"Oh, no, no!" breathed Una, with a sudden pallor. "Perhaps I shall never go again."

Mrs. Davenant looked at her curiously, and relapsed into silence until they reached home.

Then, as they entered the drawing-room, she said, with a little nervous smile:

"I have heard from my son Stephen, Una."

"From your son?"

"Yes," said Mrs. Davenant. "It is good news. He has become very rich. His uncle, Squire Davenant, has left him everything he possessed."

Una started and turned pale. Then Jack had been left nothing! That was why he had looked so grave and troubled.

"Everything?" she asked.

"Everything," said Mrs. Davenant, with a sigh: "the Hurst and the estate, and all the money, and he is very rich—very rich indeed."

Una looked before her dreamily. She could not say, "I am very glad." Mrs. Davenant waited a moment.

"There is a message for you, my dear," she said timidly, fingering the letter.

"For me!" said Una, looking up with a start.

"Yes; Stephen is so thoughtful! He never forgets others even in the midst of his great prosperity. He sends his kind regards, and trusts that you do not miss Warden, and that you will not find our quiet life too dull. He little thinks how we have plunged into gayety already. He would be surprised if he knew it."

Indeed Stephen would, with a vengeance!

"It is very kind of him," said Una, in a low voice.

Mrs. Davenant sighed.

"He is always kind and thoughtful. He tells me that he will not be able to come home just yet awhile. It seems that there is a great deal to see to. The estate was greatly neglected, and there's some business to be done with the lawyers; that keeps him there. But he says he will come as soon as he can, and, meanwhile, I am to make you as happy as I can. I hope I have done that already, dear," she added, with simple affection.

Una rose and kissed her.

"Indeed, yes; I am very happy."

Then she turned her face away to hide her tears.

"Come, you must go to bed," said Mrs. Davenant, "or you will lose all your fresh roses."

And she put her candle in her hand, and kissed her tenderly.

It was some time before Una fell asleep. The events of the night flitted like phantom visions across her eyes, and Jack's face rose to haunt her, with its tender, troubled look in the dark eyes.

The squire had willed all to Stephen then, and Jack was poor and forgotten.

The sun was high in the heavens when she awoke, and breakfast was on the table by the time she had got down.

Mrs. Davenant looked up with a smile.

"I am so glad to have you safe, dear," she said. "Come, you have got all your roses back again; and, see here, you cannot guess whom this is from;" and she held up a note. "It is from Lady Bell. It is an awful scolding for your running away last night. She says that you flew away like a bird, and that she had no sooner missed you than she heard that you had gone."

Una colored.

"Was it rude of me?" she said. "I am sorry."

"Never mind, my dear; she has evidently forgiven you, or she says she will, if you will go with her for a water picnic to-day."

Una turned pale again.

"I!" she said, below her breath.

Mrs. Davenant opened the note.

"Yes; she says she will take no denial. They are going to drive down to Richmond, and she will call for you on the way. Would you like to go, my dear?"

Una thought a moment. She longed for, yet dreaded, the meeting which she knew must take place between Jack and her if she went.

Mrs. Davenant took her silence for consent.

"There is no need of an answer, my dear," she said, with a little laugh; "Lady Bell will take no heed of a refusal. There's the note."

And she threw it across the table.

Una read the kindly-imperative little letter, and sighed as she examined the brilliant crest stamped at the head of the paper.

"It is very kind," she said. "Yes, I will go, if you are sure you do not mind my leaving you."

After breakfast, Mrs. Davenant and Jane entered into a consultation as to what Una should wear, Una standing by with a quiet smile.

At last they decided that a dainty-figured satin should be honored; and both of them, notwithstanding Una's protests, insisted upon assisting at her toilet.

They could not have chosen anything more suited to her fresh, virginal beauty than the simple, delicate dress; and when Jane had brushed the soft, silken hair until it shone and flashed like strands of golden haze, and coiled it into a knot, Mrs. Davenant could not suppress an exclamation of satisfaction and admiration.

As for Una, she had not yet learned to view her changed self without surprise, and stared at the tall, beautiful woman which the glass reflected as though she could not believe that it was herself.

They were still looking at her, and Jane's restless fingers were touching a bow here and a fold there, when they heard the rattle of heavy wheels outside, and Mrs. Davenant hurried her downstairs.

Lady Bell was already in the drawing-room, and took Una in her arms as if she were a school-girl, instead of a woman taller than herself.

"My child, I came to scold you—I meant to have a fearful scene; but you have taken it all out of me!" And she held Una by her elbows, and looked at her admiringly. "Child, you are a picture! I've half a mind to drive off without you. What will become of me? Mrs. Davenant, don't you think I am very stupid to commit suicide in this way?"

Mrs. Davenant smiled, and looked at Lady Bell's beautiful face, all bright as if with sunlight, and shook her head gently.

"Bah!" said Lady Bell, pouting. "I am nothing but a foil to her; but I shall be useful, at least. Come, we must be off. What is that—milk?"

"Yes," said Una, offering her a glass, with a smile.

"She drinks nothing else," said Mrs. Davenant.

"That accounts for her complexion," said Lady Bell. "No, it doesn't! If I drank all the dairies in London dry, I shouldn't get such milk and roses on my cheeks."

"Don't turn her head," murmured Mrs. Davenant, under her breath.

Lady Bell laughed.

"My dear Mrs. Davenant, it is just what she wants! There isn't a spark of vanity in her composition; she isn't quite a woman, for no woman is without vanity. Look at her, as grave and stern as a judge!" and she touched Una's arm with her sunshade.

Una started—she had been wondering whether Jack would be there outside, on the drag, and was listening for his voice amongst those which came floating through the open window.

Trembling inwardly she followed Lady Bell out.

The four horses were champing and pawing impatiently.

The drag was nearly full, and, for a moment, Una saw only a confused group of women in dainty morning dresses, and of men in white flannel and cheviot. A second glance convinced her that Jack was not there.

As they appeared on the steps the laughter and voices ceased, and a well-bred glance of curiosity was turned upon her.

Lady Bell was, however, equal to the occasion.

"Come along, Una," she said, gayly. "Fanny, will you make room beside you for Miss Rolfe?"

The Countess of Pierrepoint smiled.

"How do you do, Miss Rolfe!" she said graciously. "I hear you were at Lady Bell's dance last night; why did you let her hide you so completely?"

Una was silent.

Fortunately Dalrymple made so much bustle and fuss in starting, that conversation for a minute or two was impossible; and before that minute or two had passed, Una had gained her self-possession.

Seated about, she recognized several of the people Lady Bell had pointed out on the preceding evening: Lady Clarence, Mrs. Cantrip, the Marchioness of Fairfield. Beside Dalrymple, who had all his work cut out in keeping the four spirited nags in good conduct in the crowded London streets, sat, as a matter of course, Sir Arkroyd Hetley, while one or two other men—one of whom she heard addressed as the viscount—was with the ladies.

Had Una been naturally nervous, her timidity could not long have existed in such an atmosphere.

Her companions were among the highest in the land; but there was less reserve and ceremony than would have been found in a similar gathering of middle-class people. The men were laughing and chatting, ever and again turning round to make some light-hearted remark, or pass some joke round. They were all, it was evident, bent on enjoying themselves.

Very soon Una found herself brought into the conversation, Lady Bell talking to her continually, and pointing out the lions of the road.

The roses came back into Una's face in full bloom, her heart beat more lightly, and her spirits rose as the four impatient horses dashed along the roads which now ran through the beautiful vicinity of Richmond.

She had almost—almost—forgotten that Jack was not there, when happening to glance round suddenly at Lady Bell, she saw her looking dreamily before her, evidently lost in thought, with a wistful drooping of the bright red lips and a disappointed shadow in the dark eyes.

Then Una knew that it was not only she herself who felt the absence of the missing one.

However, Lady Bell soon rallied, and when they drove up to the hotel she was as bright as ever.

The luncheon had been sent up to Thames Dutton, one of the prettiest parts of the Thames, and it had been arranged that the gentlemen should row up to the island, hence the white flannel and cheviot costumes. They found boats awaiting them at the river side, and, with much laughing and gayety, started.

It was a beautiful scene, the river gleaming like a flood of silver between its banks of green meadows and stately trees, the three boats with their bright colored occupants. Una, who was of nature's own kin, was filled with delight; it was better than being at Warden. She leaned back in her comfortable seat in the stern of the foremost boat, rapt in silent enjoyment.

Lady Bell looked at her rather wistfully.

"How happy you look, child," she said, in a lower voice than usual.

"I am quite happy," said Una, simply.

"You are just the person for a picnic," said Lady Clarence. "I feel sure that you would look just as contented and serene if it rained in torrents, while the rest of us would be running about bemoaning our spoiled clothes."

Una laughed.

"I am not afraid of rain," she said.

"That's fortunate, Miss Rolfe," said Dalrymple, who was pulling stroke, and exerting himself nobly, while Hetley, pulling behind him, allowed him to do all the work. "That's fortunate, as we shall be sure to have a shower or two—always do at a water picnic."

"No prophesying, marquis!" cried Lady Bell. "There isn't a cloud in the sky; there isn't a sign of wet."

"I'm sorry for that," he said, with mock gravity, "for I'm fearfully thirsty."

They paid no attention to this broad hint, however, until they were going through Teddington Lock, when Lady Bell produced some champagne and soda water, and Hetley made a cooling cup.

When it came to Una's turn—they all drank out of the same cup, a splendid silver tankard, chased with the Earlsley arms—she glanced at it askance and shook her head.

"But you must, my dear Una," said Lady Bell. "You will be parched."

"Let me have some water," said Una, and making a cup of her hand—a trick she had learned at a very early age—she bent over the boat and as quietly and naturally drank a draught.

The countess looked at her earnestly, and Sir Arkroyd muttered to Dalrymple:

"Where did she come from?"

"I don't know," said Dalrymple, in the same tone. "I'd stick to water all the day if she'd let me drink it out of the same cup. Isn't she beautiful—perfectly lovely!"

"Hush, she'll hear you," muttered Sir Arkroyd, warningly.

But he need not have feared.

Una sat like the dream-maiden in the ballad, deaf to all but the plash of the oars and the music of the birds.

Presently the stately pile of Hampton Court Palace glided, as it were, into their view, and with a long pull Dalrymple sent the boat to the island.

The two other boats were close behind, and then these grand people who were accustomed to be waited on hand and foot, got out and dragged hampers under the shadow of the oaks and willows; and the countess and Lady Clarence laid the cloth, while Lady Bell and the rest knelt beside the hampers and pulled out the things one by one. Then Sir Arkroyd was sent to lay the champagne bottles in the shallow water, and Dalrymple was handed a dish and the ingredients for making the salad.

In a few minutes luncheon was set out to the accompaniment of much laughter, and a few accidents. One of the champagne bottles had slid into the deep water, and disappeared to the bottom of the river to astonish the fish. The corkscrew followed it; and dismay fell on all, until the viscount calmly produced another from his pocket.

"Never go to a picnic without a corkscrew," he said, shaking his head. "Generally have to produce it, too."

Then there was much dragging about of hampers, and arranging of shawls and boat cushions to provide seats for the ladies; but at last all were seated, and Dalrymple, brandishing a knife in dangerous proximity to Lady Pierrepoint's head, cut the first slice of raised pie.

Then it was discovered how easy it is to make jokes at a picnic. You can't be stately and ceremonious sitting cross-legged on the grass, and balancing your plate on your knees; especially when, in consequence of there not being quite enough knives, you have to lend the one you are using to your next-door neighbor.

As usual, too, there were not quite enough plates and those dainty gentlemen, who went into fits if a fly fell into their wineglasses at the club, bent down on their hands and knees and washed plates in the river.

"And there is no rain," said Lady Bell.

"Then one of us will have to fall into the river," said the viscount, solemnly. "Must have rain or an accident at a picnic, you know. Will you have some more cream, Lady Earlsley?"

Lady Bell shook her head, laughingly.

"No, thanks; I have enjoyed it all immensely. Why cannot we have a picnic every day?"

But Una, who sat next her, had noticed that she scarcely touched anything.

"Let us go into Bushey Park, and turn savages," said Dalrymple. "Halloa; speaking of savages, what a pity the Savage isn't here. This is just in his line."

Lady Bell bent down suddenly to take a flower from the cloth.

"Mr. Newcombe was detained in town," she said, calmly; but Una could detect the faint quiver in her voice.

"Poor old Jack," said Dalrymple, after a pause, "seems to be cut up about something lately. Do you remember how queer he was that night he came back from the country, Arkroyd?"

Lady Bell looked up suddenly.

"Let us go for a ramble. You may smoke, gentlemen," she added. "Now don't shake your heads as if you never did such a thing. I can see your cigar-case peeping out of your pocket, Lord Dalrymple."

And linking her arm in Una's, she sauntered away.

They strolled in silence for some minutes, until Una, happening to look up, saw that Lady Bell's face was quite pale, and that something suspiciously like tears were veiling the brightness of the dark eyes.

"Lady Bell!" she murmured.

"Hush!" said Lady Bell, gently. "Don't notice me, child! Oh, how sick I am of it all! What a long day it seems! How can they sit there laughing and chattering like a set of monkeys?"

"What is the matter?" said Una, in her low, musical voice.

"Nothing," said Lady Bell, softly; then she paused and tried to laugh. "Una, my sweet, innocent, I've got a complaint which you know nothing of; it is called the heartache. There is no cure for it, I am afraid; at least, not for mine. Tut! there, there! your great, grave eyes torture me; they seem to go to the bottom of my soul. Not a word more. Here they come!"

And the next instant she turned round, all life and gayety.

Una sauntered on, her heart beating wildly. Was Lady Bell's heartache produced by the absence of Jack Newcombe? Yes, that must be it!

With a sigh she drew away still further from the rest, and seating herself on the trunk of a tree by the riverside, watched the silver stream as it flowed past and was lost in the setting sun.

Suddenly she saw in the distance a white speck that looked like a bird, flitting up the middle of the stream. The speck grew larger; and she saw that it was a light boat putting toward the island.

Gradually it came nearer and nearer, and she saw that it contained one man only, and that he was clad in white flannel.

It was a light water-boat—a mere speck of white it looked now on the golden stream—and to Una, who had never seen an outrigger before, it seemed an almost impossible feat to sit in it.

But the sculler managed it with the greatest ease, and with every stroke sent it flying forward.

With regular rhythmical action he pulled on, and very soon she could see his great arms bared to the shoulders.

She watched it absently for some minutes, but presently the rower turned his head, and something in the movement struck her and made her heart bound.

Agitated and trembling she rose and stood staring down the stream.

A curve of the island hid the boat suddenly, and she stood watching for it to appear again; but the minutes passed on and it did not come. Then suddenly she heard a peal of laughter and the clatter of voices, and she knew that the boat had pulled into the island.

With a vague hope and dread commingled she sank to the seat again, and sat striving to still the wild beating of her heart.

Presently she heard her name called. It was Lady Bell's voice, and how changed; there was no false ring in it now; clear and joyous it rang out:

"Una! Una! Where are you?"

There was no escape. She knew she must go, but she waited for full three minutes. Then, nerved to an unnatural calm, she rose and moved slowly forward. They were all seated again; she could see them.

Dalrymple and Sir Arkroyd were stretched at full length, smoking; the ladies, in their dainty sateens and pompadours, were grouped near them, and a little apart sat Lady Bell, a cup in one hand and a knife in the other, her face turned toward someone eating. Though his back was toward her, Una recognized him. It was Jack Newcombe. He had turned down his sleeves and put on his white flannel jacket, and was eating and chatting at one and the same time.

"Yes, better late than never," she heard him say, and with every word of his deep, musical voice her heart leaped as if in glad response. "I found I could get away, and I jumped in the train, to learn at Richmond that you had just started. I got an outrigger, and here I am."

"Just in time to help wash up," said Dalrymple. "We've eaten all the strawberries, old man, and there isn't much cream. It's lucky for you there is any pie."

"Don't pay any attention to them, Mr. Newcombe," said Lady Bell, and how soft and sweet her voice sounded, with its undertone of tenderness. "I am so sorry you are late. Do not let them hurry you. You must be so tired. Let me give you some ham—some tongue, then?"

And she herself cut a slice and put it on his plate.

"Don't let me stop the fun," said Jack, in his grave way. "Go on with your games. What was it—kiss-in-the-ring?"

There was a laugh; the lightest joke will serve at a picnic.

"I was haunted by the dread that I should come just in time to find everything cleared up. What a beautiful day! No, no more, thanks."

"Let me give you some champagne," said Lady Bell, and reached forward with the goblet in her hand.

Jack took it, and nodded over it in true picnic fashion.

"Thanks," he said, and raised it to his lips.

At that moment Lady Bell looked up, and, seeing Una standing still and motionless, beckoned her.

Mechanically Una went round to her, and so stood in front of Jack.

His eyes were fixed at the bottom of the cup at the moment, but presently he lifted them, and, with a sharp cry, he let the cup fall to the ground and sprang to his feet.

And then he stood staring at her downcast face with startled eyes and pale countenance.

"Hallo! Take care!" cried Dalrymple. "What are you up to now, Savage? Anything bitten you?"

Lady Bell looked from one to the other, from Una's white, downcast face to Jack's pale, startled one.

"Una," she breathed, "what is it?"

But Jack recovered himself.

"Just like you fellows," he said. "Didn't you know that you had pitched me on an ants' nest? What did you say, Lady Bell? I beg your pardon. T don't think there is much spilled, and there is nothing broken."

And he knelt down and picked up the cup.

Lady Bell laughed.

"I couldn't think what was the matter," she said. "Are you really bitten?"

"Just like Jack," said Sir Arkroyd, with philosophic calmness. "He is never happy unless he is breaking something. I give you my word that he smashes more glasses at the club than any other man."

"Always was clumsy," said Jack, with a constrained laugh.

Lady Bell smiled.

"You have quite frightened my friend, Miss Rolfe," she said. "Una, this unfortunate gentleman is Mr. Newcombe."

Jack had given her time, and she was able now to look at him calmly. Jack bowed, his eyes glancing at her as if they scarcely dared trust the evidence of their own senses.

"Pray forgive me," he said. "I am very awkward. But I don't break quite so many things as they say. Is there any more champagne, Lady Earlsley? I don't deserve it, I know——"

Lady Bell took up a bottle.

"Pour this into the cup, Una," she said, with a smile. "It is true he doesn't deserve it, but we will be merciful."

Una took the bottle and leaned forward, and as she did so Jack rose and stood before her, so that he screened her trembling hand from the eyes of the rest.

His own trembled, his own heart beat wildly; all else save the beautiful face so close to his own swam before his eyes.

Was he dreaming, or was it really she? He could not trust his eyes, he felt that he must touch her.

Slowly he put out his hand, and gently, tremblingly touched her white, slender wrist.

Instantly she raised her eyes and looked at him, a long, piteous look, as if he had struck her.

Yes, it was she. It was Una, his forest-maiden!

With a long breath he raised the cup to his lips and drained it, then sank down on the grass and took up his plate, scarcely knowing what he was doing.

The laughing voices around him seemed blurred and indistinct in his ears, the green trees and silver stream seemed to fade and vanish, and give place to the silent glade in which he had sat with the same beautiful girl bending over him.

Mechanically he went through the pretense of eating until a burst of laughter recalled him to himself.

"Look here!" shouted Dalrymple in boyish glee. "Here's the Savage, busy eating nothing!"

Jack laughed, awakened to the sense of the situation. He must nerve himself, if only for her sake.

"It must be sunstroke," he said lightly, staring at his empty plate. "Will somebody give me a piece of cake? I have always doted on cake. I like a piece with the candied peel on it, Lady Bell. Thanks. Now I am just going to begin my luncheon."

"Those persons who are tired of watching the Savage satisfy his barbaric appetite are requested to withdraw!" drawled Dalrymple, and he leaped to his feet, laughing.

"Seriously, if anyone would like to go up to the palace, I've an open door. I should like a row."

There was an instant clamor. Three parts of the party wanted to see the palace, and a couple of boat loads started.

Lady Clarence, Lady Bell, Una, and Jack remained.

He still kept up the pretense of eating and drinking; and Lady Bell, kneeling opposite him, seemed never to grow weary in supplying his wants.

Una, seated at a little distance, noticed with what eager attention she hung upon every word he uttered. And Jack kept on talking as if his life depended on it. But presently his patience came to an end.

He put down his plate resolutely.

"No more, thanks, or I shall be too heavy for the outrigger. Now, then, can't I help pack up?"

But Lady Bell wouldn't hear of it.

"No, you shall light your pipe," she said, "and watch us. Come, Una. I know you are dying to help us."

Una awoke with a start and knelt down beside the plates and dishes while Lady Bell went for the hamper.

Jack seized his opportunity. Bending forward, he whispered:

"Una!"

She half turned her face, pale and dreamy.

"Well?"

"Is it really you? How did you come here? Am I dreaming?"

"It is I," she said, in her low, musical voice.

"But—but," he said, "how did you come here? I did not know you were in London. I have been looking for you."

Her heart gave a great leap. He had been looking for her.

"I have been searching for you everywhere, Una. Did you think I should not come back? I went to Warden——"

"Yes," she said eagerly.

"And I found the cottage shut up and your people gone."

"Gone?"

"Yes, gone, and I did not know what to do. So I came to town, and—and I looked for you everywhere. Ah! you thought that I had forgotten you, as you had forgotten me."

Her lovely face flushed, and she turned her dove-like eyes upon him, with a reproachful look in their depths.

"Forgotten him!"

"I cannot understand it," he went on, drawing still nearer to her, his eyes eagerly scanning her face.

She smiled faintly. A great joy welled up in her heart, every nerve was tingling with happiness, she scarcely heard him. The words, "I have been searching for you," rang in her ears.

"I scarcely understand it myself," she said; "it seems like a dream."

Jack glanced toward the bank. They had finished the packing, and would interrupt them in another minute.

"Where are you staying? You are on a visit?"

"I am staying with Mrs. Davenant," said Una, in the same low voice.

Jack started, and the unlit pipe nearly fell from his hand.

"With Mrs. Davenant?" he exclaimed. "With Stephen's mother?"

Una nodded.

"Yes; he has been very kind and good to me."

Jack stared breathless.

"Stephen good to you!" he said, fiercely. "What do you mean? Am I dreaming?"

"It was he who came to Warden with Mrs. Davenant," said Una, vaguely, troubled by the stern look of suspicion which had settled like a cloud on Jack's face.

"I don't understand," he said grimly. "Stephen—Stephen! How did he know of your existence?"

"Some friend," said Una; "I do not quite know. At any rate, it was through him. And I like Mrs. Davenant."

Jack nodded.

"Yes, she is a good woman. But Stephen——"

And he passed his hand over his brow.

Una looked at him timidly.

"Are you angry?" she asked.

"Angry! with you!" he exclaimed, bending nearer, with a look of tender devotion. "How could you think it? No, I am not angry—only puzzled. I cannot make it out. Never mind! don't look so troubled, my dear—Miss Rolfe, I mean. At any rate, I have found you. Oh, Una!—Miss Rolfe, I mean—if you knew how I have searched for you, and"—with a groan—"what a fool I have been!"

"I thought you had forgotten me," said Una, with that sweet humility of love.

Jack's eyes gleamed.

"I have not forgotten you for one moment—not for one moment! Una, I——Oh, confound it! here they are."

He broke off impatiently, as Lady Bell and the rest came back.

"What are we going to do now?" she said, with her bright smile. "Some of them have gone to the palace. Shall we wait for them, or go and meet them! What do you say, Mr. Newcombe?"

But Jack would not stir.

"They'll come back," he said, absently, his eyes drawn toward the downcast face.

How lovely it was! If they would only all go away, and leave them alone! He had so much to say—so much to ask.

But Lady Bell showed no sign of going; instead, she threw herself down on the grass beside them, and commenced to talk.

Had he enjoyed the pull up? Why had he not driven down with them? She didn't believe in particular business; and so on.

Jack pulled at his pipe, and returned absent, scarcely civil answers. At last Lady Bell noticed his abstraction, and turned her head away in silence.

Meanwhile Una sat speechless, her face turned toward the river, her whole soul absorbed by his presence. It frightened her, this feeling of absorption. She found herself waiting and listening for every word that dropped from his lips as if her life depended on it. She trembled lest he should touch her.

His manner filled her with an ecstasy of pleasure that was almost pain. How handsome he looked, stretched out at full length, his tanned face turned to the sky, his tawny mustache sweeping his clear cut lips; she felt, rather than knew, that his eyes sought her face, and she dared not turn her eyes toward him, though she longed to do so.

CHAPTER XXIV

Presently, to the relief of Una, at least, the other boats came back; the third boat was got ready, the hampers put on board, and the ladies seated.

Jack stood near the stern, and took Una's hand in his to help her to embark.

"Take care," he said, aloud, then in an undertone, he added: "I shall see you at Richmond."

"Are you going to row the outrigger down, Savage?" said Dalrymple, eying the first boat enviously.

Jack turned to him eagerly.

"No, I'll take your place in this boat; I can see you are longing for mine. Here, get in"; and before Dalrymple could refuse, Jack had almost lifted him into the outrigger, and leaped into his place in Lady Bell's boat.

All the darkness vanished from his brow. He was sitting opposite Una; so near, that when he leaned forward to make the stroke, his hand almost touched her dress.

"Are you coming with us?" said Lady Bell; "I am so glad."

"So am I," said Jack; but his eyes went to Una's face.

"Now, then," said Jack, as he bent forward.

"Steady, old man," said Sir Arkroyd; "we haven't all got blacksmith's muscles!"

But Jack was wild, delirious with joy, and he pulled, heart and soul, his great, strong arms bare to the elbows.

"What a lovely night!" said Lady Bell. "Won't anybody sing?"

Of course no one replied.

"Sing something, my dear child," she said to Una. "You have a singing face. You have no idea how beautiful it sounds on the water."

"Oh, no, no," said Una, shrinking modestly.

Jack looked up.

"Sing," he murmured, pleadingly. As if he had uttered a command, she looked at him with meek obedience, and began the song he had heard her singing in the forest.

Is there anything more exquisite on earth than the voice of a young girl? Una knew nothing of the science of song; she had had no master, no instruction of any sort; but her voice was clear and musical as a young thrush's and she sang straight from her heart.

No need to tell Jack to pull slower! He ceased rowing, and rested on his oar, his eyes fixed on her face, his lips half apart.

The other boats stopped also as the music of the sweet, young voice floated down the stream, and one and all felt the spell.

Lady Bell sat with lowered lids and pale face, and when the last note died away and she looked up, her eyes were moist.

"My dear," she said, in a low voice, "where did you learn to sing like that?"

Una, half frightened at the effect she had produced, flushed and sank back into her seat.

"I have never learned," she said, quietly.

There was a murmur, and Lady Clarence turned and looked at her curiously.

"You have a beautiful voice," she said, "and exquisite taste, or you could not sing as you do. It is a pity you have not been thoroughly trained. You should have a master."

"She shall!" said Lady Bell, impulsively. "She shall have the best. It would be criminal to let such a gift be wasted!"

Jack looked up with a flush of pleased gratitude, and Lady Bell happened to catch that glance.

With a slight start she turned pale, and looked from his face all aglow with the fervor of loving admiration to Una's downcast one, and then, with something like a shudder, she, too, sank back into the seat.

"Isn't—isn't it cold?" she said, in a strangely changed voice.

"Is it?" said Jack, musing. "We'll row on," and he bent to the oar again.

A peculiar silence fell upon them all; it seemed as if they were still listening to the sweet voice. Lady Bell closed her eyes and remained motionless, and Jack pulled as if he had undertaken to reach Richmond within a given time.

At Richmond tea was brought to them on the terrace while the horses were put to, and very soon they were dashing toward London.

Dalrymple declared that his arms were too stiff to allow him to handle the four grays properly, and Jack was unanimously voted to the box.

He looked rather inclined to refuse, but seeing that Una had been seated close behind him, he climbed up and took the reins without a word.

For the first mile or two he had quite enough to do to keep the nags in hand; but he could feel that Una was close behind him, could feel her breath on his cheek, and hear every word of the clear, low-pitched voice, and he was deliriously happy.

Presently, when he had got the horses into steady working, he turned his head and pointing with his whip, as if he were directing her attention to some object in the landscape, said in a low voice:

"Una, can you hear me?"

"Yes," she said, leaning forward.

"I have been thinking it all over," he said, "but I can't make head or tail of it. It's all a mystery. However, I know where you are now, and that's something; and I can come and see you, and that's everything—to me Are you angry with me for speaking so—so boldly?"

"No," she faltered.

"And I may come and see you? I know Mrs. Davenant; she is a good creature, though she thinks me everything that's bad—and she's not far wrong, I'm afraid——"

Una sighed faintly.

"And perhaps she'll tell me what it means, and why Stephen has sent you to be with her. Why, Una, did your father allow you to come? He loathed me for being a distant relative of the Davenants."

"I do not know," said Una, troubled.

"Never mind," said Jack, hastening to soothe her; "it's sure to be all right, if he did it. I liked your father, notwithstanding he was so rough with me. I liked him because he took such care of you. Steady, silly!" This was to the near leader, and not to Una. "What a lovely night! Are you enjoying it?—are you happy?"

A sigh, faint and tremulous, was full answer.

"Please Heaven, we'll have many a night like this. Happy! I could go half mad with delight at having you so near me. Una—I may call you Una?"

"Yes," she murmured.

"Can you guess—you sweet, innocent flower—what makes me so happy?"

"Tell me!" she answered, in a low voice, and leaning forward until her soft, silken hair almost touched his.

Jack's heart beat fast, and his blood bounded in his veins.

"It is because I love you. I love you! Do you understand? Ah, my darling! you don't know what love is. But I ought not to call you so—not yet. I can't see your face; perhaps I shouldn't dare to be so bold if I could. Speak to me, Una; speak to me. Tell me that you are not angry. Tell me that, while I have never had your sweet face out of my mind since that day we parted in Warden, you have thought once or twice of me. I don't deserve it. I'm a bad lot; but I love you, Una. Do you love me?"

There was no reply; but there was a soft nestle beside him, and then he felt her hand timidly touch his arm.

He slipped the whip and reins into one hand, and seized the little trembling hand and enclosed it as if he meant thus to swallow it up forever.

But, alas! the horses were going down hill, and were fidgeting and pulling; and with impatient exclamation at their stupidity, he was obliged to let the little hand go; but it did not go far; he could feel it touching, softly and timidly, the edge of his coat-sleeve, and that was enough for him. It was a mercy and a miracle that the drag was not upset, for he scarcely knew where or how he was driving, and it was more by instinct and habit that he brought the team safe and sound, but sweating tremendously, before the house in Park Lane.

"You must all come in," said Lady Bell.

The gentlemen looked at their white flannels apologetically, but Lady Bell laughed.

"Let us pretend that we are our own masters and mistresses for one night," she said, "and not the slaves of Fashion."

Jack stood out. He felt that, for the present, it behooved him to be discreet, and he knew that if he were not, it would be impossible for him to conceal the romantic love which burned through and through him. Besides, he knew that there would be no opportunity of speaking to Una there; and he felt that it would be agony for him to assume the conventional air of polite indifference to her for that evening, at least.

So he went. But he stood on the pavement to help her down; and as he held her in his arms, he kept her for one moment poised between heaven and earth; and as he put her down, his lips touched her arm, and she knew it.

"I'll see to the horses, Dal," he said; and he leaped up, and drove off as if he were possessed.

"That's what the Savage calls seeing to them!" grumbled Dalrymple. "He'll throw 'em down, or run over somebody, and I shall be fined five pounds for furious driving."

Jack was conscientious—where horses were concerned—and he sat on the rack and saw them rubbed down and fed with the patience of a martyr; then he jumped into a hansom, was driven to Spider Court, and, bursting into the room, fell into a chair and flung his cap at Leonard's head.

"Mad at last!" said Leonard.

"Yes, stark, staring, ramping mad, old fellow. I've found her!"

"No!" said Leonard, turning round.

"Yes! Yes! And I've spent the day with her. She's here in London, and who do you think she is staying with? With Mrs. Davenant, Stephen's mother!"

"Stephen's mother!" said Leonard, with surprise. "Nonsense."

"Fact! What do you make of it?"

Leonard Dagle mused in silence.

"I can make nothing of it," he said at last.

"Did she know Mrs. Davenant?"

"No; that's the mystery. Stephen, it seems, is the cause of her being here. He found out her father—how I can't guess—he must, of course, have known her before; there's nothing wonderful in that. But what is wonderful is that Stephen should do anyone a good turn, unless—unless—" and his face darkened suddenly and grew fierce—"unless he had some end in view."

"What end could he have in view here?" said Leonard.

"That's what I can't make out; can you?"

Leonard shook his head.

"It's a strange story throughout."

"It is," said Jack, grimly. "But, Stephen Davenant, if you mean any mischief, look out! I'm on your track, my friend! But, Len, old man, you look rather done up. What's the matter?"

Leonard passed his hand over his brow.

"Something strange and mysterious also," he said. "I went to Cheltenham Terrace an hour ago, just on the chance of getting a glimpse of—of——"

"Of Laura Treherne. Well, old man?"

"And I met with a similar shock to yours in Warden Forest. I found the house shut up, and she—gone, vanished, disappeared!"

"What!" exclaimed Jack.

Leonard paced up and down.

"I went to inquire next door, and I learned that old Mr. Treherne was dead—you remember my telling you that the blinds were down—that the funeral took place yesterday, and Miss Treherne had gone. They only lodged there, it seems, and of course she could go at any moment. Where she has gone no one seems to know. So there is an end to my little romance! But no! it shall not end there."

"No; take courage by my luck, old man," said Jack, laying his hand on his shoulder—"take courage by me! Let us talk about it."

"No, no!" said Leonard, shrinking; "I cannot—yet. You don't know how I feel. Tell me what happened today. Was she glad to see you? Did you let her see that you cared for her? Of course you did."

"Yes," said Jack, with a proud, happy smile. "Yes, I told her that I loved her, and—oh, Len! Len! I know that she cares for me!"

Leonard stared at him gravely, and put down a paper which he had taken up. But Jack saw it and took it off the table.

"What are you reading there, Len?"

Leonard took it out of his hand.

"My poor, light-hearted, unreasoning Jack," he said. "It's Levy Moss' reminder about that bill!"

Jack's face fell and he dropped into a chair.

"Quite right, Len," he said, hoarsely. "I am an unreasoning fool! What have I done? I've behaved like a blackguard! I've got this angel to admit that she loved me—me, a beggar—more than a beggar! But I swear I forgot—I forgot everything when I was near her. Oh, Heaven, Len, it's hard lines! What shall I do! If the poor old squire had but left me a few hundreds a year, how happy we could be!"

"But he hasn't," said Leonard, gravely and gently. "And what are you going to do? There's the money you lost last night——"

Jack groaned.

"What an idiot I was. Len, I swear to you that I was nearly driven out of my mind last night. First there was Lady Bell—she was more than civil, and bearing in mind all you said and wanted me to do, I made myself agreeable, and—and—she's very beautiful, Len, and when she looks right into your eyes and smiles, she seems to do what she likes with you. Len, I was nearly gone when that vision—as I thought it—came into the glass amongst the ferns. I thought it was a vision—I know now that she was there—and it drove me silly. I bolted out and made for the club, and played to forget it all."

"And made bad matters worse," said Leonard. "You're in a hole, Jack, I'm afraid. Moss won't wait; there are other bills, and there's the I. O. U. of last night, and you've lost the money you had, and you've asked this young girl to love you. You mean to marry her—I say, you mean to marry her. On what? How can you go to her father—who already doesn't seem altogether prepossessed in your favor—and ask him to give his daughter to a penniless gentleman? Mind—a gentleman! If you were a woodman like himself, your being hard up wouldn't matter. You could take an ax, or whatever they use, and earn your living. But you can't go and ask him to let her share your over-due bills and I. O. U.'s."

Jack groaned.

"What shall I do, Len? My darling, my darling!"

Leonard sighed. His heart—the heart of as true a friend as ever the world held—ached for the wild, thoughtless youth.

"Was Lady Bell there?" he asked, quietly.

Jack leaped to his feet.

"Lady Bell! I see what you mean!" he groaned. "Len, you are in love yourself, and yet you ask me to sell myself——"

Leonard flushed.

"Jack, much as I care for you, I swear that I am thinking as much of her good and happiness as of your own. If you marry her—which, after all, you *cannot*—if you could you would make her life miserable; if you marry Lady Bell, you will at least make *her*—happy."

Jack paced up and down for a moment. Then he turned, white and haggard, and held out his hand:

"You are right. Would to Heaven you were not! I see it, I cannot help it. I will not make her life miserable. But—but—I must go and tell her. Heaven help us both!"

CHAPTER XXV

Where ignorance is bliss 'tis folly to be wise. Quite ignorant and unconscious of all that was going on in London, Stephen remained down at the Hurst.

What he had written to his mother was quite true; as a matter of fact Stephen was far too clever to write direct falsehoods—he was kept at Hurst Leigh very much against his will.

Squire Ralph had left him everything—money, house, lands, everything excepting the few legacies to servants, and Stephen had been hard at work, and was still hard at work ascertaining how much that everything was.

And, as day followed day, and disclosure succeeded disclosure, he became fascinated and possessed by the immense wealth which had fallen into his hands, or, say rather, which he had seized upon.

For many years the old squire had lived upon less than half his income; the remainder he had invested and speculated with, and as often happens to the miser, the luck of Midas had fallen upon him.

Everything he touched had turned to gold. The most unlikely speculations had proved successful; properties which he had bought for a mere song, and which had been regarded by the most wary as dangerous and profitless, had become profitable and valuable.

Some of these risky speculations he had, not unnaturally, kept concealed from the prudent Hudsley, who only now, by the discovery of scrip and bonds in out-of-the-way desks and bureaus, learned what kind of man his old friend had really been.

Not a day passed but it brought to light some addition to the old man's gains, and served to swell the immense total.

Even the lands round Hurst had been manipulated by the old man, so that leases ran out almost at his death, and rents were raised.

One speculation will serve as an instance; he had purchased, some fifteen years before his death, the freehold of an estate bordering upon London; and in a locality which was then regarded as hopelessly unfashionable. A great capitalist had ruined himself by building large houses on the property, foreseeing that at some time or other the tide of the great city would reach this hitherto high and dry spot. But he had made a miscalculation, and he died before the tide which was to bring him wealth reached his property; old Ralph had then stepped in and bought it—houses, land, everything. In ten years' time the tide of fashion rolled that way, and now what had once been a neglected and forgotten quarter was the center of fashionable London.

It reads like a romance, but like many other romances, it was true.

Old Ralph himself had no idea of his own wealth, and that when he died he should leave behind him one of the most colossal fortunes in England.

Almost stunned by the immense total—so far as it had been arrived at—Stephen went about the place silent and overwhelmed.

But one thought was always ringing like a bell in his brain—"And I had nearly lost all this!"

Sometimes, in the quiet of the library, where he sat surrounded by books and papers, by accountants' statements and estimates, he would grow pale and tremble as he reflected by what a narrow chance he had secured this Midas-like wealth.

But had he secured it? and when the question presented itself, as it did a hundred, aye, a thousand times a day, he would turn ashy pale, and clutch the edge of the table to keep himself from reeling.

Where was that will—the real, true, valid will—which left everything away from him to Una?

Day by day, while going over the accounts, he found himself waiting, watching, expecting someone—whom he could not imagine—coming in and saying: "This is not yours; here is the will. I found it so and so, at such and such a time!" and he felt that if such a moment occurred it would kill him.

But as the days passed and no one came to contest his claim to the property, he grew more confident and assured, and at last he nearly succeeded in convincing himself that he really had burned the will.

"After all," he mused, over and over again, "that is the only probable, the only possible explanation. Is it likely that if anyone had the accursed thing they would keep it hidden? No! If they were honest, they would have declared it at once; if dishonest, they would have brought it to me and traded upon it. Yes, I was half mad that night. I must have destroyed it at the moment Laura knocked at the window."

But all the same he determined to make his position secure. Immediately he had arranged matters at the Hurst he would go to London and marry Una.

"She is all safe and sound there," he mused, with a satisfied smile. "My mother leads the life of a hermit. The girl herself has no friends—not one single soul in London. I shall be her only friend, and—the rest is easy."

Poor Stephen!

Then he would give a passing thought to Laura, and now and then would take from his pocket half a dozen letters, which she had written to him since the night of her journey to Hurst.

To not one of these had he replied, and the last was dated a week back.

"By this time," he thought, "she has forgotten me, or what is better, has learned that plain Stephen Davenant and Squire Davenant of Hurst Leigh are two very different men. Poor Laura! Well, well, I must do something for her. I'll make her a handsome present. Say a thousand pounds; perhaps find a husband for her. She's a sensible girl, too sensible to dream that I should think of marrying her now. After all, what harm is done? We were very happy, and amused ourselves with innocent flirtation. A mere flirtation, that is all."

And he tried to forget the pale face and flashing eyes which turned toward him that night at parting with such a strange look of warning. But he did not always succeed in forgetting. Sometimes the remembrance of that face rose like a vision between his eyes and the endless rows of figures, and made him shudder with mingled fear and annoyance.

"It has been a lesson to me," he would say, after awhile. "It is the only weakness I have ever been guilty of, and see how I am punished. I deserve it, and I must bear it."

It punished him, and it told upon him. The pallor which had come upon his face the day the will was read had settled there. The old look of composed serenity and "oiliness," as Jack called it, had gone, and in the place was a look of strained intentness, as if he were always listening, and watching, and waiting.

He was a fine actor, and would have made a fortune on the boards, and he managed to suppress this look at times, but the effort of suppression was palpable; he showed that he was affecting a calmness and serenity which he did not possess.

By two men, of all others, this change in him was especially noticed—by Mr. Hudsley and old Skettle.

The old lawyer and his clerk were necessarily with him every day; Stephen could not move a step without them. He hated Hudsley, whose keen, steel-like eyes seemed to penetrate to his inmost heart; and he detested Skettle, whose quiet, noiseless way of moving about and watching him from under his wrinkled lids, irritated Stephen to such an extent that sometimes he felt an irresistible desire to fling something at him.

But both of the men were indispensable to him at present, and he determined to wait until everything was straight before he cut all connections with them.

"Once let me get matters settled," he muttered to himself over and over again, "and those two vultures shall never darken my doors again."

And yet Hudsley was always scrupulously polite and civil, and Skettle always respectful.

With his characteristic graveness, Mr. Hudsley went through the work systematically and machine-like.

But Stephen noticed when he came to announce some fresh edition to the great Davenant property, he never even uttered a formal congratulation, or seemed pleased and gratified.

One day Stephen, nettled beyond his usual caution, said: "You must be tired of all this, Mr. Hudsley. I notice that it seems to annoy you."

And the old lawyer had looked up with grim impassibility.

"You are mistaken, Mr. Stephen. I am never tired, and I am never annoyed."

"At least you must be surprised," said Stephen; "you had no idea that my uncle had left so much."

"No, I am not even surprised," retorted Mr. Hudsley, if his calm reply could be called a retort. "I have lived too long to be surprised by anything."

And there was something in his keen, icy look which silenced Stephen, and made him bend over his papers suddenly.

Others noticed the change which had come over the once sleek, smooth-spoken young man. It got to be remarked that he rarely left the Hurst grounds, and that what exercise he took was on the terrace in front of the library, or on the lawn below it. It was said that he paced up and down this lawn for hours.

It was said, too, that he rarely addressed a servant in or out of the house. All the orders came through the valet Slummers.

Mention has been made of Slummers. It would have been difficult to describe him. He was called in the village "the Shadow," because he was so thin and noiseless, so silent and death-like.

In addition to his noiselessness, he had a trick of going about with closed eyes, or with his lids so lowered that it looked as if his eyes were closed.

Bets had been made upon the supposed color of those visional organs, but had never been decided, for never by any chance did he look anyone in the face when speaking; and when by some accident those sphinx-like lids were raised they were dropped again so quickly that examination of what lay behind them was impossible.

Secretiveness was part and parcel of this man. He never did anything openly. When he gave an order it was in a round-about way. The simplest action of his daily life was enveloped in mystery. Even his meals were taken in a room apart; only a few of the servants knew the room he occupied. Then he seemed ubiquitous. He was everywhere at once, and turned up when least expected.

With noiseless step he came and went about the house; now in the servants' hall, now in the library closeted with his master, now in the stables looking under his lids at the horses, counting, so said the grooms, every oat that went into the mangers. Not a thing was done in the house but he was acquainted with it.

And he knew everything! Not a secret was kept from him. Had anyone in the village an episode in his life, which he hoped and deemed hidden and forgotten, Slummers knew it, and managed by some dropped word or look to let the miserable man know that he knew it.

Before he had been at Hurst a week he had half the servants and villagers in his power.

Power! That was the secret mainspring of the man's existence. He loved power.

Give even the fiend his due. This man had one good quality, he was devoted to his master. Saving this one great event of his life—the theft and loss of his will—Stephen trusted him in everything.

And Slummers admired him. In his eyes Stephen was the cleverest man on earth, and being the cleverest man on earth Slummers was content to serve him. Yes, Slummers was devoted to his master, but he made up for it in his detestation of the rest of mankind in general, and of one man in particular—Jack Newcombe.

Between Jack—honest, frank, and reckless Jack—and the serpent-like Slummers there had been a feud which had commenced from the moment of their first introduction.

On that occasion Slummers had been sent with a message to Jack's room. Jack happened to be out, and Slummers whiled away the tediousness of waiting by opening a drawer in Leonard's table and reading some unimportant letters. Jack, coming in with his usual suddenness, caught him and kicked him. Jack had forgotten it long ago, but Slummers had not, and he waited for the time till he could return that kick in his own fashion.

The days passed, and Mr. Hudsley's task appeared to be nearing a conclusion.

One morning he came up to the Hurst, his hands behind his back, his head bent as usual, and asked for Stephen.

Stephen was in the library, and Slummers noiselessly ushered in the lawyer. It happened to be what Stephen would have called one of his bad mornings. He was seated at the table, not at work, but looking at the pile of papers with lack-luster eyes, that saw nothing, and pale, drawn face.

Hudsley had seen him like this before, but his keen eyes looked like steel blades.

Stephen started and put his thin, white hand across his brow.

"Good morning," he said. "Good morning. Any news? Sit down."

But Hudsley remained standing.

"I have no news," he said. "I think I may say that there are no more surprises for us. You know the extent of the fortune which you hold!"

He did not say "which is yours," or "which your uncle left you." Simply "which you hold." On Stephen's strained mind the phrase jarred. He nodded and kept his eyes downcast.

"The business that lies within my province," continued Mr. Hudsley, "is completed. What remains is the work of an accountant. My task is done."

"I am sure," said Stephen, smoothly, "that you do not need any assurance of my gratitude— —"

The old man waved his wrinkled hand.

"I have been the legal adviser of the Davenant family for the last forty years," he said, "and I know my duty. I trust I have done it so far as you are concerned," he said, sternly. "And now I have come to you to request you to receive what papers and documents are in my charge—my clerk, Skettle, will hand them to you and take your receipt—and to inform you that I wish to withdraw from my position as your legal adviser."

Stephen's pale face winced and shrunk, and he raised his eyes suspiciously.

"Mr. Hudsley, you surprise me! May I ask your reasons for this abrupt withdrawal?"

"My reasons are my own," said Hudsley, dryly; "I may say that I am growing old, and that I am disinclined to undertake the charge of so large an estate."

"Oh!" said Stephen, with a sickly smile. "Such a reason is unanswerable. But I deeply regret it—deeply. My uncle always trusted you."

"He did nothing of the sort," interrupted Mr. Hudsley, sternly. "He trusted no man."

"At any rate, I have placed implicit and well-merited confidence in you," said Stephen.

The old man looked at him and Stephen trembled.

"I—I hope I shall find your bill of costs among the papers?" he said, hoarsely.

"No," said Mr. Hudsley. "What service I have rendered you I consider as rendered to the estate. The estate has paid me sufficiently hitherto. I need, I will receive no other payment."

"But——" urged Stephen.

Mr. Hudsley waved his hand.

"I am quite resolved, sir. If you should need any information respecting any business that has occurred up to the present, I am at your service; but for the future I beg to withdraw. Good-morning."

Stephen rose, and held out his hand.

"At least, Mr. Hudsley," he said, "we part as friends, notwithstanding this hasty resolution of yours?"

"It is not hasty, sir," said Hudsley, and just touching the cold, thin hand, he bowed and left the room.

Stephen sank into a chair, and wiped the drops of cold sweat that had accumulated on his brow.

"He suspects me," he muttered. "He suspects! But he suspects only, and he can do nothing, or he would have done it. Yes; he is powerless. Let him go! let him go!" he repeated; and he paced the room.

Gradually the relief of Hudsley's withdrawal broke upon him, and his step grew lighter.

"Yes, let him go! Now I am free—I am my own master! master of wealth undreamed of! And I'll use it! By Heaven, I'll be happy! Let him go! I meant to get rid of him—he has saved me an unpleasant scene. And now to work, to work!"

He ran rather than walked across the room, and rang the bell.

Slummers opened the door almost instantly and stood motionless and silent.

"Has—has that old idiot gone?" asked Stephen.

"Yes, sir," said Slummers.

Stephen laughed hoarsely.

"Let the past go with him!" he said. "Slummers, go to my room and bring a roll of papers from my bureau-drawer. You know what they are! Plans and estimates. Do you know what I am going to do?"

Slummers raised his eyes.

"Of course you do!" said Stephen with the same laugh. "I'm going to make a clean sweep here, Slummers. I'm going to pull half this beastly place to the ground. Alterations, Slummers—alterations that will make Hurst a place for a man to live in, not a tomb, as it is at present."

"You are right, sir, it is a tomb," said Slummers, in his low, hollow voice.

Stephen shuddered.

"Yes, yes; but I mean to alter that. I'll make it fit to live in, fit to bring a young bride to. Fetch the plans, Slummers; I'll go over them at once, this minute. Yes, I will change the place till the very trees shall not know it. Fetch the plans! I'll pull the whole of it down, every stick and stone! I hate it—hate it! I'll change the name! I can do it. I can do anything now, or what is the use of this money? Fetch the plans! Fetch——" He broke off suddenly and staggered.

Slummers sprang nervously forward and caught him, and putting him into a chair, poured out some neat brandy and gave it to him.

Stephen tugged at his collar and struggled for a moment, then sank back helplessly.

"Stop!" he said, "stay here. Don't go. I—I can hear voices—an old man's voice—what is it?"

"Nothing—nothing," said Slummers. "Be calm, sir."

"Calm—I am calm!" retorted Stephen. "It's this beastly house, it's full of noises! Give me some brandy—and—get the time table. I'll go to London to-morrow, Slummers. Yes, I'll go to London!"

And the master of Hurst, the owner of a million and more, sank back in his chair and fingered the time table with trembling fingers.

CHAPTER XXVI

"Jack Newcombe!" exclaimed Mrs. Davenant, looking at the card which Mary had brought in. "Jack Newcombe!" she repeated a second time. "My dear, come here!"

Una was sitting beside the open window, a book in her lap, her eyes fixed on the sun setting just behind the chimneys.

"Yes," she said, her face flushed, her eyes glowing as if the sun were reflected in them; but she did not move.

Mrs. Davenant hurried across the room with the card in her hand.

"Una, dear, see here," she said, nervously. "Here is Jack Newcombe! You've heard me speak of him."

Una, feeling guilty and deceitful, hung her head.

Her heart beat fast. For two days she had waited and watched for him—never for a moment had he been absent from her mind.

And now he was here, in the next room.

"Yes," she said, "I—I remember."

"Well, my dear, I don't know what to do. I don't know what he wants—do you?—but of course you don't!"

Una flushed crimson to her very neck.

"I think you had better go, my dear," said Mrs. Davenant, fidgeting with the card.

Una did not move.

"Why?" she asked, raising her eyes for the first time.

Mrs. Davenant moved her head nervously.

"Because—I don't think Stephen—I mean—Jack Newcombe is the sort of man you ought to know."

"But," said Una, softly and with a steady look in her dark eyes, "I do know him already."

Mrs. Davenant stared.

"You know him? Jack Newcombe?"

Una nodded.

"Yes," she said in a low voice. "I met him up the river. I saw him at Lady Bell's—he is a friend of hers——"

"But why didn't you tell me?" said Mrs. Davenant, looking distressed and frightened.

Una felt guilty.

"I don't know," she said in reply. "I think it was because I knew you would feel angry."

Mrs. Davenant stared at her. It was like the reply of a child in its simple, naked truth.

"Well, well," she said, with a troubled voice, "of course you couldn't help it, and I couldn't help it. And"—here the door opened quietly, and Jack's head appeared, and Mrs. Davenant started.

Seeing that they were alone, Jack came in with his usual coolness, though his heart beat; and he crossed the room, and took Mrs. Davenant's hand and kissed her forehead.

And the poor woman melted in a moment, as she always did when Jack was actually present. As a matter of simple truth, she was really as fond of him as if he had been her own son, and but for Stephen, Jack would have seen her oftener.

He had lost his mother in early boyhood, and the kind-hearted, affectionate, timid Mrs. Davenant had often dried his boyish tears and held him in her arms. Even now, notwithstanding Jack's wickedness, of which Stephen made the most, her heart went out toward him.

He had not been near her for some months, nearly a year, all through Stephen, and she had almost given him up; but Jack's kiss revived all the old tenderness. And what woman could resist his handsome face and frank, manly way?

"Well, ma'am," he said—and "ma'am" sounded in her ears and in Una's almost like "mother" — "and how are you? And aren't you glad to see me?"

"Yes, Jack," said Mrs. Davenant, nervously.

"Then why do you keep me in the draughty hall for half an hour? Do you want me to catch cold?"

"Half an hour?" murmured Mrs. Davenant. "I'm sure you haven't been there three minutes."

"Two minutes and a half too long," he said, smiling. He was giving Una time to recover herself.

"You never come to see me now, Jack," said Mrs. Davenant, looking up at him sadly.

"And now I do, you keep me outside. Besides, you never ask me. Who's that in the back room, ma'am?"

Mrs. Davenant started; she had almost forgotten Una.

"You know her!" she said.

Jack had got his cue.

"Oh, it's Miss Rolfe," he said, and then he crossed the room and held out his hand.

Una rose, and without a word put her hand in his, her eyes downcast, lest the love which beamed in them should escape against her will.

"Yes," said Jack, "I have had the pleasure of meeting Miss Rolfe once or twice lately."

Then he turned away from her and began talking to Mrs. Davenant, as if Una were not in the room.

It was just what Una wanted. She felt that she could not speak, and for the present it was happiness enough to have him in the same room with her, and to hear his voice.

And Mrs. Davenant, now that the first shock was over, was glad enough to sit down and listen to the frank, musical voice—so unlike Stephen's measured, modulated tone.

Presently she said in a low, nervous tone:

"Jack, I am so sorry!"

Jack nodded, and his face dropped.

"About the poor squire? Yes! Never mind. It is all right. No! It's all wrong for me, but all right for Stephen."

"But Stephen doesn't—doesn't want it all," she murmured.

Jack looked another way; he had a different opinion.

"Never mind," he said, "don't let us worry about it—you and I. It's all past and gone, and there's no help for it."

"But you have worried," she said. "You don't look so well as you did, Jack. I hope—I do hope," and her voice faltered.

Jack's face flushed for a moment.

"You are going to scold me, as usual," he said. "Well, go on, it will be your last opportunity, ma'am. I've reformed."

There was something in his tone, something so earnest and grave, that she looked at him anxiously.

"Oh, Jack, I wish—I wish you would be more steady."

"Wait and see," he said, gravely, and in a low voice.

Mrs. Davenant wiped her eyes, and glanced at the clock. It was near the dinner hour.

"Do you want me to go?" said Jack, in his blunt way, and he took up his hat and gloves.

Mrs. Davenant hesitated a moment.

"You wouldn't stop to dinner, if I asked you," she said, with a faint smile.

Una's heart gave a great leap.

"Try me," said Jack. "Yes, I'll stay. Now don't look frightened and disappointed, or I'll go."

Mrs. Davenant rose, with her rare laugh.

"I must go and tell them," she said, "or you'd be starved," and she left the room.

Jack went and stood beside the silent, motionless figure and looked down at her with infinite yearning and infinite sorrow. He had come resolved to tell her the truth and to bid her to forget him.

"Una," he said, in a low voice.

She raised her eyes, and in an instant his grand resolution, built up with such care for the last two days, crumbled into dust. With something like a groan he was on his knee and caught her to his breast.

For a moment she resigned herself to the exquisite joy of his embrace, and with downcast eyes drooped beneath his passionate kisses, then with an effort she regained possession of the soul which had slipped from her into his, as it were, and gently disengaged herself.

"No, no, you frighten me!" she murmured, as Jack's arm drew her toward him again.

"My darling! There!" and he kissed her hands. "How can I do it? It is too much to ask of mortal man."

"Do what?" she murmured.

Jack's face paled.

"Nothing—nothing," he said.

"And are you really going to stay?" she murmured, her eyes beaming with pleasure.

"Yes," he said, "I came on purpose. If she had not asked me I meant to ask her."

"And you love her, don't you? Is she not good—and isn't it cruel to deceive her," said Una, and she hung her head.

"She's the dearest old lady in the world," said Jack, enthusiastically, who would have loved a gorilla, much less Mrs. Davenant, if it had been kind to Una. "Why, she was a second mother to me until Stephen grew up— and she has been kind to you. I can see that for myself. But you must tell me all about it—all about everything tonight. Think, my darling! we shall be together here all the evening! No noisy crowd to prevent us talking—no interference. I shall want to know everything. Hush! here she comes," and with another swift kiss he rose and went into the next room. Una stole out and upstairs to dress.

Quite unsuspicious, Mrs. Davenant came back smiling. She had ordered one or two of Jack's favorite dishes, and had come to ask him about the claret.

"There is some of the Chateau la Rose, Jack. Would you like to have it warmed a little?" she asked, anxiously.

"Let them put a bottle in the kitchen somewhere," said Jack. "It will get right there by dinner time. Eight o'clock you dine, I know. I'll just run home and dress, and be back punctually to the minute."

"It will be the first time in your life then," said Mrs. Davenant.

For the first time in his life then Jack was punctual. At five minutes to eight a hansom dashed up to the door, and Jack, in evening dress, with his light overcoat, strode up the steps and into the drawing-room.

It was empty, but a minute afterward he heard the rustle of a woman's dress, and turned as Una entered the room. She wore the dress she had worn at Lady Bell's, and Jack, who had not yet seen her in her "war paint"—as he would have described it—was startled; and Una, as she saw the look of surprise and rapt admiration, felt, like a true woman, a glow of satisfaction and pleasure. It was not that she was beautiful, but that he should think her so.

"My darling," he murmured, holding her at arm's length; "what magic charm do you possess that enables you to grow more beautiful every time I see you? Or is it all a mistake, and are you another Una than the Una of Warden Forest?"

Una put her hands on his shoulders trustfully, and turned her face up to him.

"Tell me," she murmured, "which Una do you like best?"

Jack thought a moment.

"I love them both so well," he said, "that I can't decide." And he kissed her twice. "One is for the Una of the Forest, and one for the Una of the world," he said.

She had only time to slip from his arms when Mrs. Davenant entered.

"What do you say to punctuality, ma'am?" he exclaimed, triumphantly, as he gave her his arm and lead her into the dining-room.

Jack was a favorite, for all his wickedness, wherever he went. It was no sooner known that he was to dine in the house, that the cook awoke to instant energy and enthusiasm.

"Master Jack's a gentleman worth cooking a dinner for," she declared. "It's a waste of time to worry yourself for women folk; they don't know a good dinner from a bad one; but Master Jack—oh, that's a different thing! He knows what clear soup ought to be; and he shall have it right, too."

Mrs. Davenant herself was surprised at the elaborate little dinner.

"I wish you'd dine with us every day, my dear Jack," she said.

Jack glanced demurely at Una, in time to catch the sparkle in her dark eyes.

"I'm afraid you'd soon get tired of me," he said. "But, seriously, I should improve the cooking; not this day's, I mean, but the usual ones. You've got a treasure of a cook, ma'am."

And, of course, this was carried down by Mary to the empress of the kitchen, and her majesty was rewarded for all her trouble.

"What did I tell you?" she demanded. "Master Jack knows."

Jack's appetite was always good, in love or out of it, and this evening would have been the happiest in his life but for certain twinges of conscience.

What should he say to Leonard, the faithful friend, when he got home and was asked how he had parted from Una? However, he stifled conscience—it is always easy to do that at dinner time.

"Will you have some more claret?" asked Mrs. Davenant, as she and Una prepared to leave him. "You can smoke a cigarette, if you like; but open the window afterward."

"I won't have any more claret, and I won't smoke," said Jack. "I'll just finish this glass and come with you for a cup of tea."

Five minutes of solitude spent in going over every look and word of the lovely creature he had won, were enough for Jack.

He found them seated at the window; Una in a low chair, almost at Mrs. Davenant's feet. They both looked up, as if glad to see him; and Mrs. Davenant at once rang for tea and coffee.

Una rose, and officiated with calm self-possession and accustomed ease—no one would have guessed that her acquaintance with a London drawing-room, and its accompanying forms and ceremonies, was only that of a few weeks—and brought Jack his cup.

In taking it, he tried to touch her hand, and nearly upset the cup.

"Take care, my dear Jack," said Mrs. Davenant. "Has he spoiled your dress, my dear?"

"No," said Una, her face red as a rose. "It was my fault."

"Yes; it was her fault," said Jack, significantly.

"You always were clumsy, my dear Jack," said Mrs. Davenant. "You are too big."

"I'll get myself cut down a foot or two," said Jack.

Happy! They were as happy as any two women in London, notwithstanding Jack's wickedness.

Jack glanced at the piano.

"I wish you could play," he said to Una.

Mrs. Davenant looked at him.

"How do you know she cannot?" she said.

Jack looked embarrassed.

"I rather fancy I heard U—Miss Rolfe—admit as much. But she can sing, I know."

"And you can play for her," said Mrs. Davenant. "You used to play very nicely when you were a boy," and she sighed.

Jack looked dubious for a moment, then, with sudden assurance and confidence, jumped up.

"Let me try. Will you come, Miss Rolfe?"

Una followed him to the piano, and Jack turned out all the music from the canterbury on the floor.

"Come and see if there is anything you know," he said, and Una knelt down beside him.

Of course Jack's hand was on hers in a moment.

"I nearly let the cat out of the bag just then," he said. "I must be careful."

"But why?" asked Una. "Why may we not——" she paused, then, having raised her eyes, she continued—"why may she not know?"

"So she shall," said Jack, "all in good time. I can't consent to share my secret all in one evening! Besides——"

"Cannot you find anything," said Mrs. Davenant, sleepily, from the next room.

Jack stuck up some music on the stand and sat down.

He had played well at one time, in a rough fashion, and had a wonderful ear, and, quite regardless of the music, he launched into a prelude.

"Sing the song you sang the other evening, my darling," he whispered. "I remember every note of it."

Una obeyed instantly. Free from any spark of vanity, she knew nothing of the shyness which assails self-conscious people. Jack, with his acute ear, played a running accompaniment easily enough; it was true he had remembered every note of it.

"You nightingale," he whispered, looking up at her, and the fervent admiration of his eyes made her heart throb.

"Now sing something yourself, Jack," said Mrs. Davenant.

Jack thought a moment, his fingers straying over the keys, then softening his full baritone voice as much as possible, he sang—"Yes, dear, I love but thee!"

It was an old English song, one of the sweetest of the old melodies which even now have power to rouse a *blase* audience to enthusiasm.

Una stood behind him entranced, bewitched; he sang every word to *her*.

"Yes, dear, I love but thee!"

Oh, Heaven, it was too great a joy!

Unconsciously she drew nearer and put her hand upon his shoulder, timidly, caressingly, and as the music ceased, Jack turned and caught it prisoner in his.

"Yes, dear, I love but thee!" he murmured.

"And I"—she breathed, her eyes melting with passionate tenderness—"and I love but thee."

"My darling," he whispered, "do you know what you are giving me—your precious self—and to whom you are giving it?"

The voice fell; conscience was awake again.

"Una," he went on, hurriedly, passionately. "I am not worthy of your love——"

"I love but thee!" she breathed, softly.

"You do not know, you who are so ignorant of the world, what it means to wed a man like myself, penniless, worthless—oh, Heaven, forgive me!"

"I love but thee!" she breathed, for all her answer.

Jack bent his head over her hand.

"What can I do?" he murmured, bitterly. "I cannot give her up."

Then he looked up.

"Have you no fear, Una? Do you trust me so entirely? Think, can you face poverty and all its trials. Dear, I am very poor, worse than poor."

She smiled an ineffable smile.

"And I am rich—while I have your love."

Then suddenly her voice changed, and with a look of terror she bent over him, almost clingingly.

"What is it you are saying? Jack! Jack! you will not leave me?"

Jack started to his feet, and regardless of waking Mrs. Davenant, took her in his arms.

"Never, by Heaven!" he exclaimed.

There was one moment of ecstatic joy, then suddenly Una drew back; and with a gesture of alarm, pointed to the looking-glass. Jack raised his head, and with a sudden cry drew her nearer to him as if to protect her.

Reflected in the glass was the thin figure of Stephen Davenant, looking rather like a ghost than a man—silent, motionless, with pallid face, and set, rigid eyes.

CHAPTER XXVII

White and haggard, Stephen stood in shadow-way, his eyes fixed on Jack and Una with an expression of mingled astonishment and rage beyond all description.

Jack was too astonished by what seemed as much an apparition as a reality, to withdraw his arm from round Una's waist, and it was she who first recovered self-possession enough to cross over to Mrs. Davenant and wake her.

Her movement seemed to recall Stephen to a sense of the situation, and in a moment he rose and coped with it.

Another man, a weaker man, coming thus suddenly upon what looked like the wreck of all his deeply-laid plans, upon seeing the girl, whom it was all-important he should secure for himself, in the arms of the man he hated and feared most in the world, would have given vent to his wrath and disappointment. But not so Stephen. By a vast effort, he suppressed the evil glance in his eyes, forced a smile to his compressed lips, and came across the room with outstretched hand and an expression of warmest and most affectionate greeting.

"My dear Jack!" he exclaimed, in his soft tones, almost rough in their warmth and geniality. "Now, this is a pleasant surprise. How do you do? how do you do?"

But almost before Jack knew it, Stephen had seized him by the hand, and was swinging it convulsively, smiling so that all his teeth glittered and shone in the candle-light.

Jack was taken by surprise, and returned the greeting cordially; indeed, what else could he do, seeing that he was in Stephen's mother's house, and making love to Stephen's *protegee?*

"Quite a surprise!" said Stephen, laughing; and then, still talking to Jack, he crossed over and bent down to kiss his mother. "How do you do, my dear mother? Now don't be angry at my taking you so unexpectedly."

"Angry, my dear Stephen!" faltered Mrs. Davenant; and indeed, it was not anger so much as fear that shone in the timid eyes.

Then, having got himself completely under control, Stephen raised his eyes to Una, and held out his hand.

"And how do you do, Miss Rolfe? I hope your health has not suffered in this close London of ours. May I say that there are no signs of such an ill result in your face?"

Una gave him her hand, and smiled at him in her quiet, grave way.

"I am very well, thank you," she said.

"That's right," said Stephen—"that's right!"

And he stood and looked from one to the other, rubbing his white, soft hands, and smiling as if he were over-running with the milk of human kindness.

Meanwhile Mrs. Davenant had risen, and was fluttering about nervously.

"Have you dined, Stephen? We can get some dinner, or—or something directly."

"My dear mother, I dined at my rooms two hours ago; but if you have a cup of tea, now; but don't trouble—it does not matter in the slightest."

Fresh tea was brought in, and Una, as usual, officiated. Stephen, leaning over a chair-back, talked to Jack and Mrs. Davenant, but his eyes turned continually on the graceful figure and the beautiful profile; and not one of them guessed the rage and fury which boiled and simmered under his calm and amiable exterior.

Already, as if some one had told him, he knew that Una had been out into the world. Her dress, her manner told him that; and while he smiled lovingly at his mother, he was crying out inwardly:

"Fool! fool! to trust Una to her."

He took his cup of tea, his hand as steady as a rock, and chatted with Jack, full of the pleasantest interest.

Where had he been, and what had he been doing? and was he in those eccentric but charming rooms of his in the Temple still? and how was his friend Leonard Dagle?

He was full of questions, questions which Jack answered in his curt, brief fashion. And all the while Stephen was weighing the situation, realizing all its danger and peril, and determining on a course of action.

"Just one more cup, Miss Rolfe, if you please. Tea is my favorite beverage—I am quite an old washerwoman!"

Then he took his cup, and sat down beside her.

"Yes," he said, not in a particularly low tone, but in his softest manner— "yes, I am glad to see that your health has not suffered in London. I trust you have been happy?"

Una looked up with a faint flush on her face.

"I have been—I am very, very happy," she said, and Jack's face flushed too with the delight at the accent on "I am."

"That is right," said Stephen, with the air of an old, old friend, "and I hope my mother has found some amusement for you—that she has shown you something of the great world."

"Yes," said Una, and she glanced at Mrs. Davenant, from whose pale face all traces of the calm serenity which had reigned there during the earlier part of the evening had entirely fled—"yes, I have been very gay—is not that the word? I have been to a ball, and to a picnic, and have seen all the sights."

"And where was the ball?"

"At Lady Earlsley's," said Una.

Stephen opened his eyes and smiled.

"My dear Miss Rolfe, you have penetrated the most exclusive of social rings! Lady Earlsley's! Come, that is very satisfactory; and Jack—Jack is my cousin—well, very nearly cousin, you know, I hope he has made himself useful and agreeable?"

Una glanced shyly and gravely at Jack—a glance that told everything, even if Stephen had not seen her in Jack's arms.

"Yes," she said, in a low voice, "Mr. Newcombe has been very—kind."

Stephen smiled and showed all his teeth.

"I am afraid there will be nothing left for me to do," he said.

Then, in a lower voice, he added:

"You will be glad to hear that I have news of your father."

Una looked up breathlessly. The question had been hovering on her lips.

Stephen nodded.

"Yes, he wrote me from a place in Surrey called—tut—tut! The name has escaped me! They are quite well, and send their fondest love."

Una's eyes filled.

"Why did they leave the cottage so suddenly?" she said.

"Because your father wished for a change. I told you truth, you see, when I said that your departure would be good for him, and wean him from his seclusion."

"Why does he not come to see me?" asked Una.

"He is coming, my dear Una," said Stephen. "But at present he is very much engaged, and quite satisfied with my favorable report of your health and happiness. But come, I must not make you homesick. Were you not playing when I came in?"

Una flushed.

"Jack—Mr. Newcombe—was playing," she said; "I was singing."

"Pray don't let me interrupt you," said Stephen, genially, "or I shall feel like an intruder, and walk off again. Jack, go on with your music, my dear fellow."

But Jack declined promptly, though politely.

"I'm afraid I must be off," he said, looking at his watch, and then at Una, wistfully.

"Not yet," said Stephen. "I have a whole budget of news to tell you. I dare say you wonder why I haven't been up before this, but there was so much to do—a surprising deal."

Jack nodded curtly. He certainly didn't want to finish up this particular evening by hearing Stephen's talk of the Hurst.

"No doubt," he said. "You must come and dine with me and tell me. Good-night, Mrs. Davenant!"

Mrs. Davenant gave him her hand.

"Must you go, Jack?" she said, tremulously. "You—you will come again?"

"Most certainly I will," said Jack, significantly.

Una had risen and gone to the piano to gather up the music which Jack, with his usual untidiness, had scattered about.

He followed her, and knelt down as if to help her.

"Good-night, my darling!" he murmured, touching her arm caressingly. "Don't be afraid."

Una raised her arm and touched it with her lips.

"Afraid—of whom?"

"Of—nobody!" said Jack, rather ungrammatically.

"Not of Mr. Davenant, who has been so kind?" she whispered, with a surprised look.

Jack bit his lip.

"No, no; certainly not. Oh, yes, he has been kind."

Then with a long, loving look into her sweet face he crossed the room.

"Good-night, Stephen."

"You are really going? Well, then, I'll go with you," said Stephen. "Mother will not mind my running away tonight, I am rather tired."

And he stooped and kissed her, and went to the door.

It almost seemed as if he had forgotten Una; but he turned suddenly and held out his hand, a bland, benevolent smile on his pale face.

"Good-night, good-night," he murmured, softly, and followed after Jack, who, the moment he reached the pavement, looked out for a hansom; but Stephen linked his arm in Jack's, and said:

"Are you in a hurry, my dear Jack? If not, I'll walk a little way with you; or will you come toward my rooms?"

Jack consented to the latter course, by turning in the direction of the "Albany" in silence.

He felt that Stephen was playing a part—why or wherefore he could not guess—and now that he had recovered from his surprise at Stephen's sudden appearance, his old mistrust and dislike were returning to him.

They walked on in silence for some few moments, then Stephen said:

"I wanted to have a few words with you, my dear Jack. I should have written, but I felt that I could make myself understood better by word of mouth."

Jack nodded.

"Of course, what I have to say concerns my poor uncle's death and its consequences."

Jack was silent still. He would not help him in the slightest.

"I cannot but feel that those consequences, while they have been distinctly beneficial to me, have—and to put it plainly, and I wish to speak plainly, my dear Jack—have been unfortunate for you."

"Well," said Jack, grimly.

"Well," said Stephen, softly, "I had hoped, I still hope, that you will allow me the happiness of setting right, to some extent, the wrong—yes, I will say wrong—done you by my uncle's will."

"That's impossible," said Jack, gravely.

"But, my dear Jack, why not? It is my right. Have you any idea of the fortune——"

"Not the slightest," said Jack, breaking in abruptly, "and it's no business of mine; large or small, I hope you'll enjoy it. It was the squire's to do as he liked with, and I suppose he did as he liked; and there's an end of it."

Stephen winced and bit his lip.

"And now," said Jack, quietly, but with his heart beating wildly, "I want a word with you, Stephen."

"Say on, my dear Jack. If there is anything I can do for you——"

"Yes, there is," said Jack. "I want to know—I want you to tell me—something respecting Miss Rolfe."

"Miss Rolfe!" said Stephen, softly.

"Yes," continued Jack. "You'll want to know, before I go any further, on what grounds I ask for information. I'll tell you. I have asked Miss Rolfe to be my wife."

Stephen feigned a start of astonishment.

"My dear Jack, isn't that rather sudden—rather premature?"

"It may be sudden, I don't know whether it is premature; that's for Miss Rolfe to decide. And she has decided."

Stephen moistened his lips; they burned like coals.

"She has accepted you?"

"She has," said Jack, who felt reluctant to utter one word more than was necessary.

Stephen pulled up and held out his hand.

Only One Love | 219

"My dear Jack, I congratulate you. I congratulate you," he exclaimed, fervently. "You are indeed a happy man."

Jack, confounded, allowed his hand to be wrung by the soft, white palm that burned hot and dry.

"You are a lucky fellow, my dear Jack. Miss Rolfe is one in a thousand. I question if there is a more beautiful girl in London—and her disposition. You are indeed a lucky fellow."

"Thanks, thanks!" said Jack, still overwhelmed by this flood of good will. "And now, perhaps you will tell me what I had better do in the affair! You see I find her visiting—settled, rather, at your mother's house, and neither she nor your mother seem to know why or wherefore——"

Stephen interrupted him with a pressure of the arm.

"I understand, my dear Jack; your anxiety for information is only natural. I am very glad I came up this evening—very glad! And now, as I feel rather tired, would you mind coming up to my rooms? and we'll have a hansom, after all."

Jack hailed a cab, and they were rattled to the Albany.

Of course they could not talk, and Stephen had therefore time to perfect his scheme; for he had already begun to plot and plan.

The door of the chambers was opened by Slummers, his tall, square figure dressed in black, his discreet, shifty eyes absolutely veiled under his lids.

"Let us have some Apollinaris and the liquor-case, Slummers," said Stephen, "and that box of cigars which Mr. Newcombe liked. Sit down, my dear Jack."

And he wheeled forward a chair facing the light, and took one for himself, so that his own face should be shaded.

Jack looked round the room while Slummers brought the tray.

The four walls were nearly covered with books, all of them of the dryest and most serious kind. Where any space was left, it was filled up with portraits of eminent divines and philanthropists, and every article in the room was neatly and methodically arranged. In fact, it presented as marked a contrast to Jack's rooms as it was possible to conceive.

Jack had not been inside it for years, but he remembered distinctly how he used to loathe the room and its "fixings."

"Now, my dear Jack, pray help yourself—those cigars I know you approve; I heard you praise them at the Hurst, and I brought a box at once."

"Thanks," said Jack, and he lit a cigar.

Stephen mixed the Apollinaris and brandy; and leaned back serene and amiable.

"And now, my dear Jack, I am ready to answer all questions."

Jack looked down and frowned thoughtfully. He did not know how to put them. Stephen smiled maliciously behind his hand.

"You want to know how it comes about that Miss Rolfe is under my mother's charge—under my charge, I may say?"

"Under yours?" said Jack, grimly.

Stephen nodded.

"It is a very simple affair, Jack. There is no mystery. The fact is, I have known Miss Rolfe's father for some years. He is a very good fellow, but very eccentric."

"I know," said Jack; "I've seen him."

Stephen started, and concealed his expression of surprise by reaching for his glass.

"Ah, then, no doubt, you noticed that his appearance and manner does not correspond with the station he occupies?"

"I did," said Jack.

"Yes, yes, just so. Well, my dear Jack, my poor friend Rolfe has been in early life unfortunate—money matters, which I never quite understand. Like most men of his kind, he got disgusted with the world and hid himself—there is no other word for it. But it is one thing to hide yourself and quite another to bury your children. My friend Rolfe felt this when he awoke to the fact that his daughter had grown from a child to a young woman, and like a sensible man he applied to one who was conversant with the world, and one in whom he could have, I trust, full confidence—my self."

Jack sat silently regarding the white, calm face with grim, observant eyes.

"He did not appeal to an old friendship in vain. I undertook the charge of Miss Rolfe on one condition. I may say two—one on her side, one on mine. Hers was that she should live with my mother, under her protecting wing, as it were; mine was that I should be the absolute guardian of the young girl committed to my charge."

Jack stared.

"You are Una's guardian?" he said, at last, with unconcealed surprise, as Gideon Rolfe's curse upon the race of Davenants flashed upon his memory.

Stephen Davenant smiled.

"You are surprised, my dear Jack. But think! It is very natural. Unless I had unquestionable control over the young lady, how could I answer for her safety? How guard her against the attacks of fortune hunters— —"

Jack started.

"Fortune hunters!" he exclaimed. "Do you mean to say that Una is an heiress?"

Stephen's face had flushed and turned deadly pale.

He had actually been thinking of Una Davenant while he had been talking of Una Rolfe.

"You did not hear me out, my dear Jack," he said, softly, recovering his composure instantly. "I was going to say against the attack of fortune hunters who might besiege her under the impression that, as my ward, she would be possessed of wealth, instead of being, as you know, absolutely penniless."

Jack nodded.

"At any rate," he said, grimly, "I was not so deceived."

"My dear Jack!" exclaimed Stephen, reproachfully, "do you suppose that I do not know that! You, who are the soul of honor and disinterestedness, are not likely to be mistaken for a fortune hunter by anyone, least of all by me, who know and love you so well!"

Jack winced, as the vision of Lady Bell rose before his eyes.

"Go on," he said, impatiently.

"Well, my dear Jack," said Stephen with a smile, and rubbing his hands softly, "is it not rather for you to go on? I am Una's guardian, you are her lover."

"I see," said Jack, rising and pacing up and down the room. "You want me to ask your consent formally. Well, I do so."

Stephen laughed as if at an excellent joke.

"What a grim, thorough-going old bulldog you are, my dear Jack!" he exclaimed affectionately. "You ask my consent, as if you did not know that you have it, and my best, my very heartiest wishes into the bargain. But, Jack, don't you see why I am so pleased—why this makes me so happy? It is because now you will be compelled to do me the favor of taking a share of the poor squire's money!"

Jack started as if he had been stung.

"You see, my dear fellow! you can't marry on nothing—now, can you? Love must have a cottage, and—but I beg your pardon, my dear fellow! I am, perhaps, going too far. Much to my grief and regret you have never confided in me as I should have wished, and perhaps—I hope that it may be so—you have some means——"

Jack paced up and down, the perspiration standing on his knitted brow.

In the ecstatic joy which had fallen upon him like a glamour during those few short hours with Una, he had absolutely forgotten that he was penniless, and in debt, and without a prospect in the wide world.

And now it all rushed back upon him; every softly-spoken word of Stephen's fell upon him like a drop in an icy shower bath, and awoke him from his dream to the stern reality.

What was he to do? Great Heaven, was he actually driven to accept Stephen's charity?

A shudder ran through him, a pang of worse than wounded pride.

Become a pensioner of Stephen Davenant's! No, it was simply impossible. White and haggard with the struggle that was going on within him, he turned upon the smiling face.

"What you want—what you propose, is impossible," he said, hoarsely. "I cannot and will not do it. I would rather beg my bread——"

Stephen smiled. It was a delicious moment for him, and he prolonged it.

"My dear Jack! what would Mr. Gideon Rolfe say if I gave his daughter to a beggar? I use your own words. It is ridiculous. But come, sit down. Grieved as I am at what I must call your mistaken obstinacy, I can't help being touched by it. You always were willful, my dear Jack, always. Alas! it was that very willfulness that estranged you from my uncle——"

"No more of that," said Jack, sternly.

Stephen made a gesture with his hand.

"And it would, if another man were in my place, rob you of your sweetheart; but it shall not. I am determined to prove to you, my dear Jack, that my desire to be a friend is sincere and true. Let me think. There may be some loophole in your pride which I can creep in at."

Jack went back to his seat and lit another cigar, and Stephen appeared lost in thought, but in reality he watched through his fingers, and gloated over the despair and trouble depicted on Jack's miserable countenance.

"Yes, I have it. Come, Jack, you won't refuse assistance when it comes from the hand of her Majesty? You won't object to a government appointment?"

"A government appointment?" said Jack, vaguely.

Stephen nodded.

"Yes," he went on. "By a singular chance I have acquired some influence with the present government. One of these men has a seat in Wealdshire, which really hangs on the Hurst influence. The squire never interfered, but I could do so; and—you see, my dear Jack—a snug little sinecure, say of a thousand a year! It is not much, it is true; but Una has not been accustomed to wealth so long as to feel a thousand a year to be poverty."

Jack rose and paced the room. Was he dreaming, or was this a different Stephen to the one he knew and disliked? He had heard of sudden wealth as suddenly transforming the nature of a man. Had Stephen's nature undergone this marvelous change?

He doubted and mistrusted him, but here was the absolute evidence. What could Stephen gain by this generosity? Nothing—absolutely nothing. It was strange, passing strange; but who was he that he should refuse to believe in the generosity and virtue of another man, especially when that generosity was exerted on his behalf?

Struggling against his suspicion and prejudice, Jack strode round the table and held out his hand.

"Stephen, I—I have wronged you. You must be a good fellow to behave in this way, and I—well, I have been a brute, and don't deserve this on your part."

Stephen winced under the hard grip of the warm, honest hand.

"Not a word more, my dear Jack; not a word more," he exclaimed. "This—this is really very affecting. You move me very much."

And he pressed his spotless handkerchief to his eyes.

Jack's ardor cooled at once, and the old disgust and suspicion rose; but he choked them down again, and sat down.

"Not a word more," said Stephen, with a gulp, as if he were swallowing a flood of tears. "I have long, long felt your coldness and distrust, my dear Jack, but I vowed to live it down, and prove to you that you have wronged me. Believe me that my good fortune—my unexpected fortune—was quite imbittered to me by the thought that you would misjudge me."

Jack pulled at his cigar grimly. Stephen was on the wrong track, and he saw it, and hastened to change it.

"But now, my dear Jack, we shall understand each other. You will believe me that I have your welfare deeply at heart. Who else have I to think of—except my mother, my dear mother? And we may conclude that our little negotiation as suitor and guardian is ended. Eh, Jack? You shall have the appointment and Una—lucky fellow that you are—and I shall be rewarded by seeing you happy."

Jack nodded. The mention of Una had filled him with gratitude. He could not forget that he owed her in two ways to Stephen.

"You are a good fellow, Stephen," he said, "and you deserve *your* luck. After all, you'll make a better master of Hurst than I should. You'll take care of it."

Stephen sighed. He was going to gloat again.

"I don't know. I wish to do my duty. It is an immense sum of money, Jack; immense."

Jack nodded again.

"I'm glad of it," he said, easily. "I don't envy you. I did once, and not very long ago. But I rank Una above the Hurst even, and if I have her, you are welcome to the Hurst."

Stephen winced, and looked at him from the corners of his eyes. Was there any significance in the speech? But Jack's face was open and frank, as usual.

"That's a bargain," said Stephen, laughing.

Jack thought a moment.

"But what about Mr. Rolfe?" he said, dubiously.

"Leave him to me," said Stephen, confidently. "I will manage him. And, by the way, I think for the present that we had better keep our little engagement quiet. You understand? He had better hear it from my lips, and—you quite see, Jack?"

Jack didn't quite see. He would have preferred to go to Gideon Rolfe and have the matter out—fight it out if need be—but he was, so to speak, in Stephen's hands.

"Very well," he said.

"And now have another cigar, my dear Jack, you've eaten that one."

But Jack was anxious to go. He wanted to be alone to think over this strange interview, and realize that Una was his.

"Well, if you will go," said Stephen, reluctantly; "but mind, I shall expect you to make this your second home."

Jack glanced round rather dubiously.

"And of course we shall see you at the Square?"

This invitation Jack accepted heartily, and once more he wrung Stephen's hand.

"Good-night, good-night, my dear Jack," said Stephen, and he took a candle from the table to light him down the stairs, and smiled till every tooth in his head showed like a grave-stone.

Then, as Jack's heavy step faded away and was lost, Stephen went back into the room, closed the door, and sinking into a chair sat motionless, with folded arms and haggard face.

"Yes, yes," he muttered, "I have played the best game—I have gulled him. Another man would have attempted to thwart him openly, and have raised a storm. My plan is the wiser. But to think that fate should have played me such a trick! and I thought she was safe and secure!" and he wiped the drops of cold sweat from his knitted brow. "Fool, fool that I was! Better to have left her there in the heart of the Forest! And yet—and yet—" he mused, "it is not so bad. The man might have been more powerful and cunning than the idiot whom I have in the hollow of my hand. Curse him! curse him! I never look on his face but I tremble. I hate him!" and he stretched out his closed hand as if with a curse.

As he did so it came into contact with Jack's glass.

In a paroxysm of fury he caught up the glass and dashed it into the fire-place.

It relieved and brought him to his senses.

With a gesture of self-contempt he rose and rang the bell.

Slummers stole in with his noiseless step and stood beside the table with downcast eyes, which, nevertheless, had taken in the broken tumbler.

"I've broken a glass, Slummers," said Stephen, with affected carelessness. "Never mind, leave it till the morning. Now, then, what have you learned?"

Slummers cleared his throat, and barely opening his thin lips, replied:

"A great deal, considering the time, sir. The young lady at Mrs. Davenant's— —"

"I know all about her," said Stephen, breaking in impatiently. "What about Mr. Newcombe?"

Nowise embarrassed, Slummers wiped his dry lips with a handkerchief as spotless as his master's.

"It is as you expected, sir. Mr. Newcombe is in difficulties."

"Ah!" said Stephen, with evident satisfaction.

"He has been playing and giving paper. There are some old bills out, too. These are in the hands of Moss the money-lender."

Stephen nodded and rubbed his hands.

"I know Moss—a hard man. Go on."

"But they say," continued Slummers, raising his eyes for a moment to his master's face, "that Mr. Newcombe is going to set things right by marrying an heiress."

Stephen smiled and leaned back in his chair.

"Oh, they do, do they; and who is this most fortunate young lady?"

"Lady Isabel Earlsley."

Stephen started forward.

"What!"

"Lady Isabel Earlsley," repeated Slummers, without the slightest change of voice or countenance.

"No—it's a lie!" said Stephen, with a chuckle. "Where did you hear it?"

"At the club. It is the talk of town, sir. Mr. Newcombe has been in close attendance upon her ladyship for some time. They say that her ladyship's brougham nearly ran over him, and that she took him home. It is true; her own coachman told me."

Stephen leaned back and hid his face with his hand, his busy brain at work on this last turn of the wheel.

"Go on," he said.

"That is all, sir."

Stephen was silent for a minute or two, then he turned to the writing table and wrote for some minutes.

"Go to Moss to-morrow morning," he said, "and tell him not to press Mr. Newcombe, and I don't think he will require more than the hint—but you may say I will buy all Mr. Newcombe's bills at a fair price. Mind! I want every I O U and bill that Mr. Newcombe gives. You understand?"

"I understand, Mr. Stephen," said Slummers, and a faint, malicious smile stole over his face.

"And if Mr. Moss likes to oblige Mr. Newcombe with a little loan, I will take the bill. You understand?"

Slummers nodded.

"Here is the letter to Moss for his own satisfaction. He will not mention my name."

Slummers took the note. Stephen passed his hand over his forehead, and turned his back to the light.

"Any—any other news, Slummers?"

Slummers smiled behind his hand.

"I have been to Cheltenham Terrace. We were rightly informed, sir. Old Mr. Treherne is dead, and Miss Treherne has disappeared."

Stephen drew a breath of relief.

"Indeed," he said. "Very good. Let me see, is there anything else?"

Slummers coughed.

"Nothing, sir, except to remind you that you have to speak at the charitable meeting tomorrow night."

"Ah, yes, thank you, very good, Slummers. Be good enough to hand me the last charitable reports. Good-night."

CHAPTER XXVIII

Happy! If ever two young people were happy, Una and Jack were. To Una the days passed like a happy dream time. Her sky was without a cloud; it almost seemed as if the world had been made for her, so entirely did everything lend itself to her enjoyment.

Every morning, soon after breakfast, Jack's quick, buoyant step was heard ascending the stone steps of the house in Walmington Square, and he would come marching into the breakfast room with some palpable excuse about his just happening to pass, and Mrs. Davenant would smile her gentle welcome, and Una—well, Una's eyes were eloquent, if her tongue was mute, and would speak volumes.

And Jack would lounge about for an hour, telling them all the news, and perhaps smoking a cigarette, just inside the conservatory; and Una was sure to find an excuse for being near him.

Indeed, if that young lady could be within touching distance of her god and hero, she seemed passing content. He was the very light of her life, soul of her soul; every day seemed to increase the passionate devotion of her first, her maiden love, for the wild, young ne'er-do-well.

And she was repaid. Jack thought that there never had been, since Eve began the sex, such a marvel of beauty and grace and virtue as Una. He would sit for half-an-hour smoking and watching her in silence.

"Didn't one of those clever fellows say of a certain woman that to know her was a liberal education?" he said to Mrs. Davenant. "Well, I say, that to be in Una's presence, to watch her moving about in that quiet, graceful way of hers, and then to catch a smile now and again, is like reading a first-class poem; better, indeed, for me, because I don't go in for poetry."

Not that these young lovers spent all their time in silently watching each other. Every day Jack arrived with some plan for their amusement and enjoyment. Sometimes it would be:

"Well, what are you going to do today? What do you say to taking the coach to Guildford, getting a snack there, and back in the evening?"

Una's face would light up, and Mrs. Davenant would smile agreeably, and in half-an-hour they would be ready, and Jack, as proud of Una's beauty as if it were unique, would escort them to the "White Horse" in Piccadilly, and away they would spin through the lovely Surrey valleys to that quaintest of old towns in the hills. Sometimes Jack himself would take the ribbons, and, with Una by his side, "tool the truck," as he called the handsome coach, back to town.

Then, again, he never came without a box for one of the theaters or a stall for a concert; and though not over fond of classical music himself, was quite content to sit and watch the look of rapt delight in Una's face as she listened absorbed in Joachim's wonderful violin.

But most of all, I think, they enjoyed their days on the river, when Jack, attired in his white flannels, would pull the two ladies up to Walton or Chertsey, and give them tea in one of the quiet, river-side inns.

Ah! those evenings, those moonlight nights, when the boat drifted down stream, and the two young people sat, hand in hand, whispering those endless exchanges of confidence which go to make up lovers' conversations.

It was wonderful that Mrs. Davenant did not catch cold, but Jack took great care of her, and wrapped her up in his thick ulster; and she never seemed to grow tired of witnessing their happiness.

Sometimes Jack would ask Stephen to join them, but Stephen would always find an excuse. Now it was because he had an engagement with the lawyers; at another time he had promised to speak at some philanthropic meeting, or had promised to dine at the club. He would, however, occasionally dine at the Square, or drop in and take a cup of tea; and wore always the same friendly smile and genial manner.

Jack had become quite convinced that he had done Stephen a great deal of injustice, and now thought that Stephen was everything that was kind and thoughtful.

It was only at chance times, when Jack happened to catch the pale face off its guard, that the old doubts rose to perplex and trouble him; but then he always set them to rest by asking himself what Stephen could possibly have to gain by acting as he did.

Of course, all these outings by land and water cost a great deal of money, but Jack had found Moss, the money-lender, most suddenly and strangely complaisant.

Instead of dunning him for what was owing, Moss actually pressed him to borrow more, and Jack, always too careless in money matters, was quite ready to oblige him.

"I can pay him out of my salary, when I get the appointment," he said to Leonard, in response to the latter's remonstrances and warnings.

"Yes, when you get it," said Leonard.

"What do you mean?" said Jack. "Do you mean to hint that Stephen isn't to be relied upon?"

"I haven't the honor of knowing much of Mr. Davenant," said Leonard, "and so can't say whether he is more reliable than most public men who promise places and appointments; but I do know that men have grown gray-headed while waiting for one of those said places."

"You don't know Stephen," said Jack, confidently. "He can manage anything he likes to set his mind on. He is not one of my sort. He can't let the grass grow under his feet. There, stop croaking, and come and dine at the Square."

And Leonard would go, for he and Una had, as Jack said, "cottoned to one another."

Una felt all sorts of likings and gratitude for the man who had always been Jack's friend, and none of the jealousy which some girls feel for their lover's bachelor acquaintances.

"I am sure he is good and true, Jack," she said.

"Good! There isn't a better man in England," Jack affirmed. "And he's as true as steel. Poor old Len!"

"Why do you pity him?" said Una, who had not altogether lost her way of asking direct questions.

"Well, you see, there's a lot of romance about Len," said Jack; and he told her about Leonard's meeting with Laura Treherne.

"And he has never found her?" said Una.

"Not from that day to this," answered Jack.

"And yet he still remembers and loves her," murmured Una. "Yes, I like your friend, Jack, and I do hope he will meet with this young lady and be happy. I should like all the world to be as happy as I am!"

"Ah, but don't you see all the world aren't angels like you, you know," retorted Master Jack, kissing her.

Though, in accordance with Stephen's advice, the engagement had not been made public, the outside world was beginning to get an inkling of what was going on in Walmington Square.

Jack's friends at the club chaffed him on the unfrequency of his visits.

"There's some mischief the Savage is planning," said Dalrymple. "You scarcely ever see him here now; he doesn't play, and shuns the bottle as if it were poison, and he's altogether changed. I shouldn't be surprised if he were to take to public meetings like that distant cousin of his, Stephen Davenant."

"It is my opinion," said Sir Arkroyd Hetley, "that he spends all his time at Walmington Square, for my man sees him going and coming at all hours. The Savage is in love."

And gradually those rumors spreading, like the ripple of a stone in a pool, reached Park Lane, and got to Lady Bell's ears.

She had gone out of town for a week or two, and had, of course, seen nothing of Jack or Una, but on her return she drove to the Square.

Una and Mrs. Davenant were sitting by the tea table, and wondering whether Jack would come in.

Lady Bell's entrance made quite a little flutter.

"How do you do, Mrs. Davenant, and how do you do, Wild Bird?" and she kissed Una, and holding her at arm's length, scanned her smilingly. "What have you been doing to look so fresh and happy?" Here Una's face over-spread with blushes. "What a child it is! But see, here I am just from the seaside, and as pale, or rather as yellow as a guinea, while you are like a dairy-maid. My dear girl, you positively beam with happiness."

Mrs. Davenant and Una exchanged glances—glances that were not lost upon Lady Bell's acuteness.

"Is there a secret?" she said, quickly. "Have you come into a fortune? But, no, that can't be it, for I know that I've never been thoroughly happy since I came into mine."

"You always look happy, Lady Bell," said Mrs. Davenant.

"My dear, don't judge by appearances," said Lady Bell, in her quick way. "I am not always happy; most of my time I am bored to death; I am always worried and hurried. Oh, by-the-way, speaking of worries, can you recommend me a maid? My own, a girl who came from the colonies with me, and swore, after a fashion, never to leave me, has gone and got married. I should be angry if I didn't pity her."

"Don't you believe in the happiness of the married state, then?" asked Mrs. Davenant, while Una looked on smilingly.

"No," said Lady Bell, shortly. "Men are tyrants and deceivers; there is no believing a word they say. A woman who marries is a slave, and— —"

She broke off sharply, for the door opened and Jack entered. A warm flush rose to Lady Bell's face, and she was too much occupied in concealing it to observe the similar flush which flooded Una's cheeks.

Jack was striding in with Una's name on his lips, but he stopped short at sight of Lady Bell, and the flush seemed an epidemic, for it glowed under his tan.

"I thought you were at Brighton, Lady Bell," he said, as he shook hands.

"So I was—three hours ago. I came away suddenly; got tired and bored of it before I had been there three days. If there is one place more unendurable than another it is the fashionable watering-place. I bore it until this morning, and then poor Mrs. Fellowes and I made a bolt of it, or rather I bolted and dragged her with me. I left Lord Dalrymple and Sir Arkroyd in happy unconsciousness of our desertion."

"Then, at this moment, they are wandering about the Parade in despair," said Jack, laughing. And, as he laughed, he looked from one girl to the other, making a mental comparison. Yes, Lady Bell was beautiful, with a beauty undeniable and palpable, but how it paled and grew commonplace beside Una's fresh, spiritual loveliness.

He had held her hand for a moment when he entered, and now, as he carried the tea cup, he got an opportunity of touching her arm, lovingly, caressingly.

He longed to take her by the hand and say to Lady Bell:

"This is my future wife, Lady Bell," but he remembered Stephen's advice, and was on his guard, so much so that though she watched them closely, Lady Bell saw no sign of the existing state of things.

It was singular, but since Jack's arrival she did not seem at all bored or worried, but rattled on in her gayest mood.

"And what have you been doing since I left town?" she asked Una. "I hope Mr. Newcombe has made himself useful and attentive;" and she looked at Jack, who nodded coolly enough, though Una's face crimsoned.

"Yes, I've been doing the knight errant, Lady Bell. Mrs. Davenant and I are old friends—relations, indeed."

"Ah, yes," said Lady Bell. "I hear your son, Mr. Stephen, is in London."

In a moment Mrs. Davenant's face lost its brightness.

"Yes, yes," she said, nervously; "yes, he is in London."

"Where is he?" said Lady Bell, looking round as if she expected to see him concealed behind one of the chairs. "He's always addressing public meetings, isn't he?"

"Not always, Lady Earlsley," said Stephen, from the open doorway.

"Good heavens! Speak of the—angels, and you hear the rustle of their wings!" exclaimed Lady Bell, not at all embarrassed. "How did you come in, Mr. Davenant?"

"By the door, Lady Earlsley, which was open. Mother, you will lose all your plate some day."

"And what public meeting have you come from now?" asked Lady Bell, with a smile.

"I have been walking in the park," said Stephen, "and am at your ladyship's service."

"I am glad of it," said Lady Bell, quickly, "for I want you—all of you to come and dine with me tonight."

"Tonight!" echoed Jack.

"Tonight! Why not? You have plenty of time to dress. Come, it will be charity—there's an argument for you, Mr. Davenant—for Mrs. Fellowes and I are all alone; papa has gone to some learned society meeting. Come, I'll go home at once and tell them to get your favorite wines ready. What *is* your favorite, Mr. Newcombe?"

Jack laughed.

"I'd come and dine with *you*, Lady Bell, if you gave us ginger beer," he said.

Lady Bell laughed, but she looked pleased.

"Now, that is what I call a really good compliment—for a Savage," and she glanced at Jack archly. "We'll say half-past eight tonight to give you time to finish your chat. *Au revoir*," and waving her daintily-gloved hand, she flitted from the room.

"Would he dine with me if I had only ginger beer to offer him?" she asked herself, as she went back in the brougham. "Would he? He looks so honest and so true!—so incapable of a mean, unworthy action! I wish I were as poor—as poor as Una. How quietly she sits. She has just the air of one of the great ones of the earth—the air which I, with all my title and wealth, shall never have. I wonder who she is, and whether Mr. Stephen thinks her as beautiful as I do! He looked at her as he went in—well, just as I would that *some one else* would look at me. How handsome he is, so different to Stephen Davenant. Ah, me! I know now why Brighton was so hateful; if Jack Newcombe had been there I should not have hungered and pined for London! What a miserable, infatuated being I am. I am as bad as that foolish maid of mine. Yes, just as bad, for if Jack Newcombe came and asked me, I should run away with him as she did with her young man!"

Still thinking of him, she reached home and went up to her own room, where Mrs. Fellowes, the long-suffering, hastened to meet her.

"My dear, I'm so glad you've come. How long you have been."

"My dear, you say that every time I come in. What is the matter—another maid run away?"

"No, but a maid has come, at least a young person—I was going to say lady—who wants the situation."

"Well, a lady's maid ought to be a lady," said Lady Bell, languidly. "Where is she?"

"In my room," said Mrs. Fellowes. "She came with a note from Lady Challoner. It seems the poor girl has been in trouble—she has lost her father—and not caring to go for a governess——"

"For which I don't blame her," said Lady Bell.

"She is desirous of getting an engagement as a companion or lady's maid."

"A companion's worse off than a governess, isn't she?" said Lady Bell, naively.

Mrs. Fellowes smiled.

"Yes. What is her name?" asked Lady Bell.

"Well, there's the point," said Mrs. Fellowes. "Her name is Laura Treherne, but as some of her friends—she hasn't many, she says—might think that she had done wrong in taking a menial situation she wishes to be known by some other name."

"I hate mysteries and aliases," said Lady Bell. "I don't think I shall engage her. She'll be too proud to do my hair and copy all my dresses in common material. Well, I'll see her."

"I'll send her away if you like," said Mrs. Fellowes; "but I think you'll like her."

"Do you? Then I know exactly what she's like before I see her if she has taken your fancy. Some prim old maid in black cotton and thick shoes."

Mrs. Fellowes smiled and rang the bell, and bade a servant to ask the young person who was waiting to step that way.

Lady Bell began taking off her gloves yawningly, but stopped suddenly, and looked up with an air of surprise as the door opened and a tall girl, with dark hair and eyes, entered.

CHAPTER XXIX

Lady Bell overmastered her surprise, and asking the young girl to sit down, looked at her critically as she did so.

Yes, the girl was a lady, there could be no doubt of that. But it was not only the evidence of refinement in the face and the manner of the girl that struck Lady Bell; there was an expression in the dark eyes and clear-cut lips, slightly compressed, which roused her interest and curiosity.

It was a face with a history.

For the first time she looked at Lady Challoner's note.

"I see," she said, "that Lady Challoner knows you, Miss Treherne."

"She knew my grandfather," was the quiet answer. "He is dead."

"Lately?" said Lady Bell, glancing at the note.

Laura Treherne bent her head.

"Two months ago," she said, sadly.

"And have you no friends with whom you could go and live?"

"None who would care to have me, or to whom I should wish to go."

Lady Bell was silent for a moment—the girl interested her more each minute.

"Are you taking a wise step in seeking for a situation which is considered menial?" she asked.

Laura Treherne paused for a moment.

"I do not think it degradation to serve Lady Earlsley," she said.

Lady Bell smiled, not ill pleased.

"You mean to say that you would not accept any situation?"

Laura Treherne inclined her head.

"How did you know that I wanted a maid?"

"I heard it in the house where I am lodging," she replied.

"And you knew me?"

"Yes; I had heard of you, my lady."

"Have you any other testimonials besides this note of Lady Challoner's?"

"None, my lady."

Lady Bell hesitated.

"It is quite sufficient," she said; "but I am afraid you do not understand the duties of a lady's maid."

"I think so, my lady. What I do not know now, I can soon learn."

"That's true. And I see you do not wish your real name to transpire?"

"I would rather that it did not. I would rather be known by some other name," answered Laura Treherne.

"Why?"

There was a moment's hesitation, and the dark face paled slightly.

"I thought Lady Challoner had explained. My friends— —"

"You do not care for your friends to know that you are in a situation? You think their pride would be greater than your own?"

"Exactly, my lady."

"Well, I'll engage you," she said. "When can you come? I have no maid at present."

"Now, at once, if your ladyship wishes. I will stay now, and send for my luggage, if you please."

"Very well," said Lady Bell. "Come to my room in half an hour, and we will arrange matters. You have said nothing about salary."

"That I leave in your ladyship's hands."

"Like the cabmen," said Lady Bell, laughing. "Well, come to my room in half an hour."

Laura Treherne bowed and left the room, and Mrs. Fellowes lifted up her voice in remonstrance.

"My dear Bell, that letter may be a forgery."

"It might be, but it isn't. I can read faces, and I like that young lady's. Yes, she's a lady, poor girl. Well, she might have hit upon a worse mistress; I shan't bang her about the head with a hair brush when I'm in a temper, as Lady Courtney does her maid. There, spare your remonstrances, my dear. The girl's engaged, and I mean to keep her. And now there are three or four people coming to dinner, Mr. and Mrs. Davenant, Jack—I mean Mr. Newcombe—and that strange girl, Una. What a lovely creature she is! Do you know I rather think she will become Mrs. Stephen Davenant."

"She is a very nice girl," said Mrs. Fellowes. "She ought to make a good match."

"*Ay de me,*" said Lady Bell, with a sigh. "I'm sick of that word. Men and women don't 'marry' now, they make 'good matches.' My dear, I hate your worldly way of looking at matrimony. If I were a poor girl, I'd marry the man of my heart, if he hadn't a penny. Ah, and if he were the baddest of bad lots."

"Like Jack Newcombe, for instance," said Mrs. Fellowes, archly.

"Yes," said Lady Bell, turning with the door in her hand; "like Jack Newcombe," and she ran up to her room.

Punctual to the minute, Laura Treherne knocked at the door of the dressing-room. Lady Bell was seated before the glass, surrounded by her walking clothes, which, as was her custom, she had slipped out of or flung carelessly aside.

Without a word Laura picked them up and put them in the wardrobe, and without a word took up the hair brushes. Lady Bell watched her in the glass, and gave her a hint now and then, and when her hair was dressed glanced round approvingly.

"Yes," she said, "that is very nice; and you have not hurt me once. The last maid used to pull me terribly. I suppose she was thinking of her young man. By the way, are you engaged?"

The dark face flushed for a moment, then grew pale.

"No, my lady."

"I'm glad of it. Take my advice and don't be. That sounds selfish, doesn't it. Now you want to know what I am going to wear. I don't know myself. What would you choose? Go to the wardrobe."

Laura went to the wardrobe, and came back after a minute or two with a dress of black satin and lace looped up with rosebuds of the darkest red. It was one newly arrived from Worth.

Lady Bell nodded.

"Yes, that just suits me. Give me a lady for good taste! And now choose the ornaments. There is the jewel-box."

Laura chose the set of rubies and diamonds, and Lady Bell smiled again.

"I shall look rather Spanish. Never mind. Let us try them."

With deft and gentle hands Laura helped her to dress, and Lady Bell nodded approval.

"Am I ready?"

Laura hesitated a moment.

"Will your ladyship wear the pendant?"

Lady Bell glanced in the glass.

"Ah, I see, you think that is rather too much against the rosebuds. You are right. Take it off, please. Thanks. Put the key of the jewel-box in your pocket. Stay! there is a chain for you to wear it on;" and she took out a small gold chain. "You can keep that as your own."

Laura Treherne flushed, and she inclined her head gratefully.

Lady Bell was relieved; her last maid used to overwhelm her with thanks.

"And now I will go down. By the way, will you please tell Simcox—that's the butler—that the gentlemen will want Lafitte, at least, Mr. Newcombe will. I don't know what Mr. Stephen Davenant drinks. What's the matter?" she broke off to inquire, for she heard Laura stumble and fall against the wardrobe.

There was a moment's pause; then, calmly enough, Laura said:

"My foot caught in your ladyship's dress, I think."

"Have you hurt yourself?" asked Lady Bell, kindly. "You have gone quite pale! Here, take some of this sal-volatile."

But Laura declined, respectfully. It was a mere nothing, and she would be more careful of alarming her ladyship for the future.

Lady Bell looked at her curiously. The quiet, self-contained manner, so free from nervousness or embarrassment, interested her.

She stopped her as Laura was leaving the room.

"We haven't fixed upon a name for you yet," she said.

"No, my lady; any name will do."

"It is a pity to change yours—it is a pretty one."

"Will Mary Burns do, my lady? It was my mother's name."

"Very well," said Lady Bell; "I will tell Mrs. Fellowes that you will be known by that."

"That girl has a history, I know," she thought, as she went downstairs.

Punctual almost to the minute, Mrs. Davenant's brougham arrived.

The evenings had drawn in, and a lamp was burning in the hall; and a small fire made the dining-room comfortable.

Lady Bell welcomed Una most affectionately.

"Now we will have a really enjoyable evening," she said. "I hate dinner parties, and if I had my way, would never give nor go to another one. If it were only a little colder, we'd sit round the fire and bake chestnuts. Have you ever done that, Wild Bird?"

"Often," said Una, with a quiet smile, and something like a sigh, as she thought of the long winter evenings in the cot. How long ago they seemed, almost unreal, as if they had never happened.

"Oh, Una is very accomplished," said Jack; "I believe she could make coffee if she tried."

Very snug and comfortable the dining-room looked. Lady Bell had dispensed with one of the footmen, and had evidently determined to make the meal as homely and unceremonious as possible.

Never, perhaps, had the butler seen a merrier party. Even Stephen was genial and humorous; indeed he seemed to exert himself in an extraordinary fashion. Lady Bell had given him Una to take in, and he was most attentive and entertaining—so much that Jack, who was sitting opposite, and next to Lady Bell, felt amused and interested at the change which seemed to have come over him.

Could he have seen the workings of the subtle mind concealed behind the smiling exterior, he would have felt very much less at his ease; for even now Stephen was plotting how best he could mold the material round him to serve his purpose, and while the laugh was lingering on his smooth lips, his heart was burning with hate and jealousy of the rival who sat opposite.

For it had come to this, that he desired Una, and not only for the wealth of which he had robbed her, but for herself. As deeply as it was possible for one of his nature he loved the innocent, unsuspecting girl who sat beside him.

Tonight, as he looked at the beautiful face and marked each fleeting expression that flitted like sunshine over it: as he listened to the musical voice, and felt the touch of her dress as it brushed his arm, a passionate longing seized and mastered him, and he felt that he would risk all of which he was wrongfully possessed to win her—ah, and if she were, indeed, only the daughter of a common woodman.

"Curse him!" he murmured over his wine glass, as his eyes rested on Jack's handsome face. "If he had not crossed my path, she would have been mine ere now; no matter, I will strike him out of it, as if he were a viper in my road."

Meanwhile, quite unconscious of Stephen's generous sentiments, Jack went on with his dinner, enjoying it thoroughly, and as happy as it is given to a mortal to be.

Presently the conversation turned upon their plans for the autumn.

"What are we all going to do?" said Lady Bell. "You, I suppose, Mr. Davenant, will go down to your place in Wealdshire—what is it called?"

"Hurst Leigh," said Stephen, quietly. "Yes, I must go down there, I ought to have been there before now, but I find so many attractions in town," and he smiled at Una.

"And you, my dear?" said Lady Bell to Mrs. Davenant.

"My mother will go down with me," said Stephen.

Mrs. Davenant glanced at him nervously.

"And that means Miss Wild Bird, too, I suppose?" remarked Lady Bell.

"If Miss Una will honor us," said Stephen, with an inclination of the head to Una. "Yes, we shall make quite a family party. You will join us, of course, Jack?"

Jack, who had looked up rather grim at the foregoing, bit his lip.

"I don't quite know," he said, gravely.

"Surely you will not let the poachers have all the birds this year, Jack!" said Stephen, brightly. "Besides my mother will be quite lost without you."

"Do come, Jack," whispered Mrs. Davenant.

"I'll see," said Jack, grimly, and Una looked down uneasily; she understood his reluctance to go to the old place.

"Oh, we will take no refusal," said Stephen, buoyantly. "And what are your plans, Lady Bell?"

Lady Bell looked up with rather a start and a flush.

"I—I—don't quite know," she said. "I had been thinking of going to a small place we have at Earl's Court."

"Earl's Court!" exclaimed Jack. "Why, that is only thirteen miles or so from the Hurst."

"Is it?" said Lady Bell. "I didn't know. I haven't seen it. I'm ashamed to say that I haven't made a round of inspection of the property yet. My stewards are always bothering me to do so, but I don't seem to have time."

"A sovereign cannot be expected to visit the whole of her kingdom," said Stephen, with a smile. Lady Bell sighed.

"I often wish the old earl had left me five hundred a year and a cottage somewhere," she said, quietly. "I should have been a happier woman. Oh, here is the claret. Give Mr. Newcombe the Lafitte, Simcox. Mr. Davenant——"

"I always follow Jack's suit," said Stephen, rising to open the door for the ladies. "He is an infallible guide in such matters."

"Fancy a woman lamenting the extent of her wealth," he said, with something like a sneer, as he went back to the table. "If any girl ought to be happy that girl ought to be. What a chance for some young fellow! My dear Jack, if I had been in your place——"

Jack looked up with a tinge of red in his face.

"What nonsense. Lady Bell knows better than to be caught by such chaff as I am. Besides, I am more than content. I wouldn't exchange Una for a Duchess, with the riches of Peru in her pockets. What about the commissionership, or whatever it is, Stephen?"

"All in good time, my dear Jack. Those sort of things aren't done in a moment; the matter is in hand, and we shall get it, be sure. Meanwhile, if you want any money——"

"Thanks, no," said Jack, easily.

He had only that morning negotiated a bill with Mr. Moss for another hundred pounds.

Stephen smiled evilly behind his pocket handkerchief. He held that bill in his pocketbook at that moment, in company with all Jack's previous ones.

CHAPTER XXX

The two men sat beside the fire almost in silence. Jack was trying to get over his reluctance to go to the Hurst, and wondering what would become of him if he did not, and Una left him all alone in town; and Stephen was wondering whether it was time to strike the blow he meditated.

Very soon Jack jumped up.

"If you've had enough wine, let us join the ladies," he said, and went toward the door.

Stephen followed him, but turned back to fetch his pocket handkerchief.

Lying beside it, on the table, was a rose which had fallen from the bosom of Una's dress. He took it up, and looked at it with that look which a man bestows on some trifle which has been worn by the woman he loves, and then, as if by an irresistible impulse, raised it to his lips, kissing it passionately, and put it carefully in his bosom. As he did so, he raised his eyes to the glass, which reflected one side of the room, and saw the slight figure of a woman standing in the open door and watching him.

The light from the carefully shaded lamp was too dim to allow him to see the face distinctly, but something in the figure caused him to feel a sudden chill.

He turned sharply and walked to the door; but the hall was empty and there was no sound of retreating footsteps.

"Some servant maid waiting to come in to clear the table," he muttered.

But he returned to the dining-room, and drank off a glass of liquor before going to the drawing-room, from which ripples of Jack's frank laughter were floating in the hall.

Lady Bell was seated at the piano, playing and singing in her light-hearted, careless fashion; Jack and Una were seated in a dimly-lit corner, talking in an undertone.

Stephen went up to the piano and stood apparently listening intently, but in reality watching the other two under his lowered lids.

The presence of the rose in his bosom seemed to heighten the passion which burned in his heart; and the sight of Jack bending over Una, and of her rapt, up-turned face as she looked up, drinking in his lightest word as if it were gospel, maddened him.

It was with a start that he became conscious that Lady Bell had ceased playing, and that she, like him, was watching the lovers.

"Miss Una and Mr. Newcombe seem very good friends," she said, with a forced smile.

"Do they not?" said Stephen, in his softest voice. "Too good."

Lady Bell looked up at him quickly.

"What do you mean?"

Stephen looked down at her gravely.

"Can you keep a secret, Lady Bell?" he said, hesitatingly.

"Sometimes," she said. "What is it?"

Stephen glanced across at Jack and Una.

"I'm rather anxious about our young friends," he said, his voice dropped still lower, his head bent forward with such an insidious smile that Lady Bell could not, for the life of her, help thinking of a serpent.

"Anxious!" she echoed, her heart beating. "As how?"

"Can you not guess?" he said, raising his eyebrows.

"You—you mean that they may fall in love with each other. Well, they are not badly matched," said Lady Bell, bravely, though her heart was aching.

"Not badly, in one sense," said Stephen, after a pause; "but as badly as two persons could be in all others. They are a match as regards their means. They are both penniless."

Lady Bell looked up with a start.

"Is—is Mr. Newcombe so badly off? I thought—that is, I fancied he had a wealthy uncle——" She paused.

"You mean Mr. Ralph Davenant," said Stephen, calmly, and with an air of sadness. "I am sorry to say that he left everything which he possessed to a less worthy person—to me."

Lady Bell looked at him inquiringly.

"To me," he repeated, "and poor Jack was—well, disinherited, and left penniless. It is of him I think when I say that I am anxious about them; naturally, I think of him. Miss Rolfe is a friend of my mother's, and has been used to a straitened life; but poor Jack does not know what poverty means, and in his ignorance may drift into an entanglement which may embitter her life. No man in the world is less fitted for love in a cottage, and nothing to pay the rent, than Jack Newcombe. You, who have seen something of him, must have remarked his easy-going, careless nature, his utter ignorance of the value of money, his unsuitableness for a life of poverty and privation."

Lady Bell's heart beat fast.

"But—but—" she said, "you have plenty."

"Of which Jack will not take one penny. You see he is as proud as he is poor."

"I like him for that," murmured Lady Bell.

"Yes, so do I; though it pains and grieves me. If Jack would permit me to help him, Lady Bell, he might marry Una Rolfe tomorrow; but as it is, I fear, I am anxious. Another man would be wiser, but Jack has no idea of prudence, and would plunge head first into all the misery of such a union without a thought of the morrow."

"And you—you think he loves her," murmured Lady Bell; and she waited for an answer as a man on his trial might wait for the verdict of the jury.

Stephen smiled. He could read Lady Bell's heart as if it were an open book.

"Loves her! No, certainly not—not yet. He is amused and entertained, but love has not come yet."

"And she?" asked Lady Bell, anxiously, her eyes fixed on Una's face.

Stephen smiled again.

"No, not yet. She is ignorant of the meaning of the word. I have taken some trouble to arrive at the truth, and I am sure of what I say. It is well for her that she is not, for anything like a serious engagement would be simply madness. Poor Jack! His future lies so plainly before him, and if he would follow it, the rest of his life might be happiness itself."

"You mean that he should marry for money," said Lady Bell, coldly.

"No, not for money alone," murmured Stephen. "Jack is too high-minded to be guilty of such meanness; but is it not possible to marry for love and money, too, Lady Bell?"

Lady Bell turned her head aside; her heart beating fast. The voice of the tempter sounded like music in her ear. Why should not he marry for love as well as money? She had both. She loved him passionately, and she would pour her money at his feet to do as he liked with; to squander and make ducks and drakes of, if he would but give her a little love in return.

As she looked across the room at him, that awful, wistful longing which only a woman who loves with all her heart can feel, took possession of her and mastered her.

"Why do you tell me this?" she asked, sharply turning her face, pale and working.

"Because," murmured Stephen, "because I have Jack's interest so much at heart that I am bold enough to ask for aid where I know it can be of avail."

"Do you mean that you ask *me?*" she said, tremulously. "What can I do?"

"Much, everything," he whispered, his head bent low, almost to her ear. "Ask yourself, dear Lady Bell, and you will understand me. Let me be plain and straightforward, even at the risk of offending you. There was a time, not many months ago, when I and his best friends thought Jack had made a choice at once happy and wise."

Lady Bell rose and moved to and fro, and then sank down again trembling with agitation.

"You mean that—that he was falling in love with me?"

Stephen inclined his head with lowered eyes.

"It is true," he said. "You cannot fail to have seen what all observed." And he went on quickly—"And but for this fancy—this passing fancy—all would have been well. Lady Bell, I am speaking more openly than I ever have spoken to woman before. I am risking offending you, but I do so from the affection which I bear my cousin. Lady Bell, I implore you to help me in saving him from a step which will plunge him into life-long misery. He is totally unfitted to battle with the world; married wisely and well, he would be a happy and contented man; married unwisely and badly, no one can picture the future."

Lady Bell rose, her face pale, her eyes gleaming under the strain which she was enduring.

"Don't say any more," she said; "I—I cannot bear it. You have guessed my secret; I can feel that. Yes, I would save him if I could, and if you are sure that—that there is no engagement——"

"There is none," said Stephen, lying smoothly. "There can be none; the idea is preposterous."

Lady Bell moved away as he spoke, and turned over some book on the table to conceal her agitation, and Stephen, humming a popular hymn tune, crossed the room and looked down at Jack and Una with a benedictory smile, as if he was blessing them.

"Are you aware of the time, and that Lady Bell's hall porter is uttering maledictions for our tardiness?" he said, playfully.

Jack looked at his watch.

"By Jove! No idea it was so late. Are you ready, Mrs. Davenant?"

Mrs. Davenant woke from a sleep, and she and Una went upstairs.

"I see you have a new maid," she said, when they came down again. "What a superior-looking young girl."

"Is she not?" said Lady Bell, absently. "She is more than superior, she is interesting. She has a history."

Stephen, standing by, folding and unfolding his opera hat, smiled.

"Very interesting; but take care, Lady Bell; I am always suspicious of interesting people with a history."

As he spoke, a pale, dark face looked down upon him from the upper landing for a moment, then disappeared.

"You will come with us, Stephen?" said Mrs. Davenant, nervously.

"No, thanks. I should like the walk. Good-night," and he kissed her dutifully, and shook hands with Jack and Lady Bell.

"Going to walk?" cried Mrs. Davenant. "It is very chilly, and you've only that thin overcoat."

"I've a scarf somewhere—where is it?" said Stephen.

Una stooped, and picked up a white scarf.

"Here it is," she said, laughing, and all innocently she threw it round his neck.

"Will you tie it, please?" said Stephen, in an ordinary tone, and Una, laughing still, tied it.

Stephen stood motionless, his eyes cast down; he was afraid to raise them lest the passion blazing in them should be read by all there.

"Thanks. I cannot catch cold now," he said, as he took her hand and held it for a moment.

He put them into the brougham, and under the pretext of arranging her shawl, touched her hand once again; then he stood in the chilly street and watched the brougham till it disappeared in the distance.

Then he turned and walked homeward.

"One step in the right direction," he muttered. "Take care, Master Jack; I shall outwit you yet."

As he ascended the stairs of his chambers, Slummers came out to meet him.

"There is a—person waiting for you, Mr. Stephen," he said.

Stephen stopped, and his hand closed on the balustrade; his thoughts flew to Laura Treherne.

"A—woman, Slummers?"

"No, sir, a man," said Slummers.

"Very good," said Stephen, with a breath of relief. "Who is it—do you know?"

Slummers shook his head.

"A rough sort of man, sir; says he has come on business. He has been waiting for hours."

"I am very sorry," said Stephen, aloud and blandly, for the benefit of the visitor. "I am sorry to have kept anyone waiting. But it is rather late— —"

He entered the room as he spoke, and started slightly, for standing in the center of the apartment was Gideon Rolfe.

Notwithstanding the start Stephen came forward with outstretched hand and a ready smile of welcome.

"My dear Mr. Rolfe, I am indeed sorry that you should have been kept so long. If I had only known that you were coming——"

Gideon Rolfe waived all further compliment aside with a gesture of impatience.

"I wished to see you," he said. "Time is no object to me."

Stephen shut the door carefully and stood in a listening attitude. He knew it was of no use to ask his visitor to sit down.

"You have come to inquire about your daughter?"

"No, I have not," said Gideon Rolfe, calmly. "I know that she is well—I see her daily. I came to remind you of our contract—I came to remind you of your promise that no harm should come near her."

Stephen smiled and shook his head.

"And I trust no harm has come near her, my dear Mr. Rolfe."

"But I say that it has," said Gideon Rolfe, coldly. "I have watched her daily and I know."

"To what harm do you allude?" asked Stephen, bravely.

"Do you deny that the young man Jack Newcombe is near her?"

"Oh," said Stephen, and he drew a long breath.

Then he commenced untying the scarf, his acute brain hard at work.

Here was an instrument ready to his hand, if he chose to use it properly.

"Oh, I understand. No, I do not deny it; I wish that I could do so, for your sake and for Una's," he said gravely.

"Speak plainly," said Gideon Rolfe, hoarsely.

"I will," said Stephen. "Plainly then, Mr. Newcombe has chosen to fall in love with—your daughter! That accounts for his constant attendance upon her."

Gideon Rolfe's face worked.

"I will take her back," he said, grimly.

Stephen smiled.

"Softly, softly. There are two to that bargain, my dear Mr. Rolfe. For Miss Una to go back to a state of savagery in Warden Forest is impossible. You, who have seen her in her new surroundings, and the change they have wrought in her, must admit that."

Gideon Rolfe wiped the perspiration from his brow.

"I know that she is changed," he said. "She is like a great lady now. I see her dressed in rich silks and satins, and coming and going in carriages, with servants to wait upon her, and I know that she is changed, and that she has forgotten the friends of her childhood—forgotten those who were father and mother to her——"

"You wrong Miss Una," said Stephen, smoothly. "Not a day passes but she inquires for you and deplores your absence——"

"But," went on Gideon, as if he had not been interrupted, "I have not forgotten her, nor my promise to her mother. In a weak moment, moved by your threats more than your persuasions, I consented to part with her, but I would rather she were dead than that should happen—which you say will happen."

"Pardon me," said Stephen, blandly, and with an evil smile. "I said that Mr. Newcombe had fallen in love with her; I did not say that he would marry her. I would rather she were dead than that should happen," and he turned his face for one moment to the light.

It was pale even to the lips, the eyes gleaming with resolute purpose.

Gideon Rolfe looked at him in silence for a moment.

"I do not understand," he said, in a troubled voice.

"Let me make it clear to you," said Stephen. "Against my will and wish these two have met and become acquainted. Against my will and wish that acquaintance has ripened into"—he drew a long breath as if the word hurt him—"into love, or what they mistake for love. Thus far it has gone, but it must go no further. I am at one with you there. You and I must prevent it. You cannot do it alone, you know. You have no control over Miss Una; you who are not her father and in no way related to her."

Gideon Rolfe set his teeth hard.

"You see," said Stephen, with a haggard smile, "alone you are helpless. Be sure of that. If you move in the matter without me, I will declare the secret of her birth. Stop! be calm! But you and I can put an end to this engagement."

"They are engaged?" muttered Gideon Rolfe.

Stephen smiled contemptuously.

"My good friend, this matter has passed beyond your strength. Leave it to me. Yes, they are engaged; the affair has gone so far, but it must go no further. While you have been lurking outside area gates and behind carriages I have been at work, and I will stop it. I am not too proud to accept your aid, however. When the time comes I will ask your aid. Give me an address to which to write to you."

Gideon Rolfe, with a suspicious air, drew a piece of paper from his pocket and wrote an address.

"This will find you?" said Stephen. "Good. When the time comes I will send for you; meanwhile"—and he smiled—"you can go on haunting area gates and watching carriages, but be sure of one thing, that this marriage shall never take place."

Gideon Rolfe watched the pale face grimly.

"I must know more," he said. "How will you put an end to this?"

Stephen smiled. It was not a pleasant smile.

"You want to see the *modus operandi?* How the conjurer is going to perform the wonderful feat? Well, it is very simple. My friend and somewhat cousin, for all his romance, will not care to marry a girl whose name is stained with shame. If I know my dear Jack, he will not care to make an illegitimate child of Gideon Rolfe, the woodman, Mrs. Newcombe."

Gideon Rolfe started.

"You will tell him?" he said, hoarsely.

"Yes," said Stephen; "I shall tell him the truth, of course concealing the proper names, and you must be here to confirm my statement. That is all you have to do. Mind! not a word of my uncle's connection with the matter, or all is lost. You understand?"

"Yes, I understand," said Gideon, hoarsely. "I care not by what means so that the marriage is prevented."

"Nor I," said Stephen, coolly; "and now we are agreed on that point. When I want you I will write to you. Until then—will you take any refreshment?"

Gideon Rolfe waved his hand by way of negative, and Stephen rang the bell. "Show this gentleman out, Slummers. Mind the lower stairs, the gas has been put out. Good-night, good-night."

CHAPTER XXXI

It was settled that Mrs. Davenant, Una and Stephen should go to the Hurst in a week's time. Jack had definitely declined to go to the Hurst. He felt that he would rather bear the absence of Una for a week or two than go to the old house, haunted as it was, for him, with so many memories; but lo and behold, a few days after the dinner party, had come a note from Lady Bell's father, asking him to visit Earl's Court.

Of course, Jack accepted gladly enough, without a thought of Lady Bell, and only remembering that a good nag would take him from Earl's Court to Hurst in an hour and a half, or less.

The week passed rapidly, and with something like restlessness Lady Bell organized all kinds of outings and expeditions, in all of which Jack's services were found to be indispensable.

He could not exactly tell how it happened; but he seemed to spend almost as much time with Lady Bell as with Una. Now it was to go and try a horse which Lady Bell wanted to buy; then to select some dogs to take down to Earl's Court; and, again, to buy and send down pony-carriages and dog-carts.

There was always something to take him to Park Lane, and though Jack felt inclined to kick at these demands upon his time, which would otherwise have been spent near Una, he could not see his way to refuse. Then he was fond of buying horses, and dogs, and carriages, and used to hold a *levee* at Spider Court of disreputable-looking men in fustian corduroys, much to Leonard Dagle's disgust.

"It seems to me, Jack," he said, "that you have become Lady Bell's grand vizier. Do you choose her dress for her?"

"Chaff away, old man," said Jack. "It was only the other day that you were badgering me with being cool to her."

"Yes, with a purpose," said Leonard; "but that purpose has disappeared. Have you been to the Square yet this morning?"

"No; I'm going now. No, I can't, confound it! I promised to see to the harness for the pair of ponies Lady Bell bought."

Leonard smiled rather grimly.

"How Miss Una must love Lady Bell," he said, ironically.

"So she does," said Jack, sharply. "Now don't pretend to be cynical, Len. You know as well as I do that I would spend every hour of my life by Una's side if I could; but what can I do?"

"All right!" said Len, and he fell to work again.

Strangely enough now, that Jack was so much occupied with Lady Bell's affairs, Stephen happened to find more leisure to visit his mother, and very often he accompanied her and Una to some concert or picture-gallery to which Jack was prevented from going. Stephen seemed, in addition, quite changed, and had become quite the man of pleasure in contrast to his former habits.

He rarely appeared at the Square without a nosegay or a new novel; he took the greatest interest in any subject which interested Una, and was as attentive to her as if he had been the most devoted of lovers. Now that Jack was so much absent, it was he who sat opposite her in the little brougham, who leaned over her chair at the theater, or rode beside her in the Row.

At first Una felt rather constrained by his constant attendance; she had been so used to have Jack at her side that she felt embarrassed with Stephen; but Stephen, whose tact was second only to his cunning, soon put her at her ease. She found that it was not necessary to talk to him, that she might sit by his side or ride with him for an hour without uttering a word, and was quite free to think of Jack while Stephen chatted on in his smooth, insinuating voice.

And so the very effect Stephen desired to produce came about; she got accustomed to have him near her, and got to feel at her ease in his presence. But how long the mornings seemed! and how she longed for Jack and wondered what he was doing! If anyone had openly told her she was jealous of Lady Bell, she would have repudiated the idea with scorn too deep for anything but a smile; and yet—and yet—that bright, happy look which Lady Bell had so much admired, grew fainter and fainter, and nearly disappeared, reviving only when Jack hurried in to spend a few hours with her, and then hurried off to keep some engagement with Lady Bell or on Lady Bell's affairs.

But never by word or look did Una show that his absence pained her; instead, she was always the first to remind him of his engagements and to bid him depart.

At last the day arrived for her departure to Hurst. Lady Bell did not go down to Earl's Court till three days later, and Jack, of course, had to remain in town for a day or two after that.

"It is the first time we have been parted for twenty-four hours since that happy day I learned you loved me, my darling!" he whispered as he held Una in his arms: "I almost wish that I had accepted Stephen's invitation. But—but I could not sleep under the old roof—by Heaven, I could not! You cannot understand——"

"But I do," murmured Una; "and I am glad you are not coming. If——"

And she paused.

"Well, darling?" asked Jack, kissing her.

"If you had said half a word, I would not have gone."

"Why not?" said Jack, with a sigh. "Yes, I am glad you are going. You will see the old house in which I was so happy as a boy—which I once thought would have been mine."

"Dear Jack!" she murmured; and her hand smoothed the hair from his forehead caressingly and comfortingly.

"Well, never mind," said Jack; "it is better as it is. Perhaps I should have had the Hurst, and have lost you; and I would rather lose the whole earth than you, my darling! Besides, Stephen has turned out a better fellow than I thought him, and deserves all he has got, and will make a better use of it than I should. No, I am content—I have got the greatest treasure on earth!"

And he pressed her closer to him, and kissed her again and again until, from very shame, she slid from his grasp.

Stephen had engaged a first-class carriage, had even taken the precaution to order foot-warmers, though the weather was not yet winterish, and if he had been the personal attendant on a sovereign, and that sovereign had been Una, he could not have been more anxious for her comfort. He was so thoughtful and considerate that there was nothing left for Jack to do but go down to the station and see them off.

"Four days only, my darling," he whispered, as the train was starting; "they will seem years to me."

And he clung to her hand to the last moment, much to the disgust of the guard and porters, who expected to see him dragged under the train. Then he went back to Spider Court, feeling cold, chilly and miserable, as if the sun had been put out.

"Len, I wish I had gone!" he exclaimed, as he opened the door.

But there was no Len to hear him—the room was empty.

"Great Heaven! has everyone disappeared?" he exclaimed, irritably, and flung himself out of the house and into a hansom.

"Where to?" said the cabman, and Jack, half absently, answered:

"Park Lane."

The man had often driven him before, and he drove straight to Lady Bell's.

Jack walked into the drawing-room quite naturally—the room was familiar to him—and sat down before the fire; and Lady Bell came in with outstretched hand.

It was a comfort to have someone left, and Jack greeted her warmly, more warmly than he knew or intended. Lady Bell's face flushed as he held her hand longer than was absolutely necessary.

"Thank Heaven! there is someone left," he said, devoutly. "They have all gone, and Len is out, and——"

"I am left," said Lady Bell. "Well, you are just in time for luncheon. I half expected you, and I have told them to make a curry."

Curry was one of Jack's weaknesses.

"That is very kind of you," he said, gratefully. He felt, very unreasonably, neglected somehow. "You always seem to know what a fellow likes."

"That's because I have a good memory," said Lady Bell, smiling down at him. "I shall take care to have plenty of curries at Earl's Court. And, by the way, will you choose a paper for the smoking-room down there? I have told them that they must do it at once."

Jack rose without a word; he had been choosing papers and decorations for a week past, and it did not seem strange. Luncheon was announced while they were discussing the paper, and Jack gave her his arm. Mrs. Fellowes was the only other person present, and she sat reading a novel, deaf and blind to all else. Not but what she might have heard every word, for the young people talked of the most commonplace subjects, and Jack was very absent-minded, thinking of Una, and quite unconscious of the light which beamed in Lady Bell's eyes when they rested on him.

Then they rode in the Row; he could do no less than offer to accompany her, and Mrs. Fellowes wanted to see a piece at one of the theaters, and Jack went to book seats, and took one for himself, and sat staring at the stage and thinking of Una; but he sat behind Lady Bell's chair, and spoke to her occasionally, and Lady Bell was content.

Hetley and Arkroyd were in the stalls, and saw him.

"Jack's making the running," said Lord Dalrymple, eying the box through his opera glass. "He's the winning horse, and we, the field, are nowhere."

And not only those two, but many others, remarked on Jack's close attendance on the great heiress, and not a few who would have gone to the box if he had not been there, kept away.

Meanwhile, Jack, simple, unsuspecting Jack, was bestowing scarcely a thought on the beautiful woman by his side, and thinking of Una miles away.

The theater over, and Lady Bell put into the carriage, he looked in at the club, sauntered into the card-room, smoked a cigar in the smoking-room, and then went home to Spider Court.

Much to his surprise he found Leonard up, not only up, but pacing the room, his face flushed and agitated.

"Hallo!" exclaimed Jack, "what's the matter? And where on earth have you been?"

"Jack, I have found her!"

"That's just what I said some months ago!"

"Yes, I know. I have been thinking how strangely alike our love affairs have been. It is my turn now. I have found her!"

"What, this young lady, Laura Treherne?"

"Yes," said Leonard, with a long breath.

"Tell me all about it," said Jack. "Hold hard a minute, till I get something to drink. Now, fire away."

"Well," said Leonard, still pacing up and down, and seeming scarcely conscious of Jack's presence, "I was walking in the park. You know the place, that quiet walk under the beeches. I was thinking of you and your love affairs, when I saw, sitting under a tree, a figure that I knew at once. For a moment I could not move, and scarcely think; then I wondered how I should get to speak to her; but presently, when I had pulled myself together, I saw that she had dropped her handkerchief, and I went and picked it up and took it to her."

"A fine opening," muttered Jack.

Leonard Dagle evidently did not hear him.

"Well, she started when I approached her, and merely thanked me with a bow, but I was determined not to let her go this time, and I said, 'Pardon me, but we have met before.' 'Where?' said she. 'In a railway carriage,' I said, and she looked at me, and trembled. 'I remember,' she said, and I swear I saw her shudder. 'Since then,' I said, 'I have sought you far and near.' 'Why should you do that?' she asked."

"A very natural question," interjected Jack.

"Then I told her. I told her that from that hour I had been unable to rid my mind of her face, that it had haunted me; that I had followed her and learned her address; and that though I had lost her I had sought her all over London."

"Was she angry?" asked Jack.

"At first she was," said Leonard, "very angry, but something in my voice or my face—Heaven knows I was earnest enough! convinced her that I meant no harm, and she listened."

"Well," said Jack, interested and excited.

"Well," said Leonard, "we sat talking for an hour, perhaps more, and she has promised to meet me again; at least she admitted that she walked in the park every afternoon. I tried to get her address, but she told me plainly that she would not give it to me."

"And is that all you learned?" asked Jack, with something like good-natured contempt.

"No!" replied Leonard. "I learned that she had been injured—oh, not in the way you think—and that she had some purpose to effect—some wrong to right."

"And of course you offered to help her?" said Jack.

"I offered to help her; I laid my services, my whole time and strength, at her disposal; I went so far as to beseech her to tell me what this purpose, this wrong was; but she would not tell me, and so we parted. But we are to meet again. She is much changed; paler and thinner than when I saw her in the railway carriage, but still more beautiful in my eyes than any other woman in the world."

"It is a strange affair," mused Jack. "Quite a romance in its way. Isn't it funny, Len, that both our love affairs should be romantic, and so much alike!"

"Yes," said Leonard, "very. But mine has scarcely begun, while yours has ended happily, or will do so, if you do not play the fool!"

"What do you mean?" asked Jack, sharply.

"Where have you been to-night?" asked Leonard.

"To the theater with Lady Bell."

"I expected as much," said Leonard, and he fell to at his writing, and would say no more, though Jack stormed and raved.

Meanwhile the Davenant party had, thanks to Stephen, made a comfortable journey. They found a carriage and pair waiting for them at the station; not the ramshackle vehicle of the old squire's time, but a new carriage from the best man in Long Acre, and they were rolled along the country lanes in a style Ralph Davenant would have marveled at.

Presently they came in sight of the Hurst, and Mrs. Davenant uttered an exclamation.

"Why, Stephen, it is altered!" she said.

Stephen smiled proudly.

Short as the time had been he had effected a radical change in the old house; a hundred workmen had been busy, and the ramshackle old mansion had been transformed. Wings had been added, the grounds had been newly laid out; the road, even, had been altered, and they drove through an avenue of thriving young limes.

Una, silent and interested, kept her eyes fixed on the house. She had often heard Jack describe it, but this palatial residence did not answer to his description. Stephen's money and energy had entirely transformed the place.

The carriage pulled up at the entrance, and half a dozen grooms flew to the horses' heads: footmen in handsome liveries stood in attendance, and the servants formed a lane for their master to pass through. Una had often read of such a reception, but here was a reality.

Stephen helped her to alight, and took her and his mother on his arm, his head erect, a warm flush on his cheek.

Suddenly the flush disappeared and a frown took its place as he saw amongst the crowd gathered together at the entrance the parchment-like visage of old Skettle.

But the frown disappeared as he entered the house, and stood silent, listening to the approving comments of Mrs. Davenant.

"My dear Stephen," she said, "you have certainly altered the place—I should not have known it. And is this what was the gloomy old Hall?"

"Yes," said Stephen, proudly, and he glanced round at the alterations with an air of satisfaction, and looked at Una's face for some sign of approval.

But Una was looking around anxiously. If it was so much altered, then it was not the old home that Jack knew and remembered.

"You will find everything altered and improved, I hope," said Stephen.

Altered, indeed! They have even shifted the old staircase, so that it would have been difficult to have found the room in which the old squire died, exclaiming:

"You thief! you thief! what have you done with the will?"

Yes, indeed, there was great alteration. The old squire, if he had come to life again, would not have known Hurst as Stephen had made it. Masons, carpenters, and decorators had been at work to some purpose. Everything was changed, and unmistakably for the better.

Stephen looked around with an air of pride.

"They have been very quick," he said. "I placed it in good hands. You will find everything you require up-stairs. You must know," he said, turning to Una, "that I found the place little better than a barn, and have done my best to make it fit to receive you! You are looking at the portraits," he added, seeing Una's gaze wandering along the double line of dead and gone Davenants. Most of them you would not have seen two months ago, they had been terribly neglected, but I have had them cleaned and renewed. That is the old squire, my poor uncle," and he sighed comfortably.

Una paused before this, the last portrait of the series, and looked at it long and curiously, and the other two stood and watched her, Stephen with a keen glance of scrutiny and with a nervous tremor about his heart. If she could but know that she was looking at the portrait of her own father! Una turned away at last with a faint sigh. She was thinking that this was the old man who had once loved Jack and left him to poverty.

Mrs. Davenant shuddered slightly.

"He was a terrible old man, my dear," she murmured, "and always frightened me. I trembled when he looked at me."

"He does not look so terrible," said Una, sadly.

Stephen fidgeted slightly.

"Come," he said, "you must not catch cold. Your maids are here by this time. Will you go up to your room? The housekeeper will show them to you, and I hope you will find everything comfortable."

Very slowly, looking to right and left of her, Una followed Mrs. Davenant up the broad staircase.

The place seemed to have a strange fascination for her; she could almost have persuaded herself that she had been in it before, and it seemed familiar, though so much changed from all likeness to Jack's description of it.

They found the rooms upstairs beautifully decorated, and furnished in the most approved and luxurious style. Lady Bell's house in Park Lane even was eclipsed.

"Stephen has made it a palace," said Mrs. Davenant. "How I used to hate it in the old time! it was so dark and grim and gloomy, always felt dull and damp. Stephen tells me that he has had it thoroughly drained after the new fashion, and that it is quite dry. Such a palace as this wants a mistress; I wish he would marry."

"Why do you not tell him so?" said Una, with a smile.

Mrs. Davenant shook her head nervously.

"That would do no good, my dear," she said. "I sometimes think he will never marry."

And she glanced at Una with some embarrassment. A dim suspicion had of late crossed her mind that if Una had been free, Stephen might have stood in Jack's place. She could not help noticing Stephen's close attendance on Una—a mother's eyes are sharp to note such things.

If the old squire could have seen the dining-room and the elaborate *menu* that evening, he would have stared and sworn. Stephen had engaged a French cook; the appointments were as perfect as they could be; the servants admirably trained, and as to the wines the Hurst cellar stood second to none in the country.

It almost seemed as if he were sparing no pains to impress on Una all that the wife of Stephen Davenant would possess. And Una, more than half the dinner-time, was thinking of Jack, and fondly picturing the little house they had so often talked of setting up when the commissionership came home. Just at the same time, Jack was leaning over Lady Bell's chair in the theater.

Stephen was in his best mood, and exerted himself to the uttermost. He described the neighborhood, planned excursions and expeditions; told innumerable anecdotes of the village folk, and played the host to perfection.

In a thousand ways he showed his anxiety for Una's comfort; and after dinner he had the place lit up, and went over it, asking her opinion on this point and the other, and humbly begging her to suggest alterations. So much so that Una began to grow shy and reserved, and shrank closer to Mrs. Davenant; and Stephen, quick to see when he was going too fast, left them and went to the library to write letters.

Now, strange to say, of all the rooms in the house, this one room remained unaltered. He had not allowed it to be touched—indeed it was kept closely locked, and the key never left him night and day. Just as it had been on the night of the squire's death, when Stephen stood with the stolen will in his hand, so it was now.

He never entered it without a shudder, and all the time he was in it his eyes unconsciously wandered over the floor and furniture as if mechanically searching for something.

It exerted a strange, weird influence over him, and seemed to draw him into it. Tonight he paced up and down, looking at the familiar objects, and making no attempt to write his letters.

His brain was busy, not with schemes of ambition and avarice, but of love. The blood ran riot in his veins as he thought that Una was under the same roof as himself, and one mighty resolve took possession of him.

"She shall never leave it but to come back as my wife," was his resolve.

Even the lost will did not trouble him tonight. He had Una in his grasp, Una upon whom everything turned.

It was far into the morning before he went to bed, and at the head of the stairs he turned and looked round with a proud smile.

"All—all mine!" he muttered, "and I will have her, too," and he went to sleep and dreamed, not of Una, but of Laura Treherne.

All through the watches of the night the pale, dark face haunted him. At times he saw it peering at him through the library window, at others it was pursuing him along an endless road; but always it wore a threatening aspect and filled him with a vague terror.

Some men's conscience only awake at night.

CHAPTER XXXII

If Una had been a queen visiting some distant part of her realm, more elaborate preparations for her amusement could not have been made.

Not a day passed but Stephen had got some proposition for pleasuring, and he never tired of hunting up some place to go.

One morning they would drive to some romantic and historic spot; another there would be some flower show or *fete*, which he insisted upon them seeing; on others, they would play lawn tennis in the now beautiful grounds. The fame of the new Hurst had spread abroad, and those of the county families who were in residence called at once, and dinner parties were given and accepted. So the week glided by quickly, even to Una, who reckoned time by the day on which she would see Jack.

Every morning there came a scrawl—Jack's handwriting was mysterious and terrible—from him; in every letter he expressed his longing to see her, and the hateful time he was having in town. But every letter had some mention of Lady Bell; and it was evident that he spent most of his time at Park Lane.

But Una was not jealous—she put away from her resolutely any feeling of that kind.

"I am so glad that Lady Bell is in town, and that Jack has some place to go to," she said to Mrs. Davenant.

And Mrs. Davenant smiled; but sighed at the same time. To her, as to others, it seemed that Jack spent too much time in attendance upon the great heiress.

Stephen's money flew, it was scattered about in every direction; but still he was not popular. Men touched their hats, but they never smiled as they had done at the old squire, and as they had done at Jack. There was something about Stephen that the Hurst folk could not and would not take to; and even while they were drinking with his money, they talked of Master Jack and shook their heads regretfully.

And Stephen knew it, and hated them all; but most of all hated old Skettle. It seemed as if the old man was ubiquitous; he was everywhere. Stephen could not take a walk outside the grounds but he came upon the old man; and, though Skettle always raised his hat and gave him "Good-day," Stephen felt the small, keen eyes watching him. Of Hudsley he had seen nothing.

At last the county papers announced the important fact that Lady Earlsley had arrived at Earl's Court, and Una knew that in two days she would see Jack.

That night Stephen was more attentive than ever. They had been dining out at a neighbor's, and were sitting in the drawing-room, talking over the evening. The prospect of Jack's coming had brought a glad light to Una's eyes—a brighter color to her face. In two days she should see him! In her happiness she felt amiable and tender to all around her, and, for the first time, she responded to Stephen's unceasing devotion. He had brought in from the new library a whole pile of books relating to the county, and was showing and explaining the illustrations.

"That is Earl's Court," he said; "a beautiful place, isn't it? But Lady Bell has several grander places than that."

"She is very rich," said Una.

"Very," he said, thoughtfully. "It's a pity that she does not marry."

Una smiled.

"She says that she will never marry," she said.

Stephen looked up.

"And yet a little while ago they were saying that she would be married before the year was out."

"Indeed!" said Una.

"It would be a grand match for any one," said Stephen. "It would have been a great match for him."

"For him?" said Una. "Who was it?"

Stephen started and looked embarrassed, as if he had made a slip of the tongue.

"Well," he said, with a little, awkward laugh; "but—are you jealous? Perhaps I ought not to tell tales out of school, though the affair is off long ago, and he has made a happier choice."

Una put the fire screen on one side and looked at him calmly. He was sitting almost at her feet. Mrs. Davenant was dozing in her accustomed arm-chair.

"Of whom do you speak?" she asked.

Stephen hesitated, as if reluctant to reply.

"Well," he said, "it is mere gossip, of course, but gossip awarded the great prize of the season to a near and dear friend of yours."

Una's heart beat fast. She guessed what was coming.

"Tell me," she said, in a low voice.

"Tut!" said Stephen, as if ashamed to retail such idle gossip.

"Well, they said that Jack meant to marry the great heiress."

"It is not true," Una said; but her color went, and left her quite pale and cold.

"Of course not," said Stephen, cheerfully; "though I would not say but there was some excuse for the rumor. Jack was a great deal at Park Lane until he met—one who shall be nameless." And he looked up at her with a smile. "Why, they went so far as to congratulate him," he said, laughing as if at an excellent joke. "And indeed I think if Jack had said 'Yes,' Lady Bell would not have said 'No.' So, you see, that you have made a veritable conquest!"

And he laughed again.

But there was no answering smile on Una's pale face. It was not of Lady Bell she thought, but of herself and Jack.

It was true she had stepped in between Jack and wealth and prosperity—she, the penniless daughter of a woodman, had prevented his marrying the great heiress and becoming the master of Earl's Court and all the Earlsley wealth! A chill passed over her, and she raised the screen to hide her face from Stephen's eye.

"Yes, it would have been a great match for Jack," he said, carelessly—"it would have set him on his feet, as they say. But he is still more fortunate." And he sighed.

Una rose.

"I think I will go up now," she said; and she went and woke Mrs. Davenant.

Stephen escorted them to the head of the stairs, smiling as if nothing had been said, and then went straight to the old library and rang the bell.

It was understood that no one was to answer the library bell but Slummers, and Slummers now appeared.

Stephen wrote two letters; one ran thus:

"My Dear Mr. Rolfe:—Be kind enough to be at my chambers tomorrow morning at eight o'clock."

The other was still more short; it was addressed to Mr. Levy Moss:

"Put on the screw at once."

Calmly and leisurely he put them in their envelopes, as if the fate and happiness of two souls were not hanging upon them, and gave them to Slummers.

"Take the morning express and deliver these yourself," he said, quietly. "I shall follow you by the midday train. When you have done so, find Mr. Newcombe and keep him in sight. You understand?"

"Quite, sir," said Slummers, and disappeared as silently as usual.

CHAPTER XXXIII

It was Jack's last day in town. Tomorrow he would be at Earl's Court, and in the evening would be riding as fast as a horse could carry him to Una.

The hours seemed to drift with leaden wings.

It was no use going to Park Lane, for the blinds were down, and Lady Bell was at Earl's Court. It was no use going to the club, for the whitewashers had taken possession of it; never had Jack been so utterly bored and wearied. At last he strolled into the park, and sat on one of the seats and stared at the Row, giving himself up to thoughts of Una, and picturing their meeting on the morrow.

He lingered in the park till dusk: then he went home to dress.

"Still writing, old man?" he said, as he entered, and laid his hand on Leonard's shoulder.

"Halloa! is that you, Jack?" said Leonard, throwing down his pen. "I have been expecting you."

"Why for?" asked Jack, yawning. Then he looked up curiously. "I wish I'd known it; I'd have come home. Look here, Len, we'll go and dine somewhere; if there is anything left to eat in this howling desert of a London. If ever any man was bored to death and sick of it, I am this day. Twenty-four hours more of it, and I should chuck myself into the Serpentine! I never spent such a day— —"

He stopped suddenly, for he became conscious that Leonard was standing, looking down at him with a grave and earnest regard.

"What's the matter, old man?" he asked.

Leonard hesitated.

"Jack," he said, at last, "Moss has been here."

"Oh, has he?" said Jack, carelessly.

"Yes, and there is trouble about. He is pressing for his money."

"What!" exclaimed Jack.

Leonard nodded.

"Yes, he means mischief; he made quite a fuss here. Said he had a heavy claim to meet— —"

"Oh, I know that old yarn."

"And that he must and would have money to meet those bills of yours."

Jack looked grave.

"Did he mean it?"

"Yes," said Leonard. "Thanks to you, I know Mr. Levy Moss by this time, and I am sure he was in earnest."

"Confound him!" muttered Jack.

"Confounding him won't pay him," said Leonard, sensibly.

Jack rose and paced the room.

"What am I to do, Len?"

"I don't know," said Leonard. "If I could help you—but all I have wouldn't meet one bill."

"And I wouldn't take it if it would," said Jack. "But I can't understand it! Only last week he was bothering me to take a hundred or two."

Leonard shook his head.

"All I can tell you is, that he was simply furious. He said that he must and would have some money, that if you did not pay him he would— —"

"Well?" said Jack, grimly.

"That he would put you through the Court," said Leonard.

Jack turned pale.

"What am I to do?" he said. "I have been relying on the commissionership that Stephen promised, and Moss seemed quite willing to wait. I can't find any money."

Leonard shook his head.

"The man was furious. Worse than I have ever seen him. You will have to find some money somewhere. How much do you owe him?"

Jack tilted his hat on one side and scratched his head.

"Hanged if I know. He has let me have a great deal lately. Five hundred, perhaps."

"Jack, you have been a fool," said Leonard. "I told you that it was no use counting upon the place your cousin Stephen promised you."

"I don't so much care for myself, but Una, Una," said Jack, with a groan. Then he jumped up. "Let us go and get some dinner, and think it over."

They went to a well-known house in Strand, and Jack, careless Jack, ordered a dinner fit for a prince, and enjoyed it as he would have enjoyed it if he had been going to be hanged on the morrow.

"I don't understand Moss," he said. "He was everything that was agreeable and pleasant a few days ago."

"And today he was like a wolf hunting for a bone," said Leonard. "Hello, who's this?" for a gentleman had entered the dining-room and approached their table.

"Why, it's Stephen!" exclaimed Jack, forgetting Moss in a moment. "Just in time, Stephen, we'll have another bottle of claret up. What on earth brings you to town? And how is—how are they all?"

Stephen sat down with a grave smile, and just sipped the claret, the best the house had on its list. And he sat and talked till the wine was finished, the greater part of which Jack drank, then he said:

"Jack, I want you to come to my chambers; I have something to tell you."

"All right," said Jack. "Leonard can find his way home very well."

Stephen called a hansom, and they were rattled away to the Albany.

As they ascended the stairs, Stephen laid his hand on Jack's arm.

"Jack, I am sorry to say I have bad news for you. You will be calm."

"Bad news!" said Jack, and his heart stood still. "What is it? Una——"

"Yes," said Stephen; "it is about Una. You will be calm, my dear Jack?"

Jack leaned against the balustrade and drew a long breath.

"Is she ill—dead?" he gasped.

"Neither," said Stephen. "Come, be a man."

"I am ready," said Jack. "If she is neither ill nor dead I can bear anything else."

Stephen opened the door, and Jack, entering, saw Gideon Rolfe standing on the hearthrug.

"Mr. Rolfe!" he exclaimed. "How do you do? I am very glad to see you!" and he held out his hand.

Gideon Rolfe nodded and turned aside.

"What is it? What is the matter?" asked Jack, turning to Stephen, who had carefully closed the door and stood with knitted brow and sad countenance.

At Jack's question he glanced at Rolfe, and then, with a sigh, said:

"Yes, Jack, I will tell you. It will come better from me than Mr. Rolfe. Jack, you were right in suspecting that the business referred to Una. She is quite well—and happy. But—but I am afraid your engagement must cease."

At this, Jack's calmness came back to him, and with something like a smile, he said, scornfully:

"Indeed!"

"Yes," said Gideon Rolfe, but Stephen held up his hand and silenced him.

"Perhaps you will tell me for what reason?" said Jack, quietly.

"For a sad, very sad reason," said Stephen, in a subdued and mournful tone. "Jack, my heart bleeds for you——"

"Never mind your heart," said Jack, curtly. "Come to the point, Stephen."

"I sympathize with you deeply," continued Stephen, not at all affronted. "The fact is, Mr. Rolfe has tonight made a communication respecting our dear young friend, which has completely overwhelmed me——"

"Let me see if it will overwhelm me," said Jack. "What is it?"

"My dear Jack, it is a story involving shame——"

"Shame!" echoed Jack, and his brow darkened. "To whom?"

"To those who can feel shame no longer," said Stephen; "but alas! its shadow falls on a young life as innocent and pure as the angels."

"On Una?" demanded Jack, fiercely.

Stephen bowed his head.

"Yes, Jack. Una is a nameless child—she is illegitimate."

Jack reeled and fell into a chair, and there he sat for a moment.

"It is a lie!" he said at last.

"It is true!" said the deep voice of Gideon Rolfe; and Jack, fixing his startled eyes on the rough, ragged face, knew that it was the truth.

With a groan he covered his face with his hands; then he started up and struck the table a blow that made Stephen wince.

"Well," he exclaimed, with a short laugh—"well, what business is it of anyone's but mine and Una's? What do I care whether she is illegitimate or not? Let her be the daughter of whom she may, married or unmarried, it matters not to me. She *is* Una, and that is enough!"

His voice rang out loud and clear as a bell's tone, and he looked from one to the other defiantly.

"And now that is settled," he said, sternly. "Let us come to particulars, to proof. Mr. Rolfe, though I know you are averse to our marriage, I believe you. I do not think you are capable of inventing a lie—a base, fiendish lie—to serve your ends. But all the same I ask, and not without reason, some proofs. First, who are Una's parents?"

Gideon Rolfe was about to reply, but a glance from Stephen stopped him.

"That is the question I have implored Mr. Rolfe to answer," he said. "I have entreated him to give us some information, but he declines. It is a secret which he says shall go down to the grave with him, unless——"

"Unless what?" demanded Jack, hoarsely.

"Unless you are still determined to hold Una to her engagement. Then——"

He paused, and Jack looked from one to the other.

"Well?"

"Then he declares he will go to Una and inform her of the shame that clings to her name."

Jack uttered a low cry and sank back in his chair. He saw by what heavy chains he was bound. To get possession of Una he must inflict the agony of shame upon her.

If ever a man loved truly and nobly Jack loved Una. He would have died the death to spare her a moment's pain; and here was this man threatening to darken and curse her whole life if he, Jack, did not relinquish her.

"Are you human?" he said, turning his eyes upon Gideon Rolfe with a wild, hunted gaze.

Gideon Rolfe smiled bitterly.

"I am human enough to prevent this marriage."

Jack rose and confronted him.

"I will not give her up," he said hoarsely. "I defy you!"

"Good!" said Gideon Rolfe. "Then I go to the girl and acquaint her with the true story of her birth. If I know her—and I do—she has sufficient pride to prevent her staining so honorable a family as the Davenants by marrying into it," and he sneered bitterly.

Jack's face flushed.

"You professed to love her," he said. "Are you totally indifferent to her happiness?"

"No happiness could follow her union to one of your race," said Gideon Rolfe.

Stephen trembled. He was playing a dangerous and desperate game. A word from Rolfe might put Jack in possession of Una's real parentage, and Stephen would be ruined.

"My dear Jack," he said, sorrowfully, "I have besought Mr. Rolfe, almost on my knees, to hold his hand, but he is like stone—immovable."

There was a pause.

Jack stood, his brain in a whirl, his heart beating wildly. His frenzied brain saw the whole thing clearly. On one side stood his passionate love and his life-long happiness, on the other Una's shame and agony.

"I love her so!" he moaned.

"You say that you love her," said Gideon Rolfe, sternly. "Prove it by saving her from the knowledge of the shame which clings to her name. If your love is worth anything it will make that sacrifice. Remember, it is on your side only. She is young—a mere girl, a few weeks, months at most, and she will have learned to forget you."

"That's a lie, at least," groaned Jack. "I know her better than you."

"No matter," said Gideon Rolfe, coldly. "Time will heal a disappointed love; no time can heal an undying shame."

Jack rose and paced the room.

"Leave me alone for a few minutes," he said hoarsely. "I must think this out; nothing you can say can influence me."

At a signal from Stephen, Gideon Rolfe remained silent.

Five minutes passed and then Jack came to the light.

The handsome face was haggard and white and so changed that ten years might have passed over his head in those few minutes.

"Mr. Rolfe," he said, and his voice was broken and hollow, "why you bear me such deadly enmity I cannot imagine, and you will not tell me?"

Gideon Rolfe made a gesture of assent.

"It is a mystery to me; I only know its results. Once more I ask you to relent, and spare the unhappiness of both of us."

"I am resolved," said Gideon. "Either relinquish her or I tell her all. The decision is in your hands. I do not doubt you will seize your happiness, even at the cost of her shame."

"Then you wrong me," said Jack. "Rather than she should know the shadow which hangs on her life I relinquish her."

A light gleamed in Stephen's eyes, and his lips twitched.

"This I do," continued Jack, in a voice so low and broken that it scarcely reached them, "placing implicit trust in your assertion that she is—as you state."

He drew a long breath.

"I dare not risk it; but if in the future I should find that you have played me false—if, I say, this should prove a lie, then I tell you beware, for, as there is a Heaven above us, I will take my vengeance."

"So be it," said Gideon Rolfe, grimly. "Now write," and he pointed to a bureau on which stood pen and paper, as if prepared for use.

Jack started.

"You will not take my word?" he said, bitterly.

Gideon Rolfe hesitated; but, at a glance from Stephen, said:

"Let the knowledge that the engagement is at an end come from you; it will be better so."

Jack went to the bureau and sank into a chair.

Yes, if the blow must be dealt it better be by his hands, as tenderly as possible.

He sat for some moments with his head in his hands, as utterly oblivious of the presence of the others as if they were absent.

Before him rose the lovely face with its trustful eyes; in his ears rang the musical voice which he should never hear again.

What should he write? Why should he write?

Stephen stole behind him.

"You will be careful to conceal the truth, my dear Jack," he murmured.

Jack started, and turned upon him with a look that caused Stephen to shrink back behind the table.

"For what am I giving up what is most precious in life?" he said hoarsely.

Then in sheer despair he seized the pen, and wrote in a trembling hand:

"My Dearest:—Since you left me, circumstances have occurred which have changed the current of both our lives. I dare not tell you more, but I pray, I beseech, you not to misjudge me. If you knew the position in which I am placed, you would understand why I am acting thus, and instead of condemning, pity me. Una, from this moment our lives are separate. Heaven send you happiness, and—as I know your true, loving heart—forgetfulness. I cannot tell you more—would to Heaven that I could. From the first I have been unworthy of you; I am more unworthy now than ever. I dare not ask of you to remember me; forget me, Una, forget that such a person as I ever crossed your path. Would to Heaven that we had never met! Don't think hardly of me, my darling, whatever you may hear. What I am doing is as much for your good as for mine. Good-bye. I shall never cease to remember and love you, whatever happens. Good-bye!

"Jack."

Blotted and smeared, he enclosed it in an envelope, and dropped it before Gideon Rolfe; then he looked round for his hat.

"A glass of wine, Jack?" murmured Stephen.

But Jack took no more notice than if he had been deaf, and seizing his hat staggered from the room.

Stephen drew a long breath.

"Well, Mr. Rolfe," he said, "we have conquered. As for this note, I will see that it is delivered at a proper opportunity."

"Good," said Gideon Rolfe; then he paused, and frowned sternly. "I am sorry for the young man."

Stephen smiled, and waved his hand.

"A mere fancy," he said, lightly. "My dear Jack is apt to take these matters as very serious, but he generally manages to get over them. And now what will you take to drink, Mr. Rolfe?"

Gideon Rolfe waved his hand and put on his hat.

"I leave the letter with you," he said. "Good-night."

Stephen filled a wine glass with brandy, and drank it off, his hand shaking. Then he eyed Jack's letter curiously, and at last held the envelope over the steam of the hot water, and drew it apart.

"A very sensible letter," he muttered, as he read. "Ambiguous, but all the better for that. Really, anyone reading this, would conclude that Jack had made up his mind to marry Lady Bell, and was ashamed to say so."

Then he reclosed the envelope, and went to bed, and slept the sleep of the just.

Meanwhile Jack strode around the streets of London, his brain in a whirl, half mad with "the desperation of despair," as a poet has it.

At last he reached home, and found the rooms dark and lonesome, and Leonard in bed.

He sat down and wrote a short note to Lady Bell, telling her that things had turned up which prevented him coming to Earl's Court—giving no reason, but just simply the fact. Then he turned out, and he walked about till daylight.

When he came in Leonard was at breakfast, and stared aghast at Jack's haggard face and changed appearance.

"My dear old man," he commenced, but Jack cut him short.

"Len, I'm the most miserable wretch in existence. Don't ask me the why and the wherefore; but all is over between me and Una."

"Impossible!" said Leonard.

"Impossible, but true," retorted Jack. "All is over between us, and if you value our friendship you will not mention her name again."

"But——" said Leonard.

"Enough," said Jack. "I tell you that it is so."

"Moss has been here again," Leonard said.

"I don't care."

"But, my dear fellow——"

"I don't care," said Jack, stolidly. "A hundred Mosses wouldn't matter to me now. Let him do his worst."

"You don't know what his worst is," said Leonard. "He has got you in his power."

"All right," said Jack, coolly. "Let him exercise it to his uttermost."

Leonard had never seen Jack like this.

"Listen to me," he said. "If Moss does all he can do, he can expel you from any club in London, can make you an utter out-cast. Come, Jack, be reasonable."

"I can't be reasonable!" retorted Jack. "I am utterly ruined and undone. With Una everything that is worth living for has gone. I care nothing for Moss or anything he can do."

CHAPTER XXXIV

"In another hour he will be here," said Una, as she stood at her dressing-room window, and looked out upon the lawns and park of Hurst, where they stretched down toward the road.

"Another hour!" and at the thought, a smile—yet scarcely a smile, but a suitable light like a sun ray stole over her face.

The great poet Tennyson has, in one of his greatest poems, portrayed a girl who, all unconscious of the bitter moments awaiting her, decked herself in her brightest ribbons to receive her expected lover.

Bright ribbons are out of fashion now, but Una had paid some, for her, extraordinary attention to her toilet. Jack was never tired of calling her beautiful; had even gone so far as to speak of her loveliness, and it had raised no vanity in her; but this evening she felt she would like to appear really and truly beautiful in his eyes, so beautiful that even Lady Bell's spirited face should be forgotten.

She had chosen the dress he liked best; had selected, with unusual care, a couple of flowers from the costly bouquet, which, morning and evening, was sent to her room from the hot-houses, and had decked herself in the locket and bracelet, and ring which Jack had given her.

Mrs. Davenant had made her many presents of jewelry, some of it costly, and even rare; but she would not wear anything but Jack's own gifts tonight.

"He will come fresh from Lady Bell's diamonds and sapphires, and would think little of mine, beautiful as they are; but he will like to see his locket and his bracelet, and will know that I love him best."

Not once, but twice and thrice she had moved from the window to the glass, and looked into it. Not with any expression of pleased vanity, but rather with merciless criticism. For the first time, she would like to be as beautiful as Jack thought her. For the last few days she had been rather silent, and somewhat pale. Stephen's cunning hints respecting Jack and Lady Bell had had their effect; but tonight's expectation, and the nearness of Jack's approach, had brought a faint rose-like tint to her cheeks, and her eyes shone with the subtle light of love and hope.

Mrs. Davenant looked up at her as she entered the drawing-room and smiled affectionately.

"How well you look tonight, dear," she said, as she kissed her and drew her down beside her. "I'm inclined to believe Jack, when he says that you grow more beautiful than ever."

"Hush," said Una, but with a blush. "Jack says so many foolish things, dear."

"If he never said anything more foolish than that he would be a wise man," said Mrs. Davenant. "How long would he be now, dear?"

Una glanced at the clock.

"Just forty minutes," she said simply.

Mrs. Davenant smiled and patted her hand.

"Counting the very minutes," she murmured, gently. "What a thing love is! What would life be without it?"

"Death," said Una, with a grave smile. "Worse than death."

Mrs. Davenant sighed.

"Jack is a happy man," she said. "I wonder whether Stephen will come down this evening?"

"Do you not know?" said Una, absently.

"No," replied Mrs. Davenant. "I thought, perhaps, he might have told you."

"Me!" said Una, with open eyes. "Oh, no. Why should he?"

"I didn't know," said Mrs. Davenant, quietly. "He tells you everything, I think."

Una smiled.

"He is very good and kind," she said, still a little absently. "Oh, very kind. No one could have taken more trouble to make me happy."

"Yes, Stephen likes to see you happy," said Mrs. Davenant, softly. "Poor Stephen!" and she sighed.

But Una heard neither the expression of pity nor the sigh. She had risen, and was moving about the room with that suppressed impatience which marks the one who wafts an expected joy.

Presently her quick ears heard the rattle of approaching wheels, and with a throbbing heart she looked at the clock. It wanted ten minutes to the appointed time for Jack's arrival. With a quick flush of gratitude for his punctuality she moved to the door, and stole swiftly and softly to her own room, to regain composure. She heard the carriage pull up and go away to the stables—heard the hurried tread of footsteps in the marble hall—and then, with the faint flush grown into a full-blown blush, went downstairs and entered the drawing-room.

A sudden shock of disappointment chilled her. Stephen was standing before the fire warming his hands, but Jack was not there.

Stephen, in the glass, saw her enter, saw the sudden start and disappearance of the warm flush, and turned to meet her.

He looked tired, pale and worn, and the smile with which he met her was a singular one, one that would have been almost triumphant but for the expression of anxiety underlying it.

"I have got back, you see," he said. "And are you quite well?"

Una murmured an inaudible response, and he went back to the fire and bent over it, warming his hands, his face grown, if anything, still paler.

"How beautiful she looks!" he thought. "How beautiful! Worth risking all for—all!"

"Won't you go up and dress, Stephen?" said Mrs. Davenant. "There is a large fire in your room, and in Jack's too; I have just been into both of them."

"Yes, yes," he said, not nervously, but with almost an absent air, and he left the room.

"Stephen looks tired," said Mrs. Davenant. "I'm afraid he has had some business that has worried him. I can always tell by his face."

"I am very sorry," said Una, gently. "Yes, he did look tired and worried," she added, but with her eyes on the clock. The hands went round to the hour—an hour beyond Jack's time—and the butler announced dinner.

"Oh, we will wait a little while for Mr. Newcombe!" said Mrs. Davenant, but Una, with a little flush, murmured:

"No, do not, please; Mr. Davenant must want his dinner. Please do not wait;" and Mrs. Davenant, never able to stand out against anyone's will, rose and put her arm in Una's and they went into the dining-room. Stephen followed and sat down without making any remark on Jack's absence; even when Mrs. Davenant said to the butler—"Let them be sure and keep the soup hot for Mr. Newcombe," Stephen made no observation.

Dish after dish disappeared, and Una made a faint pretence at eating as usual, and joined in the conversation between Stephen and Mrs. Davenant, but her eyes were continually straying toward the clock, her ears straining for the sound of wheels or a galloping horse.

The dinner was a thing of the past, and the soup had been kept hot in vain; no Jack arrived. Gradually silence had fallen on the three, and when Mrs. Davenant rose it was with a sigh of loving sympathy with the troubled heart that ached so near her own.

"I cannot think what has kept him," she said, when they were alone together in the drawing-room. "If it were anyone but Jack I should feel nervous—but even I cannot feel nervous about *him*. It is a plain, easy road from Earl's Court, and he rides like a—a centaur."

"Perhaps," said Una, with her eyes fixed on the fire—"perhaps Lady Bell pressed him to stay to dinner, and he will be here presently."

"That must be it," said Mrs. Davenant, hopefully. "He will come in directly, making a most tremendous noise, and raging against whatever has been keeping him. Jack's rages are dreadful while they last—they don't last long!"

Una smiled, and listened.

Stephen entered—so noiselessly that she almost started—and stooped over his mother.

"There are some things in the breakfast room I brought from London, will you go and see to them?"

Mrs. Davenant rose instantly.

"Una, dear," she said, "see to the tea, I will be back directly."

Una nodded, and sat down at the gypsy table. Stephen stood beside the fire, one white hand stretched out to the blaze, his face turned toward her, his eyes watching her under their lowered lids. His heart beat nervously, the task before him seemed to overmaster him, and he shrank from it; with one hand he felt Jack's letter, lying like an asp in his breast coat pocket.

"There is a cold wind tonight," he said absently. "Jack said the wind had gone round this morning."

"Jack," said Una, raising her eyes, with a sudden flame of color in her face. "Have you seen him? You have been to Earl's Court?"

Stephen frowned as if angry at making a slip.

"No—no," he said with gentle hesitation. "No; I saw him in London. He is not at Earl's Court."

"Not at Earl's Court!" said Una, with surprise. "How is that? Oh, he is not ill?"

And her breath came sharply.

Stephen turned to the fire, with knitted brow and compressed lip, and fidgeted with the poker.

"No," he replied, slowly, and as if uncertain what to say—"he is not ill."

"Then why did he not go?" asked Una.

Stephen remained silent; and still keeping her eyes fixed on his pale face, she rose and glided to his side.

"You have something to tell me," she said, laying her hand on his arm, and speaking in a low, panting voice. "What is it? You will tell me, will you not? Has anything happened to Lady Bell? Is she at Earl's Court?"

"Yes, she is at Earl's Court," he said, almost bitterly, "and she is quite well, I believe."

"Then," said Una, in a low voice, which she tried vainly to keep steady—"then it is something concerning Jack. Oh, why do you keep me in suspense?" Her misery maddened him.

"I will tell you that he is quite well," he said, almost sharply. "I left him in perfect health. I dined with him, and he made an excellent dinner."

"You are angry with him! What has he done to make you angry?" she asked.

He raised her hand, and let it fall with a gesture of noble indignation.

"What has he done?" he repeated, as if to himself. "I can find no words to describe it adequately. My poor Una!"

And he turned to her, and laid his hand caressingly and pityingly on her arm.

Una, white and cold, was all unconscious of his touch.

Stephen drew her gently to a low seat, and stood over her, his hand resting with the same caressing pity on her arm.

"Yes, I must tell you," he said, his voice low and gentle. "Would to Heaven I had been spared the task. Dear Una! you will be calm—I know your brave spirit and true, courageous heart. You will summon all your strength to bear the blow it is left for me to deal you—me who would lay down my life to spare you a moment's pain!"

She scarcely heeded him. Her eyes, fixed on his face, were dilated with fear and dread, her lips white and apart with suspense.

"Tell me," she murmured. "It is something to do with Jack?"

"It is," he said. "It is."

"He is dead!" she breathed.

And her eyes closed, as a shudder ran through her frame.

"Would to Heaven he had died, ere this night's work," said Stephen, in a low, fierce voice. "No; I have told you the truth. I left him well and—Heaven forgive him—happy."

Una drew a long breath, and smiled wearily.

"What can you have to tell me about him that is so dreadful, if he is alive and happy?"

"He is alive, but he must be dead to you, dear Una," said Stephen.

"Dead to me!" repeated Una, as if the words had no meaning for her. "Dead to me! I—I do not understand."

Then, as he stood silent, with a look of gentle pity and sorrow on his pale face, a sharp expression of apprehension flashed across her face.

"Say that again," she said. "You—you mean to tell me that he has left me?"

Stephen lowered his head.

Una was silent, while the clock ticked three, then three words came swiftly and sharply from her white lips:

"It is false!"

Stephen started.

"Would to Heaven it were," he murmured.

"Gone! left me without a word," said Una, with a smile of scorn. "Can you ask—can you expect me to believe it?"

"No," said Stephen. "No one would believe such base and hideous treachery without proof."

"Proof!" she echoed, faintly, and with sudden sinking of the heart. "Proof! Give it to me!"

Stephen drew the letter from his pocket slowly and reluctantly.

Una saw it and shivered.

"It is from him; give it to me," she said.

And she held out her hand.

Stephen took it in his, and held it for a moment.

"Wait—for Heaven's sake wait," he murmured, with agitation. "I meant to break it to you—to explain— —"

"Give it to me," was all she said, and she shook his hand off impatiently.

"Take it," said Stephen, with a tremor in his voice, "take it, and would to Heaven he had found some other messenger to bear it."

Una took the letter and slowly but steadily carried it to another part of the room.

There she stood and looked at it as if she were waiting to gain strength to open it.

At last, after what seemed an eternity to Stephen, who was watching her in the glass, she broke open the envelope and read.

Not twice, but thrice she read it, as if she meant to engrave every line on her heart, then she thrust the letter in her bosom and came back to the fire.

Stephen turned, and with a low cry of alarm at sight of her altered face, moved toward her; but she put up her hand to keep him back.

Altered! Not only in face but in bravery. A minute ago she had been a gentle-hearted, suffering, tortured girl, now she was an injured, deserted woman.

"Thanks," she said, and the words fell like ice from her lips. "You spoke of an explanation. Will you tell me all you know, Stephen?"

"Pray—not now," he murmured. "Tomorrow— —"

But she stopped him with a smile, awful to see in its utter despair and unnatural calmness.

"Now, please."

"It—it is too easy of explanation," said Stephen hoarsely. "He was tempted and he has fallen. He has bartered his honor for gold. Ask me no more."

Una drew a long breath.

"It is needless," she said. "You mean that he has left me, because I am poor, for Lady Earlsley, who can make him rich."

Stephen turned away and sighed heavily.

Una looked at him for a moment, then sat down at the tea-table.

"You will have some tea?" she said calmly.

Stephen started and looked at her. She had taken up the cream ewer with an unfaltering hand. Great Heaven! could it be possible that she did not feel it—that she did not really love Jack after all! A wild feeling of exultation rose within his heart.

"Thank Heaven!" he murmured, "you can meet such treachery as it deserves—with scorn and contempt."

She looked up at him with a strange smile on her cold, white face, and held out a tea-cup. But as he came near her, the cup dropped from her hand with a crash, and she fell back like one stricken unto death.

That same evening, Lady Bell stood in the drawing-room of Earl's Court. She was richly dressed, more richly than was usual with her; upon her white neck and arms sparkled the diamond set which she wore only on the most special occasions. The room was full. Four or five of the country families had been dining with her, and the buzz of conversation and sound of music rose and fell together confusedly.

Surrounded, as usual, by a little circle of courtiers, she reigned, by the right of her beauty, her birth, and her wealth, a queen of society.

Brilliant and witty she, so to speak, kept her devoted adherents at bay, her beautiful face lit up with the smile which so many found so falsely fascinating, her eyes shining like the gems in her hair. Never had she appeared so beautiful, so irresistible.

Regarding her even most critically one would have assented to the proposition that certainly if any woman in the world was happy that night it was Lady Isabel Earlsley.

And yet beneath all her brilliance Lady Bell was hiding an aching heart. Half the country was there at her feet, and only one of all her invited guests absent, and he a poor, tireless, ne'er-do-well. But Lady Bell would willingly, joyfully have exchanged them all for that one man, for that scapegrace with the bold, handsome face and frank, fearless eyes.

Since mid-day she had been expecting him. Like Una, her eyes had wandered to the clock, and she had told the minutes over; but he had not come, and now, with that false gayety of despair, she was striving, fighting hard to forget him.

But her eyes and ears refused to obey her will, and were still watching and waiting, and suddenly her glance, wandering over her fan, saw a figure standing in the doorway.

It was not a man's, it was that of Laura Treherne's—Mary Burns.

Not one of them around her noticed any difference in her smile or guessed why she dismissed them so easily and naturally. She did not even march straight for the door, but making a circuit, gradually reached the hall.

Pale and calm and self-possessed as usual, the strange maid was waiting for her.

"Well!" said Lady Bell, and her voice was scarcely above a whisper. "Has—has he come?"

"No," said Laura Treherne. "But though your ladyship told me only to let you know of Mr. Newcombe's arrival, I thought it best to bring you this letter."

Lady Bell almost snatched it from her hand.

"You did right," she said.

With trembling hands she broke open the envelope, not noting that it opened easily as if it had been tampered with, and read the note.

"Dear Lady Bell—I am sorry I cannot come as arranged. I am in great trouble, and cannot leave London.

"Yours truly,
Jack Newcombe."

Lady Bell looked at the few lines for full a minute, then she pressed the letter to her lips. As she did so, she saw that the slight figure in its dark dress was still standing in front of her, and she started.

"Why are you waiting?" she said angrily.

Laura Treherne turned to go, but Lady Bell called to her.

"Wait. I beg your pardon. I am going to London tomorrow by the first train. Will you have everything ready?"

Laura Treherne bowed.

"Yes, my lady."

"And—and—you need not sit up," said Lady Bell.

"Thanks, my lady," was the calm response. And the dim figure disappeared in the distance.

CHAPTER XXXV

Christmas was near at hand; but notwithstanding that nearly everybody who had a country house, or an invitation to one, was away in the shires, London was by no means empty. There were still "chariots and horsemen" in the park; and the clubs were pretty well frequented. Not a few have come to the conclusion that after all London is at its best and cheerfulest in midwinter; and that plum pudding and roast beef can be enjoyed in a London square as well, if not better, than in the country.

Among these was Lady Bell. Although she had two or three country houses which she might have filled with guests, she, for sundry reasons, preferred to remain in Park Lane.

Perhaps, like Leonard Dagle, she thought that there was no place like London. He would have his idea that there was no place in it like Spider Court. Spring, summer, autumn, and winter, with perhaps, just a short interregnum of a fortnight in summer, Leonard stuck to Spider Court; and on this winter evening he was sitting in his accustomed place, busily driving the pen.

There was a certain change about Leonard which was worthy of remark. He looked, not older than we saw him last, but younger. In place of the weary, abstracted air, which had settled upon him during the long months of the search of Laura Treherne, there was an expression of hopefulness and energy which was distinctly palpable. The room too looked changed. It was neater and less muddled; and though the boxing gloves and portraits of actresses and fair ladies of the ballet still adorned the walls, the floor and chairs were no longer lumbered with Jack's boots and gloves, cigar boxes, and other impedimenta.

Perhaps Leonard missed these untidy objects, for he was wont to look up from his work and round the room with a sigh, and not seldom would rise and stalk into the bed-room beyond his own; the bed-room which Jack kept in a similar litter, but which now was neat and tidy—and unoccupied.

At such times Leonard would sigh and murmur to himself, "Poor Jack!" and betaking himself to his writing desk again would pull out a locket and gaze long and earnestly on a face enshrined therein, a face which strikingly resembled that of Laura Treherne, and so would gain comfort and fall to work again.

Tonight, he had wandered into the unoccupied room and had glanced at the portrait two or three times, for he felt lonely and would have given a five-pound note to hear Jack's tread upon the stairs, and his voice shouting for the housekeeper to bring him hot water.

"Poor Jack!" he murmured, "where is he now?" For some months had elapsed since he had found a few lines of sad farewell from Jack lying on his writing desk, but pregnant with despair and reckless helplessness. And Jack had gone whither not even Mr. Levy Moss, who sought him far and wide, could discover; and not Mr. Moss alone, but Lady Bell Earlsley; fast as she had traveled from Earl's Court to London, she arrived too late to see Jack, too late to learn from his lips the nature of the trouble which he had spoken of in his short note to her. And from Leonard even, she could not learn much. He could only tell her that Jack and Una's engagement was broken off, and by Jack himself, but for what reason he could not tell or guess. And with that Lady Bell had to be, not content, but patient.

"You were his dearest friend," she said to Leonard, "can you not guess where he has gone?"

And Leonard had shaken his head sorrowfully. "I cannot even guess. He was utterly miserable and reckless; he once spoke, half in jest, of enlisting. He was in great trouble."

"Money trouble?" Lady Bell had asked.

"Money trouble," assented Len, and Lady Bell had sunk into Leonard's chair and wrung her white hands.

"Money! money! how I hate the word! and here I am with more of the vile stuff than I know what to do with!"

"That would make no difference to Jack," Leonard said, quietly; and Lady Bell had sighed—she almost sobbed—and gone on her way as near broken-hearted as a woman could be.

And then she had sought for him as openly as she dared, but with no result, save discovering that there were hundreds of young men who answered to Jack's description, and who were all indignant when they applied in response to the advertisements and found that they were not the men wanted.

And so the months had rolled on, and the "Savage" was nearly forgotten at the Club, excepting at odd times when Hetley or Dalrymple remembered how well he used to tool a team to the "Sheaves," or row stroke in a scratch eight. My friend, if you want to find out of how little importance you are in your little world, disappear for a few months, and when you come back you will find that your place has been excellently well filled, excepting in the hearts of the one or two faithful men and women who loved you.

The world went on very well without Jack, and only two or three hearts ached, really ached, at his absence—Len, honest Len, in his den in Spider Court; Lady Bell, in Park Lane; and that other tender, loving, and tortured heart in the old new house at Hurst.

Leonard often thought of that tender heart, and sighed over it as he sighed for Jack. It was still a mystery to him, their separation; he knew that Una was still at the Hurst, but that was all. No news of her ever reached him. At times he ran across Stephen in London, and exchanged a word or a bow with him, and had noticed that he was looking better and sleeker, and less pale—more flourishing in fact, than he had done for some time.

He, too had come to Spider Court, and expressed profound grief at Jack's disappearance, and had gone away after wringing Leonard's hand sympathetically.

Leonard sat thinking over this far more than was good to the work he had in hand, when he heard the door open, and half starting, said absently:

"Nothing more wanted tonight, Mrs. Brown "

But a step, certainly not Mrs. Brown's, crossed the room, and a heavy hand was laid on his shoulder, and looking up, he saw Jack's face above him.

"Jack!" he exclaimed, clutching him as if he expected to see him disappear again. "It is you, really you? Great Heaven!"

There was reason for the exclamation; for though it was Jack, he was so altered as to have rendered the description of him in the advertisements quite useless. Thin, pale, careworn, it was no more the old Jack than the living skeleton is Daniel Lambert.

"Great Heaven! Is it really you, Jack?"

"Yes, it is I! what is left of me, Len. You—you are looking well, old man. And the old room; how cheery it seems."

And he laughed—the shadow of the old laugh—even more pitiable than tears.

"For Heaven's sake be quiet; don't speak just yet," said Len, with a husky voice. "Sit down. You've frightened me, Jack. Have you been ill?"

"Slightly," said Jack, with a smile.

"And where have you been? Tell me all about it—no, don't tell me anything yet."

And he went to the cupboard, and brought out the whisky, and mixed a stiff glass.

"Now, then, old man, where's the cigars? here—here's a light. Now then—no; take off your boots. I'll tell Mrs. Brown to air the bed and get your dressing-gown. And what about supper?"

And with a suspicious moisture in his eyes, Len turned from the room.

"Staunch as a woman, tender as a man." It was a wise saying, whoever wrote it.

Jack sipped his whisky and water, and smoked his cigar, and pulled himself together, which was just what Len wanted to get him to do; and then Len came back.

"Now then, old man, out with it. Where have you been?"

"I've been to America," said Jack. "Don't ask me any particulars, Len; I wouldn't tell you much if you did. I've been nearly out of my mind half the time, and down with one of their charming fevers the remainder. You won't get enough information out of me to write even a magazine article, old man."

And he smiled, with a faint attempt at badinage.

"Great Heaven!" exclaimed Len, again; "and—and is that all?"

"That's all it amounts to," said Jack, wearily. "You want to know how I came back, and why? Well, I can scarcely tell why. I got so sick of trying to get knocked on the head, and failing miserably, that I got disgusted with the country, weary of wandering about, and resolved that it would be better to come and give Levy Moss his revenge. He's still alive, I hope?"

"And you got back?" said Len.

"I worked my passage over," said Jack, curtly. "I was a bad hand, and caught cold on the top of the last affair, and just managed to pull myself together to reach London, and here I am. Not very lucid, Len, is it? But there's no more to tell."

Leonard looked at him with infinite pity, and mixed another glass of whisky.

"Poor old Jack," he murmured.

"And now it's your turn," said Jack, lighting another cigar. "Tell me all the news, Len, about yourself first. How are Hetley, and Dalrymple, and the rest of them? But yourself first, Len. You look well—better than when I left. Things have gone right with you."

"Then you have not forgotten?" said Len, gratefully.

"It is not likely," he said, quietly. "I have thought of you many a night as I lay burning with that confounded fever. Are you married?" and he looked round the room as if he expected to see Mrs. Dagle in some dim corner.

Leonard blushed.

"Nonsense! No, Jack, I'm not married. But—I'm very happy, old man—should have been quite happy, but for missing you."

Jack nodded.

"I'm glad of that. Glad it has all worked round, and that you have missed me, too. Where is she—Laura Treherne? You see I remember her name."

Leonard hesitated, and looked troubled.

"I—I'm afraid I mustn't tell you. You see, Jack, there's still some kind of mystery hanging about this love affair of mine. It is Laura's wish that I should keep silent as to her whereabouts. I give you my word I don't understand why. But I don't want to talk of myself and my affairs, Jack. There is something and someone else you want to hear about."

Jack looked up with a sudden start, and held up his hand.

"No, not a word!" he said. "Don't tell me a word. I—that affair is over—dead and buried. Don't speak her name, Len, for Heaven's sake. Let that rest forever between us."

Len sighed.

"Tell me more about yourself," said Jack, impatiently, as if anxious to get away from the other subject. "There is some mystery, secret, you say."

"Yes," said Leonard, humoring him, "there is a mystery and secret, which, much as I love her, and I hope and believe she loves me, Laura will not trust—well, I will not say 'trust'—which she does not feel authorized to confide to me."

"I remember," said Jack, "your telling me that she had some task, or mission, or something to accomplish—sounds strange."

"Yes," said Leonard, with a sigh, "and that mission is still unaccomplished, and blocks the marriage. But I am content to wait and trust, and I am happy."

Jack sighed.

"You deserve to be, old fellow!" he said.

"No, I don't!" exclaimed Leonard, remorsefully, "for flaunting my happiness in your face, Jack. And now, here's the supper," he added, as a waiter from a neighboring chop-house brought in a tray.

Jack sat down, and Leonard waited upon him, hanging over him, and watching him as if every mouthful he ate did him, Leonard, good; meanwhile chatting cheerfully.

"London pretty full, Jack; lots of people up this year."

"Yes," said Jack, then he looked up. "I suppose I shan't be able to show up, because of Moss, Len?"

"Oh, he won't know you are here! And we'll cut it. We'll go down to the country somewhere, Jack, before anyone sees you. You haven't met anyone, have you?"

"Met them, no. But I have seen Stephen."

"Stephen Davenant?"

"Yes, I saw him, but I don't think he saw me. He is looking well."

Leonard nodded.

"He did not see you—but it wouldn't have mattered."

"No," said Jack, with a sigh. "Len, this is the first 'square meal,' as they say over the sea, that I've enjoyed since I left. I'm very tired."

"I can see that," said Leonard. "Go off to bed, old man. We'll have no more questions tonight."

Jack rose and took his candle.

"Yes, one more," he said, as he held Leonard's hand, tightly. "Is—is she well, Len?"

Leonard nodded.

"Yes, I think so——"

"That's all," said Jack, resolutely. "Good-night, Len, good-night," and he turned away quickly.

Leonard stole into Jack's room several times that night and looked down upon the tired, weary face, still handsome for all its lines and haggardness, handsomer some might have thought, for suffering sets a seal of dignity upon a man's face if there be sterling stuff in him. Leonard looked down at it pityingly.

"Poor old man; he has had a hard time of it if any man has."

Jack turned up at breakfast time looking much refreshed.

"First good night's rest I've had since—oh, too long to remember, Len. Dreamed that all that has happened was only a dream, and that I was waking up and going to see——" he broke off suddenly and sighed.

Leonard was delighted to see him so much better.

"We'll leave town directly, Jack," he said. "I've just done my usual batch of work, and am free. We'll spend our Christmas at some old inn——"

Jack looked at him gratefully.

"You're a staunch old man, Len," he said, quietly. "You'd sacrifice your sweetheart to your friend."

Len colored.

"I'm sure she'd be the first to urge us to go," he said. "Laura is so unselfish."

"She shan't be sacrificed for me," said Jack. "No, Len, I'll go off by myself, before anyone knows I'm back—hallo! what's that?"

It was a footstep on the stairs, Len motioned for Jack to retreat into the bedroom, and only just in time, for, barely stopping to knock, Mr. Levy Moss opened the door.

CHAPTER XXXVI

"Good-morning, Mr. Dagle," said Moss, his eyes roaming about the room. "Here I am again, you see, Mr. Dagle; and where is Mr. Newcombe? He's here, I know."

"If you know so much you've no need to ask," said Leonard. "Who told you he was here?"

Levy Moss winked one bleared eye cunningly.

"I'm smart, Mr. Dagle; I keep my eyes open and my feet a-moving."

"Just so," said Leonard, "and if you'll be good enough to move them out of my room I shall be obliged. Please observe that these are *my* rooms, Mr. Moss, and not Mr. Newcombe's, and that I am not desirous of further visits from you."

"You're sharp, too, Mr. Dagle," said Moss; "but Mr. Newcombe's here; you don't want two cups and saucers, and two plates, you know, for your breakfast, eh?"

"Get out!" said Len, who, when he was roused was, like most quiet men, rather hot-headed. "Get out! and, by the way, if you meet Mr. Newcombe, I'd advise you to keep clear of him; he's back from America and carries two revolvers and a bowie knife, and I needn't tell you, who know him so well, that he'd as soon put a bullet through your head or stick the knife in between your ribs as look at you—far rather, perhaps."

Moss turned pale.

"I hope Mr. Jack won't do anything rash."

"I won't answer for him. They don't think much of killing your sort of people on the other side, Moss. Get out," and Mr. Moss shuffled out; Leonard bolting the door after him.

Jack came in and sat down quietly and gravely.

"I've frightened him," said Leonard, smiling. "He'll keep clear of you for a day or two. But how did he know you were back? He couldn't have been keeping watch for all these months."

"I don't know; someone must have seen me, and told him; I don't know who, Len. I'm going out."

"Now, Jack?" said Leonard, fearfully.

Jack smiled.

"No, Len; I won't cut it again without telling you and saying 'good-by.' I'm only going for a walk; and I'll be back to dinner."

Leonard looked after him, still rather anxiously; there was a look of determination on the pale, thoughtful face which alarmed him.

Jack walked to Regent street—please mark that he didn't call a hansom; though Len had pressed some money upon him—and then into Piccadilly, and still with the thoughtful look of determination on his face, into Park Lane, and ascended the steps of Lady Bell's villa.

A footman, who knew not Jack, opened the door, and Jack, who had not any cards, gave his name, which the footman gave to Lady Bell's maid as "Mr. Bluecut."

Jack walked into the drawing-room, every article of which was familiar to him; and sat down in the chair which he had so often drawn close to Lady Bell's, only a few months back; and yet how long, long ago it seemed.

Presently the door opened, and Lady Bell came in.

He saw her in the glass before she saw him.

Tastefully and simply dressed, she looked, if anything, more beautiful than ever, but not so bright and restless; Jack noticed that. There was an undefinable change about her, just as if she had gone through some trouble, or had done battle with some grief.

Suddenly she looked round and saw him, and stopped; one hand holding a chair, her face going from white to crimson.

Jack rose.

"I've startled you; I'm very sorry."

Lady Bell recovered herself, and went to him with outstretched hand and a look in her dark eyes that she tried to keep out of them.

"Jack," she said, almost involuntarily.

"Yes, it's I; like the bad penny, back again, Lady Bell."

And he sat down and laughed.

She sank into a chair beside him, and looked at his careworn face.

"Where have you been?" she asked, softly.

"To America," said Jack.

"You have been ill?" she said, still more softly.

Jack nodded.

"Yes. I'm all right now. And you? You don't look quite the thing?"

"Do I not?" she said, with a smile. "I am quite well. And is that all you are going to tell me of your wanderings?"

"No. I'll tell you everything some other time," said Jack, quietly.

"You are not going away again, then?" she asked, looking at him, and then away from him.

Jack flushed.

"That depends," he said, quietly.

"Depends on what?" she asked.

"On you," he said.

Lady Bell started, and the crimson flush flooded her face and neck. Her lips trembled, and she looked away.

"On me?" she murmured, faintly.

"On you," said Jack, earnestly. "Lady Bell, I have come back to ask you to be my wife."

She was silent; her face turned from him, so that he could not see the tears that welled up in her eyes.

Jack took her hand.

"Lady Bell, I know that I am not worthy of you—know it quite well. There isn't a man in the world who is; I, least of all. I know, too, what the world would say if you should answer 'Yes.' It will impute all sorts of base motives to me. But, as Heaven is my witness, it is not for your wealth that I ask you to be my wife. I am poor, and in all sorts of trouble; but if you were poorer than I am I would still ask you."

"You would?" she murmured.

"Yes," he said, quietly. "Yes, I can say that, though I tell you in the same breath that I am, at this moment, being hunted for money. And I think you will believe me."

She made a gesture of assent with her hand.

"Dear Lady Bell," he continued, "during the last few months I have been looking back to those happy days we spent together; and when a man's down with the fever he looks back with keen and wise insight into the turn of things, and knows when he was happy in the past, and with whom; and I swore that, if ever I pulled through and got back, I would ask you if you did not think we might be as happy in the future as in the past. Dear Bell, I would try and make you happy. Will you be my wife?"

Trembling in every limb, she sat silent, and with averted face. Then, suddenly and yet slowly, she turned her eyes upon him—eyes full of ineffable love and sadness.

Slowly, softly, she put her other hand in his, and smiled at him.

"You ask me to be your wife, Jack?"

"I do," he said. "Your answer, dear Bell?"

"Is—No," she said.

Jack started, and his eyes fell before the deep love and tenderness in hers. He would have drawn his hand away, but she still held it gently.

"Do you ask me why, Jack? I will tell you. It is because you do not love me."

He looked up with a start, and turned pale.

Lady Bell shook her head gently.

"Do not speak—it is useless. Besides, you would not tell me a lie, Jack. Listen; I, too, have been looking back; I, too, have learned a lesson—a truth—while you have been away. And that truth is, that others may love as truly and deeply as myself; and that others may find it as impossible to forget——"

Jack, pale and agitated, stopped her.

"The past is buried," he said, hoarsely—"let it rest."

"It is not buried—it cannot be. See! it revives—springs up, even without the mention of her name. Jack, you do not love me—you cannot; for all your love has been given, is still given, to Una."

"For Heaven's sake!" he implored, rising and pacing the room.

Lady Bell looked at him.

"Ah, how you love her still, Jack! See how right I was; and yet you would come to me."

And the tears fall slowly.

"Forgive me," said Jack, bending over her humbly, imploringly—"forgive me! You—you are right. But I swear I thought it was over for me. You knew me better than I knew myself."

"Yes, for a good reason, Jack," she murmured; "for I love you."

Jack winced.

"I have been a brute!" he murmured.

"No, Jack," she said—and she put her hand on his arm and looked up at him with a smile—"you meant well and honestly. You did not know how it stood with you. I could not have loved you so well if you had been false—if you had forgotten her. I have been thinking it out, Jack; and I know now that to love once—as you and I love—is to love forever."

"But it is past," he said, "utterly, irrevocably past. You do not know the barrier that stands immovably between her and me."

"Do I not?" she murmured, inaudibly. "Be it what it will, your love and hers stand firm on either side of it. But no more of that, Jack. I am glad you have come to me—very, very glad. And though I cannot be your wife, Jack"—with what tenderness and sadness those two words were breathed—"I can be your friend. I want you to promise me something."

Jack pressed her hand. He could not trust himself to speak.

"I want you to promise that you will not go away again, that you will not leave London whatever happens—mind, whatever happens—without letting me know! I may ask that much, Jack?"

"You may ask anything," he said, huskily; "I will do anything you ask of me—simply anything."

"I think you would," she said. "Then I have your promise? And, Jack, this must make no difference between us; you will come and see me?"

"I do not deserve to come within a mile of you."

She smiled.

"And so punish me for not saying 'yes,'" she said, with a little attempt at archness. "That would be hard for me, Jack. I should lose lover and friend as well."

"You are the truest-hearted woman in the world," said Jack, deeply moved.

"Except one," said Lady Bell. "There, go now, Jack, and come to dinner tonight, and bring Leonard Dagle with you—another true heart."

"I will," said Jack, simply. And he held out his hand.

She held out both of hers, and looked at him with a strange, wistful yearning in her eyes.

"Jack," she breathed, softly, "will you kiss me for the first and last time?"

Jack drew her toward him and kissed her. Then, with a little sigh, she left him. How Jack got out he knew not, for his eyes were strangely dim and useless.

CHAPTER XXXVII

A dim light was burning in the drawing-room of the Hurst. Outside, the storm was raging wild and pitiless, making the warm room seem like a harbor of refuge. Beside the fire sat Mrs. Davenant, half dozing over a piece of finest needlework for the village working club. She was alone in the room, and every now and then glanced anxiously toward the door. Presently it opened, and the tall figure of Stephen entered and crossed over to her.

"Mother," he said, and there was a tremulous ring in his voice and a quiver in his lips that were in marked contrast to his usual smooth calm.

Mrs. Davenant looked up with a glance of alarm. "Una!" she exclaimed.

"Hush!" he said, laying his hand on her shoulder. "Una," and his voice dwelt on the name. "Una is asleep. She has gone to her own room for a little while. Mother," he said, slowly, "she has consented."

Mrs. Davenant looked up and trembled: "Oh, Stephen!"

He nodded, and stood before the fire, looking up with a smile of undisguised triumph and joy. "Yes, she has consented. It was—well, hard work; but my love overmastered her. I told her that you agreed with me that the sooner the marriage took place the better. You do, do you not?"

"Yes," murmured Mrs. Davenant.

"She wants change; nothing but entire change of life and thought will do her good. Mother, if she remained here, if something were not done, she would"—he paused, and went on hoarsely, "she would die!"

Mrs. Davenant shuddered and her eyes filled. "My poor, poor Una!" she murmured.

Stephen moved impatiently. "She will not need your pity, mother. A few weeks hence and you will have no reason to pity her. I'll stake my life that I bring her back here with the roses in her cheeks, with the smile in her eyes, as of old. Mother, you do not know what such love as mine can do!" and his voice trembled with suppressed passion.

Mrs. Davenant looked up at him, tearfully.

"You—you are much changed, Stephen," she murmured.

"I am," he said, with a curt laugh. "I am changed, am I not? I scarcely know myself. And she has done it. She! My beautiful queen, my lily! Yes, she shall be happy, if man can make her." He was silent a moment, dwelling on his love and future, and looked, as he spoke, much changed. Then he awoke at a question from his mother.

"When is it to be, Stephen?"

"Tomorrow," he said, quietly.

"Tomorrow!" gasped. Mrs. Davenant. "Impossible!"

"Not at all," he said, curtly. "Remember, I told you not to be surprised, that it would come suddenly."

"But——"

He made a movement of impatience.

"Do you think I have not made preparations? See," and he took a paper from his pocket, "I have had the license for a week past. It is no ordinary marriage. We want no bridesmaid and wedding favors. She would not have them—or me, if you insisted upon it. It is principally on the condition that the ceremony shall be quite private—secret almost—that she has consented."

Mrs. Davenant stared at the fire.

Stephen smiled.

"You do not understand me, even yet, mother," he said. "Did you ever know anything fail me?"

Mrs. Davenant shuddered, or was it the play of the fire-light?

"Never," she said, in a low voice.

Stephen smiled again.

"I have seen this coming, have seen my way to it for months past; I have swept every barrier away——" He stopped suddenly and bit his lip—"and now for our plans, mother. Try and collect yourself; this has surprised and upset you," he said, sharply.

Mrs. Davenant sat up and looked at him attentively.

"Tomorrow we start, without fuss or bother, for Clumley. I have ordered them to take a pair of horses to the half-way house, so that we can change without loss of time. I have also sent a letter to the clergyman telling him to be prepared for us, and keep his own counsel. We shall reach Clumley, traveling easily, by half-past ten. There will be no wedding breakfast—thank Heaven! no fuss or ceremony. We shall go straight from the church to London, and thence to Paris. Excepting ourselves and clergyman no one can know anything of the matter until the marriage is over, then——" and he drew a long breath and smiled.

Mrs. Davenant, pale and trembling, stared up at him.

"And—and Una? Does she agree to all this?"

"Una agrees to everything," he said, impatiently. "She herself stipulated that it should be done quietly, and"—with a smile—"if this is not quietly, I do not know what is. And now, my dear mother, go and make what preparations are absolutely necessary, and make them yourself, and unaided. Remember there must be no approach to any wedding party. We are only going to take an outing for a day or two. You understand?"

"I understand," she faltered; "and when will you be back, Stephen?" she asked, pitiably. "I—I—you won't be away long, Stephen? I shall miss her so."

Stephen patted her on the shoulder.

"Don't be afraid, mother. We shall not be away too long. I am too proud of my beautiful bride to hide her away. I want to see her here, mistress of the Hurst. My wife! my wife! Hush! here she comes. Do not upset her."

And, with a quick, noiseless step, he went out as Una entered.

Framed in the doorway, she stood for a moment like a picture. Paler and slighter than in the old days, she had lost none of her beauty. Stephen had cause to be proud of his bride. There would be no lovelier woman in Wealdshire than the future mistress of the Hurst. And yet, if Jack could have seen her that moment, what agony her face would have cost him; for his eyes, quickened by his passionate love, would have read and understood that subtle change that had fallen on the beautiful face; would have read the settled melancholy which sat enthroned on the dark eyes, and gave them the dreamy, far-away look which never left them for a moment.

> "Communing with the past, she walked;
> Alive, yet dead to all the world."

Slowly she crossed the room, and stood just where Stephen had stood, and looked into the fire; but not as he had looked—triumphantly, joyfully; but with an absent, dreamy air.

Mrs. Davenant put out her hand, and touched her arm.

"Una!"

She turned her head, and looked at her questioningly, with a weary, uninterested gaze.

"Una, he—Stephen has told me. Oh, my darling, I hope you will be happy!"

Una smiled—a cold, mechanical smile.

"Happy? Yes, he says I shall be happy. Do you think," and she looked calmly at the anxious, nervous face, "do you think I shall be happy?"

Mrs. Davenant drew her toward her.

"My dear, you frighten me. You—you are so—so strange and cold. Cold! Your hands are like ice. Oh, Una, do you know what it means—this that you are going to do? It is not too late. Think, Una. You know how I love you, dear. That I would give all the world to call you—what you are, my heart of hearts—my own daughter. But, oh, Una! if you think, if you are not quite sure that you will be happy——"

Una looked straight at the fire.

"He says so," she said, in the same hard, cold voice; "he is clever and wise. He is your son; why do you doubt him?"

Mrs. Davenant shivered.

"I—I don't doubt him, dear. Yes, he is my son; he has been a good son to me. But you are to be his wife; think."

"I have thought," said Una, quietly. "It will make him happy—he says so; and the rest does not matter to me. Yes, I have thought; I am tired with thinking"; and she put her hand to her brow with a sharp gesture, half wild, half weary. "I will make him happy, and I shall always be with you, whom I love. What does the rest matter?"

Mrs. Davenant uttered a little moan.

"And—and have you quite forgotten?"

Una looked at her calmly, but with a faint shadow in her eyes and a touch of pain on her lips.

"Forgotten! No, I shall not forget until I am dead; perhaps not then; who knows?" and the dreamy look came back. "But that cannot matter. He, Stephen, is content; I have told him all, and he is content. He is easily satisfied." And for the first time a smile of bitterness crossed her lips. "Why should he love me so?" she said, curtly. "Why should he be so anxious to make me his wife? I cannot understand it. Is it because he thinks that I am beautiful? I looked in the glass just now, and it seemed a dead face."

"Una!"

She turned and smiled.

"It is true. But I have made you cry. Don't do that, dear. At least, we shall be together, shall we not?"

In answer, the poor woman took her in her arms, and cried over her; but Una shed not a single tear.

No, Stephen was not likely to fail. There were not likely to be any hitches in anything he undertook.

Even the weather seemed to conform to his plans and wishes, for the morning broke clear and bright, so that he might say:

"Happy is the bride whom the sun shines on."

Without fuss or bustle, the traveling chariot, with its pair of handsome bays, drew up to the door; a couple of portmanteaus, no larger than was necessary for a day or two's outing, were put in the box; and Slummers, in his tall hat and black overcoat, looking very much like the old-fashioned banker's clerk, stood with the carriage door in his hand.

Presently Stephen came down the steps, dressed in a traveling suit, and looking as calm as usual, but for the touch of color in his face. He had grown younger in appearance, less prim and formal, and altogether better-looking. If he could have lost the trick of looking from under his lowered eyelids, he would have been worth calling handsome. He exchanged a word with Slummers.

"All right, sir. The horses are at Netherton; everything is arranged exactly according to your wishes."

"And no one suspects anything?"

"Not a soul," said Slummers, with a smile.

This morning's work was the sort of thing Slummers liked. He was enjoying himself, and as happy as his master.

Stephen went into the house again, and presently Mrs. Davenant and Una appeared. Notwithstanding Stephen's warning, Mrs. Davenant's eyes were red; but Una showed no traces of emotion; pale, almost white, she looked calmly around her.

In the night she had started out of her sleep, calling wildly, piteously, on Jack to come and save her. But there was no Jack here—only Stephen, smiling and watchful as he came to meet her and help her into the carriage. For a moment her hand touched his bare wrist, and he felt it cold as ice even through her glove; but he smiled still as if he had no fear.

"Once mine," he thought, "and all will be well!"

Quietly, with no fuss or bustle, Slummers closed the door, mounted the box, and the horses started off.

Stephen looked at his watch, and smiled.

"Punctual almost to the minute," he said. "Are you warm enough, my darling?"

And he bent forward, and arranged the costly furs round the slight form.

"Quite," she said; but she shrank into her corner with a little shiver.

Stephen left her to herself, but would not remain silent, chatting with, or rather to, Mrs. Davenant, in a strain of easy cheerfulness, his eyes wandering to the pale face just showing above the pile of furs.

Their hoofs ringing on the road, which a few hours of early frost had made hard, the horses, the finest pair in the county, for Stephen was critical in such matters and liked the best, spun the distance, and again, almost punctual to the minute, the village of Netherton, to which Stephen had sent the change of horses, was reached.

Slummers stepped down from the box, and was seen to enter the inn yard.

"The horses ought to be out and waiting," said Stephen, with a little impatience.

A moment or two passed, and then Slummers came to the carriage door.

Stephen jumped out.

"What is it? Why do you not put the horses to?"—for the others had been taken out and were standing in the stable.

Slummers, for the first time in his life, changed color and hesitated.

"There has been some mistake, sir."

"Mistake!"

"The horses are not here."

Stephen glared at him.

"I can't understand it, sir. I gave your orders most minutely, but George has taken the horses on to Clumley."

Stephen bit his lip and glanced at the carriage.

"Put the others back," he said, "and tell Masters to drive for his life."

Slummers hesitated and went to the coachman, coming back in a moment with an uneasy countenance.

"I'm—I'm afraid they won't reach Clumley in time, sir," he said. "Masters says that it is impossible. Calculating on fresh horses, he has forced them a bit on the road, and they are used up. If you will look at them, sir— —"

Stephen uttered an oath, and his face twitched.

The coachman came up, troubled but respectful. It was no fault of his.

"I thought I should get the change here, sir. I couldn't do it, unless the horses had a quarter of an hour and a wipe down, and then— —"

He paused and shook his head.

Stephen controlled himself, though his face was white.

"A quarter of an hour," he said. "We will wait so long, and not a moment longer. Then drive as if your life depended on it. Do not spare the horses."

Then he went to the carriage and forced a smile.

"A little delay," he said, cheerfully. "Would you like to get out for a quarter of an hour, darling?"

Una shook her head.

"I do not care"; but Mrs. Davenant looked at her and spoke out.

"Yes, Stephen," she said. "My dear, you are half frozen."

Stephen went to the window of the inn and looked into the room, then went back.

"Come," he said. "There is a pleasant fire. A rest and the warmth will do you good. Come," and, wrapping a huge fur round her, he took her on his arm and entered the inn.

Mrs. Davenant followed into the room. A fire was burning in the old-fashioned grate. Stephen drew a chair near to the welcome blaze and led Una to it. White and indifferent she sat and looked at the flames.

"It is only for a few minutes, darling, then we shall be off. Come, drink some of this," and he held a glass of hot spirit and water to her hand.

Una shook her head.

"Thanks, I could not," she said, simply.

Stephen motioned to his mother.

"See that she takes some," he said, in a low voice. "I will go and look after the horses," and he turned. As he did so the door opened, and a lady entered.

For a moment, in the dim light of the low room, Stephen did not recognize her, then a chill fell on him as if a cold hand had laid on his heart. He staggered back, and then she raised her veil and looked at him.

Not a word passed. Face to face, eye to eye, they stood. A moment passed. Una had not looked round, only Mrs. Davenant stood speechless and trembling. Then, as if with an effort, Stephen regained possession of his quaking soul, and stole nearer to her.

"Laura," he whispered, glancing behind him. "You here? You want me? Well, let us come outside."

A smile, calm and scornful, flashed from her dark face.

"You cannot pass," she said.

A wild devil leaped, full grown, into his bosom, and he raised his hand to strike her, but the next instant he was grasped by the shoulder and flung aside, and Gideon Rolfe stood over him.

The room whirled round; scarcely conscious that other figures had entered and surrounded him, he staggered to his feet. Then a cry, two words, "Father! Jack!" smote upon his ear, and with an effort he turned and saw Jack's tall form towering in the low room, with Una clasped tightly, lying prone in his arms.

It was all over. Just as the criminal in the dock, when he sees the judge placing the black cap on his head, knows that his doom is sealed, Stephen knew that all was lost. But the will was not all subdued yet.

There was Davenant blood in his veins. White to the very lips, he stood and glared at them, one hand grasping the table, the other thrust in his breast. Then an evil smile curled the cunning mouth.

"Cleverly planned," he said, speaking as if every word cost him a pang. "You have beaten me, thus far. Gideon Rolfe, I congratulate you upon the success of your maneuvers; in another hour your daughter would have been the mistress of Hurst; she will, now, I presume, be the wife of a beggar."

Gideon Rolfe looked at him with stern, immovable eyes.

Stephen smiled and took up his hat.

"You have robbed me of my bride," he said; "permit me to return to the home which still remains to me."

There was an intense silence. Then a slight stir as Jack, carrying Una in his arms, left the room, followed by Mrs. Davenant. With haggard eyes Stephen watched them, then, with a convulsive movement, he took up his hat.

"You will find me at the Hurst," he said; "I will go there. If there is any law in the land which can punish you, I will have it, though it cost me a fortune. Yes, I will go home."

Still they were silent. Whether from pity, or awe at the sight of his misery, they were silent. He looked round and, as if he had called, Slummers glided to his side. They had already reached the door, when a voice said:

"Tell him."

It was Jack who had returned to the room.

At the sound of the voice, grave and pitying, Stephen swung round as if he had been stung.

"You are here still," he said, and a glance of malignant hatred distorted his face. "I thought you were in jail by this time. You were waiting to take your wife with you. It would have been wiser to allow her to go to the Hurst."

"Tell him," said Jack.

With a slow, almost reluctant movement, Laura Treherne drew a paper from under her jacket and held it up.

Stephen looked at it for a moment as if his sight had failed him, then he smiled.

"The plot thickens," he said. "You have robbed me of my wife; you have, no doubt, some ready-forged document to rob me of my estate. Am I to give the credit to you for this?" Then he broke out wildly, with a mad laugh. "It is a forgery! a forgery! I will swear it. There is no such will. The marriage never took place. You've to prove both yet! You are not so clever as I thought. You should have stopped short where you were. You have got her, be satisfied; the rest is mine! Mine, and you cannot take it from me," and he held his clinched fist toward Jack as he held all Hurst in his grasp.

"Show him," said Gideon Rolfe.

Stephen waved his hand contemptuously.

"A stale trick," he said. "A clumsy forgery. You cannot connect it with my uncle's death. Go to your lawyer—Hudsley, if you will; he will be ready enough to help you—and he will tell you that proof is impossible."

As he spoke his voice grew clearer. It was a relief to his overwrought brain to fight them on ground he had often mentally surveyed. With an insolent smile on his face he leaned both hands on the table and looked at them.

"Come," he said, "you have not won everything yet. The Hurst is mine; I laugh your forgery to scorn. I will spend every penny of the estate to contest it. I assert that this paper was forged—last night—if you like. You cannot prove it was in existence an hour sooner; I defy you. You have overreached yourselves. Take care! This is your hour. Mine will come when I see you in the dock."

In his excitement he had not noticed the entrance of the bent figure of Skettle, and he turned with a start as the thin, dry voice, close to his elbow, croaked:

"Quite right, Mr. Stephen. That's their weak point—want of connection. If they could carry it back, say to the night of the squire's death, now, it would be different."

Stephen looked round with a cunning smile of defiance.

"This old fool will bear me out. Show him your will."

"A daring forgery this, Mr. Stephen, if it is a forgery. Leaves the Hurst to Miss Una, the squire's legitimate daughter. Fifty thousand to Master Jack; and a set of sermons to you."

"No doubt," he said, with a hoarse laugh; "it was not worth their while to do things by halves."

"Been scorched, too," said Skettle. "Bit torn out by the seal. Now, if they could find that bit in the possession of a respectable man, who could prove that he found it on the night, say, of the squire's death, well—it would go hard with you, Mr. Stephen."

"But they cannot."

"I don't know," said Skettle; and slowly drawing out a leather pocket book of ancient date, he took out a piece of paper and fitted it to the will.

"It is a conspiracy!"

"It is the will I saw you looking for the night of the squire's death."

"Let me go." And leaning heavily on the arm of his fellow-knave, he moved with the gait and bearing of an old man, to the door.

"Great Heaven, this is awful!" said Jack.

Winter had passed and spring had clothed the earth with her soft, green mantle, and in her glad sunlight that sat like a benediction on the great elms and smooth lawn of Hurst, a party of ladies and gentlemen were standing on the stone steps that led up to the entrance.

It was, in a word, the wedding day of Squire Jack Newcombe and Miss Una Davenant, and these good and tried friends were waiting about the steps to see the bride and bridegroom start for their honeymoon.

That Len and Laura and Lady Bell should be there calls for no surprise, but how comes it that Gideon Rolfe should be a willing witness to the marriage of Una with one of the hated race of Davenants? Well, when the cause of hatred is removed, all hate vanishes from the heart of an honest man.

On the day he learned that the old squire had not wronged the girl he had stolen from Gideon, Gideon's hatred had flown, and in its place had sprung up a longing for atonement; and what better step could he take toward burying the old animosity than in giving his adopted daughter to the man of her choice—the man who would make her, as her mother had been before her, the Squire of Hurst's wife?

And thus it came to pass that he stood silently, but not grimly waiting for his daughter—for she was still his daughter—to pass out to the new life of happiness. And presently there rose a buzz and a hum of excitement in the house, and the stalwart figure of Jack appeared on the top step. A moment later and the beautiful face of Una was by his side. No longer pale, but bright with blushes, and glowing with health and happiness, she stood, half timidly, pressing close to the proud fellow beside her.

Is it all a dream in her eyes, dimmed as they are by happy tears? Can it be true that Jack is all her own—that these good friends and true are really clustering round her, bidding her Godspeed and yet hindering her going as if they were loth to let her go? Perhaps she does not realize it all until they part and let her pass to where the old bent figure of Stephen's mother stands waiting to see the last of the girl whom she has loved and still loves as a daughter.

Then as Una takes the trembling figure in her arms and kisses the pale face, she realizes it all, and through sobs she hears the faltering voice murmuring:

"God bless you, my darling! God bless and keep you!"

And as the broken benediction falls from the trembling lips, the crowd stand back, silent and tearful, and Jack and his bride are allowed to enter the carriage at last. Then breaks forth the cheer from outside the gates, and so, wafted around by blessings and good wishes, they commence their real life. A month later they will come back to find those friends who saw them depart, eager to welcome them back.

"No coming home to a silent house, my wild bird!" says Jack. "We'll have them all here, everyone of them. I'd have all the world to see my darling, if I could."

"My darling! my darling! they might take all the rest if they would leave me you."

And Stephen? There is no difficulty in finding Stephen—he is too public a man. You can see and hear him any evening during the month of charitable meetings, if you will but go to the proper places.

There amongst philosophers and social reformers, you will see a tall, thin gentleman, with a white face and spotless linen, who, when he comes forward to make his speech, is received with deafening cheers, and who never fails to draw tears from the audience by his pathos and tender-souled eloquence; and when the meeting is over, if you wait beside the private entrance to the hall, you will see another tall, thin, black-coated man, who is like a reflection of the great philanthropist for whom he is waiting, and who, when he emerges, will take him by the arm and lead him to his brougham. For, excepting when he is before the public, Stephen is an injured, broken-down man, only at times able to whine out the story of the wrongs wrought him by the hands of those he most trusted. By his own account he has been robbed of his wife, his estate, his all, and left to the charity of a generous public; and it is only Slummers, besides Stephen himself, who knows that a check arrives punctually each quarter from Jack's lawyer for the support of the man who returns forgiveness and generosity with undying hate and calumny. Yes, Stephen Davenant is regarded as a deeply injured man, and when he appears, with his pale face, and soft, mournful voice, there is always a show of handkerchiefs.

But Jack and Una are quite content, and whenever his name is mentioned, it is with more pity than anger. There is no room for aught else in their hearts but love.